A FEARF...

There was silence, Aurora barely moving as she took shallow breaths of air, then Lord Killingham looked at her once again, and seemed to recall where he was. He reached out a hand towards the lovely girl before him, desiring to touch the throat that glowed white against the fire. Aurora could feel her heart pounding as if to burst as she pressed hard against the back of her chair in a futile attempt to escape Killingham's touch, loathing and dread in her eyes. She was paralized and unable to flee, but a knock on the door stayed Lord Killingham's hand at the crucial instant . . .

Unless she could be saved in time, Aurora's fate would be sealed. She would be brutally forced to marry the horrible Killingham, and remain separated from her true love forever.

Also by Adora Sheridan
Published by Ballantine Books:

THE SIGNET RING

THE
Season

Adora Sheridan

BALLANTINE BOOKS • NEW YORK

Library of Congress Catalog Card Number: 78-65319

ISBN 0-345-27787-2

Manufactured in the United States of America

First Edition: June 1979

This book is dedicated to
Ms. Susan Carlson, a closet
romantic of the first water!

CHAPTER 1

"NEVER was there a more contrary, obstinate child! What have I done that I should be afflicted with such a show of utter disregard? I am sure I do not know!"

This exasperated statement, declared as it was in tones of the utmost despair by the Countess of Trevelyn, assailed the ears of her ever-attentive if less than sympathetic spouse, Roland, Earl of Trevelyn. Being used to such fits of pique, the Earl was not overly surprised that his wife should choose to throw a pet even amidst what had originally promised to be an entertaining gathering.

After a moment's pause for breath, the Countess continued to give voice to her grievances. "Am I an unnatural parent?" she asked, not waiting for a reply. "Am I unreasonable? Am I, God forbid, a cruel spiteful thing to any of my daughters?" she demanded, her face brightening for an instant as she waved with one gloved hand toward a fleeting figure in patterned muslin who waltzed past her; then resumed her former peevish expression.

Watching his wife's agitation with no little amusement, the Earl could not help but be struck by her appearance. Magnificent in a gown of emerald-green silk, tiny pearls accentuating the provocative décolletage, the Countess was dazzling even as she picked savagely at the blossom she had chosen from one of the many floral arrangements situated about the ballroom.

"I can hardly think that our host will appreciate the destruction of his decorations, my love," the Earl commented as several soft white petals fluttered wounded to the polished floor.

1

Discarding the mangled stem with no sign of remorse, the Countess proceeded methodically to choose another victim from the nearby vase. Several acquaintances passed quietly by the couple, aware of the Countess's ill humor.

"Diana," the Earl murmured placatingly as the Countess proceeded to open and close with impatient abruptness the fan which dangled from one slender wrist. "Lettice is not one to be ordered to do that to which she is little inclined," the Earl pointed out. "She is very much of a similar humor to yourself in matters of the heart, truth be told."

The Countess looked up to frown, her hands manipulating the fan with agitated movements.

"Let her sit with her friends about her for a while," the Earl urged. "She does not disobey you to throw you into a passion, and I am sure she will dance with some fortunate male before the evening's end."

These comments did nothing to smooth the lady's ruffled feathers. Rather, the Earl's words appeared to have the opposite effect. At the mention of her daughter's current and perturbing behavior, the Countess became agitated to such a degree as to cause her to close her fan with a sharp snap. This action was done with such violence that a single delicately painted section shattered, the carved spine unequal to the lady's irritation. The Earl's lip twitched ever so slightly in silent amusement.

Observing her husband's unseemly mirth from out of the corner of her eye, the Countess lost all patience and stamped one delicately shod foot with rage. "It is all very well an' you should be amused, Roland," the Countess said with asperity, "but I am not. It is the outside of enough that Lettice should have refused Lord Alston's suit not a fortnight ago, a perfectly eligible party, and so very suitable. What is worse, you evince not the slightest concern that your eldest daughter may end her days like that Hoaxly girl. Such an absolute dragon of a woman!" She shuddered at the thought.

At this comparison the Earl's expression became one of incredulity. "Never compare Lettice to Hoaxly's daughter, my love," he said with exaggerated offense.

"Is she not flesh of my flesh as well, my dear? I am not, I hope, to be compared to that toad-figure of a parent, Lord Hoaxly."

The Countess smiled despite herself, but quickly replaced it with a reproving look. "If only I could be sure that Lettice does not miss her chance for happiness, my love," the Countess sighed. "She cannot continue to refuse all her suitors."

It was obvious to the Earl that the Countess was not to be easily appeased on this occasion. "It is most unlike you my dear to be so ill-natured at such a fete," the Earl admonished gently. "I for one did not quite like Lord Alston's manner if you must know, and if Lettice should choose to play deep and refuse to marry him, I cannot say that I am displeased. As for the others, suffice it to say, I suffer no pangs of parental displeasure at her decisions. I cannot dictate to Lettice on whom she shall bestow her heart, and neither, I fear, can you, my dear. In any case, our daughter is a knowing 'un, a downier one I do not know. I have no such fears that she will 'miss' her opportunity."

The smile with which the Earl tempered his words to his wife moved the Countess to hang her head somewhat guiltily, a repentant look in her eyes. Extending her hand gracefully to the Earl's velvet-clad arm, the Countess indicated her desire to join the set that was beginning to form for a quadrille.

"I suppose you are correct, Roland," the Countess murmured. "I cannot expect to rule Lettice. Still, I wish she had taken a fancy to Alston. It seems most unusual to me that she should not have found one man in five for whom she could form a tendre."

Observing her eldest daughter seated at the farthest end of the ballroom, the Countess conceded that she could not compare in appearance with her younger sisters, who were experiencing their first season, but she did possess a certain allure nonetheless.

Relatively tall with a Junoesque figure, Lettice could move with a grace inherited from the Countess, but to her mother's infinite distress, Lettice rarely danced enough to show this asset to advantage. Black hair and brown eyes, not spectacular in themselves, were props with which Lettice displayed her unique personality.

Proclaimed animated and witty by several knowing mamas, Lettice had attracted many a roving eye; even those individuals thought to be confirmed bachelors had succumbed to her special presence. Full lips with an impish twist had brought not less than five besotted gentlemen up to scratch, all equally eligible, yet Lettice had refused them all without any apparent qualm and with unnerving regularity. She neither actively sought nor discouraged any gentleman's interest, but her apparent indifference to the idea of becoming a maiden aunt had caused the Countess innumerable moments of vexation and worry. The thought even now had the Countess near vapors and it was only with the utmost difficulty and concentration that the Countess turned her mind to the opening figures of the dance.

Sighing audibly, the Countess could not help praying aloud. "I can only hope, my dear, that Aurora and Patrice do not follow their sister's lead. They are both originals, and that is an advantage when one is being presented to society. A parrot is such a bore. They will have a multitude of offers. I only hope they don't refuse them all like Lettice."

Smiling, the Earl reminded the Countess, "Had you accepted the first suitor, I should not have had the great privilege of offering for your hand, which, I might add, is as ravishing tonight as ever it was." Bending gracefully, the Earl kissed the hand he so admired.

This gallant comment, accompanied as it was by the Earl's passionate salute of that dainty member, wiped all thoughts of her unresponsive daughter's behavior from the Countess's mind. With a smile radiant as sunlight, the Countess of Trevelyn thought no more of Lettice.

That object of so much parental concern was, for the moment, holding court along with her two sisters at the end of the ballroom, oblivious to her mother's watchful eye. This lack of awareness was due in part to the fact that all three ladies were surrounded by admirers of varying rank and prominence.

Lettice was not the only one of the Trevelyn sisters who had attracted a number of suitors. Aurora, the second-born child, had at present three gentlemen of consequence vying for her hand, and would no doubt have many more by the end of the season.

Only one look at Aurora was necessary to explain why these gentlemen were so willing to give up their bachelorhood for her. An unusual beauty at nineteen, Lady Aurora would stand out even amongst the loveliest ladies in all of London. But a lovely face was not her only asset, by any means. She possessed intelligence, wit, and strength of body, attributes which were sorely lacking in many a well-bred woman and man alike.

Eighteen-year-old Patrice, the youngest Trevelyn sister, was considered the sweetest and gentlest of the three. With her delicate bone structure and voluptuous figure she fascinated men of all ranks, her kind nature keeping a hold on them after the initial physical attraction.

It was natural that all this beauty, wit and charm the sisters possessed would disgruntle some of the other women while enthralling the men. This was just the case as the Trevelyn ladies sat chatting, unaware that vitriolic glances were cast in their direction from several discontented mamas.

One gentleman in the group, however, was very much aware of these ladies' impotent fury, and derived such pleasure from the sight as to cause slight sputtering sounds to emit from his closely compressed lips.

A single glance from his companion seated beside him quelled this outburst instantly, and Lord Ringwood assumed a properly interested look as Lady Lettice Trevelyn asked with arched brow, "What are you sputtering about Stuart? Surely you cannot have found the fact that Sir Francis has bought a new white gelding and had it dyed pink to match his curricle humorous?"

Lettice waited with exaggerated attention for Lord Ringwood's reply, certain that Stuart had been paying so little heed to the conversation that he was only just now attending to this absurdity.

Overcome for a moment with the utter ridiculousness of the idea, Lord Ringwood was speechless.

"It is all the crack, I can assure you Lord Ringwood," Francis Trent insisted, a slightly offended look on his face at Lord Ringwood's lack of response. Lord Ringwood continued to gape.

"And if it is not, Francis, I am sure you shall show us all the way and it very soon *will* be the thing," Lettice assured the annoyed young aristocrat, patting his hand soothingly to emphasize her words.

Aurora Trevelyn glanced heavenwards at such nonsense while Patrice contented herself with an attempt to alleviate the situation.

Turning to Sir Francis with that stunning smile for which she was renowned, Patrice said placatingly, "I am sure, Francis, that Stuart simply could not find the words to do justice to such a unique and original idea. Is that not so Lord Ringwood?"

As she turned large green eyes flecked with dazzling gold onto the hapless young man, Lord Ringwood seemed at last able to make an answer.

"Yes, of course that was the thing, Trent," Lord Ringwood sputtered gamely. "Totally astounded by the originality of the idea. Damn well certain I have never heard the like before; Would have remembered that!" he added feelingly.

Taking the comment at face value, Sir Francis seemed almost to preen himself. His demeanor was decidedly proud and Lettice noted with amusement the droll way in which Sir Francis posed himself.

With a self-depreciating gesture of his quizzing glass, Sir Francis coughed modestly. "In the blood you know," he murmured with a languid air. "Father was ever the one to create new fashion. Inherited talent. I mean, must be, stands to reason."

Patrice smiled encouragingly at this, Aurora allowed her lovely head to tilt ever so slightly, and Lettice smiled wickedly at Lord Ringwood.

Sir Francis turned to Aurora's companion, Lord Simmons, and removed a delicately enameled snuff box from an inner pocket of his evening jacket. With a carefully practiced flourish, he presented the open receptacle before the Lord's half-closed eyes.

Lord Simmons, a dandy of the first order and the arch rival in sartorial splendor to Sir Francis, eyed the gold box with a faint sneer, observing that Sir Francis chose to use a silver scoop in his partaking of snuff.

This was no doubt yet another atrocity that Sir Francis had created in the name of fashion, and Lord Simmons waved his refusal with one superbly manicured, dead-white hand.

Clothed in an evening jacket of Parisian cut, Lord Simmons was quietly elegant, not a crease or fold out of place, the ivory striping of his stockings echoed in his crisp neck cloth and accentuated by a single diamond amidst the snowy folds. Gazing at his adversary, Lord Simmons' critical eye took in every detail of the horrible sight that was Sir Francis.

In his love for the new and flamboyant, Sir Francis was complete to a shade in canary-yellow evening jacket with orange striping and stockings to match. This material manifestation of Sir Francis' tastes was too much for Lord Simmons, and he averted his eyes with a wince.

"I suppose I need not ask your opinion of my mounts, Lord Simmons," Sir Francis sniffed, turning to Aurora as he spoke. "The whole of London is aware that Lord Simmons has a steadfast partiality to chestnut." Sir Francis' disdain was obvious and was returned in kind by Lord Simmons.

"I am partial to both pink and chestnut, gentlemen," Aurora commented with a smile, "and I am sure there is room enough for both on Rotten Row."

"But with which will you ride, Lady Aurora?" Sir Francis asked impetuously, his rivalry with Lord Simmons for Aurora's favors becoming ever more pronounced.

"Why, with either or both, of course, you silly ninny," Lettice admonished gaily, observing Aurora's rising irritation at being pressured. "Of course, you will first have to invent a way to divide my sister into equal portions if you should both wish her company at the same time, but that should be no difficult task for so inventive a fellow as yourself Sir Francis," Lettice concluded.

This seemed effectively to silence Sir Francis for the time being, and Lettice beckoned for Lord Simmons to come closer to her seat, fluttering her fan insistently as she played for time so Aurora could regain her good humor.

7

"That is better," she sighed with contentment as Lord Simmons drew nearer. "One does want to have one's friends near, you know. It gives the matrons something to frown about," she laughed.

Her mirth was shared by all but the Marquess of Wainfleet who was considered to be, by general consensus, a dashed dull dog. He had hardly spoken five words past those of the common civilities since joining their group, and seemed to resent even this meager call upon his sociability.

Patrice eyed this pattern-card of propriety dressed in a tan evening coat of conservative cut. Obviously *not* Weston, she decided, and wondered afresh if the Marquess was indeed as tight-fisted as she had heard. I do wish he would but leave us, she thought irritably, glancing anxiously about the crowded ballroom for a more interesting individual who had promised to make an appearance this evening.

The Marquess continued to keep his own counsel for the most part. This was so much so that only the most astute of matrons would recognize his silent vigil as a mode of paying court to Lady Aurora, who was only vaguely aware of his motive. With an impoverished estate, the Marquess was hardly considered an eligible parti, and was doomed from the start in his endeavors to fix the attentions of any young heiress by the very nature of his personality.

Lettice and Aurora continued to entertain their gathering for some time, Patrice occasionally adding some comment of her own but obviously much more absorbed in her study of the various guests, searching for that particular face.

Equally absorbed in a perusal of the many figures, but less obvious in her occupation, Lettice chanced to spy the much sought-after individual first.

"Patrice," Lady Lettice observed aloud, "is not that Count Eustice to the left of Miss Wildham?" Pointing discreetly with her fan, she attempted to direct her sister's gaze away from that area of the room where she had seen the object of her sister's search.

The ruse served, as Patrice shifted her gaze to the veriest gargantuan of a gentleman in bright orange beside a callow young woman in poison-green taffeta.

8

All eyes turned toward the couple as the giant made his leg to the woman, a task no less difficult in execution than the moving of a mountain.

"I believe it is the Count," Sir Francis affirmed, peering through the curved surface of his quizzing glass at the parody of a bow. "I do not, I think, mistake his style. It must indeed be Anthony," he quipped.

Turning from the sight, Sir Francis scanned the rest of the room, his eye coming to rest on a gentleman approaching the group. "An' I do not mistake, that gentleman is Lieutenant Torquill. We were introduced as I recall when I chanced upon the lieutenant and Lady Patrice walking on one of the footpaths in Hyde Park," Sir Francis remarked, his glass never wavering.

It was charity that such was the case for he was not aware of the two sets of angry glances shot his way through veiled lids. Both Lettice and Aurora groaned inwardly as Patrice turned eagerly toward the uniformed officer as he neared. Waving one small gloved hand, Patrice's cheeks flushed with pleasure as she succeeded in gaining the lieutenant's attention.

Presenting himself before Patrice, Lieutenant Torquill bowed stiffly over her hand.

Aurora curled a well-shaped lip. Military, she thought scornfully. Not an ounce of grace.

Patrice did not seem to notice this lack of finesse as she smiled her approval. Her voice a trifle breathless, she said, "You have come, no doubt, to claim the dance I promised you earlier in the evening."

The lieutenant smiled his assent, and Patrice seemed almost to melt at his gaze, much to the combined disgust of her two sisters and the almost imperceptible distress of Lord Ringwood, who chewed on his lower lip unconsciously.

"And does the military teach its lieutenants to waltz creditably?" Lettice asked with light sarcasm. The lieutenant smiled yet again, aware of Lady Lettice's hostility. Aurora reflected with satisfaction that the lieutenant's gums showed when he smiled, and that it was not to the good.

"Lady Lettice," the lieutenant answered with a resonant baritone voice, "the military omits no aspect of a gentleman's training. As your father was a captain and danced tolerably well, you should be aware of this."

This rather smug rejoinder caused Lettice to comment through dangerously pursed lips. "You have unusual wit, sir. I have always held that the military could do wonders with the deportment of an individual, but I had not expected such a miracle as this."

There was a general titter of laughter as the lieutenant reddened slightly. Lettice continued. "As for my father, he does indeed dance well; however, that is expected as he was a gentleman prior to his captaincy, whereas you could have no prior advantage, hence my inquiry," she drawled, touching her fan lightly to her half-parted lips.

Lieutenant Torquill colored hotly at this, his teeth gritted to bite back any retort. His determination to remain congenial toward Lady Patrice's sister wavered visibly.

"This is our dance, I believe, Lieutenant Torquill." Patrice's pleading tone and the insistent pressure of her hand on his caused the lieutenant to bow slightly and lead his partner onto the ballroom floor without comment.

At the imploring look Patrice threw to her sisters as she was squired to the dance floor, Lettice was tempted to feel some remorse; however, her resolve to end such an unsuitable match was unshaken. Glancing meaningfully at her younger sister, Aurora rose gracefully from her chair, Lord Simmons rising instantly to attend her, fully aware of the sisters' disapproval of the lieutenant and amenable to their protective instincts so long as they furthered his own suit with Aurora.

Taking her hand, Lord Simmons took Lady Aurora to the floor, following carefully in the wake of Lieutenant Torquill and Patrice.

So quickly did this scene occur that Sir Francis could do little to protest, and the Marquess had already excused himself once it had become apparent that there was little hope of Aurora's quitting Lord Simmons' company that evening.

Sir Francis' only satisfaction was in witnessing Lord Simmons' shirt points wilting in the heat of the assembled bodies, and the sure knowledge of the distress it would cause that gentleman.

Sir Francis departed to try his luck at the card tables, leaving Lettice in the company of Lord Ringwood who continued to cannibalize his lower lip.

"Such unsociability!" Lettice commented with amusement as she watched Sir Francis wend his way through the crowd. Turning to her remaining companion she saw that Stuart Ringwood still attempted to follow the graceful movements of Patrice and the lieutenant, a worried expression on his face as he observed the exchange of intimate glances. So absorbed in this self-torture was he that he was unaware to what extent his feelings were revealed on his countenance.

Patrice and Lieutenant Torquill appeared an enchanting couple, and as Patrice looked adoringly up into the young man's face, she was once again struck by the incredible refinement she found in his features. The lieutenant was aware of her gaze and smiled easily.

"Are you enjoying yourself, my dearest?" he whispered close to her ear as he whirled her across the floor. He hardly needed to ask as he was fully certain of the state of infatuation he had induced in the young girl. Her reply was as expected.

"Now that you are here, I am," Patrice answered in a soft, breathless voice. "You are very handsome tonight, Basil," she continued shyly, lowering her eyes but waiting hopefully.

Lieutenant Torquill's smile broadened, and he did not disappoint her. "You are beyond compare tonight!" he said, placing a finger beneath her chin to raise her eyes to his. "You are the most precious of jewels, and if no one else appreciates your worth, then at least I do. I would compare you to Helen of Troy for I would gladly fight an army for your hand."

Lettice might have laughed at such verbose and contrived compliments, but for Patrice's romantic soul they were exactly what she had always longed to hear, and it was a smile of satisfaction that Basil Torquill wore as he congratulated himself on the success of his courtship thus far.

The couple continued to dance, Patrice never taking

her eyes from her partner; and Lord Ringwood continued to watch as well, oblivious to Lettice's presence.

Taking pity on her oldest friend, Lettice patted Stuart's hand in a comforting manner. She had been aware for some time of the passionate attachment Lord Ringwood had developed for Patrice, feelings he did not yet dare to express from fear. Patrice's attraction to the lieutenant was obvious and Lord Ringwood despaired of ever finding an opportunity to declare himself.

"Stuart," Lettice said at last, "we are old friends, are we not?"

"Of course, Lettice, very old and very good friends," Lord Ringwood replied, somewhat surprised.

"And you will let me say this for the friendship you bear me, I hope," she added. At the questioning look on his face, Lettice continued. "I am sure that you have formed a tendre for Patrice, Stuart." Lord Ringwood paled somewhat at this statement, and Lettice squeezed his hand reassuringly. "No, I have not told her, but why do you not let Patrice know of your feelings for her? I am sure that you and she would suit each other very well and she is really quite fond of you already."

"Lettice, she is fond of me as a sister is fond of a brother," Lord Ringwood replied dispiritedly. "She is in love with Lieutenant Torquill in any case, so it don't signify even if she does like me a bit."

"Nonsense," Lettice retorted gruffly, the mere mention of Lieutenant Torquill setting her back up. "You have only to become more loverlike in manner; then I am certain you could win her heart, Stuart," she insisted, but Lettice could see that there was no use pursuing the matter further that evening as Lord Ringwood was in no mood to listen to reason.

He continued to watch the couple waltz lightly across on the ballroom floor. Patrice fairly floated, glowing in a gown of white embroidered muslin, silver threads depicting rosebuds and hearts. Adorning her blond hair were pink roses, and ribbons trailed in delicate streamers from her waist, swirling about her partner's coat sleeves as if delivering intimate caresses. He turned away finally, an unhappy look in his eyes.

Lettice observed all of this with growing dismay, and her already considerable dislike for the lieutenant became even more profound in witnessing Stuart Ringwood's torture.

Of course, in form and feature there could be no possible objection to the lieutenant. He was, in fact, every young girl's dream of love personified, and though Lettice eyed him critically, she could not in all honesty find faults. Golden curls, well-shaped head, and a body like an Adonis. I suppose one can hardly blame Patrice for being attracted to such a man, Lettice mused, But such a twit! she thought with impatience, recalling tales from friends and acquaintances regarding the officer's character which Patrice chose to ignore. Autocratic, demanding, utterly overpowering, how can it be that he could hide all these traits? Lettice wondered with suspicion. If his behavior toward Patrice is any indication, he must be wanting a wife of means quite badly to make himself so very amenable . . . for the time being at least. Though she longed to ask Lord Ringwood if the lieutenant was a gazetted fortune hunter, she dared not.

By his very nature, Lord Ringwood was really incapable of any attack on Basil Torquill's motives, unlike Lettice who could occupy her time quite nicely with the assassination of the lieutenant's intentions.

He is thoroughly unsuitable, Lettice concluded mentally with characteristic abruptness. Mama would never allow the match, so I shall not fret on it further and neither should anyone else of consequence.

Fanning herself absent-mindedly, Lettice could not help comparing Lord Ringwood to Lieutenant Torquill. Undeniably, Stuart was far superior in personality. Amiable, well-liked, and respected, he would make a considerate, devoted husband. Everything which Lettice was sure would suit her sister's disposition. If the rumors were correct, Lieutenant Torquill would show his true colors only after the vows were said, and Patrice, if she married him, would live a life dominated utterly by her spouse.

A life she is not at all accustomed to, Lettice thought, her brows contracting into a frown. She would not like to play the mouse, and I daresay I should not

13

like to witness it. If only she were a bit more perceptive, how can she not see that Stuart is the better of the two? This question was one which Lettice found difficult to answer.

The young officer was a handsome devil and provokingly magnetic as well, but Lord Ringwood was by far more likable in Lettice's estimation, and a more loyal fellow she could not imagine.

However, taking stock of Stuart's physical attributes, Lettice reflected that he could not in all good conscience have been described as handsome. Yet in that same nicety of feeling, she refused to think of Stuart as being less than attractive, so amiable was his demeanor.

Relatively tall and of a willowy build, Lord Ringwood was reportedly athletic enough to have gained considerable praise from friends, but it was in his face that there seemed to be something lacking. With a head shaped into an elongated oval, Lord Ringwood gave the appearance of having been stretched rather too far. His jaw, while strong enough, did not seem able to accommodate his teeth, they having a tendency to protrude through a too-small mouth. Thick, straight eyebrows surmounted open friendly eyes the color of mint leaves which sparkled most definitely when he was happy and deepened in hue when he was disturbed. With hair of an uninspired brown, a nose which was overly wide, and ears which seemed to persist in jutting too far from his head, Stuart Ringwood was hardly the lover a girl would fancy. Yet, there was no denying his affability which won him an inordinately large number of male friends, if it did nothing to further him in more than friendship in the hearts of the young ladies of his acquaintance.

Titled, wealthy, Lord Ringwood had never been in the "Petticoat Line," and most knowing mamas had given up entirely on his ever coming up to scratch. Lettice had known Stuart for some years, she supplying the amusement and variety that Lord Ringwood appreciated and he, in return, responding with the very best in his own nature. It was a knack that Lettice possessed to an uncommon degree, the ability to draw people out or to make them vastly uncomfortable, should she so choose. Luckily, she had taken a liking to Lord Ringwood; she found his geniality endearing. Patrice was, she was sure, fond of Stuart as well, and Aurora was drawn to him through their mutual love of good horseflesh.

As the waltz came to a close, Stuart sighed his relief as he saw Lord Simmons and Aurora catch up with the handsome couple.

"Oh, yes," Lettice said, drawing Lord Ringwood's attention away from a situation he could do nothing to alleviate. "When, dear boy, will you be able to show Aurora your new horse? You know she desires it above all else, and she is very impatient that you have not raised the issue before this," Lettice admonished in mock severity.

At the mention of his horse, Stuart turned his full attentions to the conversation. "Truth of the matter is ma dear, the brute is not fit to see," he commented unhappily.

"But you described him as such a wonder, Stuart! Big and bold and powerful. Never tell me you were bamming. Aurora will most certainly serve you trick and tie for such a deception," Lettice warned unnecessarily.

"Wasn't bamming," Lord Ringwood replied defensively. "Splendid-looking beast. Thing is, unruly. Can't seem to tame the fellow down. Whenever one of the men approaches the animal, it plunges about, won't let anyone come near. Tried everything."

"And what will you do now?" Lettice asked curiously.

"Sell the beast. Only thing to do," Stuart replied. "Ought to fetch something at the auction tomorrow."

Looking down into the sherry-colored velvet of her full skirts, Lettice carefully smoothed the rumpled surface of the material, glancing up almost coyly from out the corner of her eye at Lord Ringwood. "I might be persuaded to purchase the animal myself, Stuart," Lettice said cautiously, her keen eyes watching to see her friend's reaction to the suggestion. "I would need to have our groom look at the horse first, but I have had a mind to make a few purchases for our stables at home."

"Well, he'd be a bacon-brained fellow if he did advise you to buy such a horse. It's as plain as a pikestaff that the beast ain't fit for a lady to ride. Better stick to the gentler steeds," Lord Ringwood advised sagely, but with a look of alarm in the back of his eyes.

"I am sure that he could be managed," Lettice insisted, angered at Lord Ringwood's steadfast insistence that the horse was beyond a female's capabilities to tame. "Well, it doesn't signify in the least if you won't sell me your horse, Stuart," Lettice said with dangerous sweetness. "After all, how could he be a suitable mount indeed if *you* cannot manage him?"

"That's the ticket," Lord Ringwood said with relief.

"Never mind that you cannot ride Gypsy while Aurora can," Lettice added airily, observing Lord Ringwood's discomfiture.

"A hit," Lord Ringwood acknowledged. "Aurora might well be able to tame the creature."

"Well, she is the true horsewoman of the Trevelyns, you know," Lettice admitted. "She will not like to hear that you will not let her see the animal. And don't think you can tell her some Banbury tale, for it won't fadge. She would smell the bubble out almost immediately and it would only vex her."

"I shall think of something to serve, never fear Lettice," Lord Ringwood said with more assurance than he felt.

"I do not envy you an' you set her back up," Lettice commented. "I am sure she would serve you up dreadfully."

Lord Ringwood shuddered slightly at the idea of the lady's reaction, reflecting that there were worse things than allowing Aurora to see his horse.

At that moment, the selfsame unpredictable lady, along with Patrice, having a desire for refreshments to revive them after their strenuous activity, sent their two cavaliers to procure some punch. Standing by the terrace overlooking a garden, the sisters awaited their return.

Fanning herself faintly, Patrice seated herself on a small chair, Aurora remaining by the balcony. "Aurora," she asked pensively, examining the design on the face of her fan, "I know that Lettice does not like

Basil, but I am persuaded that she might if only she would allow him in her company for more than five minutes at a time. Do you not think so?"

Leaning against the thin barrier of the terrace, Aurora, unable to think of an adequate reply for her love-struck sister, did not immediately answer as she looked out over the garden below. Though she did not fancy the lieutenant at all herself, she was not so blunt in her dislike as Lettice, who was inclined to cut those persons she found distasteful.

After a moment of silence, Aurora reluctantly answered. "Well, my dear, you know Lettice. It isn't that she could not like the lieutenant, for I am sure she could if she wished. Thing is, she doesn't wish it, and there is nothing for it, I am afraid."

Sitting beside her sister, Aurora placed a comforting arm about her shoulders. "Not to worry, though," Aurora encouraged, trying to put a little heart into Patrice's woebegone face. "If you really love the lieutenant, I am sure that you need not concern yourself over Lettice. She will change her mind about him, I imagine."

Patrice seemed unconvinced of this eventuality, and so intent were the two ladies in their thoughts that they did not at first notice the arrival of another person on the terrace. Looking up at the sound of oddly uneven footsteps, the two sisters observed before them an extremely tall and extremely foxed gentleman with whom they were unacquainted.

Reeking of alcohol, the man loomed above the seated women, swaying slightly from side to side as he attempted to focus a pair of bleary gray eyes.

Unable to produce the desired effect, the stranger thrust his face closer to the ladies, bending at the waist and perilously close to toppling over. Squinting in a most incredible manner, he exclaimed delightedly, "Well, by Jove! What have we here?" His words slurred together as if running upstream.

Pulling herself up with as much dignity as she could muster, Aurora said in icy tones, "I do not believe we have been introduced, sir."

This chilly attitude did not seem to bother the stranger in the least. Eyeing both ladies with an avidity which Aurora found disquieting and which caused Pa-

17

trice to shrink in her seat, the drunken fellow made an exaggerated bow.

"And what might your names be?" he said with difficulty, beads of sweat standing out on his drink-reddened forehead. He waited for a reply. None was forthcoming and he continued loudly. "Modesty! You have a great deal of maidenly, maidenly . . . damnation!" he swore, unable to recall the word he wished to use.

Thoroughly disgusted and nearly suffocated by the strong fumes on his breath, Aurora thrust the man out of her way and dragged her sister after her. Attempting to escape, she found it difficult to pass the drunk as Patrice was near-paralyzed from fear, hampering any effective efforts.

With a familiarity more appropriate to the streets, the stranger pursued the two women across the balcony.

"You are quite a lovely bit of muslin indeed," he commented to Aurora, a lascivious look on his face.

At those words, Aurora realized that he was so soused with drink that he had mistaken her for a low-born woman of the streets. Indignation and revulsion rose in her throat, and it was with a sudden instinctive flash that Aurora realized her danger. The intruder, his lips bearing a lecherous leer, lunged at the two women in hopes of catching them in his wide-opened arms.

Aurora thrust Patrice toward the French doors and out of danger as she deftly avoided the drunkard's embrace. Patrice hurried inside, giving one frightened glance behind her in time to see Aurora elude the inebriate once again. Staggering a bit, he continued to pursue the young woman until she could feel the cold stone of the balustrade at her back, her avenues of escape cut off.

The obtruder approached Aurora for the third time, sure of success. Quick as light, Aurora ducked low as he made his last approach. Moving too quickly to stop, he lost his balance, toppling over the railing.

For a split second, Aurora was most alarmed, thinking he surely would die from such a fall. She was soon relieved from her worries, however, by the sound of a large splash. Leaning over the balustrade she saw that

18

the sot had fallen into the lily pond, situated directly beneath the balcony. He lay motionless in the water for a time, then to Aurora's immense relief he began struggling to his feet. Extricating himself from the long stems and waterbugs, he staggered off into the night, mumbling curses audibly to himself as he went.

Aurora stood for a moment longer watching the drunken man stumble away; she was half persuaded to laugh at the sight. She heard a commotion behind her at that instant and turned to see Lord Ringwood followed by the lieutenant, Lord Simmons, and her sister, all approaching with purposeful strides.

Stuart reached Aurora first, looking about the area in search of the offender. He had obviously been informed of the situation by Patrice who had evidently gone in search of him as discreetly as possible once she had escaped the balcony.

"Well, where the deuce is he?" Lord Ringwood demanded as he determined that there was no one else in the vicinity.

As the others reached her side, Aurora responded to Lord Ringwood's question somewhat bemusedly. "In the pond, at least that was where he was a moment ago. He was a trifle overzealous in his attentions to me."

Looking over to the tiny pool of water, Lord Ringwood raised a brow and Lord Simmons let out a low whistle. "Serve him right if he takes a chill," Stuart asserted at last, turning back to Aurora. "You're all right, then?"

"But of course," Aurora replied with consummate nonchalance. Hooking her arm in Lord Ringwood's, she smiled. "If you would be so good, Stuart, I would like you to take me to Lettice. I am sure she would not wish to miss such a tale as I have to tell her." Glancing furtively over to Patrice, Lord Ringwood managed to convey to Aurora his worry at leaving her to Lieutenant Torquill's company. "Lord Simmons," Aurora asked sweetly, "would you please escort my sister back to my parents? I am sure we shall be leaving soon."

Lord Simmons bowed slightly over the glass of punch and plate of confections he had neglected to abandon in his haste to come to Aurora's assistance. "I

19

should be happy to," he assured her, much to Basil Torquill's discontent.

"I am sure we are not yet leaving," Patrice said with surprise as Lord Simmons steered her firmly back toward the ballroom.

"And I would be glad to escort Patrice myself," Lieutenant Torquill interjected firmly.

"Since I have asked Lord Simmons, and would not deprive him of my sister's company, you could not be so cruel as to deny him that pleasure, I am sure. Besides, two escorts are far better than just one," Aurora concluded breezily.

With that, Aurora turned with Lord Ringwood and reentered the ballroom to search for Lettice. It was with a sigh of relief that Aurora departed. She had had quite enough of the lieutenant's incredulous and disapproving looks as she had stood on the balcony. Gapeseed, she thought disparagingly.

Having no desire to remain vexed all evening, Aurora shrugged off her irritation, and turning to Stuart, who was looking about the room for a sign of Lettice, asked, "Well, my lord, when will I at last be privileged enough to see that new stallion of yours? You have put me off time and time again and now I vow I absolutely must see him." Aurora waited patiently for an answer. "I am free tomorrow afternoon," she pressed as no reply seemed to be forthcoming.

Fidgeting uncomfortably, Lord Ringwood craned his neck in desperation for the familiar figure of the eldest Trevelyn sister, without result.

"You'll get no reprieve from Lettice," Aurora warned. "Well?"

"Well you simply cannot see the animal tomorrow," Stuart replied gruffly.

"And why not?" Aurora demanded with disconcerting directness.

Without pausing to choose his words, Lord Ringwood replied, "Because of the race, of course. I haven't the bloody time to—"

"A race?" Aurora exclaimed ecstatically. "How marvelous!"

Realizing his mistake, Lord Ringwood instantly regretted his haste. "There is no use getting excited, for you are not going," he insisted.

"Not going? Don't be absurd, Stuart." Aurora dismissed the idea with a scornful glance. "You know how I love a good race."

"But there will be no other ladies present. Not the thing. Surely you can see that," Lord Ringwood pleaded with the feeling of a trapped creature.

"I see no such thing," Aurora replied with some heat. "Why must I be penalized simply because no other women will be in attendance?" she asked suspiciously. "Unless there is something you are not telling me."

Lord Ringwood stepped up his pace and seemed to look about with even more vigor for Lettice.

"I am persuaded that there is some mystery here, Stuart," Aurora asserted with deepening conviction.

"No mystery at all," Lord Ringwood countered uneasily, one hand going to his collar which had suddenly become too tight.

"But there is. Come now, what is it?" Aurora wheedled. "I shan't tell anyone. Promise, 'pon my honor."

Glancing uneasily about in a last effort for salvation, Lord Ringwood's unhappy face showed his reluctance to speak. Finally he sighed. "Well, I suppose it's inevitable. If you must know, there are certain special rules for the running of this particular race."

"Rules?"

"Yes, well, the entrants are to have one arm tied behind their backs, you see," Lord Ringwood murmured in a low voice, coughing slightly.

"I see," Aurora commented thoughtfully. "That could be quite difficult, to say the least."

"Well, I should rather think so!" Lord Ringwood exclaimed. "A fellow could be done to a cow's thumb if he wasn't careful."

"Then you simply cannot be so cruel as to say you will not take me to see this race if it is to be such an event," Aurora maintained, her persuasive tone pulling and twisting Stuart's already naturally yielding disposition to her way of thinking.

With a decisive nod of his head, he decided. "Right.

You may come along," he said, "but only if you let me hide you from view and if you promise not to go missish on me during the race."

To this Aurora readily agreed, and the two young people discussed arrangements for Lord Ringwood to come by with his curricle in the morning. It was also decided that the plans should be kept from Lettice as she was apt to disapprove of such a lark, though Aurora personally believed that she would do the same herself, given the opportunity. "I'll just tell everyone we are going riding together," she told Stuart.

When at last Lord Ringwood had ferreted out Lettice, the plans had been made. Lettice had been occupied in the card room where she had watched with fascination as the Honorable Bertram Boniface had lost to a gentleman she suspected of being a Captain Sharp.

Normally, Lettice might have noted with some suspicion the smile of contentment Aurora wore and the apprehensive look which adorned Lord Ringwood's face, so vastly different were these expressions; however, as it was, she was too absorbed in recounting to her friend and sister Mr. Boniface's ineptitude at faro, and in listening to Aurora's tale of this drunk on the terrace.

The hour was late by this time, and the crowd of guests was beginning to thin. Lettice and Aurora returned to their parents' side, Patrice already donning her cloak in the hallway with the assistance of Lieutenant Torquill.

Drawing Lord Ringwood to the side of the hall for a last word, Lettice inquired with interest, "Well, then, have you told Aurora about your horse?" She waited for an answer, catching sight of Lieutenant Torquill as he made his farewell to Patrice. Giving one last passionate salute to Patrice's gloved hand, he left her. Lettice frowned.

Lord Ringwood did not answer immediately, distracted, as he also had witnessed this overly fond departure. Turning from the sight uncomfortably, he answered, "Yes, I have discussed the matter and she will see the horse tomorrow morning. I will pick her up with ma rig and take her to the stables."

"Fine, then I shall meet you both there later for the auction," Lettice said happily. "Perhaps you would like

Patrice to come along as well?" Lettice suggested compassionately to her love-struck friend.

The result of her words was such as to baffle anyone. Stuart jumped slightly, as if he had been stuck with a pin.

"No!" he ejaculated abruptly. Then clearing his throat, he hastily added, "No, no, really. Patrice ain't at all interested in horses. Would be bored silly."

Eyeing her friend with contracted brow, Lettice looked at him with puzzlement, then shrugged slightly.

"I do hope you are going home now, Stuart," she commented with concern, observing his pale, slightly sweating face. "You seem under the weather. Not yourself. Won't do to go burning yourself to the socket," she admonished gently, patting his arm slightly and walking to the door.

Lord Ringwood followed Lettice to her carriage, assisting her as she entered. "I will be going to White's for a bit, Lettice," he said, observing the Countess's watchful eye from the carriage window. With a formal bow, he took his leave, assuring Lettice that he would no doubt leave directly after for home.

"See that you do so, Stuart," Lettice called out in a gay voice as the horseman cracked his whip, disregarding the exasperated sigh from the Countess at her impropriety of manner. "And do try to keep Aurora from getting into any scrapes tomorrow. You know how I depend upon your discretion to guide this wayward child," Lettice mocked, placing a teasing hand on Aurora's arm. If Aurora seemed strangely unaffected by her sister's jibes, it went unnoticed.

With another motion of his whip, the driver set the carriage in motion, and Stuart Ringwood found it thankfully unnecessary to make any reply to Lettice's final words as that lady waved back to him.

Keep her out of scrapes, Lord Ringwood thought. Shaking his head at this, he reentered the house to retrieve his topcoat and hat.

Standing before the large hallway mirror, he carefully placed his hat at an angle on his head in a vain attempt to achieve a somewhat rakish affect. Making a dissatisfied face, Lord Ringwood adjusted the offending hat several times, but gave up this endeavor for futile.

" 'T'won't serve, Stuart," a voice declared from behind him. Looking into the glass, Lord Ringwood observed the figure of Lord Simmons, his own hat set at the particular angle that Stuart could not himself achieve.

"Damn this hat anyway," Lord Ringwood swore with irritation.

" 'T'ain't the hat, you know," Lord Simmons drawled, minutely checking his own attire in the reflective surface. With a satisfied nod, he stepped back from the mirror. "It is, I am very much afraid, your head which fails to come up to scratch, my lord." The dandy's smile was disarming, and Stuart took the jest good-naturedly.

"If there wasn't so much truth to what you say, I daresay I should have to call you out for such a gross insult to ma physiognomy," Lord Ringwood declared in fun, shaking his substantially solid fist in Lord Simmons' face. The bark of laughter which escaped Lord Simmons' lips echoed in the hall.

"I take no exception to your fivers, Stuart, just with your head," he quipped, knowing the threat to be an empty one. "Coming to White's?" he inquired, passing through the open doorway and acknowledging the slight bow accorded by the butler. Following him out, Stuart nodded.

"Yes. Want to place a bet on the race tomorrow?" he said, walking abreast with Lord Simmons and keeping pace with long-limbed strides.

"Have the odds changed?" Lord Simmons asked with interest.

"Not an' I know of it," Lord Ringwood replied, his face screwed up in concentration. "The field is so well matched that I haven't a clue as to who will win it, but I will place a small wager nonetheless."

"On which man, though?" Lord Simmons questioned.

"Well, I don't know, but I will decide once at the club. Whomever suits ma fancy at that moment, I suppose," Stuart Ringwood commented unconcernedly. Not a betting man, the amounts that he usually wagered were not worth the worry entailed by their loss. He bet only enough to make the race exciting, not enough to cause him undue concern should he lose.

Nearing the club, Lord Simmons chided his companion. "Really Stuart, if you are going to bet at all, why not make it worth your—I say. What is going on?" Lord Simmons asked, squinting at a scene up ahead at the entrance to White's.

"What is it indeed?" Lord Ringwood inquired, craning his neck to see, and slowing his pace in apprehension.

Coming to a full halt, Lord Simmons cocked his head to the side in wonder. "Gad, looks like some fellow is being refused admittance," he said at last. Coming closer, Lord Ringwood could hear the strained and unsure voice of the footman at the door.

"Sir, I do not recall your face at all, and I am well acquainted with every member of this club. I am afraid I cannot permit you to enter."

There was a gesture from a gentleman cloaked in the many-caped coat of a Corinthian. It had a decidedly French cut to the discerning eye of Lord Simmons, marking the man as a gentleman.

The footman continued to speak, his tone formally chilling. "If you could perhaps obtain the invitation of one of our members, I am sure that you will be most welcome. However, without such recognition, I am afraid I cannot let you pass."

The figure turned at this last statement, apparently to depart.

With a puzzled frown, Lord Ringwood watched as the man started down the steps of the club. Something in his manner, in the very way in which he walked, stirred a memory in the deeper recesses of his mind, a long forgotten familiarity which echoed *friend.*

"I know that man," he whispered softly, so faintly that Lord Simmons doubted that he had heard aright. With a hesitant step forward, then another, Stuart Ringwood found himself running to catch up with the retreating figure. Lord Simmons and the footman gaped in astonishment.

"A moment, sir," he called out, wondering at his own behavior and vaguely aware that the situation could become vastly uncomfortable, should this man not be an acquaintance of his. The time for discretion was past as the figure stopped in the shadows and turned to face the approaching lord.

Stopping dead in his tracks, Lord Ringwood seemed as one stunned. In a voice reflecting his mixed emotions, he called out, "Richard, my God, you have come back!"

꧁꧂ CHAPTER 2

TOOLING his curricle down the street, Lord Ringwood cursed mildly as one brightly painted wheel jolted quickly in and out of a pothole, the vibrations sending his hat askew for the third time that morning. Straightening it resolutely with one hand, he frowned and attempted to pay more heed to where he was going; but it was really too much to ask as his mind was still occupied with the events of the previous evening.

Smiling, Lord Ringwood recalled his surprise at seeing Richard, now the new Duke of Melburry, after so long an absence. Four years abroad was quite a while, and though Richard had written consistently, Stuart had had no inkling of his return. There had been little change in Richard's physical appearance. A trifle taller, perhaps a bit broader in the shoulders, but still the Richard he remembered. His manner had been as easy as ever, with that hint of the devil within. He had walked into White's with the air of a man who had never been away, and the other members had taken their cue from him.

Amidst the usual back pounding and hearty hellos there had not been the slightest reference to the scandal which had caused Richard to leave England. Stuart himself would never mention it, but he felt that Lord Simmons would have asked for some details had not the look in the Duke's eyes changed his mind for him.

It had not been a warning glance precisely, but it had left Lord Simmons uneasy enough to curtail any thoughts of discussing bygone events.

In any case, Stuart reflected, there can be no doubt that Richard has changed, no matter if he appears the same as ever.

This conviction was due to the six neat bundles of letters Lord Ringwood had received over the past few years from Richard from various locations in France.

The change also became evident to a few of the older members of the club and particularly to one Sir Gibbon who had once had a taste of Richard's sense of the absurd: some years back Sir Gibbon had commented on the excellence of his own fox hounds within earshot of Richard and the following evening had been the unwilling recipient of an unruly pack of mongrel dogs which had been delivered to his townhouse from some "unknown" benefactor.

Recalling the incident to Richard, Sir Gibbon made a frosty reference to that night, and much to his surprise, but not to Stuart's, Richard made a proper and correct apology for his little escapade, a thing unheard of from the "old" Richard.

Taken aback by this oddity, Sir Gibbon harrumphed, "Well, I see your sojourn in France has changed you a bit."

"To be sure, Sir Gibbon," Richard replied with familiar aplomb. "It has been an education indeed, though I am sure you are aware of the benefits yourself, having made the tour in your own youth."

Sir Gibbon barked a laugh, well aware of his own peccadilloes in his salad days. "Well, Melburry, you must come up to the house when you find the time."

Richard had accepted, of course, and Lord Ringwood thought he could even detect pleasure on his friend's face at the prospect. He had been pleased himself by the reception Richard had received from everyone, pleased, that is, until Giles Killingham and his cohort, Percival Snogging, had entered the club. All eyes were instantly trained on Richard and Killingham for the confrontation they knew must occur.

Richard had appeared to be oblivious to Killingham's presence, avidly discussing the race that was to take place on the following day with Lord Simmons. However, Lord Ringwood had seen the slight stiffening of his friend's back as he had taken note of Killingham's arrival.

Killingham himself had not immediately seen Richard on entering the club, but the Honorable Percival Snogging soon made him aware by incessantly tugging at his sleeve. Responding to the silent call for his attention, Lord Killingham had glanced irritably in the direction of His Grace. Small bloodshot eyes peered at Richard for one incredulous moment as if unable to comprehend what they saw, and then, to Lord Ringwood's utter dismay, Lord Killingham had approached the small group by the fire. Glancing quickly at Richard, Stuart had been put somewhat at ease by what he saw there. No sign of discomfort or fear was present and it was as if the tenseness that Lord Ringwood had detected a moment before had never existed.

Though Stuart was usually of a peaceable nature and abhorred scenes of any sort, he had been determined to lend any assistance Richard should require. Nibbling resolutely on one bedraggled fingernail, Lord Ringwood steeled himself for the fray. Fortunately, no such aid had been necessary.

Killingham had sauntered almost casually up to Richard who had been prepared to lay a wager on the upcoming race. The other men there, Lord Simmons and Sir Francis, greeted him with studied nonchalance, no more anxious for a mill in the midst of the club than Lord Ringwood.

"Gentlemen," Lord Killingham greeted the group, his eyes never leaving the Duke's face. "Your Grace, I see you have returned from your 'trip'," he had said, his red-rimmed eyes narrowing slightly.

If he had expected a reaction from Richard, Stuart reflected, he had been sorely disappointed. The Duke had looked with unflappable calm into Killingham's eyes, never flinching or indicating anything other than total control. This incredible reaction to the presence of Lord Killingham had its effect on the members of the club. Of course a confrontation would have had to occur, but all the men who had assumed Richard's guilt in the past scandal found to their amazement that they were having second thoughts on the matter.

Speculative looks flew across the room, but Lord Ringwood could think of nothing to say. Richard, however, seemed to be in command of the situation.

"I have indeed returned, Lord Killingham. Your eyes do not deceive you, and I see that you have not changed," Richard replied with a languidness implying boredom. "Correct me if I am wrong," he added, just as Killingham would have spoken, "but is it now *à la mode* to sport one's hair wet down with water? We have not yet heard of it on the continent."

All eyes had turned to gaze at Lord Killingham's sodden coiffure. It had apparently suffered a soaking and lay on his head in untidy disarray. Lord Ringwood's suspicions had been aroused at the sight, as he recalled Aurora's unidentified admirer of earlier in the evening.

"Perhaps it is raining outside?" Lord Simmons added with mock helpfulness.

"No, it is not a new style, neither is it raining," Lord Killingham had replied with the barest civility. He did not care to be the butt of a joke and appeared determined to extract some sign of discomfiture from Richard. "You would be better versed in the fashions, Your Grace, after your stay in France. Tell me, why did you return? Were not the attractions of the demimonde enough to entice you to stay?"

After a moment's pause, Richard had replied with quiet dignity. "I have come to put the estate in order, Lord Killingham."

Killingham stared back coldly, but Sir Francis had murmured, "Of course, of course," a somewhat stricken expression on his powdered face. "Your father, the late Duke—"

"Precisely," Lord Ringwood had put in, finding his voice enough to cover the embarrased silence. "But that is all beside the point. You are back and that is all right and tight," he had finished bravely, daring anyone to say him nay.

There were no dissenters, and many had found Lord Killingham's references to the late Duke uncalled for.

"Quite pleased you are back," Francis Trent had

29

chipped in. "And I will be more than glad to relieve you of some of your blunt, Melbury, in francs or pounds, it doesn't matter a whit," he had added with strained jocularity. "You were about to place a bet, Your Grace, on your brother Peregrine, and if that don't mean you'll lose I do not know my horses."

"What he means," Lord Simmons had remarked with exaggerated skepticism, "is that he fully intends to win the race himself."

"And what is so extraordinary about that, my lord?" Killingham had asked, venom still in his eyes. "It is hardly likely, after all, that a Melbury would be able to best Sir Francis. The Melbury talents lie in other directions, surely?"

The insinuation was strong, and the Honorable Percival Snogging gave his unasked-for opinion as well, the scent of a possible kill encouraging him to speak. "As I recall it, Your Grace, you used to participate in daredevil races in your youth, as well as other things. In fact, I believe you are considered something of a buck." Mr. Snogging's eyes had shifted about the gathered faces, flitting uneasily from each man's eyes as would a fly afraid of being swatted.

As Lord Ringwood drove, now recalling the little man, he felt disgust rise in his throat anew and just barely managed to avoid nicking the wheels of another passing carriage. Pulling hurriedly on the reins of his rig, he reflected that Richard's passion for horses and riding had not abated over the years spent in France. The idea of participating in the race had, of course, appealed to the more reckless side of his friend, and Stuart had been able to tell that Richard was tempted. Then the deciding card was dealt.

Blandly examining his pearl-gray gloved hand, Lord Killingham had added, "I am, myself, riding tomorrow." The challenge was unmistakable.

"There is room for yet another rider," Mr. Snogging had informed the Duke unnecessarily.

Only a moment's hesitation showed his indecision to Lord Ringwood, and then with a characteristic cocky tilt of his head, Richard had replied, "That would be up to the members of the club, of course."

The question had been put up to the members of

White's with all haste, spurred on by Percival Snogging, and the arrangements had been made for Richard to participate in the race.

Stuart would have liked to have left the club with Richard, as there were so many things he would have liked to say. Unfortunately, Richard had slipped away later in the evening, leaving a note for Lord Ringwood to visit him the evening after the race.

Stuart sighed as he pulled his matched chestnuts into the street where the Trevelyns resided. He supposed he should have known that some sort of power confrontation was inevitable between the two men and that perhaps he should be thankful it was only to be a horse race. Still, he could not help being nervous; it was his nature.

Manipulating the reins in his hands with care, Lord Ringwood placed the curricle precisely before the Trevelyn manor, fitting neatly between a barouche of advanced age and a decidedly feminine landaulet. Leaping from the high perch, Stuart's thoughts turned from Richard's problems to his own precarious predicament. Aiding Aurora Trevelyn in another one of her famous scrapes was not the best of ideas, but then it would have been far worse for him if he had refused, as he would then have had to face that lady's considerable irritation.

Awkwardly straightening his neckcloth and checking his boots to see that the high polish he had at last achieved was still present, Lord Ringwood approached the door, attempting to wipe all signs of the guilt he felt from his telltale face.

Looking out of her sister's sitting-room window, Patrice Trevelyn called out to Aurora who was busily searching about in a chest of drawers, "Stuart is here. You had best make all haste and find that riding whip or he shall be tempted to go off without you."

Making a face at her younger sister's comment, Aurora turned back to her task of pillaging Lettice's drawers for the elusive whip.

"And where is *your* riding crop, Aurora, if I may ask?" a voice inquired from the doorway.

"Lost," Aurora replied to Lettice with perfect aplomb. With a casual flourish, she removed an intriguingly colorful piece of silk from one drawer and let it fall on a nearby table.

"Here now, let me do it or we will have half the contents of the thing on the table," Lettice insisted impatiently and with some exasperation to her sister who smiled puckishly at her vexation. A few seconds of searching and Lettice produced the desired object. "There you are. You have only to be searching for something, Aurora, for it to be in exactly the last place you would look," Lettice teased. "Tell me, when did you lose your whip?" Lettice asked, replacing the articles that Aurora had so cheerfully removed. "It is not like you."

"I did not lose it myself. I am not such a clumsy as to lose a perfectly good crop, I will have you know," Aurora answered, carefully setting her riding hat upon her head before the gilt mirror. "I lent it to Ann Snogging when we were at Concordance for the fox hunt. The silly creature dropped it among the trees during the hunt; said the horn had startled her."

Aurora's scorn was heavy and neither sister felt up to dealing with the ravings and rantings that would surely ensue, should either of them attempt to defend Mrs. Snogging. Indeed, none of the Trevelyn sisters had any love to bestow on that lady as she had been a nuisance more often than not, and tended to gossip behind even her friends' backs.

"To change the topic," Lettice announced, "Stuart is below waiting on you, Aurora. Do hurry and save him from Mama."

"I am aware of Stuart's arrival, my dear. Do come and help me set this hat to rights. You have a touch for it," Aurora said as she was frustrated in her attempts to satisfy her own exacting standards.

"Shall I see you at the auction this afternoon?" Lettice asked as she came forward to adjust the bothersome article. "Though Derek is an excellent groom, and certainly knows his horses, I would feel better if I could have your opinion as well. After all, you ride them more than I do and I must admit that Derek loses me when he speaks of one having a bit more 'leg' or another not having enough 'wind' for running."

"I should love to come," Aurora replied, pleased

with her sister's acknowledgment of her expertise. "You may depend upon it that I will speak to Stuart."

"Fine," Lettice replied, pleased. "I need not ask if you will come, Patrice," Lettice said, turning to her unattentive sibling who was, as she knew, intent on searching the street below for signs of her lieutenant. "I know your interests lie elsewhere today."

Looking up from her vigil, Patrice's eyes seemed dreamy and distant.

"You shall strain your eyes, dear, if you don't stop searching for every little bit of braid and red that comes down the street," Aurora scolded playfully. "He will come when he comes and not a moment sooner, for all your attentions." Pausing a moment, she added, "Considering Mama, perhaps it is best he come later than sooner, for his own sake."

"I cannot help it, I am afraid," Patrice apologized with a sigh. "I do hope Mama will like him. Do you think she shall?" she asked Lettice, a hopeful look in her eyes.

"She may, but you know Mama," Lettice answered doubtfully.

The crestfallen expression on Patrice's face prompted Aurora to add compassionately, "Bound to like him if she feels he is suitable. Mama is not unreasonable after all, so he does have a chance."

"He is not titled or plump in the pockets," Patrice murmured awkwardly. "I know it signifies to Mama that I marry well."

"Just what is it that you do like about him, Patrice?" Aurora asked curiously.

"Why, I like everything about him," Patrice answered with an enchanted smile. "He has all the qualities I have always wanted in a man."

"And what qualities are those?" Lettice queried with a cocked brow.

"Well," she replied reflectively, "he is very romantic and attentive to my wishes. He says such lovely things—complimenting me and telling me how much he cares for me. He does things for me, too. He's on my side. When I don't feel strong enough to do something, he will do it for me. I suppose you could say he is what every girl wants," she sighed.

"He's not what I would want, I can tell you that," Lettice put in emphatically.

"No? Then what are you looking for in a man, Lettice?" Patrice inquired.

"Let me think . . . I'd like a handsome man, to be sure, but it is not really necessary as long as he has the other qualities I require. He must have an aura of confidence and a good deal of wit. He would be a knowing 'un socially, and naturally he must be faithful to me and adore me utterly." She laughed at the last, but the statement was true, nonetheless, and serious.

"And what about you, Aurora? What sort of a gentleman would you fall in love with?" Patrice asked, turning to her other sister.

Aurora stood angling her hat before the mirror and frowned with exaggerated severity. "Well, I've given it a great deal of thought and I know what I want, I daresay. He must be a sensitive creature. That is imperative," she declared. "He must understand my feelings and share many of them as well. He should be open and honest with his emotions. I must have loyalty from one I would love, too. Yes," she continued thoughtfully, "loyalty is very high on my list. It is important that he be true to me." Her knit brows conveyed how strongly she felt about this subject.

The gravity of Aurora's attitude made tears well up in Patrice's eyes as she recalled her own situation to mind. "I am sure you can see then how important it is, now that I've found a man who possesses everything I need, that I not allow Mama to keep me from him."

"But Mama does want you to be happy," Lettice reminded hurriedly. "Don't cry, my dear. Only think how badly you look when you are all weepy, and your Basil about to arrive at any moment."

"Yes, do cheer up," Aurora encouraged. "Only a very few people can cry without looking quite appalling, and I am sorry to have to say that you do not possess this singular talent. Come, help Lettice with my hat, maybe between the two of you it can be set to rights."

"You are right, of course," Patrice said with a tiny smile. "Red eyes would never do." Drying her tears with the edge of her lace handkerchief, Patrice rose, and between the sisters' combined efforts, they succeeded in making Aurora presentable in her own eyes.

Stepping back to admire the effect in the glass, Aurora appeared unconcerned that Lord Ringwood would have to bear the company of her mother while she did so.

Below, Stuart Ringwood was almost at wit's end for a subject to speak on with the Countess who insisted upon engaging him in conversation. Though she knew nothing of horses or men's fashions, the only two subjects that Stuart was somewhat conversant on, she endeavored to keep the lord occupied. Having exhausted the merits of the newest fashions in slippers and thoroughly expounded on the necessity for young ladies of fashion *not* to be allowed to wear silk ballroom gowns that possessed revealing décolletages, both parties felt totally at a standstill. Silence hung like a pall for a few seconds, Lord Ringwood allowing his attention to wander.

"And what do you think of the new leather goods from Morocco?" the Countess asked so suddenly that Stuart appeared to start quite some inches from his seat as he came to attention.

"Eh?" he replied inelegantly, then clearing his voice and blushing he sputtered, "Ah, yes. Moroccan leather. Quite the thing I am sure, Countess. Lord Simmons, I believe, has brought it into fashion. Can't say that I really fancy the stuff ma self, though. A bit on the gaudy side, don't you think, Madam?"

His inquiry was received with a stillness that was unnatural for a woman accustomed to speaking even when she had little constructive to contribute. The icy stare that Stuart beheld raised his apprehension and after a moment the Countess spoke. "There are those individuals, Lord Ringwood, who favor the new fashion."

This was said in such a voice that Stuart's eyes moved reluctantly, but with a fair certainty of what he would discover, down to the Countess's feet, shod in patterned Moroccan leather.

"Umm, well, yes," Lord Ringwood mumbled meekly, "quite so."

Squirming, Stuart prayed fervently for Aurora to hurry her preparations, seeming to sink in his seat as the Countess eyed him coolly.

Lord Ringwood's silent entreaty was soon answered as Aurora hurried down the stairs to greet her friend.

"Stuart, how prompt you are," Aurora praised as she allowed the relieved young man chastely to salute one gloved hand.

"And where are you off to today?" the Countess asked politely. "Or need I ask?" she commented, noting her daughter's riding attire.

With arched brow, Aurora gave Lord Ringwood a speaking glance, causing that already skittish gentleman's considerable nose to twitch slightly, as a rabbit's does when sensing danger.

Twirling gracefully before her mother, Aurora replied blithely, "As you can see, Mama, we shall be with horses. No doubt we shall ride, and . . ." she added with an impish smile, "the rest I leave to your imagination."

The Countess laughed, uneasily granted, but she seemed reassured when her daughter kissed her lightly on a powdered cheek before taking Lord Ringwood's arm.

Watching them depart, the Countess voiced to unhearing air much the same sentiment as Lettice had to Lord Ringwood the previous evening. "Well, I suppose she could not get into any scrapes with Lord Ringwood." The Countess frowned as her daughter's untrammeled laughter floated up through the open windows to her anxious ears.

Helping Aurora into a curricle, which those in the know had announced as "slap up to dash," Lord Ringwood noted with approval the light brown riding habit Aurora wore. Inconspicuous, good, he thought as he took his place beside her.

"Will you not let me take the reins, Stuart?" Aurora instantly asked as he took up the stout leather in his own hands. "You know I can manage a pair very well. I drive all the time in the country, but Mama will not hear of it in town," she implored.

Looking at his companion, Stuart shook his head emphatically, ruining his neckcloth in the process.

"The Countess would rake me down if I did," he said in his defense. "Besides, you don't know the way, and we will be later than I like as it is."

With a flick of his wrists he started the chestnuts down the road at a brisk rate.

"Oh, you're no fun anymore," Aurora declared peevishly, but to no avail.

Sighing, Aurora witnessed the set expression on Lord Ringwood's face that insured her defeat. It was not one of anger or stubbornness so much as it was a resolved look, and Aurora knew better than to pursue a futile goal. Settling herself in the soft red leather of the seat, she proceeded to enjoy the excellent handling Lord Ringwood exhibited in driving his matched pair, vicariously deriving some modicum of pleasure.

"Tell me, Stuart. Do I know any of the gentlemen who are running today?" Aurora asked as they reached the outskirts of town, her curiosity roused as they neared their destination.

Keeping the horses at a steady pace, Lord Ringwood replied, without taking his eyes from the road ahead, "You know a few of them, I daresay." Avoiding a pothole in the road by the thinnest of margins, he continued, "Of course, don't know just who you are familiar with, this being your first season and all, but Lettice knows the majority."

"Yes, well, I am not Lettice so you must describe them all to me, you silly goose," Aurora remonstrated with mock exasperation. "Now tell me who is to race."

"Well, there is Lord Simmons naturally," Stuart replied after a moment's careful thought.

"And he did not even mention it to me," Aurora interrupted indignantly.

"And so he shouldn't," Stuart replied primly. "And if I didn't have such a cursed loose jaw, I shouldn't have let you get wind of it either."

"Do go on, who else will be there?" Aurora urged, sensing dangerous second thoughts on Lord Ringwood's part.

"Alan Wainfleet is also running, though what could have possessed him to do so I am sure I don't know."

"Nor I," Aurora agreed feelingly. "He is such a dashed dull dog that I am quite at a standstill as to what could have induced him to do anything which smacks so thoroughly of frivolity and amusement," she added with disdain.

Stuart Ringwood eyed the young woman with surprise. "Thought you liked the Marquess," he remarked with confusion. "Must have been mistaken."

"Indeed, I don't think anyone can like that man. He throws a damper on everything," Aurora said with a decisive nod of her lovely head.

"Nonetheless, he is running," her companion continued undaunted, "and Francis wants to defeat both Wainfleet and Simmons with a passion."

"Somehow I cannot see Francis thrown into a passion by anything," Aurora replied doubtfully. "Except, perhaps, if either gentleman should insult his attire. Who else? This begins to become entertaining."

"There are a few fellows I don't believe you know," Lord Ringwood continued. "The Duke of Melbury, his younger brother Peregrine, and . . . Giles Killingham."

"They are unfamiliar to me, I am afraid. However, you seem to dislike this Giles Killingham. May I ask why, Stuart? You dislike so few people that this man must be quite dreadful indeed. Tell me about him," Aurora coaxed, eager as ever to satisfy her constant curiosity.

For a few moments, Stuart was at a loss, then sensing that Aurora was impatient for an answer, said reluctantly, "If you must know, Lord Killingham is not much liked by anyone. He is reputed to have behaved in a less than chivalrous manner to various *ladies*, and is in ma opinion something of an outsider."

Aurora considered his words before answering. "When you say 'various ladies', Stuart, are you telling me that the man has the gall to come the ugly with his mistresses?" Aurora asked in a shockingly knowing manner.

"I made no such comment," Lord Ringwood sputtered, then with a stern expression he admonished, "and you should know better than to talk in that mode."

"I don't speak in such a manner to anyone but you, an' you know it is so, Stuart. I know you shan't blush

38

to hear the truth. That *is* the truth of the matter, is it not?" she asked, her discerning eye catching Lord Ringwood's mute assent. "I thought as much," she said, a note of satisfaction in her voice. With a disdainful expression, she added, "How I detest a cad! Or is it a rake?" she asked, unsure of the precise definitions.

"T'ain't a rake, to be sure. Not the sort of phiz the women go batty over," Lord Ringwood replied after contemplating the question.

"I suppose he is a cad, then," Aurora interjected, "and I am glad you told me about him. Now I can snub him if we meet, and do so without the usual twinge of conscience that I so often have after giving someone a set-down."

This course of action settled on, Aurora continued, "You will have to point out to me those gentlemen I don't know so I will know who has won."

Ignoring the incredulous look on her friend's face at this request, Aurora considered the matter settled.

"Dash it, Aurora. A fellow can't go about signaling or whispering into bushes. The others will think me a looby," Stuart Ringwood objected.

"How else am I to know who is who, then? And what is all this talk about bushes?" Aurora demanded suspiciously. "I thought I was to hide in the stables and watch the race."

Caught off guard, Lord Ringwood sputtered a bit. "Well, we had to change the location of the race at the last moment," he explained rather apologetically. "If you are to watch, you will have to be hidden in the bushes."

"I had not bargained for that," Aurora announced, somewhat disgruntled at the thought of possibly soiling her habit. At the exasperated sigh from Lord Ringwood, however, she assured him quickly, "but if that is the only way . . . Oh well." She said enthusiastically, "It will be exciting even if I must sit on the ground." Tilting her head, she asked, "And why are you not in the race? Surely you can ride as well as any of the others, Stuart, or are you fretful that you will take a spill and ruin your ensemble?" Aurora looked at him, a smile of wicked delight playing about her full lips.

"I prefer to leave such antics to others," Lord Ringwood commented with a straight-laced air. "I shall *watch* the proceedings, an occupation I much prefer to risking ma neck for such a silly thing as a daredevil race."

"Well, I think it excessively kind of you to bring me so I may enjoy it too, Stuart, and I thank you heartily in advance," Aurora said, smiling sweetly at her companion who was completely unmanned by the unexpectedness of her gratitude.

Murmuring a few self-deprecating words, Lord Ringwood found himself nearing the spot where the race would be held. Drawing in the reins, the young lord brought his curricle to a halt before a large group of dense hedges directly adjacent to the makeshift course that someone had obligingly marked out with poles, scraps of white muslin tied to them so that the riders could clearly observe their path.

Descending from the highly sprung vehicle, Aurora surveyed the area, noting with a thrill of approval the difficulty of the course which included three crumbling stone walls, one of which banked the edges of a shallow irrigation ditch. The height of the lichen-covered obstruction was quite adequate to foul any rider, even as excellent a seat as Sir Francis was purported to be.

Looking nervously about and checking his timepiece, Lord Ringwood pulled insistently at Aurora's sleeve, guiding her over to the clump of bushes. Parting the dense foliage so that she could hide herself from view, Aurora half knelt among the greenery, the brown of her habit camouflaging her effectively. Uncomfortable though she was, she found that by moving some of the leaves aside she had an excellent view of the course.

"Can you see?" Lord Ringwood whispered, looking furtively toward the sound of approaching voices. In the distance he could see men and horses coming, accompanied by the sounds of jovial intercourse.

"I can see just fine. It is marvelous, really," Aurora replied delightedly to her harried conspirator. "Though it is a bit cramped in here to say the least, and my legs are beginning to feel numb already," she added, shifting her position slightly.

The crackling of leaves that followed this move caused Lord Ringwood to cringe slightly.

"Try not to look so odd, Stuart, or you will quite give us away, and that would be a great pity indeed," Aurora encouraged, as she could see Lord Ringwood's nerves were beginning to fray.

Taking this advice to heart, Stuart turned from the hedge in time to see the Duke of Melburry approach, holding bindings in one hand and leading a large chestnut mare with the other.

Aurora's eyes went first to the horse, a great hulking beast with muscles that rippled fantastically in the sunlight as it sidled up affectionately to its master.

As Aurora watched, the master petted the huge muzzle absent-mindedly.

What a fine blood horse, Aurora thought enviously as she observed the strong flanks and excellent lines on the animal. Made for running, without any doubt.

Almost as an afterthought, she noticed the prospective rider. Lord Ringwood proceeded to bind Richard's right arm behind his back, talking all the while. Aurora faintly heard a joking reference to "Your Grace's giant of a mare," and knew that this must be the Duke of Melburry.

As Aurora watched the proceedings, she took in the newcomer's features. He is what they would call a Corinthian, I suppose, Aurora thought as she observed the Duke's lean physique displayed in the casual riding attire sported by such gentlemen who favored the hunt and seemed as if they were bred, as much as their horses, to the sport. He did not seem to top six feet and was built along the same thin lines as Lord Ringwood, though not as gangly by half. Even as he was being bound, he had an air of nonchalance that Aurora felt was as much a part of the man's nature as breathing.

The Duke was quite handsome, though his features, considered individually, might make one wonder why one thought so. He possessed a squarish jaw with a pointed chin and a rather pinched-looking nose which were not precisely in the classic mold. However, put together with his curling brown hair, reminiscent of the Greek gods, and his pleasing hazel eyes, he cut an altogether personable figure.

Besides all this, he had an undeniable charm which

permeated his very being even at a distance, making his physical attributes all the more attractive.

Wearing a brown riding jacket with huge mother-of-pearl buttons, fawn-colored breeches, and shining riding boots, His Grace appeared no less than splendid. And if he seems a bit arrogant, Aurora thought, perhaps he has a right.

Farther off, Aurora could see other riders being prepared in a similar manner. Straining her ears, she could make out some of the conversation between Lord Ringwood and the Duke.

"There!" Stuart announced as he stood back to look at his handiwork. "Done up as fine as a Christmas package."

"Forgive me, Stuart," the Duke replied, wincing as he attempted to move his arm, "but any child receiving a yuletide gift from you would be struggling to open it still by spring."

"A bit tight, is it?" Lord Ringwood asked with a laugh.

As he spoke another figure strode up and Aurora recognized him to be Lord Simmons.

"So much the better," Lord Simmons commented as he checked the Duke's bindings as he had been doing with all the competitors. "It won't be likely to come undone accidentally as you go over the walls. Wouldn't want you disqualified on a technicality, you know." With a toothy grin, Lord Simmons completed his inspection. "Everything is all fine here," he said after a moment. "Need any help mounting?" he asked as His Grace struggled, attempting to get astride his horse.

The animal seemed skittish at seeing its master in so unusual a condition, but without a word the Duke succeeded, disdaining the offer of assistance with a self-sufficient manner.

"Has Peregrine been prepared yet?" Richard asked, steadying his mare with his unfettered hand.

Looking about, Stuart shrugged and tilted his head askance. "I don't see him, Richard. I'm sure he is about somewhere. Have you seen him Lord Simmons?"

"I believe he has just mounted that white monster over there," Lord Simmons commented, pointing to a rider and horse that approached the group. "Why is it,

Richard, that all the horses you and your brother possess are such large animals? That creature your brother is riding is enormous."

The men turned as if one body to look, and Aurora joined their numbers as she too observed the nearing figure. Silhouetted against the bright sun, Aurora could not make out the man's features at first. Then, as horse and rider turned and crossed into the shade, Aurora found her eyes riveted upon the handsomest man she had ever beheld.

Though it was difficult to tell, he seemed of a size comparable to his brother as he drew his mount abreast of His Grace. Seen in profile, he appeared exquisite in blue velvet, and Aurora found herself staring, eyes wide with amazement. An admiring sigh escaped her as she noted the difference between the two brothers. Even at a distance she could see the broad, strong shoulders that held the immense horse in check. Powerful-looking hands held the reins and when Lord Melbury turned to face her hiding place, she could look squarely into eyes of bright blue, deep-set in a face as fair as an angel's.

For one startling moment Aurora had the conviction that the young man's dusty blue eyes had spotted her, nestled among the bushes. His eyes were extraordinarily large and brilliantly compelling, appearing to look past all obstacles and deceptions.

Flushing, Aurora felt her throat tighten oddly and realized that she had caught her breath. Peregrine made no sign that he was aware of her presence, however, and Aurora dismissed her thought as an illusion. As if to confirm this, Peregrine turned to speak to Richard, oblivious to the young woman's steady gaze.

Dark brown hair blowing gently in the morning breeze, the young lord spoke with his brother the Duke, a teasing, almost shy smile playing about his full, well-shaped lips. For a moment, the Duke appeared to play the clown for his sibling's benefit, making broad gestures as if recounting an amusing tale. Peregrine's laughter floated to Aurora's ears as he tossed his head back like a restive colt, the sound of his voice sending a thrill along her every nerve. Aurora felt a strange tenderness fill her as she noticed the

43

manner in which the corners of Lord Melburry's eyes sloped downwards, giving him a perpetually wistful expression which tugged disturbingly at her heart. Pale translucent skin contrasted with the Duke's darker coloration, and a straight, small nose harmonized with the whole to create a memorable picture.

Too far away to hear his words, Aurora thought she could still discern a gravelly quality to the young man's voice that she found vastly attractive, and she wondered that she had not been made aware of such an obviously eligible parti.

The sickening possibility that Lord Melburry was already wed or otherwise engaged Aurora thrust from her mind. She felt excitement rise within herself as she perceived that the race was about to begin.

As her blood began to surge, the thought struck her that she might easily be about to witness a spectacle that would be less than exhilarating, the dangerously childish aspects of the whole thing whirling in her mind. With a mixture of fear and expectancy, Aurora watched the riders line up close to her hiding place, making out familiar faces as the men strove to keep their horses in check. As her eyes scanned the field, she found them suddenly arrested by a face all too disgustingly familiar.

Astride a brown speckled animal was none other than the man who had made drunken advances to her the previous evening. As Sherwood "Sherry" Davenant, judge of the forthcoming race, inspected the gentleman to see if all the rules were being observed, she heard him call the man "Lord Killingham."

"So *he* is Giles Killingham," Aurora spoke out loud with revulsion. "Now I know why Stuart does not like him."

Turning from Lord Killingham, Sherry checked the bindings of the other gentlemen one final time. Walking down the row of men and horses, he halted abruptly before Sir Francis and gaped. "Sir Francis, what the devil is all this?" he inquired in a tone of incredulity.

"Lord Davenant," Sir Francis replied peevishly, "it behooves me to ask you to be more specific in your questioning." It was obvious that Sir Francis was impatient for the race to begin. "As you can plainly see, an' you have eyes in your head, my bindings are tight enough."

"Indeed sir, that I can readily observe, but you are the only gentleman among us using gold cord."

"To match your jacket, I suppose," Lord Simmons commented with open mockery. "You could have saved yourself the trouble. 'Tis the wrong shade sir."

Thrusting his chin out in his most aggressive manner at this taunt, Sir Francis glared at his opponent and Aurora fancied she could hear his teeth grind. She stifled a titter at the thought.

"At least I make the effort, sir," Sir Francis replied with strained civility. "There are those who make no pretense at style, though they be touted by the masses as veritable fashion plates." Looking at Lord Simmons' grey riding jacket and muted accessories with derision, Sir Francis seemed gratified by his lordship's lack of color.

"Leave off now, Francis," Davenant interrupted hastily, sensing a battle royal was about to develop. "This is neither the time nor the place for such goings on."

There was a murmuring of agreement from the others assembled, and Lord Davenant completed his inspection without further mishap.

Aurora allowed herself one last searching look into the face of each rider, assessing their strengths and weaknesses, then lingering not unjustifiably on the captivatingly handsome face of Peregrine Melburry.

Never moving her eyes from him, she heard rather than saw Lord Davenant pull the hammer back on the starting pistol.

"Ready, gentlemen?" he asked briskly.

There was a muttering of assent.

The horses were tense, sensing their riders' anticipation, and Aurora caught the slight movement of Lord Davenant's arm as he raised the pistol heavenwards. A near-deafening roar filled the air as Sherry discharged the gun and Aurora watched with fascination as all six horses surged forward in a mass of rippling, straining muscle and sinew, striving to gather momentum and speed.

Her blood pounding in rhythm to the horses' hooves

as they thundered toward the walls at the far end of the field, Aurora watched, eyes wide and alert. Three walls, one almost after the other, then around the large oak tree and back for one more turn, that was the route planned for the race and Aurora could tell even before they reached the first jump who the actual contenders would be. From her vantage point, Aurora watched as both Lord Simmons and the Marquess reined in their horses before the first wall, their caution prompting them to take the jump slowly. Aurora shook her head. Though both these riders had initially led the pack by virtue of their horses' apparent superiority in sprinting power, they had now lost the majority of their lead.

" 'T'won't do," Aurora noted decisively. "One must throw one's heart over entirely. They won't win by being overly cautious, and their horses sense it as well."

Even as she said this, Lord Simmons' horse staggered before another wall, taking it at an awkward angle. With only one hand, Lord Simmons struggled futilely and took a walloping-huge fall. The Marquess barely managed to avoid the same fate as his own horse cleared the wall, the rear hooves nicking the top of the stones.

The four remaining riders took the three walls with more grace, and were only a hair's breadth behind the Marquess who had lost considerable ground taking all three of the walls at a reduced speed.

Lord Simmons had picked himself up with difficulty and had moved his mount to the center of the course's circular path, his attire unmarred as he had fallen safely onto dried grass. He watched intently the progress of those still in the race.

Both the Marquess and Sir Francis were lagging behind. Lord Killingham's horse's legs were spattered by mud where the animal had stumbled after clearing the third wall, but he was riding closely behind the Duke and Peregrine.

His Grace and Lord Melburry rode with similar styles, both with evident skill and irreproachable judgment. As Aurora watched, the two figures, nearing the walls for the final run, vied for the first jump.

She looked away from the brothers for a moment to confirm that Killingham was advancing slowly on them. A few seconds more and he had drawn abreast with them, making it a dash to the finish among the three.

They took the first wall at a dead heat and with balletlike grace. The second wall was taken with no visible sign of hesitation.

Though the riders were too far away for Aurora to see their faces well, she could still discern Peregrine Melburry's determined posture and the grim set of his jaw.

Killingham's forehead gleamed in the sun from beads of perspiration, his thoroughbred's every step seeming to shake him to the core with its force. Even from that distance Aurora thought he looked half mad in his unnaturally strong desire to win.

Aurora continued to watch as they cleared the remaining wall. Shifting her gaze to the Duke's face, she saw he displayed no emotion, curls swept back from his forehead by the force of the wind, except concentration. Hazel eyes narrowed against the sun, the Duke rode with a surety and confidence that were intimidating.

As the trio rounded the oak tree and headed for the finish, Aurora was vaguely aware of the sound of cheering from the spectators. It was then that she realized that one of the riders was lagging behind, the horse's uneven gait attesting to some sort of problem. Instinctively she knew the rider was Peregrine, though she could not tear her gaze from the remaining two riders as they came up quickly, neck and neck.

Lord Killingham was wearing a horribly strained smile as he fought to pull ahead, using his weight to goad his horse onward. Just as he might have overtaken the Duke, Lord Killingham made the mistake of glancing over to his opponent for a fraction of a second. It was enough. Almost imperceptibly, the Duke's horse began to pass Lord Killingham's. There was no time to rectify his mistake as Killingham watched His Grace's horse pull ahead to cross the line, the winner by only a few scant inches.

The din that resulted at this deed was enough to rouse Aurora from her trancelike state, so hypnotic had the spectacle been. Her breath slowly returning to normal, it was a few moments before she realized that she had dug her fingernails into the palms of her hands, tiny crimson crescents visible against their paleness.

Ignoring the niggling pain, she looked back on the group of the remaining riders now coming in. Dismounting, they offered their congratulations to the winner, slapping him on the back and shaking the Duke's hand with a great deal of enthusiasm.

Stuart appeared greatly pleased, due in part no doubt to having won his bet.

Observing Lord Killingham for a moment, Aurora was shocked to see the look of intense hatred that he cast in the Duke's direction.

There is more than a race at stake here, she thought as she shifted slightly.

She continued to observe him with fascination as one often becomes absorbed with watching something repulsive. He moved away from the other men, not intending in the least to acknowledge the Duke's victory. Pulling his horse along with him, Lord Killingham kept looking furtively behind himself as if he did not want to be seen.

The group of men began to disperse, heading toward the stables, and Lord Killingham watched them go.

"Good," Aurora heard him mumble as he passed her bush. Tying his horse to a tree a scant few feet from where she was hiding, a particularly vicious look came over his face.

"You worthless—" He was unable to think of a word harsh enough to convey his feelings to the unfortunate animal. He blamed his horse, rather than his own less than expert riding, for the Duke of Melburry's winning. "You lost me that race," he said. Raising his whip, Lord Killingham savagely struck the animal. Then he struck it again and kicked its flank, oblivious to its terrified whinnies.

Aurora was about to cry out and fly to the assistance of the animal, regardless of discovery, but suddenly Lord Killingham stopped and looked up, a startled expression on his face.

Now Aurora also heard what had stayed his hand,

the sound of someone approaching. Looking about, she could see Peregrine Melbury in the distance, returning with his slightly limping mount.

Muttering another curse, Killingham untied his still-frightened horse, mounted it with difficulty and rode away. He did not want anyone to witness his doing something socially unacceptable, at least while he was sober, so a hasty retreat was definitely in order.

"That man belongs in Bedlam," Aurora said to herself, quite appalled by the scene she had just witnessed.

Lord Melbury continued to approach, unaware of Lord Killingham's activities. Stopping before Aurora's bush, he stooped to inspect his horse's leg.

The physical discomfort that Aurora had forgotten during the excitement of the race returned, and she began to feel very cramped as her muscles protested with irresistible reminders of their confinement. Shifting her weight once more, Aurora attempted to move herself into a more favorable posture. As she did so, she felt a terrible pain shoot through her numb left leg. It had fallen asleep under her, and with a small cry she fell forward, crashing through the brush into the full and startled view of Lord Peregrine Melbury.

For a moment that young man did not move, so amazed was he by the sudden appearance of a woman in so inappropriate a setting. It was some seconds before he could grasp the delicacy of the situation, and as he did he grappled for the correct manner in which to approach the downed lady before him.

Aurora stared directly into the young lord's eyes and read his thoughts clearly. If anything, he was even more handsome than she had first believed, and though she knew herself to be in a most mortifying and embarrassing circumstance, she could not help feeling a thrill at the man's presence.

Aurora would have liked to stare into Lord Melbury's startled blue eyes for the bulk of the afternoon, such was the pleasure that she derived from that sweet pastime, but a sharp twinge of pain forced her to attend to her leg which she proceeded to rub vigorously in an attempt to restore her circulation. Averting her eyes as much from shyness as from necessity, Aurora felt a slight flush of color rise to her cheeks as Lord Melbury continued to look at her.

Aurora's sudden activity seemed to rouse Peregrine, and he hurried forward to her side so that he might assist her in rising. Looking down at the young woman, her head bent toward her task, Lord Melbury cleared his throat.

"Are you hurt?" he asked, his words sounding awkward and strained even to his own ears.

Without looking up, Aurora replied with admirable calm, "No, I am uninjured, sir. My leg is just a bit stiff."

These reassuring words were followed by an attempt to get up, and Peregrine quickly bent to Aurora's assistance. Taking hold of one arm, he steadied her movements as she tried to walk a few paces. The prickling sensation was receding, and Aurora managed to walk alone after a few steps.

"There you go. Right as rain," Lord Melbury remarked, relieved that there was genuinely nothing wrong.

"Yes, that is much better," Aurora agreed, taking some more steps just to be sure. "Thank you for your help," she added, looking up into Peregrine's smiling face.

The effect of this natural action was quite enough to stun Lord Melbury who had not previously been aware of Aurora's considerable beauty. Observing her upturned face, Peregrine seemed as one mesmerized, drinking in the dazzling blue of her eyes, the delicate curve of her cheek, and the captivatingly impish smile with which she favored him.

"I no longer require assistance, thank you. I believe I can stand on my own now," Aurora said after an instant, her sense of propriety compelling her to end the prolonged moment of silence that had followed. It was with some embarrassment that Lord Melbury released his hold on Aurora's arm. However, it seemed to her that there existed in Peregrine a definite reluctance to part from her company, as he continued to accompany her as she moved toward his injured steed.

"Is your horse very badly off?" she inquired, feeling

the want of conversation as she kneeled to examine the beast's hoof.

Startled a bit by the lady's casual way with a horse that he himself would not have taken such a liberty with, Peregrine managed to croak a no in response. "I think he had a pebble in his shoe. Though at present he seems to be as unhurt as you are, madam," he remarked with a wry expression.

"How unfortunate that you could not complete the race," Aurora said, once again looking into Peregrine's eyes. "I am sure that you had an excellent chance of winning."

"And were you hidden all that time?" Peregrine inquired curiously, incredulity showing on his countenance.

"But of course. I came specifically to see you all race, and those bushes, although cramped, were perfect for my needs," Aurora replied without the least hint of hesitation.

"I hope we did not disappoint you, then," Peregrine replied with a smile. "But you must know that all the matrons would gasp at such conduct as you have indulged in this morning, madam."

This admonition was made with such exaggerated emphasis as to make Aurora laugh a bit.

"No doubt they would all refuse me vouchers at Almack's an' they knew of it," Aurora agreed cheerfully. "But they will not know of it unless you, sir, should be so ungallant as to reveal my secret, and I do not believe you shall."

Looking for all the world like some playful sprite, Aurora's eyes seemed to know that Lord Melburry would not contradict her. Entering into the fun of the moment, Peregrine pretended to censure Aurora's actions.

"A young lady of quality and consequence would not witness such an improper activity as a private race," Peregrine sermonized, and Aurora could almost picture him behind a pulpit, except for the playful gleam in the young lord's long-lashed eyes. It was definitely more the look of the sinner than the saint and Aurora countered skillfully.

"If my conduct was improper, my lord, only think

51

what the matrons would make of *your* behavior. Where I was only a spectator, you were actually a participant, so your guilt must be much greater than mine."

"Ah, well, you may be right," Peregrine admitted, "however, you will at least agree that their criticism of you would still be more severe as you are bound by somewhat stricter rules."

Aurora's smile faded for a moment, but returned quickly. "We each have rules we live by, my lord, some of them are not as fair as others, but we deal with them in any case."

Aurora spoke lightly, intending to pass the comment off. However, Lord Melburry surprised her with his reaction.

"I commend you in the manner you have learned to deal with those unfair rules. You have uncommon courage," he said, his face quite serious. Then, as if to dispel the atmosphere which was becoming decidedly more disturbing, Lord Melburry smiled broadly. "Just don't let the dragons get wind of it," he said in a conspiratorial tone.

"I knew you would keep my secret," Aurora laughed.

"You are correct in that," Peregrine replied, "but may I know whose secret I have the privilege of preserving? I know we have not been introduced before."

"Are you so sure we have not?" Aurora teased. "I know your name and it does not worry you at all that we may have been introduced and you have been so gauche as to have quite forgotten me?"

She had to laugh aloud at the sincerely appalled look on the gentleman's face at such a possibility. Repenting her words a bit, she assured the young lord, "Of course we have not met. My name is Aurora Trevelyn. My father is the Earl of Trevelyn."

With exaggerated formality, Lord Melburry made his bow before Aurora, his expression convincingly solemn. "Charmed," he replied, pressing his lips briefly against the white kid gloves she wore. "May I present myself? I am Peregrine Melburry, second son of the late Duke of Melburry and just recently from a tour of France."

"Acquiring the continental touch?" Aurora inquired with arched brow.

"Just so," was the polite response.

For a moment both parties managed to contain themselves, then as Aurora observed Lord Melburry's lip tremble with pent-up amusement, she let loose her own laughter.

It was a few seconds before either young person could regain composure, and Peregrine was the first to speak.

"Tell me, then, Lady Aurora, who told you about our little activity?" he asked curiously, truly mystified.

"Did I imply that anyone informed me of it?" Aurora asked, uneasy at the idea of divulging Lord Ringwood's involvement.

"As we changed the location of the race only last night, I am afraid that not even common gossip, fast as it does spread, would explain your being here, Lady Aurora." Lord Melburry's words were not unkindly but they were firm. "I don't criticize but I do wonder who it was."

Before Aurora could make a reply to this unanswerable question, she was interrupted by the sound of someone approaching. Turning, they saw that it was Lord Ringwood, coming to escort Aurora home.

Halting before the couple, a concerned look on his face, Lord Ringwood was quite taken aback by Lord Melburry's presence.

"Ah, I see we have the culprit here," Peregrine jested as Stuart strolled to Aurora's side.

"It is entirely my fault that Lady Aurora is here," Stuart began, fully intending to take the blame before any was assigned.

"That is chivalrous of you, Lord Ringwood," Peregrine interjected, but it is unnecessary since I have already promised to say nothing of this. You may rest easy."

"I appreciate your discretion," Aurora said, extending her hand to Lord Melburry. "Perhaps someday I shall be able to repay your kindness."

Taking her hand, the young man replied, "Your appreciation is already past what I deserve, Lady Aurora."

With that, he bestowed a kiss on the bared skin above her dainty glove.

If Aurora was displeased by this boldness, by the impudently possessive pressure of his hand upon hers or by the kiss which lingered warmly on her wrist, she did not show it in the least. And if Lord Melburry looked a bit audaciously into her eyes as he straightened, Lady Aurora looked no less saucily into his.

"Yes, well . . ." Lord Ringwood interrupted nervously, uncomfortable with such ready familiarity. "I will be seeing you later at the auction, I suppose, Peregrine."

"Eh?" Lord Melburry asked, not seeming to have heard, his gaze drawn reluctantly from Aurora's face where he had just been admiring that young lady's intriguing dimples. "Oh, yes. The auction," he said as he observed Lord Ringwood's obvious desire for him to absent himself.

With a small bow, Lord Melburry took his leave, mounting his horse with a fluid motion. Looking down from his perch, he could discern a strange but pleasurable feeling about his heart as he gazed at Aurora once more.

"I do hope to see you soon," he said suddenly, as if the words had been forced from him. "Please allow me to call on you," he pleaded.

Lord Ringwood's surprised expression at such an earnest tone did not deter Peregrine from casting a speaking look to Aurora. The manner in which their eyes seemed to lock was most extraordinary to Lord Ringwood who had never seen the like.

To Aurora, who was experiencing a hitherto unknown elation at the evidence of her effect on Lord Melburry, his words were like wine to her senses, and she barely managed to nod her assent to his request.

"May I call on you sometime next week?" he asked, anxious with anticipation.

"I will, of course, need to discuss it with Mama; though I am sure that it may be arranged," Aurora answered, her mind reeling with the impetuosity of this virtual stranger.

"I shall wait on your summons," Peregrine replied resolutely.

"And I will look forward to your visit, though perhaps you shall see me sooner than you anticipate," Aurora commented cryptically.

Lord Melburry tilted his head slightly at this, looking for all the world like a small inquisitive bird. "Until we meet again, then," he said with a nod of his head. Spurring his horse forward, Peregrine rode off in the direction of the stables to join his friends.

"Well, if that don't beat the Dutch!" Stuart exclaimed as he watched Lord Melburry ride away, a look of utter amazement on his face. Scratching his head, Lord Ringwood seemed lost in thought for a moment. Turning back to Aurora, he declared, "You seem to have the Devil's own luck. Good thing it was Peregrine who chanced upon you. He'll keep his word, never fear, though I don't know how you managed it."

"I will tell you some other time, Stuart," she promised. "I am relieved that Mother and Father will not hear of it."

"I dare say so," Lord Ringwood agreed, "especially after last night," he added with unthinking clumsiness.

Before he could apologize for his faux pas, however, Aurora turned to him abruptly, her memory stirred.

"Stuart! You will never guess! I have discovered the most revolting thing," Aurora burst out, disgust evident on her face. "That creature who attacked me last night at the ball, that was Lord Killingham. I recognized him during the race."

"Are you sure?" Lord Ringwood asked, his own suspicions confirmed.

"Positive," Aurora replied with certainty. "I would know that wretch anywhere. He has tiny pig eyes and I absolutely loathe him. I am glad that he lost to the Duke of Melburry."

Aurora's vehemence was not surprising to Lord Ringwood, as he was well acquainted with the lady's tendency to feel everything strongly. Discretion's being the better part of valor, Stuart refrained from comment on the subject of Lord Killingham. He was far too tired to listen to the tirade that would ensue.

"We had best be going," Stuart said, motioning for

Aurora to mount his horse. "I will take us back to the curricle and then bring you home. You've had enough excitement for one day, I'll be bound."

These cheery words were halted abruptly as Lord Ringwood observed the wheedling smile that graced Aurora's lips. Moving forward to take hold of the sleeve of Stuart's jacket, Aurora patted his arm reassuringly, much in the same manner that her sister Lettice had often employed when persuading that gentleman of something.

"Stuart! I am surprised that you credit me with so little stamina!" Aurora exclaimed. "I am sure that I have appetite enough for more activity than you have planned for me, sir. As a matter of fact, Lettice is expecting me to attend the auction at the stables. We spoke of it this morning before I left."

"But it has been a trying day," Stuart pleaded unavailingly.

"Perhaps it has been for you, however, I am still quite fresh," Aurora replied stubbornly. "The day has hardly begun, and I am not sculptured from porcelain. I shan't break, you know, Stuart, and if I recall rightly you have promised me a look at your stallion."

Lord Ringwood hesitated, unsure how to untangle himself from a situation that could prove fraught with unseen dangers. Still, it was a comforting thought that Lettice would be present. She could curb her sister's impetuosity, and there would not be so much danger of Aurora's getting into any scrapes. With that in mind, Lord Ringwood was inclined to give in to Aurora's insistence.

"I promise to be ever so discreet," Aurora enticed, sensing a victory.

"You are sure that Lettice will be there?" Lord Ringwood asked, still leery of the idea.

"Certainly. She wants my opinion on the horses. Well? Will she be sufficient chaperone and will you take me?" Aurora asked eagerly.

"Very well. If she is to be there then I have no objection to your going," Lord Ringwood decided. "I only hope that Peregrine doesn't let anything slip out. It would never do for you to be subject for gossip."

"I am sure he will be careful," she replied with a

note of confidence that Stuart sincerely hoped was warranted. "You know, Stuart, this will be diverting for us both," Aurora assured the unhappy lord. "You shall see Lettice whom you like very well, and I shall have an opportunity to speak with Lord Melburry again, under more correct circumstances of course. Does that not sound like a pleasant afternoon?"

"A rare treat," Lord Ringwood replied gloomily.

The prospect of seeing Peregrine distressed Lord Ringwood as much as it appeared to delight Aurora. His instincts were to forget all Aurora's pleadings and return her to the bosom of her family. Still, he reasoned, there was not much mischief that could be had while Lettice was present. Lettice was always a stable, reliable, and level-headed person, up to every trick socially.

Perhaps I am worrying about nothing, Lord Ringwood thought, as they made their way along the path, but the frown on his face did not altogether disappear and neither did his apprehension.

CHAPTER 3

IT WAS with the utmost caution that Lord Simmons leaned against the confining rail beside the Duke of Melburry, carefully avoiding any unnecessary soiling of his still-immaculate riding breeches.

Noting the delicacy with which that gentleman assumed his place, the Duke's lip twitched into a half smile that conveyed a tinge of mockery. Several fine-looking bays stood placidly within the paddock and Richard Melburry examined them with the schooled eye of an expert.

Lord Simmons' interest in horses was generally as great as the Duke's, however at this time there was an object which claimed his attention and his curiosity more keenly than the excellent horseflesh before him.

"You know, Richard, I would not have thought it, but I do believe that Peregrine's constitution is less robust than one would first credit," Lord Simmons remarked cautiously as he watched that young man standing apart from the general mass of men milling about the stables.

"My lord, I am not aware of any unnatural weakness on the part of my brother. I have always considered him to be uncommonly healthy, truth be told," the Duke replied, never taking his eyes from the magnificent animals which were beginning to paw restlessly at the dry turf.

"He appears quite distracted to me," Lord Simmons countered. "Only look how pale he is, and there . . . he is doing it again, staring off into space. I say, Richard, do look at least."

At this insistence, the Duke looked over at Peregrine, intending only a cursory glance. However, he found to his surprise that his sibling did indeed lack his usual healthful coloration, and that he appeared to be present not in sensibility, but in form only. Richard could even detect a faint pulling at the corners of his brother's mouth suggesting some sort of remembered pleasure.

Lord Simmons had noticed this as well, unconsciously raising his quizzing glass to his straining eyes before recalling himself. He let the glass fall as inconspicuously as possible, an embarrassed cough escaping him.

"I think I shall have a small talk with Peregrine," the Duke said, excusing himself abruptly and taking deliberate steps toward his all but oblivious relative.

Nearing the oddly still figure, Richard was struck by the dreamy quality in his sibling's eyes, something akin to drug-induced stupefaction, though his lordship was fairly certain that this was not a vice in which Peregrine indulged.

Not that Peregrine had many vices. He was into nothing more serious than the usual scrapes and larks of a young gentleman down from his first trip abroad, kicking up a dust here and there. The Duke had, of course, guided his brother unobtrusively through the dangers of the French court, and Peregrine had never been guilty of more than overzealousness stimulated by youth. All told, the Duke had been pleased with Peregrine. He had emerged from his experiences with a passable air and a goodly amount of knowingness.

Nothing, however, came to mind to explain Peregrine's present state and as His Grace stopped before his brother, looking him squarely in the face, he received not so much as a blink in reaction. Tugging on one limp-armed sleeve, he attempted to rouse him from his reverie.

"Peregrine, do tell me if I obstruct your view," Richard commented as his brother attempted to focus foggy eyes. "Do you feel all right?" he inquired with concern.

A hesitant nod was his reply, and the Duke let the matter drop as he spied a familiar rig approaching the stables. "There is Stuart," the Duke informed his brother. "I wonder who that is?" he added, noticing the lady beside his friend. Turning to his brother he added, "Ah, well, no doubt we shall be introduced presently." To his surprise, Peregrine had regained his color and was peering avidly in the direction of Lord Ringwood's carriage, more specifically at the lovely young lady accompanying Stuart. Suddenly matters became quite clear to the Duke as he at last recognized Peregrine's odd condition for what it was: unabashed fascination with, if not outright adoration of, the undeniable vision, who was at that moment being assisted by his lanky friend from the high perch of the curricle.

"Perhaps it would be more appropriate if I requested that you make the introductions," Richard suggested with a wicked smile.

Peregrine flushed slightly, but the elder Melburry could not tell if it was from being harassed, or from the presence of the young lady.

Lord Ringwood meanwhile escorted Aurora toward the two men with the greatest trepidation. He was sorely in need of moral support at that moment, for the morning's events had been quite enough to unsettle his calm for the rest of the day. As it was, rescue came unexpectedly in the familiar and welcome form of Let-

59

tice. Sailing across the open space left in the yard, Lettice was followed dutifully by the solid country figure of the family's favorite ostler.

The three parties converged at the same moment, the Duke and his brother waiting patiently as Lettice exchanged greetings with Lord Ringwood and her sister.

"Well, Aurora, Stuart, I hope you have enjoyed your morning ride," Lettice offered as she looked about her at the gathering crowd of people. She waited for an introduction to be made, and Lord Ringwood cleared his throat slightly as all eyes turned toward him.

"Lettice, Aurora, may I present to you the Duke of Melburry and his younger brother, Lord Peregrine Melburry?" Lord Ringwood murmured at last. "Your Grace, Peregrine, the Ladies Lettice and Aurora Trevelyn."

The gentlemen bowed formally over the extended hands, Peregrine exhibiting more than the usual attention over Aurora's dainty member.

The sweetly shy expression on Aurora's visage confirmed all that the Duke had supposed, and he looked at the young woman intently, trying to gain a feeling of what she was like.

Lettice, noting her sister's growing discomfort at the Duke's intense appraisal, interrupted his concentration by asking, "Well, Your Grace. Are you here to take in the atmosphere, or are you seeking to build up your stables?"

Looking at Lettice as if for the first time, the Duke was instantly struck by the contrast in features between the sisters.

Lettice recognized the inquisitive look and with some slight irritation spoke. "Yes, Your Grace, we really are sisters. I, however, can lay claim to my father's side of the family for my appearance while Aurora can thank our mother for hers."

Richard's hazel eyes registered surprise at the attack, and a distinct dislike seemed to make them narrow. Lettice did not miss this sign, and the tilt of her beautiful head became distinctly more arrogant.

"Madam, I certainly do not question your relationship, though I had noticed that your sister was formed along more 'delicate' lines than yourself."

Aurora felt herself filled with foreboding as she watched her sister's reaction to this less than gallant reference to Lettice's considerable height. Lesser men had been subjected to her sister's wrath and had fared quite poorly.

"Indeed, Your Grace, I believe that it is the usual occurrence that the eldest child is less refined in appearance than his or her brothers or sisters. I am sure you have noticed that it is true with yourself." The archness in Lettice's voice was quite evident and the Duke, though loath to acknowledge the hit, did, in fact, nod once.

"Well, I believe we came down here for a purpose," Lord Ringwood interrupted hurriedly, hoping to avert a full-fledged war.

"Yes, Stuart. As I was about to answer Lady Trevelyn. I do intend to build up my stables and will be most interested in seeing the animals up for auction," Richard commented mildly. "Is that your purpose as well?"

"Yes, it is," she replied in an equally calm manner.

"And you have brought along someone to help you, I see," the Duke added, his tone rather pointed.

Stuart sighed a bit and glanced over at Peregrine. Lord Melburry was too absorbed in memorizing Aurora's every feature to be bothered with his elder brother's conduct, and Lord Ringwood knew he could not garner any help from that quarter.

"I perceive that you feel you need no such assistance in choosing your breeding stock, Your Grace," Lettice said in a voice that implied skepticism.

"As you can see, I have not brought anyone from my stables," the Duke replied, motioning to empty space, the mocking expression on his face causing Lettice's brown eyes to blaze.

"Stuart," Aurora interrupted abruptly, "you have promised me a look at your stallion and you have not yet fulfilled your duty."

"That is indeed naughty of you, Stuart," Lettice added, buying time to think of an adequately scathing remark for the Duke. "You must show the beast now, before the auction, as I will also soon be needing Aurora's opinion on the horses, and there may not be time later."

"I think we should all like to see this animal," Peregrine added, more than willing to advocate anything Aurora should desire.

"It would seem that you must accede to the majority," the Duke said, smiling.

"Are you the horsewoman of the Trevelyns?" Peregrine impishly inquired of Aurora as Lord Ringwood left the group to fetch the horse.

"But of course," Lettice replied as her sister seemed to be smiling for some strange reason and appeared not to be able to speak for herself. "It cannot be our sister Patrice, as she detests the exertion involved in the hunt, and it could not possibly be myself, as the Duke has been so kind as to point out."

"I have been told that I have some small knowledge of horses, Lord Melburry," Aurora remarked, giving a significant look in the Duke's direction, "though Lettice's understanding is by no means less than mine. Certainly it must be the wisest course to receive counsel from anyone who knows horses as well as our stableman, Derek, there."

Before the Duke could respond to this defense of Lettice, Stuart returned leading with difficulty a spirited white horse.

Lettice had only to look at the animal to know that Aurora would more than likely fall in love with it, and she was not surprised to hear the exclamation that followed once her sister had taken in the spectacle of this magnificent but untamed brute.

"He is gorgeous, Stuart!" Aurora exclaimed as she impulsively strode up to the horse. Seeing the fast-approaching figure, the animal tried vigorously to pull the bridle from Lord Ringwood's strong hands, taking several small steps back only to be thwarted.

"Unruly creature," Lettice remarked aloud.

"Perhaps you had best not to go any closer, Lady Trevelyn," the Duke advised Aurora who had stopped short of the horse.

Though Lettice had been about to give the same advice, she found that hearing those words from the Duke inclined her to change her mind.

"I am sure he is just a little restive, Your Grace," Aurora assured Richard Melbury, coming closer to the horse. Extending one soft white hand, Aurora stroked the snowy muzzle, cooing, "Aren't you the sweetest thing?"

Lettice enjoyed the dumbfounded expression which graced the Duke's visage as the horse came instantly to rest, ceasing its skittish prancing. Of course, Lettice was used to the effect Aurora had on all animals, but this did not decrease one whit her enjoyment as she observed the Duke's reaction.

As she glanced at Peregrine, she saw the admiration in the young lord's eyes. He was a pretty youth; and in a moment, with her usual quickness of resolve, Lettice decided that she liked the idea of a match between her sister and this boy. They would make a charming couple, she thought, then winced when she realized she would of a necessity be related to the Duke.

Stuart, though aware of Aurora's special charm with horses, was astonished at the change. "If that don't beat the Dutch!" he exclaimed as Aurora proceeded to take the now-slack reins from his hands.

Aurora herself was tempted to mount the stallion on the spot, saddle or no, trained or not. But though she was sure he would be excellent in time, she was not so foolish as to think she could ride the beast so soon.

"Well, Stuart," Lettice said at last, a note of pride and triumph in her voice, "what do you think now? Will the animal suit Aurora?"

"What is more important, does Lady Trevelyn find the animal to her liking?" Peregrine inquired, cocking an inquisitive head at that beautiful lady.

"Most definitely I do, Lord Melbury," Aurora replied, her gaze on his person as appreciative as it was when trained on the horse.

"Well, then, that settles it," Lord Ringwood decided. "He is yours, Aurora, if you wish it."

"I very much do, Stuart. I thank you for the opportunity to possess such an incredible creature."

"An unusual horse for a very unusual lady," Lord Melbury remarked with a seriousness of bearing that left no room for mistaking his complete and utter surrender to this fascinating woman.

"It would appear that all of the Trevelyn women are unique," Richard remarked wryly, eyeing Lettice warily.

"Let us just say that our judgment in the area of horseflesh is not to be trifled with," Lettice replied, staring coolly back into the Duke's eyes, measuring this possible adversary with her own uncanny judgment.

Perhaps it was best that Lettice had made that distinction, for the Countess of Trevelyn was fast finding that not all of the Trevelyn women had the best of judgment or expertise in all areas. More specifically, she was finding that her youngest daughter, Patrice, was rising to rebellion, a most unexpected and astonishing outcome of her entanglement with Lieutenant Basil Torquill. A more unfortunate attachment had never been made, or so the Countess felt, and she had fervently hoped that the passion would prove only temporary. However, she had this expectation dispelled upon her very first opportunity to see the two young people together.

Patrice's lieutenant had at last arrived at the Trevelyn town house, making the traditional call upon the Countess for tea in the early afternoon. On being ushered into the drawing room, he had been pointedly ignored by Lettice, who was just leaving the house for the auction. Though he made his bow stiffly, Lettice had not deigned to acknowledge it, sallying forth from the house without so much as a blink in return.

As much as the lieutenant's arrival thrilled Patrice, it did not do the same for the Countess, who found the intrusion less than satisfactory. The Earl was not present at the tea, having excused himself for some important and urgent matter which needed his immediate attention, thus the Countess was forced to entertain alone.

The lieutenant's presence spoiled her morning. The Countess found this especially irritating since the previous evening had been a particularly romantic one and had left her in the morning with a pleasant glow, somewhat reminiscent of her early years as the Earl's bride.

The enthralled expression on Patrice's face as she looked at the lieutenant, which the Countess recognized for what it was, did not sit well with her, as she totally opposed any such match. It was not so much that the man was a paltry lieutenant, but that the Countess did not like his air. Soon after the tea was poured and the conversation begun, the Countess became convinced of Lieutenant Torquill's unsuitability for her daughter.

"Well, lieutenant," the Countess began, handing the young man his cup. "Patrice has told me a great deal about you, but she has not said just how long you have been with the military."

"Quite a while, Madam," Basil Torquill replied as he sat at attention on the soft-cushioned chair. As he lifted his cup to his lips, the Countess observed that he even consumed that beverage at attention. "I started in the lower ranks and elevated myself through a conscientious observation of my duties."

"Of course," Countess Trevelyn replied, at a loss for what next to ask of such a very strange man.

"Lieutenant Torquill has been commended several times by his officers, Mama," Patrice added helpfully, but blushed as the lieutenant gave her a stern glance.

"Thank you, Lady Trevelyn, but I believe I can best answer the Countess's questions," he said unkindly.

The Countess did not like the manner in which Patrice replied—with a hurried, "Of course . . . of course, Basil, rather, Lieutenant Torquill." Though Patrice had always been a timid child, she seemed even more so under the hand of this man.

In any case, the interview was short, the Countess suddenly developing a migraine of enormous proportions in the middle of the jam tarts and the buttered croissants. It was induced, no doubt, by having to speak to the junior officer for so extended a time, though Patrice dared not imply that it was deliberate on her mother's part.

As the footman ushered Torquill out, Patrice found her mother's disapproving eye on her and knew that a lecture was to come. But it was the Countess who was the recipient of an unexpectedly forceful display of emotion. Before she could speak one word, Patrice burst out, "I shall not give him up, Mama. I love Basil and he loves me."

"I wish I could believe that he loved you, Patrice," the Countess replied, "but I don't believe you know as much about that gentleman as you think. He did not speak in the most loverlike tones that I have ever heard, and I should not be surprised to find that he is a fortune hunter."

Patrice was aghast at the insult. "I refuse to listen to your unfounded suspicions, Mama," she cried passionately.

That comment was a mistake, for the Countess, unused to such rebellion from Patrice, instantly lost all patience. "I forbid you ever to see that man again, Patrice," she commanded. "You are being just silly. Look at you, you are not even behaving like yourself at all."

Turning in tears from her mother, Patrice ran upstairs, her mother's voice pursuing her even to the threshold of her door.

"Understand, I will not tolerate it, Patrice." The Countess did not receive a reply, nor did she expect one. What she did expect, and felt she would fully receive, was obedience. Though she regretted that she needed to use such tactics, she felt some measure of relief that she had managed to be firm. However, she felt uneasy as she waited anxiously for the Earl's return, sure that he could put things easily to rights once he was aware of the situation.

"If only I had paid more heed to Lettice," the Countess murmured in exasperation, recalling her eldest's warnings about the infatuation. "She should have been here to help instead of running off to see some silly horses. I'm sure she could have talked to Patrice and we should not have had such a vexing time of it. Now Patrice has thrown a pet which is quite unlike her."

The Countess had more than enough time to dwell on Lettice's shortcomings as that lady was in no danger of returning home too soon, so thoroughly absorbed was she in comparing the "young 'uns", as Lord Ringwood had so aptly put it, which were in the process of being auctioned off.

The crowd of gentlemen present was large enough to make the bidding lively from the start, though the really best horses were being saved for last. She had been tempted several times to make an offer for some showy animal or another, but on each occasion, she had looked to her groom for his opinion, and that knowledgeable individual's dour glance had not permitted it. Lettice had no doubt that she was wise in taking Derek's opinions to heart, however it did not stop the niggling irritation she developed as she was certain that the Duke of Melburry looked on her collaborations with mild amusement, several times detecting the hint of a smirk as she glanced in the Duke's direction. To her surprise, Lettice found that she had set her teeth together so hard that her jaw ached—a habit she had when anyone had set her back up.

Surveying the Duke for a moment in an effort to know better her adversary—for an adversary she was fairly convinced he could become, should his brother form a tendre for Aurora—Lettice only now noted Richard Melburry more than amply displayed an easy air; a lazy kind of attractiveness that she was sure would gain him the attentions of the majority of young ladies in society. Standing a little way off, he was speaking to Aurora as though in frivolous conversation, but Lettice found that his eyes occasionally belied his blasé attitude, shooting appraising looks at her sister. For a moment, the thought struck Lettice that the Duke might find Aurora attractive as much as his brother, and the idea made her more irritable than before.

Impulsively, Lettice walked over to the pair, leaving her startled groom to keep watch over the proceedings.

"Well, Your Grace, for a gentleman bent on restocking his stables, you show very little interest in the auction," Lettice offered, looking him directly, and some would have said brazenly, in the eyes.

"On the contrary, I have been paying very careful attention to the bidding, Lady Trevelyn," Richard protested, a startled brow creeping ever higher at her abrupt statement. "Of course, none of the animals being displayed is suitable for my needs," he added defensively.

"The best horses are saved for last in any case," Lord Ringwood commented hurriedly.

Glancing back at the proceedings, Lettice perceived the majority of the general stock had been dealt with, and that the rest of the animals were being prepared to be shown.

"It would appear that you have not much longer to enjoy Aurora's conversation, Your Grace, as the serious activity is about to commence."

"Then I should escort you back to your groom, so that perhaps some of his expertise may rub off on me," the Duke suggested, an annoyed edge on his voice. "I am sure you would like to consult with him before making such a monumental decision as purchasing a horse."

Taking one delicately gloved hand deliberately in his, Richard led Lettice toward the center of the throng, totally unaffected by her furious but controlled gaze at his last remark. Trailing behind them, hoping to avert a possible disaster, Lord Ringwood nervously cracked his knuckles. Halting beside his friend, Stuart attempted to whisper a word of caution to Richard, but a quelling glance from Lettice warned him to mind his own affairs. She would settle with the Duke in her own fashion.

"Derek," Lettice said, turning to her groom again, "you will, of course, bid for me, using in part your own discretion. But I am to have the final decision, is that understood?"

Lettice had not raised her voice, but the manner in which she had announced her intentions could only have been meant for the Duke to understand.

"Of course, Lady Trevelyn," was the uneasy reply. Though he had been pleased to accompany the master's eldest daughter on this occasion, the stableman knew well that Lettice had a tendency to be attracted to horses with more show than substance. Even as a child, it had been more important to her that her mounts suit her in form rather than in running or jumping ability. Looking at his mistress now, he became even more disturbed to see a somewhat vengeful glint in her eye.

The Duke was terribly tempted to commend Lady

Trevelyn on her "bravery" in the face of her own igno-
rance. However, Richard knew that the strain on
Stuart would be grievous, so he relented, allowing himself only a slight betrayal of cynicism.

As the bidding began, and the various animals were
presented, Lord Ringwood's anxiety and Derek's
diminished somewhat. Neither the Duke nor Lettice
appeared to be interested in the same animal, Lady
Trevelyn intent on purchasing suitable carriage steeds
and the Duke turning in favor of hunting horses, here a
matched set of grays, there a dasher of a hunter. Had
Stuart known Lettice's personality less, he might have
been almost comfortable since there was more than one
rivalry being tried that day, one which even he, prover-
bial peacemaker that he was, could enjoy.

This was, of course, the ever-present competition between Lord Simmons and Sir Francis to see which
gentleman could obtain the most impressive horse for
his sallies into Hyde Park at the fashionable hour.
Lord Simmons could have actually cared less, but he
derived some unfathomable pleasure in making Sir
Francis livid as he outbid him for one delicately boned
mare which he had devined—from Sir Francis'
twitching nostrils—his rival held a distinct desire for.

Provoked by this thwarting of his hopes, Sir Francis
stalked up to Lord Simmons. Even Lettice had to hide
a grin as Sir Francis stamped his foot in rage. The
words that passed between the men could not be heard,
but the pantomime of the dandy and the piqued fop
was quite enough to cause a rumble of laughter to
emerge from the Duke.

"Amusing, is it not?" Lettice asked with so much
sweetness in her attitude that Lord Ringwood would
have been hard-pressed to say just what she had up her
sleeve.

"Very entertaining, let us say," Richard Melburry
replied. "I wonder at Francis' allowing Simmons to win
out, though."

Lettice looked the Duke in the eye with an innocent
surprise. "And you have never allowed yourself to be
outbid for a horse, Your Grace?"

"Lady Trevelyn, I am seldom at a loss, and usually
can obtain that which I want with little trouble," he re-

plied in the drawl he had assumed in her presence more often than not.

The tilt of Lettice's head caused the foreboding to return to Stuart, and when the stable assistant led out an enormous, long-legged beast with a flowing mane and a capering walk, Stuart felt that Richard's fate was sealed.

To see the stallion was to want to possess it, such was the spirit in its every movement. The effect on Richard was plain, but he was not oblivious to the timeliness of its appearance. Gazing down into Lady Trevelyn's brown eyes, he read an unmistakable challenge in them.

"Were you aware this horse would be up for auction today, Lady Trevelyn?" he asked, knowing the answer in advance.

"I have been awaiting the occasion for some time to purchase it, Your Grace," Lettice replied carefully, "and I have come prepared to obtain the beast. Lord Quibble is a close neighbor and I have seen this horse as a foal. Quite impressive, is it not so?"

"Quite," the Duke replied. "May I wish you luck?"

"Gallant opponent," Lettice remarked, raising her chin a bit and looking steadily at the Duke through half-closed eyes. "Luck then, to both of us," she agreed, extending her hand to him, not knowing why she should suddenly wonder at her own plan. Richard's next remark dispelled her reluctance.

"Of course, the winner is predestined, I warn you Lady Trevelyn," the Duke said, the slightly pitying tone setting Lettice's back up more than ever.

"We shall see, Your Grace. I do not believe in predestination in the least, and you would do well to doubt it as well," Lettice replied tartly.

Moving away from her opponent a bit, Lettice conferred with Derek as the auctioneer opened at eight hundred guineas, a reasonable sum to start from. With a nudge from one elegantly covered elbow, the Trevelyn groom made an offer of nine hundred guineas.

"She doesn't mince matters," the Duke murmured to Lord Ringwood, who winced slightly at the comment. There was little else Stuart could do as Richard made a substantial opposing offer.

"One thousand guineas." The Duke's voice was very clear and cut through the silence which had descended on the other gentlemen gathered. It was apparent to all that there was something afoot.

The distressed expression on Derek's face attested to his feeling that the bidding was going too high, that the horse was scarcely worth the money, but another prodding from his mistress and he reluctantly raised the bid another three hundred guineas.

"One thousand five hundred guineas," the Duke countered steadily, his face a mask to his feelings. Lord Ringwood was sure that Richard had not thought that the bidding would become quite so trying, but as he watched his friend, Stuart was sure that Richard was already riding the beast in his imagination, that it was his, and he could not give up.

There was a pause as the Trevelyn groom whispered frantically to his mistress, a stubborn, set expression to his face. He had not felt that the stallion was worth the amount quoted already, however he had just at that moment noticed something about the creature which made him adamant about not continuing. The animal had been run briskly about the paddock and Richard had not noticed the oddly labored breathing that resulted.

The crowd waited patiently, the auctioneer warning Lettice that this was her last opportunity to make a bid. Her reluctance showed on her face, but it was plain that the groom had made his point. There was no counter bid.

"The horse is yours, Your Grace," the auctioneer announced, motioning for the assistant to place the animal with the other purchases.

Richard did not gloat, but neither did he seem displeased. Recalling himself, and realizing that Lettice must feel quite put out, he approached the lady with the intent of saying a few words to soften the loss. To his utter amazement, she was all graciousness.

"Congratulations, Your Grace. I may begin to put more merit in predestination," she said as he reached her side. Curiously, there was no sign of envy or remorse in her voice, no anger or mortification at having been bested.

71

"It is a pity that only one of us could possess the animal, Lady Trevelyn," he replied. "You put up quite a battle. I paid dearly for that horse." The sincerity of those words seemed to take Lettice aback, and Stuart thought he saw guilt flicker on her face.

"But it was worth it, was it not?" Lettice questioned, her interest evident in the way she searched the Duke's face.

"Yes, it was worth it," Richard conceded, wondering at the gravity in her manner.

"Then there is nothing else to say," she said abruptly. "Let us rejoin your brother and my sister. They will have thought that we have quite forgotten them by now, I vow."

"Of course," the Duke agreed, puzzled by her seeming lack of emotion. She did not wait to take his hand but seemed in a rush, hurrying somewhat past Richard to her sister's side.

"Lettice, what a shame you could not have him," Aurora exclaimed as soon as she reached her. "Of all the most beautiful animals. Oh well, I suppose there will be others," she added, attempting to be philosophical about the situation. Ordinarily, such an event would have been tragic, but Aurora had other matters more pressing to consider on this day. Her eyes continually crept back to Peregrine's face, darting shyly away if he appeared to return her gaze as was often the very case.

"It doesn't bother me in the least," Lettice responded. "We have enough horses, so it doesn't signify a whit."

The offhand manner in which Lettice announced this fact surprised Aurora as much as it had the Duke of Melburry. It was so unlike her older sister that she held her tongue for the time being.

"Well, I will tell you what does signify," Peregrine declared with a smile enhanced by straight white teeth. "If we don't go off and make arrangements to have the beasts transported home, we shall be here for the remainder of the afternoon. Much as I enjoy the stables, the thought of spending the night holds no particular allure for me."

Looking directly at Lord Ringwood and his brother, Peregrine cocked a knowing brow.

"As you can see, my brother is an insistent and persuasive individual," Richard said with some humor. "We should indeed make arrangements, so if you will excuse us, we will take our leave for a moment."

He made a parting bow, but so pointedly that Lettice flushed a bit at the sure knowledge that he was singling her out for the distinction.

"It will be for only a very short moment, I assure you," Peregrine added to Aurora as he took the easily granted liberty of kissing her gloved hand.

Lettice did not have to observe her sister's pleasure to be aware that it existed, and Lord Ringwood had the distinct feeling of being trapped among events which he could not hope to control.

Giving in to the inevitable, Stuart turned to Aurora. "I will take care of your horse for you, Aurora," he promised as Peregrine pulled insistently at his sleeve. "Are you sure you will be all right for a bit?" he added, aware of his responsibility and of the Countess's disapproval, should anything befall her child in his care.

"We will be quite fine, Stuart," Lettice responded quickly, before Aurora might suggest that Lord Melburry remain behind as she suspected her sister might.

"Well, if you are sure," Lord Ringwood said, reluctantly allowing himself to be led off to do his duty.

As he left with his friends, Lettice was aware of Aurora's reproachful gaze. "And why should Lord Melburry not remain behind, I ask you?" that young lady inquired petulantly. "I daresay the Duke is capable of making the arrangements himself. Besides, I would leifer he stayed to bear us company," she added wistfully, an unhappy pout gracing her lips.

"I have no doubt that they have things to say to one another," Lettice explained reasonably. "After all, the Duke appears to be many things, but I, too, am sure he can manage such a paltry affair as this."

Even as she said the words, Lettice's brow wrinkled with lines of worry, and she wished quite heartily that she might be able to hear what indeed the Duke might be saying.

Well she might wish it, but it would not have afforded her much insight as the Duke himself was confounded beyond anything he had previously experienced in his dealings with the fairer sex, and they had been extensive to say the least. One did not, he reflected as he walked toward the holding paddock, spend seven instructive years on the continent without feeling one knew at least some of the workings of the female mind. Nevertheless, in this particular instance he found himself at a loss to explain both the lady's behavior and even his own reaction to it all.

Gnawing silently and reflectively on his lower lip, the Duke was called to attention by his brother. "Here now, much more of that and you will have no lips left at all, not that there is much to begin with, but a lipless Corinthian is an oddity, even among the eccentrics," Peregrine quipped, pleased at his own witticism as he ducked a halfhearted swing of the Duke's fist.

"Jackanapes," Richard declared. "I would have thought you had more respect for your elders."

"I have a great deal of respect for you, Richard," Peregrine replied promptly. "After all, I modeled myself after you."

The Duke laughed at this, and Lord Ringwood shook his head at such antics. "I would have thought that you had *both* outgrown such things," Stuart sighed. "If we do not get to the business at hand, we shall all be in the basket."

With this said, Lord Ringwood went off to attend to matters. As he discussed arrangements with the stable assistant, the Melburrys waited their turn.

Looking at his still-smiling brother, Peregrine nodded with approval. "Now that is more like it, I should think," he commented. "Much better than that grim clock you had a moment ago. Shouldn't think but what you would put the ladies off entirely and throw a damper on the day."

"And that is forbidden at all costs, no doubt," Richard responded, his humor up. "If you hadn't noticed, Peregrine, I am out quite a lot of blunt due to one of those 'ladies'. If that isn't throwing a damper on *my* day, then I know not what I speak."

"You can well afford it, Richard, if I do say so myself. Quite plump in the pockets, so you can't persuade me that it is such a loss. It won't fadge, 'Your Grace',"

Peregrine said mockingly. "Besides, I have an idea that you enjoyed the whole thing more than you say."

"I profess I did not," Richard insisted, but he did not look his brother in the eye and Peregrine noted the disturbed expression on his face.

"Then why were you smiling at the last?" Peregrine pursued. "Smoky bit of business, if you ask me." This last comment was a hit, Lord Melburry deduced, as he neatly avoided yet another of Richard's attempts to cuff him.

"You will never threaten the pets of the fancy at this rate," Peregrine laughed. "So, Lettice Trevelyn may have made a conquest."

"No more but what Aurora Trevelyn has added a lap dog to her collection in you," Richard responded gruffly, a bit ruffled at the idea presented by his sibling.

To the Duke's surprise, Peregrine did not deny the statement, rather he appeared more than a little pleased at the suggestion. "Do you think so?" he asked, looking hopefully at his brother as if he were indeed a pet entreating for a bonbon or something sweet.

"It is as plain as the pikestaff," Richard answered bluntly, scrutinizing Peregrine more closely. The young man only smiled blissfully, his hopes on earth apparently fulfilled. "Perhaps I will be wishing you well soon and reading your name in the banns," the Duke half-teased.

"Perhaps you will at that, and sooner than you might imagine," Peregrine retaliated. "Here now, Stuart is finished, let us have done and settle up. Mustn't keep the ladies waiting, you know," he added, leaving any other comments Richard might have for later.

As eager as his brother might have appeared to cultivate his interest in Aurora, Richard was not so anxious to do the same with Lettice. There were things, inescapable things, that he had to deal with before he could consider even the mildest entanglement. With a sigh, he followed his brother, his piqued interest fighting his common sense.

He might have taken some comfort in the fact that he was not singularly alone in this attempt. Standing with her sister and trying to occupy her attention on other matters, Lettice was distinctly uncomfortable and seemed incapable of standing still.

"You seem vastly impatient, for a person who allowed an angel to pass from our presence," Aurora remonstrated gently. "Why do you fidget so?"

Staring carefully into her sister's face, Aurora noted the irritable expression, the somewhat resentful look that Lettice habitually wore when feeling guilty for some offense. This thought reminded Aurora of something she had been wanting to ask. "And while you are explaining that, perhaps you can explain that statement you made about the stallion not mattering? I have never heard such a bag of moonshine in my life. Admit it, that was all a hum." Aurora awaited her reply and it came, though not without reluctance.

"Well, I admit it. It was all a bubble about the horse, you see," Lettice admitted, looking for understanding in her sister's eyes.

"A sham? But how?" Aurora asked, unsure of what her sister was inferring.

"That horse, I have known it since it was a foal. After all, Lord Quibble lives only a stone's throw away," Lettice started.

"Yes, I know that. So you have seen the horse before. What does that signify? It is a magnificent animal," Aurora interjected.

"It looks well, that is true," Lettice continued, "but it has no wind, can't run half a mile without huffing and puffing like a chimney."

Understanding dawned on Aurora's face, and incredulity at her sister's revenge. "You deliberately made the price high. You bid the animal up knowing that the Duke would offer more."

"I was carried away, it was not deliberate, really. Luckily, Derek reminded me to stop. In any case, the Duke needs more counsel on his horses than he thought," Lettice said with a defiant toss of her head, but there was still the shadow of guilt in her demeanor.

"Well, he deserved it, I dare swear," Aurora admitted. "He will be horribly perturbed, to say the least, when he discovers the defect, and I am sure he will realize what you did. But then I suppose you don't care an' he does, or do you?"

The way in which Lettice hung her head and examined the toe of her shoe answered Aurora. "Well, there is nothing for it, I suppose," she said at last. Then, seeing the dismay on Lettice's face, she comforted, "He can well afford to lose the money you know, and perhaps he will know he deserved it."

Looking Aurora squarely in the eyes, Lettice murmured, "I don't know why I should feel badly. It went as I wished it, but somehow, at the end it was almost as if I had mistaken the Duke. Perhaps I should tell him." Then, seeming to buck up a bit, Lettice appeared to reconsider with a toss of her head. "Well, I will not worry now, it is most certainly done and I cannot put it to rights, so I will enjoy the rest of the day as I had intended."

"That's right. Let us enjoy ourselves while we may," Aurora agreed more heartily than she felt.

"We shall have every opportunity," Lettice said with less enthusiasm than she might have, as she noted the return of the Duke, his brother and Lord Ringwood.

"Your groom is still occupied," Stuart said as he halted by Lettice's side. "He is a thorough fellow, examining every one of those creatures as if they were to be the last."

"That is why we employ him," Aurora announced. "Of course, his father held the post before him, so that has something to do with it as well. But he does his work very well, don't you agree, Your Grace?" She gazed at the Duke directly on this inquiry.

"No doubt he was very useful in his manner," Richard replied, watching Lettice's expression for the slightest change. "To be truthful, I have asked the opinion of my own stableman on occasion."

"And yet you criticized my decision to make use of ours!" Lettice remarked.

Gazing into her warm brown eyes for a moment, the Duke put on his most engaging of smiles. "For that error I hope you will forgive me."

Lettice was somewhat taken aback by this, so surprising was the comment after his original behavior. Richard was himself surprised at his own words, but the prospect of cultivating Lettice's friendship was too strong for him to resist. With an appealing look at the reluctant lady, he waited for a reply.

She was well aware of an obligation to say something, but was at a loss for words. As luck would have it, she was relieved of this responsibility as a form appeared directly behind the Duke.

"Well, Your Grace, congratulations on your purchase," the stranger said in a low voice.

The reaction to those words was quite startling, Lettice observed. Richard Melburry stiffened and then turned quickly to confront the intruder. Stuart, too, seemed uneasy. However, Lettice was most concerned with Aurora's reaction. A sharp intake of breath on her sister's part had assured Lettice that here was an individual whom Aurora must find unpleasant for some reason.

"Lord Killingham," Richard responded with a nod of the head. He appeared completely collected now, his initial surprise having been bested.

"Killingham, I wasn't aware that you had remained for the auction," Stuart remarked. "Did you have some special interest or are you simply intent on occupying your time?"

The suspicious tone in which this was said did not escape Lettice's notice. There was definitely something afoot.

"You have it precisely, Lord Ringwood," Lord Killingham replied, his attention focused unwaveringly on Aurora's lovely visage. "What better way of spending one's time than in the presence of pleasant company?"

Lord Killingham had not been so drunk the night before that he did not recognize the lovely woman he had accosted. He thought her even more beautiful than ever now that his eyes were not glazed over with drink, and he was instantly smitten.

Lettice glanced at her sister to see how she would respond to the man's indirect compliment. The comment only caused Aurora to shrink back slightly in disgust, and reply, "I would have thought, sir, that you had quite enough of my company last night on the terrace."

Lord Ringwood felt his heart sink as Lettice's eyes

widened and flew to her sister's blue orbs. At the disdainful tilt of Aurora's chin, Lettice confirmed that this stranger was indeed the offensive gentleman who had dared to insult her sister. It was not an affront that Lettice would bear without a word, as Stuart well knew. And though Aurora was no more fond of scenes than Lord Ringwood, that gentleman was sure she would have no compunction against aiding her elder sister, should she take it into her head to kick up a dust.

Unaware of what events had passed, the Duke was aware only that Lord Killingham appeared to have every intention of remaining with the group. "You must forgive my manners, Lady Trevelyn," Richard directed to Lettice after a pause. "Have you been introduced to this gentleman?"

"I am sure that we have not, though you seem to know my sister, sir," Lettice replied looking from the Duke to Lord Killingham. Her reserved manner did not bespeak an eagerness to become acquainted, but she was resigned.

Introductions were made, and Killingham made a motion to press his lips onto the back of Aurora's riding glove as he bowed over it. Before he could complete his intention, however, the hand was hastily withdrawn, a look of intense disgust flickering across Aurora's face. This apparent dislike did not daunt Lord Killingham in the least, nor did the dagger look with which Peregrine Melburry gazed at him.

Noting Aurora's habit, Killingham smiled slightly. "You are a horsewoman?" he asked conversationally. "I have few women in my acquaintance who relish the pastime, so it is refreshing to see someone who actually does."

"I do enjoy a good run on occasion," Aurora replied curtly, utterly nauseated by Lord Killingham and incredulous over his overt familiarity.

"Aurora is an excellent rider," Stuart remarked faithfully.

"Oh, I have no doubt of that at all, Lord Ringwood," Killingham said quickly, almost too eagerly. "I also enjoy an occasional ride. Do you not do the round at Hyde Park?"

"Do you, Lord Killingham?" Lettice interrupted, watching the man with antipathy.

"But of course," Lord Killingham responded, his eyes still on Aurora. His appreciative gaze was embarrassing in the extreme.

Determined to turn his attention from Aurora, Lettice turned tactfully to the Duke for assistance. "Your Grace, I do not believe I have seen you in the park. Do you frequent it?"

"Not recently. Now that I am aware that you frequent it, I will attempt to make amends for my absence."

Lettice had only hoped to divert the gentleman's attention for a moment to allow Aurora time to rally her wits and make short work of this slimy, obnoxious fellow, but her ploy worked amazingly well as she watched Lord Killingham turn to the Duke. Though the man still wore a smile, there was an anger that exuded from his unwavering eye.

"His Grace has, of course, been abroad for some time, so you cannot really fault him, Lady Trevelyn," Killingham announced, something like satisfaction in his voice.

"Abroad? Where did you reside there, Your Grace?" Lettice queried, her curiosity engaged.

"In France," he replied quietly. Something flickered in his eyes and then was still. Lettice was not sure just what, perhaps unease.

Lettice was aware that this point was one which Lord Killingham had deliberately stressed. Though unaware of the significance, she was confident in her decision on how to accept this information.

"That is quite fascinating, Your Grace. Perhaps we can discuss that on another occasion, but now, Lord Killingham, you have not said if you consider yourself a horseman of repute," she pointed out. Looking at his mud-spattered clothing, less than elegant to be sure, and then to the Duke's immaculate attire, Lettice allowed her brow to arch.

"That I cannot say, Lady Trevelyn. Modesty forbids," Killingham answered with mock humility.

"I can answer for him, however," Peregrine interjected, "since I am an independent observer of Lord Killingham's style, and I am sure he is far too retiring to say anything himself."

All eyes turned to Peregrine in polite interest. "There is not a jump that exists but that Lord Killingham is able to maneuver it, in one way or another. I recall Killingham, at Sir Francis' country estate, the fox hunt. There was this hedge along the run and your horse balked to jump it."

"I do recall it," Killingham replied with chilling coldness, the muscles in his face slackening his smile. Lettice thought she could detect a grinding of teeth and was delighted. Aurora was already beginning to smile, anticipating a hit.

"But ladies," Peregrine continued with relish, "far from thwarting Lord Killingham, he with his inimitable ingenuity was able to go down the hedge a mile to find an almost concealed opening through which to secrete himself and his horse. As I said, he is never at a loss." All this was said with the most earnest tone, all the more infuriating in its supposed adulation.

"You are too kind in your comments," Lord Killingham managed to say through clenched teeth.

"Not at all, not at all," Peregrine said with an easy wave of his hand, a smirk ill-hidden in the corner of his mouth.

"And what of the Duke?" Aurora asked, a twinkle in her blue eyes that almost caused Lord Melburry to forget himself, so intent was he on appreciating her merriment.

"The Duke? Ah . . . yes. Richard is not so original, I fear. He did the usual, jumped the hedge. Most common," Peregrine admitted apologetically.

Lettice looked over at the elder Melburry, who shrugged. "I am afraid that is the long and short of it," he agreed.

"Not to feel badly," Aurora consoled. "I quite often do the same myself." With that remark Aurora tittered into one hand.

Killingham forced a smile, though Lettice would have wagered that he did not feel it inside in the least.

"I will warrant that Your Grace has not received many invitations to hunt of late. How quickly old friends forget," Killingham remarked with a sly expression on his face. Lettice was surprised at this provoking remark, but the Duke did not seem unduly put out.

"Perhaps some of your acquaintances have short memories, Lord Killingham, but apparently my friends do not suffer from that fault. I have been offered the use of Lord Anselm's pack whenever I should find it convenient to visit." This was a hit, as Lord Killingham's startled and distinctly disappointed expression conveyed.

"If you have retained a fancy for hunting, perhaps you could join Lord Anselm and the Duke," Lettice interjected, eyes wide with innocence.

Lord Killingham appeared nonplussed a moment and there was a long pause. In that time Lettice noted that there were deep wrinkles in the corners of the man's eyes and that the flesh of his face had lost the resilience of youth.

"I don't believe that Lord Anselm is acquainted with Lord Killingham. They do not travel in the same circles," Richard remarked, at last breaking the silence. The inference that Lord Anselm would scorn Lord Killingham's presence was enough to feed the hatred that Lettice could see growing within Lord Killingham, but it was not enough to enrage him altogether.

Killingham continued to stare at Richard with venom, then turned to Aurora abruptly. "Lord Anselm is addicted to hunting overmuch. I prefer to ride for the pleasure of it. Perhaps you would care to come riding the Thursday after next?" Aurora was astonished by such an impudent invitation, but the man continued. "A trot in the park, and then perhaps I could meet the Countess, your mother?"

This was a doubler in its rudeness, and Aurora was so amazed at Lord Killingham's utter gall that she was at a loss. Fortunately, Lettice was not, and she covertly poked Lord Melburry in the side, making him jump slightly.

"Ah . . ." he began, quite startled himself. Glancing only briefly at Lettice's face, he understood instantly what she was suggesting. "I am afraid that before Lady Aurora can respond to your invitation, Lord Killingham, she must give me an answer to mine."

Aurora looked attentively at Lord Melbury in an attempt to catch the drift of his plan. "Of course, how silly of me. I have not yet given you my answer."

"Indeed, madam, and you have made me suffer grievously in waiting," Peregrine avowed.

A smile spread on Aurora's face. "I am much sorrowed if I have done so, my lord," she said with incredible seriousness.

"Forgiven only if you will end the torture now, madam. Will you indeed ride with my brother and me in the park on Thursday next?" Peregrine asked gravely.

Looking to her sister, Aurora asked, "What do you advise, Lettice?"

Inspecting Peregrine with a thorough eye, Lettice replied, "I think you had best comply, for he is beginning to show signs of a decline, I dare swear."

"Then it is yes!" Peregrine declared delightedly.

"It would appear so, Lord Melbury. I could not live with myself if I should be the cause of a profound melancholy on your part," Aurora responded. "I am afraid I will be engaged next week, Lord Killingham."

"Perhaps I can come out and meet the Countess in any case," Killingham remarked, not one to go down without a fight. Aurora almost gasped at the man's impudence.

"I am sure that can be arranged, Lord Killingham," Lettice assured him airily. "I will let Mama know of your wishes and she will issue the invitation personally."

"I will await the invitation eagerly," Killingham said, realizing that his overbold move had been outmaneuvered.

He will await it indefinitely, Lettice thought as she smiled back. "It is getting late, I really feel it is time that we left, don't you think so, Aurora?"

"Most certainly. I think I have had quite enough excitement now," Aurora agreed.

Since there was little else he could do, Lord Killingham took his leave; this time, however, he was successful in kissing Aurora's gloved hand before he left. "I will be waiting on the invitation, Lady Trevelyn," he murmured in parting, his sensuous gaze lingering on Aurora's figure.

Lettice noted Peregrine's clenching his fists behind his back at the sight, and wondered at his restraint. His verbal assault on Lord Killingham, while clever, was not as severe as it could have been. He must have a reason for checking himself, but Lettice was at a loss to know why.

"It really is time that we left," Lettice observed as she watched the retreating form of Lord Killingham. "Aurora can return in our carriage, Stuart."

"Then let us at least walk to your vehicle," Peregrine insisted.

To this the sisters readily acquiesced, Aurora walking a little ahead of her sister with Lord Melburry while Lettice was left with Lord Ringwood and the Duke for company.

"Stuart," Richard said as they walked, "don't you think that you should see to your own carriage?"

"It is in the same general direction, Richard," Lord Ringwood assured his friend with his annoying lack of perspicacity. A speaking glance, however, made Stuart realize that something was required of him. "Oh, yes. I suppose I had best attend to it," he said, confused as to the reason for Richard's request. "I will see you later in the week, Lettice," he said as he left.

Walking alone with the Duke, Lettice was decidedly uneasy, and was made more so because he appeared to be struggling with something he wished to say, a serious expression on his face. She decided to try for a lighter mood.

"Well, your brother has quite a ready wit," Lettice said. "And a great deal of chivalry as well," she added. "You will, of course, tell him that he is under no obligation whatever to attend us on Thursday."

Looking into Richard's eyes, Lettice saw that he was now smiling. "I am sure that your sister has said something similar to Peregrine just now, and I am also positive that he has no desire to be divested of that delightful task for which he volunteered so willingly. If you have not noticed, Lady Trevelyn, my younger brother appears to be quite taken with your sister." Richard spoke these words with an easy air which made it quite natural for Lettice to smile in response.

Unexpectedly, the Duke seemed to make a decision while looking at her. "You know, Lady Trevelyn, I do believe I have made a grievous mistake."

"Indeed, what would that be?" she inquired warily, his voice putting her on guard.

"I have made a mistake in purchasing that stallion."

Lettice paled and her eyes widened. However, she had averted her face, and the Duke did not see the change. Stopping, Richard stood before her as Lettice met his eyes, her iron control restoring her composure.

"I have made a mistake," he repeated. "The horse is definitely more suited to you, Lady Trevelyn. I would not dream of changing fate, and I am ever more convinced upon reflection that you, not I, were meant to possess that animal."

This time the surprise was undisguised, but what Richard mistook for delight was in reality more like relief. Even so, Lettice was aware that the Duke was no fool.

"Your Grace," she protested in a halfhearted manner, "are you sure that you wish to sell it to me? Quite sure?"

"Lady Trevelyn, I wish you would accept the horse as a gift."

As he stood there with the most serious of expressions, Lettice could not doubt the sincerity of his words, but she was terribly flustered by this offer. To purchase the steed for a fair price was one thing, to except such a costly gift from an absolute stranger was impossible. "I cannot," she said at last. "It is not possible. What would my family think of me?" Though she had hoped not to offend the Duke by her refusal, he did appear somewhat dejected.

"You are angry, then, and punish me by refusing the horse," he asserted.

"But . . . No!" she exclaimed. "It is only . . ."

The Duke did not allow her to finish. "Then it is settled, you will accept it as a token of, of my esteem for you, and hopefully of friendship."

Lettice paused a moment. She had refused an easy way out of her dilemma once, she was not such a fool as to refuse the opportunity a second time. "In friendship, then, I accept your gift," Lettice said, still a little wary, extending her hand to him.

With a large smile, the Duke accepted and held it for a moment, sealing the bargain.

"I will arrange for the animal to be with the other animals you purchased today," Richard promised, and Lettice decided to allow her parents to believe that the animal was a personal purchase of her own so as to avoid any arguments. They would never ask, as it was her usual custom to purchase her own mounts with the "pin money" she had accumulated.

The Duke still held her hand and once engaged in this pleasant attitude, Lettice was at a loss on how best to disengage her hand, for he showed no inclination toward releasing it. In fact, Richard seemed to find the opportunity a perfect one to examine Lettice's countenance more closely. He was rewarded with a slight blush.

"Your Grace," Lettice murmured, "do you not think that we should attend our siblings?" Though she had found that small contact rather pleasant, she was not so easily won over. She would reserve her opinion of Richard Melburry until such time as she felt she knew him better.

Recalling himself, the Duke removed his hand from hers. "Oh, yes. I suppose we should," he replied, looking about for the young couple. "There they are," he said as he spotted them near the stable where the carriages had been left. To Richard's surprise, he saw that Lord Simmons was with Peregrine and Aurora, deeply engrossed in a discussion with the younger Trevelyn sister.

Lettice was slightly amused to see that Lord Melburry was not taking the intrusion well, and he looked distinctly jealous as Lord Simmons took his leave, firmly kissing Aurora's gloved hand as if to stake a claim.

Rising from his elegant, if stooped, position, Lord Simmons greeted Richard and Lettice. "Lady Trevelyn, Your Grace. I was just enjoying the company of your sister," he said as he looked at Lettice. "You will both be going to the card party tonight, will you not?" he inquired hopefully.

"We shall be present, all three of us, Lord Simmons," Lettice answered cheerfully, feeling much brighter since the worry over the Duke's new purchase had been lifted from her shoulders. "We hardly ever appear without one another, you know. Today is an obvious change from our common way."

"If you shall all be there, then I am content to wait to see you tonight," Lord Simmons avowed. "Lady Trevelyn, Aurora." Nodding to the two gentlemen, Lord Simmons left the small group.

"You will not be attending the card party, Lord Melbury?" Lettice asked, turning to look at the young gentleman who seemed to be watching Lord Simmons' departure with a bad-tempered expression.

Turning his attention to her inquiry, Peregrine Melburry shook his head in such a woeful manner that Lettice was tempted to laugh. "I am afraid I shall be engaged in other matters this evening, Lady Trevelyn."

"We shall miss your company, then," Aurora said with a simple straightforwardness which the Duke's brother found entrancing.

"Indeed we shall," Lettice agreed wholeheartedly, "but leave we must, now. It is, I will repeat, quite late."

Walking over to the carriages, the Duke assisted Lettice in ascending the few steps while Peregrine bent to kiss Aurora's hand.

"One moment," Aurora said, hastily withdrawing her hand. To Lord Melbury's astonishment, she removed the leather glove with some difficulty, and presented her hand once again for his salute. He kissed the soft, smooth skin and rose, a questioning look in his eyes.

Throwing the glove to the ground, Aurora explained, "Lord Killingham has irreparably soiled it with his touch, and it is not fit for one such as you to kiss."

They both smiled, then with the last glance in parting, Lord Melbury assisted Aurora to step up into the carriage. With a motion of the leads, their coachman started for home. Watching the vehicle depart, Peregrine burst out laughing as he saw the remaining glove go sailing out the carriage window.

There was little to be said on the ride home. Lettice

astonished her sister with the knowledge of the Duke's gift, but felt that Aurora was much too distracted with her own thoughts to wish to discuss it. So it was that the Trevelyn sisters spent most of the journey in their own reflections.

It was fortunate that they were allowed some quiet, for the chaos that they returned to was something to cut up any sensible person's peace.

Stepping through the door, Lettice was immediately besieged by the Countess who demanded her eldest daughter do something about Patrice and her stubborn refusal to give up "her" lieutenant, while Aurora was begged by a tearful Patrice to side with her in convincing the Countess that she had found the only man to whom she could possibly be wed.

"But what has happened here?" Lettice demanded loudly as she had to raise her voice to be heard over the din of wailing and weeping.

"Patrice insists on marrying Lieutenant Torquill. I have forbidden it, of course," the Countess huffed, the very thought of the lieutenant's boldness inflaming her once more.

"Of course," Lettice said, "and of course, Patrice, you will not give him up," she deduced.

"Lettice, I love Basil and I will continue to see him," Patrice declared with unusual bravado, but Lettice could see that her sister was weakening under such an unaccustomed stance.

"Can we not discuss this calmly?" Aurora asked, dabbing futilely with a pitifully inadequate handkerchief at the tears flowing down Patrice's cheeks.

There was a moment's complete silence as everyone attempted to rally herself. Then, the Earl walked into the room, having returned from his business.

"Oh, Papa," Patrice instantly wailed and commenced to cry again.

The house was in an uproar once again, both the Countess and Patrice attempting to speak at once. Lettice sighed, resigning herself to an evening of turmoil. It did not appear that they would be able to attend the card party after all, Aurora reflected, and she hoped that Lord Melburry was having a more enjoyable evening than the one she herself was about to endure.

Lord Melburry was not in the position of enjoying himself that evening, however, as he reluctantly stopped his carriage before a small but fashionably constructed home on the outskirts of London. Swearing slightly at the lost opportunity to pursue his acquaintance with Aurora, he found himself even more uncomfortable with the task before him. After he knocked briefly on the large whitewashed door, it was opened and an elderly butler looked him up and down.

"You are expected, sir," he said without inquiring name or purpose. "I shall have one of the footmen remove your carriage from the front of the house. You will understand that we practice the utmost discretion."

Peregrine did not reply to this, and without another word the butler admitted him. Though he had little previous experience with women of the demimonde, Lord Melburry was surprised to find this woman's house furnished luxuriously yet tastefully, with a slightly oriental flavor.

Inspecting a porcelain vase, Peregrine was suddenly aware of footsteps and, looking up toward the doorway, his eyes were met by those of a dark-haired beauty. She glided across the room to the sofa.

"Lord Melburry, I believe you have come to discuss an urgent matter. Please, be seated," she said, motioning for him to sit beside her. As he did so, the woman indicated to her footman to leave them.

꙳꙳꙳꙳ CHAPTER 4

"ON PAIN of death, you will not move one more time, Stuart!" Lettice threatened irritably, throwing the soft-leaded sketching pencil she held at her subject so that it bounced with some force off one broad shoulder.

With her portfolio open and sheets of parchment and sketch paper strewn about with ruined likenesses,

Lettice was at her wit's end in her efforts to reproduce the features of her twitching friend. Kneeling awkwardly on the carpeted floor of the sitting-room alcove, Lettice groped with one arm under the sofa where the pencil had rolled, cursing silently to herself for having been importuned by Patrice into producing a portrait of Lord Ringwood for her album.

"Here, let me get it," Stuart offered helpfully.

"No, stay right where you are," Lettice ordered, a dire edge on her voice. "If you move one particle, I shall not be held responsible for my actions. Simply sit there still enough for me to catch a good likeness and. I shall be content and you can go off and have your supper as I am sure you desire."

With a sigh, Lord Ringwood did as he was requested, the twitch in his cheek acting up only slightly as Lettice rose, red-faced and somewhat disheveled from her stooped position. That he wished above all else to do what he was told was evident in his shallow, almost inadequate breathing, the better for Lettice to catch the "real" him. Unfortunately, this caused Stuart to yawn quite a bit which exasperated Lettice quite beyond all endurance.

Lord Ringwood did not flatter himself in thinking that Patrice had any motives other than friendship in wishing to have a picture of him, however, even this pitifully small interest was enough to fluster him and this did not make the sitting any easier.

Seating herself once more across the table and taking up an unsullied sheet of paper, Lettice tried once more to capture the essence that was Lord Ringwood and bind it to parchment.

After a few careful strokes, Lettice seemed to relax a bit, occasionally glancing up at Stuart as the pencil scratched quickly and lightly on the surface of the paper.

"Well, now, I did not say you couldn't talk, you know," she said reproachfully as the silence in the room grew so thick that it became oppressive.

"If I talk, then I am moving, and you have already pointed out that this would be lethal," Stuart protested, his lips hardly stirring in the process.

"I am a woman of my word, too," Lettice agreed

with a faint smile, "but I have completed that funny little mouth to my satisfaction, so you may speak with impunity."

Continuing with easy accuracy, Lettice noted that Lord Ringwood was watching the minutes tick by on the mantel clock with apprehension. "You have other appointments?" she inquired curiously. "If you do, we can desist for now, and you can sit for me again another day. Of course," she added with mischief gleaming in her eyes, "Patrice will have to wait for her portrait of you all the longer and I know she very much desires to have it."

"By all means, continue," Stuart insisted. "I would not want to sit for this again, and there is yet time enough for me to prepare ma self before meeting with Richard. Besides, he is not so very choosy about my appearance as you are."

At the mention of the Duke, Lettice glanced up. Suddenly, she turned her attention to her work again, deliberately avoiding Stuart's eye as she asked casually, "Richard, that is the Duke of Melburry, is it not?"

Shifting his eyes rather painfully so that he could see Lettice from out the corner, Lord Ringwood showed some surprise. "Yes, it is, and I should think you would remember the man. It isn't everybody who gives you a stallion on your first meeting, you know," Stuart pointed out unnecessarily.

"I am aware," she replied. "Still, I cannot be as conversant with the Duke as you appear to be. How long have you known him? You seem to be well acquainted, but you have never mentioned him to me. Why have we never met before?"

"I *have* known Richard a good while, and I haven't mentioned him because he has been out of the country, as you know."

"My memory is not deficient, but he must have been abroad a long time or we should have met ere now," Lettice countered, the tilt of her chin and the contemplative look on her face causing Lord Ringwood some qualms.

He was not ready to discuss Richard's past with Lettice, such as it was, and especially when he knew not himself in what light Richard himself viewed it.

"Richard has been away from home some four years, so there was no opportunity for the two of you to meet before now," Stuart said with caution.

"He must have enjoyed living in France a great deal, to stay so very long," Lettice commented, her pencil poised with unnerving inactivity over the paper as she continued to contemplate Lord Ringwood's features.

"Richard was ever one for France," he claimed lamely. "He speaks the tongue like a native, says I could do the same if I applied ma self. Thing is, ain't interested in the Froggies like he is."

This comment went unheeded as Lettice suddenly commenced to sketch once again, noting that the sun was beginning to fade and that she would soon lose her light.

"You will have to forgive my curiosity," Lettice said at last as she completed her work with a satisfied flourish under her signature. Turning the picture toward Stuart, who leaned forward better to view it, she asked, "What think you?"

"Now, how would I know?" he questioned. "I suppose it is fine, but are you sure that ma nose is that large?"

This last was asked with such a pitiful expression that Lettice gave in to a small deception.

"Actually, it is a trifle too large, now you mention it, but I can right it in a moment," she replied, and with a few strokes, she softened the offending feature, making reality less harsh for her friend. "There, now with this to guide me I will be able to paint a faithful miniature for Patrice as she asked," she said with satisfaction.

Stretching catlike, Stuart stood up from his position of the last hour.

Clearing the remaining pictures and packing them neatly away into her portfolio, Lettice motioned for Lord Ringwood to sit on the couch.

"Sit down. Patrice said that she would come down to look at my masterpiece, and you can still spare the time I'll warrant."

Unable to forego such a pleasure, Lord Ringwood did as he was bade, Lettice joining him for a comfortable tête-à-tête. Stuart shifted uneasily in his seat for he had a feeling Lettice's curiosity had not yet been satisfied.

He was correct in his assumption as she asked in her most inquisitive tones, "Stuart, is there some old dislike between the Duke and that Killingham individual?"

"Well, yes there is," he admitted. "But how did you guess? They said nothing about it, no hard words at all. Peregrine was more difficult than Richard."

"True," she agreed, "the Duke was all politeness, but there was still the way that they looked at one another. Such coldness and such hostility! Tell me, was it a woman?" Lettice waited attentively for a reply as Stuart debated how far he could go without betraying Richard's secrets.

He had decided that he would answer as best he could when he was saved by the entrance of Patrice, resplendent in a softly gathered dress of fine white muslin, the shirred bodice decorously high and enhancing the fresh youthfulness of her bearing.

"Dear Stuart, have you endured the agony of Lettice's scrutiny for me?" Patrice asked with more gaiety than her sister expected.

In truth, though Patrice may have been downcast, she would never dream of showing such a face to Lord Ringwood. It would have distressed her even more to think of her friend disturbed for her well-being.

"Lord, yes, and have had enough of it, thank you kindly," he replied with the brotherly banter to which he had resorted in hiding his passion from Patrice.

Handing her the portrait, Lettice asked, "Is it like?"

She knew full well that Patrice would be happy whatever the quality of the picture. She had always been an easily pleased child, always lavish in her praise, and was no different now as she looked at her sister's work.

"Lettice, you have just captured Stuart. It is very like him, and I shall treasure the miniature always once you complete it," Patrice said sincerely.

Turning to Lord Ringwood who seemed entranced with looking at Patrice, Lettice pointed out archly, "You were about to say, Stuart, before Patrice came into the room, something about the Duke of Melburry."

Recalling himself, Lord Ringwood gathered his wits, such as they were. "I really haven't time now, Lettice," he replied, sidling toward the door in an effort to elude her questioning. "I have to be off now, can't present myself to dine like this. Another time, I'm sure," he said, reaching for his hat and gloves where he had laid them on an occasional table.

"That is quite all right, I understand completely," Lettice responded amiably. "I will have the opportunity of asking the Duke himself when he and his brother come to call on Thursday." Lettice smiled at the surprise on Stuart's face. "The Duke sent a messenger to the house to ask if he might accompany Aurora and me when we ride in the park with Lord Melbury. Enjoy your meal, Stuart," she finished, walking over and opening the doors to the room with a satisfied smile.

"Yes, well, I hope to see you again soon, Lettice, Patrice," he mumbled awkwardly, taking a last admiring glance at Patrice who held out her hand for him to kiss as was her wont.

As he bent awkwardly over the hand he so coveted, Patrice looked at his bent head with sisterly affection. "Recall, Stuart, that I have asked you to praise Aurora before the Duke's brother, not that she really needs such extra comments, but it does not hurt. From what Aurora has said of him, it sounds as if they suit one another, do you not think so?" Patrice asked her unknown admirer.

"As you wish, though I fancy that there is no need, as Peregrine does indeed seem taken," Stuart answered, his eyes cast down on the Turkey carpet at his feet.

Taking his leave, he made good his escape at last. To linger in Patrice's presence would have been too difficult, the mixture of pleasure and despair causing him an exquisite type of agony, as Patrice could be expected to expound on the virtues of Basil Torquill.

Turning to Lettice as the doors closed, Patrice fixed her sister with a mischievous glance. "I need not ask if I should have recommended that Stuart do the same service for you, Lettice," she commented, her teasing voice baiting her sister for a reply. She knew of Lettice's encounter with the Duke, her sisters having described the events in graphic detail on their arrival home.

Even when attempting to get the better of Lettice, Patrice was still gentle in her dealings, and her sister was not offended in the least.

"We all know that such a service would be unappreciated, Patrice," Lettice responded with such primness that both had to laugh at the absurdity.

"He shall be crushed to know that you do not find him pleasing," Patrice warned sagely.

"Hardly crushed, I would not even think he would be slightly bruised in feelings," Lettice countered. "No, I definitely must disagree with such a ridiculous idea. The Duke currys my favor for a light flirtation and no more, of that I am convinced." Lettice's assured manner caused her sister to raise her brow with surprise.

"Why do you think it? Do you have some information to which I have not been privy?" she inquired curiously.

"One can assume these things, Patrice," Lettice assured in a knowing manner. "The Duke, I am sure, has cultivated the art of flirtation during his stay in France, though I have a feeling that he had more than his share of experience before his trip abroad. Suffice it to say that I am not to be a mild flirtation for the Duke's amusement."

"Indeed?" Patrice questioned doubtfully. "You will not succumb to his charm? I hear from Aurora that his magnetism is considerable, almost as great as she finds Lord Melburry's."

"I will not be persuaded by the Duke's winning manner, if that is what you mean. And if I should choose to flirt a bit myself, it will be only in sport. Certainly, I would not be such a fool as to lose my heart to a rake," Lettice said with some scorn.

"Come, you are too harsh!" Patrice exclaimed. "A rake! Going it a bit brown as Stuart would say."

"La, and you talking flash now!" Lettice said with astonishment. "I would watch myself if I were you. If Mama should hear you, it shall go badly, and that is the last thing you need now."

"It cannot go worse," Patrice lamented sorrowfully. With that comment, she walked with a lagging step to the pianoforte and sat on the low bench. "I have not seen nor heard from Basil in a week, and Mama swears this is how it shall be. She has no heart!" she declared bitterly, letting fall a large teardrop.

"Now that is not true!" Lettice insisted. "Mama simply doesn't show her emotions, you know. She cares and has heart enough too."

"If she shows nothing, then it matters not a whit if she feels," Patrice disagreed. "It is as if it were nothing to her that I love Basil."

"It is something to her, but it is more to her that you wish to marry a man of whom she disapproves," Lettice admonished, beginning to tire of her task of lecturing.

"It is the money," Patrice burst out, burying her head in her hands and letting a torrent of tears flood her green eyes. Her sobbing grew louder, and though Lettice could understand her sister's unhappiness, she was annoyed nonetheless, unable to see, herself, just what sterling virtues the lieutenant could possibly possess that should make him such a prize.

Once the crying seemed less, Lettice made one more effort to talk reasonably. "Patrice, I will tell you this once again. Mama cares about the money, it is true, but only because she cares for your future comfort. She cares about rank because she is sure, as am I, that you would be unhappy married to someone who is too far beneath you. Perhaps if you were of a different caste, Mama should not care, but you are what you are, and there is nothing for it. Finally, she doesn't feel that the lieutenant would make you a loving husband. On the first two points she might be convinced to reverse her decision, however, on the last she is adamant and so you would do best to forget Basil."

As gently as she had said it, Lettice knew that her sister considered her words as a betrayal.

"I had hoped you would help me, but I see I am wrong. I have no allies in this," Patrice said between sobs. "Basil would make a wonderful husband. He tells Mama things I could never say. If he wants me to attend a party with him, he can tell Mama to her face. If he wishes to go for a ride with me, there is no fear in him in asking it, nay, demanding it from Mama or

Papa. I have always had to do as Mama and Papa have said, but with Basil it is different. He is strong for me."

Viewing the tear-stained face and quivering lip of her sister, Lettice decided that more discussion would be futile. "Very well, you must fight your battles as you feel fit, but excuse me if I leave you for better company. I cannot have sympathy for your lieutenant, though I do not like to see you in such pain. If you insist on grieving for him, then there is nothing constructive I can do."

With that, Lettice quit the room leaving only the walls to witness her sister's weeping. Entering the foyer, Lettice scowled so that the mirrors might have been expected to shatter at her ire. She had never enjoyed the role of mother's helper; she was not by nature a disciplinarian and disliked meddling in her sister's affairs. However, as the eldest, it was expected that she would reinforce the Countess's strictures. She had often balked at the situation, but on this occasion she found herself in accord with her mother, unusual in itself, and it appeared that a watchful eye was needed.

"So I am to be the enemy, for I am sure Mama will not be sufficiently aware of what is going on and someone must be," Lettice sighed resignedly as she began to mount the stairs. And who will take care to watch me? she wondered. Though she had made a great show of immunity toward the Duke's behavior, she knew that in truth she was more attracted to him than she cared to admit. It was a most unsatisfactory feeling, this gravitation toward Richard Melburry. Lettice felt sure that Lord Ringwood's behavior when discussing the Duke's past with her was something of a warning. Unintentional perhaps, but she was convinced that the Duke's absence from England must have had something to do with his involvement with a woman. If his conduct had been beyond reproach, then Stuart would have said so. Lettice could only conclude that the Duke was one who enjoyed a dalliance or affair while treating women's hearts with a careless hand.

"Well, he shall not do so to me," she mumbled determinedly to herself as she reached the first landing.

Suddenly, from below, there was a tremendous bustling about. The main doors flew open before the hurrying figure of Aurora, the servants trailing behind much bedraggled-looking and laden with bandboxes and parcels from all of the most fashionable establishments in London.

"You have had an enjoyable afternoon?" Lettice inquired drolly, inspecting the packages as the footmen labored up the stairs with their burdens.

"Immensely," Aurora replied with satisfaction, racing up to her sister's side in a most unladylike manner to supervise the transporting of her prizes. "I now have four gowns to choose from for the garden party tomorrow and as many bonnets and parasols to match. I shall at last feel as though I have something to wear," she exulted.

"Odd, you should of a sudden decide that your clothing needed to be supplemented," Lettice mused aloud. "In case you were wondering, I have it on the best authority that Lord Melburry will *not* be attending the affair. I trust that has no bearing in any case on your selection of attire."

The disappointment was glaring on Aurora's face. "You are a beast to tell me so," she said dejectedly then, reconsidering, she shook her head. "No, I take that back. It is just that I was hoping to see Lord Melburry before Thursday."

"Don't fret. Even if you don't see him tomorrow, it will be soon enough and you can still don one of your new gowns. So, now give us a smile for I am sure I cannot take any more tearful or sullen faces today," Lettice cajoled, taking her sister's hand in hers and squeezing it.

A smile appeared hesitantly, then more brightly on Aurora's face as she seemed to consider Lettice's words. "You are right, of course. I need not be so anxious to see Lord Melburry."

Continuing up the stairs together, Aurora noted that Lettice's face seemed drawn, and the meaning of her previous words dawned on her. "Patrice is fretting over her lieutenant again, is she?" she inquired sympathetically.

"Yes, she is, and I am the resident ogre today, so don't get too near lest I eat you alive. I am sure that I have just completed a thorough job of ripping her heart from her breast. Should you talk to her, I know she will accuse me of the grossest inconsideration of her feelings. In short, I am very bad to her today," Lettice concluded with a roll of her eyes heavenwards, as if to ask for a relief of her charge.

Patting her sister's shoulder comfortingly, Aurora attempted to console Lettice. "She will come around. You mark my words."

"I sincerely hope so," Lettice prayed. "Oh, yes! She gave Stuart strict orders to further you in Lord Melburry's eyes. I thought you would like to know that, since Stuart always does her bidding."

This information did not displease Aurora who took it in renewed good humor. "I hope you told her that it would be unnecessary," she said confidently.

"You are so very sure?" Lettice asked with surprise.

"I am not sure, but I have the strangest feeling that I can risk the pretense of being sure. I know not why, but I do know I have never felt so wonderful in my life."

The glow on Aurora's face convinced Lettice that this was true, and a little envy crept into her voice as she replied, "Would that we could all be so sure of what was true. You have an innate feeling on the matter. Patrice is convinced she loves the lieutenant. And, the only thing I am sure of is that I have loved no man at all who has wanted to wed me. They all profess to adore me, worship at my feet, so why I cannot believe them is beyond me. I wish I were blessed with such surety as the two of you seem to have," Lettice groaned, as she reached her room.

Aurora eyed her sister with uncertainty. "I had thought that perhaps you had taken a liking to the Duke. After all, he did bestow a very handsome horse on you, and was very much more polite and flattering toward the end of the day. Though, to be sure, I don't know why he did, as you tried your best to be as contrary as possible," Aurora commented with a knowing smile.

"The Duke is engaging, nothing more than that. In fact, Lord Simmons can be said to have more style in his speaking than the Duke, and more wit, I believe," Lettice asserted strongly, only half believing her own words.

She reflected that the only reason she was saying this was to give her sister an opportunity to contradict her as Aurora readily proceeded to do; pointing out that the Duke was by far the sharper of the two gentlemen and cut a much handsomer figure to boot.

"In fact, I don't think that a fair comparison can even be made," she said at last. "The Duke is nothing like Lord Simmons, or anyone else, for that matter, within my remembrance."

Lettice agreed with apparent reluctance, but Aurora was not fooled in the least. "Why, you are just funning, I suppose! Silly child, I cannot tell you what you like. You already know too well. You just have to make up your mind whether or not you like the Duke, so I won't pick at you any longer." With an exasperated shake of her glossy blond curls, Aurora left her sister to attend to her own toilette before supper.

Sighing at Aurora's departure, Lettice thought that it was really a pity that she couldn't decide yet whether or not the Duke appealed to her sensibilities. Indubitably he was handsome, he had a quick wit, and could have a scathing tongue, a definite sign of a sharp and agile mind. He could certainly be charming when he desired, and perhaps this easy ability was the thing which annoyed her the most.

"Why should he have my good fellowship simply at his own whim?" she asked herself aloud, entering her room and sitting before her vanity. "Well, he will have to work a bit to earn my friendship," she said with a huff to her reflection. "If everyone else chooses to like him, then he is simply fortunate. He cannot claim much charisma in having Stuart for a friend, for Stuart is such a good-natured creature that he would befriend almost anyone at all, given the opportunity."

Lettice knew this last thought was untrue, but she was not prepared to like the Duke just yet. She dismissed the entire issue from her mind as she brushed vigorously at her black locks, frowning quite severely into the glass before her.

Lord Ringwood's features were formed into a frown as well, as he hurried his horses along the darkening streets toward the Duke's townhouse, uncomfortably tardy in making his promised appearance. Stuart's lean body seemed to strain forward as if somehow to urge his pair to step up its already considerable pace. Though Lord Ringwood was by no means a perfectionist, he did try to be as punctual as possible, so it was with some relief that he finally reached his destination. Handing his hat and overcoat to the footman, he was informed by the butler that Lord Melburry and the Duke had just at that moment entered the dining room.

"They waited on your arrival as long as possible, your lordship," the butler remarked as he was shown the way, passing through the well lit hallway to the heavy oaken doors of the small dining hall. "The master prefers to keep the grand hall for larger parties," the butler informed Stuart as he glanced over the contents of the room. Small but comfortable enough for entertaining one's friends, the rectangular table of mahogany gleamed with high polish, the labor of many hours, no doubt. However, it was not the meticulous shine which caused Lord Ringwood's eyes to widen with surprise.

Seated at either end of the small table were the Duke and his brother, and they observed their friend's somewhat bemused look as they greeted him.

"Well, Stuart. How do you like it?" Richard inquired wryly, motioning broadly at the dishes on the table. Before him, Stuart stared at an enormously elaborate setting consisting of heavy gold plate, oppressive as was the usual for such outmoded articles, but nonetheless opulent.

"Good God!" Stuart exclaimed when he found his voice. Seating himself at his place on the right of Richard, he hefted one very weighty knife, the edge only slightly blunted from use. "We are good friends, but I hardly warrant such a display, Richard," Stuart said, looking a bit overwhelmed as he lifted a solid gold cup to his lips and took a sip of much-needed wine.

"You sell yourself short, Stuart," Peregrine insisted with a smile hovering about his lips. "You and I both quite deserve to dine in this manner. Of course, it doesn't matter that these dishes were the only ones to be had in the entire place." This last was added with a look to Richard. "I suppose you will be rectifying this before we dine next with you?" Peregrine said with a sigh.

"Unfortunately for you, I shall be," the Duke replied to his incorrigible sibling. Turning to Stuart he added, "My father was very stubborn; he insisted on the traditional setting whenever we dined. Needless to say, meals here have usually been quite formal."

"So I would imagine," Stuart answered feelingly. "Your father wasn't by any chance related to Midas, I suppose? No, no, I don't think I really want to know."

Stuart sat back in the carved wood chair as the footmen—their livery reflecting brightly the Melburry colors—began serving the covered dishes that had been prepared. Peregrine looked over to Stuart through the heavy candelabras on the table with a grin as he cut into a delicately broiled slice of veal.

"So, Stuart, no explanation for your abominable behavior?" Peregrine asked, his humor showing through his admonishing tone. "You have slighted us both with your unpunctuality. What engrossing occupation has caused this outrage?" he demanded with a stern expression, losing the effect by the constant twitching of his lips with mirth.

Conveying another deliciously rare morsel of meat to his lips, Lord Ringwood mumbled a reply through a mouthful of food. "Had to sit for a portrait. Lettice insisted that I do so for Patrice, you see. Couldn't very well run out."

"Of course not," Richard agreed to this reasonable explanation. "I don't blame you for not wishing to set Lady Lettice's back up. I have myself had a taste of her irritation," he admitted, observing one of the offered dishes, frowning and waving it away.

"Actually, I rather fancy that Stuart was lingering in hopes of catching a glimpse of Lady Patrice rather than remaining out of a sense of duty," Peregrine insisted, both he and Richard being well aware of Lord Ringwood's standing passion for the lady.

Stuart turned an interestingly intense shade of pink up to the tips of his ears at these words.

"And I suppose you wouldn't have been late if it had been a portrait of yourself for the Lady Aurora?" the Duke queried, effectively silencing Peregrine and causing his impish brother to pay more heed to the dish before him.

Peregrine was perfectly capable of retaliating in kind to his brother, but he had noted of late that Richard was not to be toyed with on the subject of the Lady Lettice Trevelyn, and as much as it amused Peregrine to tease him, he was inclined toward compassion this time. Stuart, of course, was not the sort to make jest of what appeared to be a budding passion on Richard's part for Lettice, amazed as he was.

There was silence for the rest of the meal except for a few innocuous remarks on the weather and the shocking coil that Pomroy Fitzhugh had gotten himself into. Though Richard agreed with Peregrine that it was a damnable situation when a man was faced with the paternity of twin baby boys from a former mistress, his mind was only half engaged, the other portion preoccupied with thoughts he could not altogether suppress.

Though some time had passed since Richard had met Lady Lettice, he was disturbed to find that his curiosity about her had not waned in the least, as was usually his wont in such situations. Rather than finding another fancy to occupy his mind, the Duke had found his head filled with visions of Lettice on horseback, of her particularly becoming features, somehow compelling in their defiant nature.

He did not pretend to understand her fluctuating behavior, going all at once from anger and indignant scorn to grudging respect, to mysterious calm. He was attracted, he knew, but it was not the usual thing for him. He had finally given in to the impulse to see her again, having sent a note requesting that he be allowed to accompany his brother and the two sisters on their ride in Hyde Park.

Sitting back and sipping casually on his wine, Richard reflected that he could not call Lady Lettice "pretty" for she was not pretty in the sense that her features were small and pert. She was not ethereal as was her sister Aurora, nor was she delicate as he had been assured by Stuart that Patrice was. Richard was accustomed to the petite and sophisticated Parisian ladies he had lived among for the past few years. Many of his former tendres had been for such women; their youth, flirting behavior, and gaiety attracting him and helping him to fill his days with meaningless but pleasant patter.

No, this woman was far from pleasant at times, and she was full of disquieting behavior, but she was terribly interesting as well. Richard had found himself trying to understand her nature, an occupation he had never dreamed of indulging in with his former inamoratas.

The Duke was roused suddenly from his thoughts by a sharp cracking sound, and then another. As he looked over at Stuart, Lord Ringwood glanced up from the walnuts he was breaking in his hands, elbows askance, the shoulders of his coat wrinkling in a most irreparable manner.

The footman was instantly at Richard's side as he drained the last of the wine from his cup in an amiable salute to Lord Ringwood. Covering the cup with his hand, Richard looked over to Peregrine who toyed at the cheese and slivers of almonds on his plate, the footman scuttling quietly away to fetch the sherry and cordial glasses.

Tossing half a nutmeat into his mouth, Stuart glanced at the large clock over in a corner. "It's early," he declared, finishing off the remains of his repast and refreshing his palate with more wine. "I suppose we could go down to White's."

"Or stay here and play a few hands," Peregrine suggested, loathing to venture into the cold night air after such a comforting meal.

"I am for that, unless it seems too tame for you, Stuart?" Richard said, rising to stretch his long legs.

Clad in blue bath cloth of impeccable cut with shining Hessians up the knees, the Duke was quiet in his elegance, and not for the first time Lord Ringwood reflected that there had indeed been some changes in Richard's style. Not noticeable at first glance, they were subtle changes, but they were there.

Where he used to be something of a peacock, Richard was much quieter in dress, and though to others he still appeared somewhat more than lively and a bit wild, he did not spend his private hours in constant rounds of partying or other pleasures less harmless. He had even appeared to have lost what little interest in gaming he had originally possessed.

"You know Richard," Stuart was compelled to remark, "you are still a downy one, but damn me if you haven't become more tame in your dotage."

"You yourself were never a wild one in your day, Stuart," Richard replied, surprised at Lord Ringwood's observation. "I have simply gotten a bit older, and things are not so new and exciting for me now."

Rising to their feet as well, Stuart and Peregrine followed Richard into the sitting room to enjoy their sherry, undisturbed by the bustle of the servants as they cleared the table.

Settling into the plush chair by the fireplace, Stuart heaved a contented sigh as Richard placed a table before him and laid out the small deck of cards. Tracing out the blue stamped pattern on the back with one rather knobby finger, Lord Ringwood was vaguely aware that the design was French. "I know you've been away, but do we have to contend with French playing cards?"

"You have an objection to them, Stuart?" Richard asked, pulling up two chairs and sitting across from his loose-limbed guest.

Picking up a card, Peregrine remarked, "They look all right to me," turning it over in his hands to look at the face.

"You can't tell me that the people on them don't look a trifle odd," Stuart asserted stubbornly.

"They appear to be French, Stuart. Is that so peculiar considering who produced them?" Richard asked reasonably. Lord Ringwood was not to be appeased on this count, however, and giving in to his insistence, Richard produced a less elegant but distinctly more English deck of cards and proceeded with consummate skill to deal out the lots to the players.

This pastime consumed the better part of an hour, and Stuart Ringwood was gradually aware that the

Duke was not playing with any relish. He did not take the game seriously, but it was pleasant enough in any case as Peregrine played with the determination that is habitual with the young when competing, pouncing on his winning cards with little chuckles of glee that he would never have allowed to escape his lips at White's.

Tossing down his cards in disgust, Lord Ringwood found that his luck was definitely not with him tonight.

"What? Stopping already?" Peregrine asked with an innocent voice as he counted up his points with a busy air.

"Yes, already," Stuart actually snorted. "It's a good thing we were only playing for the enjoyment of it all or you should have run me off at the legs in a few more hands. Where did you learn to play?"

"From Richard, of course," Peregrine replied, grinning at his brother affectionately. "He may not be a Captain Sharp or an Ivory Turner, but he plays well enough for the likes of you, Stuart."

The Duke took this compliment with a small bow, the mocking smile he bestowed on Stuart causing Lord Ringwood to comment, "Wouldn't have thought it the way you played this evening, Richard. You seem to have lost your touch since you've been away."

There was a slight pause before Richard answered, "The French do not play seriously at cards, at least not as a parlor game, and they play much too seriously in the gaming halls. Being so long abroad, I suppose I *have* lost the eagerness for play that I once possessed."

The following silence was so dense that the Duke regretted having spoken so seriously and would have made light of it except for Peregrine.

"This is the outside of enough, having to muck around the subject all the time with your own brother and your best friend," Peregrine objected with sincere concern. "If you can't speak of it openly to us, then I fail to see what use we are at all to you, Richard. Do you *want* to talk about it?"

This question had been burning within Stuart's breast for some time as well, but he had been unable to bring himself to broach the subject. He had hoped when he had met Richard earlier in the week at home that he would mention his extended absence and the disturbing circumstances surrounding his departure, but he had not, and they had spent the evening as if he had never been away. It made things comfortable for Lord Ringwood to slip into the old routine of easy laughing and pleasantries, but he had known that Richard must be as human as the next man and in need of a talk. Though they knew the story, as they had been in the midst of it all, not once had the three of them ever discussed the affair.

Richard appeared distinctly uncomfortable and unsure of how to proceed, his usually confident air for the moment absent as he looked at the serious faces around him.

"I would prefer to forget about the entire episode, myself."

"Killingham has no intention of letting the scandal die," Peregrine remarked needlessly. Richard was well aware of Lord Killingham's loud remarks of late at the club and at other public places. "He is out to provoke you, Richard, but so far you have not really dealt directly with the man."

"I am aware of that as much as you are, Peregrine," Richard replied. "And what about you, Stuart? What have you to say?"

Looking to his friend, Richard could see that Stuart was torn between respecting the delicacy of Richard's feelings and wanting to help the Duke sort things out.

"I have to agree with Peregrine, Richard," Stuart replied at last. "It may sound blunt, but Killingham's not the sort of fellow to take being made a cuckold."

"I was never his wife's lover," Richard replied abruptly, "as well you both know."

"But Killingham don't believe that a'tall," Stuart pointed out. "It doesn't matter if she had others. He didn't know of 'um. And if he did, it is different when you are made a public spectacle."

"Besides, Renshaw, Davidson, and the rest, she never spoke of them to her husband. Only you, Richard," Peregrine added. "It was because of you that she wanted a divorce. Of course, Killingham would have named you as the corespondent."

"And I am the only one who never was involved with her. Of course, I had a light flirtation, the sort of thing that all aging beauties expect from a young man," Richard admitted, a frown creasing his brow as he recalled the past. "But she was always very strange, highly strung. She took the matter too strongly."

The Duke's eyes were clouded with memories as they flashed through his mind, and Stuart read the pain even now as Richard remembered.

"You still blame yourself for her death," Stuart said. It was not a question, the answer was obvious on Richard's face. "She was mad. It was not your fault that she killed herself," Stuart insisted, but he could tell that he was not convincing his friend.

"Perhaps if I had not left London, if I had stayed and talked with her . . ." Richard's voice trailed off in his wonderings. One might have expected something pitiable in his voice, but the Duke had lived so long with the horror that he could speak of it with a certain calm detachment, doubtless born out of a need to be able to live with the memory of the deed.

Walking over to the mantel, Richard continued, "Of course I could not have stayed. I only wish I could have been with Father at the end. If I had only known his time was short . . . there were many things left unsaid."

The regret in the Duke's voice merely hinted at the deep sorrow he had endured. Richard's letters to his brother had indirectly told the story of his grief, there in a foreign land without anyone there to comfort him.

Peregrine had been silent for the most part, but now spoke as Richard stared into the glowing embers of the fire.

"Father saw no other alternative but for you to leave. In doing what he wished, you could not have been doing wrong."

Peregrine spoke with the voice of authority, and Richard seemed to take heart from this, straightening himself and returning to his brother's side.

"You may be right. It is done in any case," he continued. "All, that is, except for Killingham. I am not sure what I shall do about him, so I will simply have to wait and see what happens."

"Wait and see what his next move is?" Peregrine asked.

"And then I shall know how to reply."

Looking his brother in the eyes, Peregrine hesitated before saying, "You know, Richard, I still don't think that you should blame yourself for Lady Killingham. Something had always bothered me about the entire incident as you know. Can't place a finger on just what, but that's beside the point."

"The point is," Stuart interjected, "that you not be so hard on yourself. You hardly go out now, you avoid public places."

"I had not noticed that I did," Richard responded coolly. But the knowledge that the words Stuart spoke were true prompted the Duke to add, "Doubtless the ton will soon have their fill of me Thursday when Peregrine and I accompany the Trevelyn sisters."

"And you won't denounce Killingham's sly accusations of your involvement with Lady Killingham and your motives in leaving London?" Peregrine asked curiously.

"Peregrine," Richard said patiently, "I do not intend to spend my entire life explaining to others what is so and what is not. It is enough that my intimates know the truth. For the rest, I haven't a concern. I would hardly have time left to attend to my own affairs if I was required to explain myself to every person. How could I denounce his wife's fantasying anyway, or my reason for leaving London in the wake of an imminent scandal? He would not believe me, and I am not sure that I wish to explain myself even to Killingham."

"There seems nothing left to say then," Stuart remarked, rising from his chair. Crossing over to Richard's side, he gripped his hand firmly. "I must go now, getting late and all. Take care, Richard, I shall see you in all probability when you take the view in Hyde Park."

"And I shall have the ladies wave to you on Rotten Row," Peregrine assured Lord Ringwood, "though why they should deign to recognize such a connection I am sure I can't conceive."

This last quip earned Lord Melbury an amused smile from Richard, so it served its purpose. "Will you be off to White's, Stuart?" Peregrine asked, pouring himself a small glass of wine from the decanter. "I could stand the company."

Lord Ringwood shook his head. "Oh, I think not Peregrine. You go off on your own. I'm quite done in."

Stuart was shown the door, and as he took up his reins, he wondered if he should indeed join Peregrine in a visit to the club. After a moment's reflection, however, he chose to start for home and his own warm bed. "Others might only be beginning the evening, but I shall be knocked into horse nails as it is, I dare swear," he said to himself as he started up his pair.

Waiting within the townhouse for a footman to fetch one of the Duke's coaches, Lord Melburry attempted for the fourth time to convince his reticent brother to accompany him. The look of perturbation on Richard's face did not deter Peregrine in the least. He was used to some small amount of resistance from Richard and could usually harass the Duke into doing things his way. However, on this occasion, Lord Melburry found his brother adamant.

"No, Peregrine. I have no intention of going to the club this evening. I have no interest in any further gaming and I certainly prefer to remain within the comfortable confines of home," the Duke said, steadfast against his brother's insistence.

"You've not been out of this damned drafty house in days, Richard," Peregrine said with asperity. "If you continue like this, I will bring sackcloth and ashes on my next visit."

This threat did not faze the Duke as he shook his head with finality. "I have had quite enough sociability for the time being. Only recall, infant, what a shambles that evening spent with Sir Gibbons was. That should be enough to cure anyone of the desire to be sociable."

The Duke's expression was blandly amused, but Peregrine knew his brother too well not to hear the disappointment in Richard's voice.

"Bad, I know it, but surely Sir Gibbons and his wife did the best they could," Peregrine remarked lamely.

"Of course, but I should never have accepted the invitation. I should have realized that they would not know what to talk about. No topic of discussion could be touched upon that did not bring up the fact that I had been away from the country. Killingham aggravated things when he spoke to Sir Gibbons some days previously, so the entire incident was fresh in his mind. I could see the embarrassment clearly. I should not have placed Sir Gibbons in such an uncomfortable situation, and I will not place older friends in the same position at the club."

The Duke could not be persuaded differently, and there was no time in any case as the footman returned with the coach. Entering the richly upholstered vehicle, Peregrine reflected that Richard had not been totally honest. He could not blame him, since he knew that Richard was assailed by doubts of his own about the entire scandal. However, if Richard had always tended to put others off before they could have the opportunity to cut him, the scandal had only aggravated a natural tendency on his part toward reclusiveness.

This was not to say that Richard had not been sociable, he was hardly ever to be found at home in times past, gaming and attending on some beauty of the town with a regularity that bespoke a deceptive gregarity on his part. Those who attempted a closer familiarity were kept at a chilling distance.

He did not ask others to understand him, and he rarely bothered with strangers. He would make the effort with only a few people, and how much *they* knew of him God only knew, Peregrine thought as he looked out the carriage window at the gas lights in the darkness. The dull glow fatigued his eyes so he closed them for a moment, almost lulled into the beginnings of sleep by the coach's sway.

With a start, Peregrine realized that the vehicle had halted before the doors of the club. He hesitated at the portal, the thought that perhaps Killingham might be present sending a slight chill up his spine and causing the hair on the back of his neck to bristle a bit. He did not desire a confrontation at this time, and he had certain arrangements to make if he hoped to deal effectively with Giles Killingham in the future. Resolutely squaring his shoulders, Lord Melburry entered the club with the utmost calm.

Sauntering into the main room, Peregrine's eyes

were initially assailed by a sight which almost undid his studied composure.

"Gad, Francis! What sort of a rig is that supposed to be!" Lord Melburry exclaimed, positively spellbound by the absurd figure that Sir Francis Trent cut in a jacket cut so full at the skirts as to have the appearance of a dandelion gone to seed, the layers of stiffened white satin beneath the initial fabric radiating from the skinny center which was Sir Francis' torso.

"I suppose I should know better than to seek some aesthetic appreciation from someone who feels riding toggery is the correct attire for *all* social occasions," Sir Francis sniffed disdainfully at the Hessians that encased Peregrine's considerable calves. "For your information this will be all the crack in a scant two or three weeks," Sir Francis assured the gaping young lord.

Coming up behind Trent, Lord Simmons' ever-present quizzing glass rose to a jaundiced eye. Nothing was remarkable to such a seasoned dandy, though he could not help curl a lip in disdain for the ensemble he was now inspecting. "Not that I have anything to say in the matter, Francis," Lord Simmons remarked with certainty. "More than one gentleman must wear the garb before it becomes 'fashion' and I will advocate that any ships from France bearing such atrocities be blockaded from our shores."

This ridicule was not appreciated, and Sir Francis appeared almost moved to violence, his smallish fists clenching till bony knuckles shone white.

Peregrine could perceive that the fop, if pushed, would resort to an act Francis patently abhorred, physical violence. His nonviolent nature stemmed not solely from the fact that he would probably be bested in any pugilistic endeavor, but also from the inevitability that he would have ruined his appearance and the fit of his flawless ensemble. However, there had been occasions when Francis had made an exception, and Peregrine took Lord Simmons, the source of Sir Francis' irritation, away to another room.

"Ah, Peregrine," Lord Simmons admonished sadly as he was dragged by the persistent young man toward the faro table. "You're definitely no fun anymore.

Have you been taking lessons from your brother, the Duke?" he inquired. "We have not seen him in a fortnight. Has he gone into seclusion?"

Marquess Wainfleet was one of the gentlemen watching the play of cards and he turned at this remark.

"Richard did not feel like coming down. It is as simple as that," Peregrine said uneasily. His brother's absences were conspicuous, especially since it was all about town that he had returned and that Killingham had been quite vocal in his comments on past events.

"One can understand his reticence," Marquess Wainfleet proferred, his unsolicited remark issued in such a disdainful tone that Peregrine was quite beside himself with rage. The bore did not note the flush of anger that washed the young man's face, and continued along his disastrous track. "I am sure that he cares not at all to be reminded of his, shall we say, less than 'gentlemanly' behavior in the past."

Condescension oozed from Marquess Wainfleet's every pore, and Lord Melburry debated the judiciousness of committing murder before the eyes of all in the club.

Peregrine faced Wainfleet with flashing eyes. The play about the room had ceased and all eyes were on the two men. The desire to plant his fist in Wainfleet's sour and disapproving face was so great that Peregrine visibly shook with the emotions he felt.

By his side, Lord Simmons could read intense fury in the young lord's face and was deeply shocked. He had not realized that Peregrine felt the barbs so much. Any action on Peregrine's part at this point would simply be more fuel for the gossips on the morrow.

"Marquess Wainfleet," Lord Simmons announced loudly to the room in general, "is giving vent to excesses of emotion tonight. I am sure we all know why." The loudness surprised the men present, and their attention wavered for a moment, then turned to Lord Simmons who had the look of a man with an amusing secret about to be divulged. "You give your opinion where it is little wanted, but then such bitter and biting remarks are not unusual in a man thwarted in love." He looked pointedly at Marquess Wainfleet and saw that he had made a hit. "You resent young

Melburry here, and you have good reason, I must admit. After all, when a young lady of such beauty and accomplishment as Lady Aurora Trevelyn shows a decided preference for a man she has known only a few days over one who has been suing for her attentions for no less than a year . . . well, it can raise considerable bad feelings."

There was a snicker from somewhere within the room, and Wainfleet winced angrily at it, his control not quite as good as that of Lord Melburry. He could say nothing, however, for it was true, and perforce chose to absent himself from the room. He left tight-lipped and livid.

Watching Marquess Wainfleet stalk off, Peregrine himself was silent. Inconspicuously, the other men in the room went back to their gaming, and Lord Simmons did not have to coax Lord Melburry to follow him into the hallway at a leisurely pace.

Once alone, Peregrine tried to thank Lord Simmons, but was unsure as to how to go about it. As he fumbled for words, Lord Simmons did not appear to wish to hear such pap, however.

"Really, Peregrine. You oughtn't to thank a fellow for saying what is true," Lord Simmons declared, then noted a slight wrinkle in his coat causing him to groan at the hall mirror. Smoothing it with great deliberation, he continued, looking at Lord Melburry's reflection as he spoke. "You showed remarkable restraint, Peregrine. However, you should not let such remarks enrage you. This situation is only temporary. The original scandal blew over in three months' time, and this will disappear in even less, given the chance. Of course there is Giles to contend with, but something will be managed." This lecture did not seem to comfort Lord Melburry, who listened patiently but did not appear in the least convinced. Noting the stubborn look, Lord Simmons said with some exasperation, as if to a thick-headed student, "There is nothing for it, so why not let it be, until it dies a natural death? The ton will not long find it interesting."

"Perhaps not," Lord Melburry burst out heatedly, "but there may yet be something I can do to bury the subject once and for all. If you will give me leave, I have an important engagement now that I had forgotten."

With that, Lord Melburry rushed off, ordering a footman to hail a carriage for him. Lord Simmons followed Peregrine to the threshold of the club and watched him ascend the hired coach, puzzled by the purposeful if angry expression that he wore. The cockney request as to " 'is lordship's" destination and the curt reply were made, and Lord Simmons' ears pricked up as he recognized the area of town toward which Lord Melburry was headed.

Watching him go, Lord Simmons shrugged to himself. "If he wishes to lighten his sorrows in the arms of one of the demimonde, I suppose there are worse things he could be doing," he reflected.

But not to Aurora, a voice in the back of his mind insisted.

He had grown to like Peregrine quite well, despite the boy's courting of Aurora. Lord Simmons liked him enough to take his side against Wainfleet, and even against formidable Giles Killingham, but he did not like him enough to stand by and watch him break Aurora's heart. His loyalty always belonged to Aurora, no matter who else might be involved in *any* given situation.

Although his own pursuit of the lady's affections appeared to be leisurely, she had nonetheless captured his heart completely. As she had never shown any passion for him, he had kept the extent of his feelings inside for the most part. His love for her was unselfish enough so that he wanted her to be happy, even if it meant she would find her happiness with another man. Knowing her as he did, he was positive that she would never be happy with one who paid ardent court to her by day, then indulged in the pleasures of the demimonde by night.

"No, I will not allow Peregrine to deceive Aurora," he said firmly. With disturbing thoughts still troubling his mind, Lord Simmons turned and reentered the club.

The hired carriage halted before a well-furnished home. The driver was quite familiar with the street as he had occasion to transport many of the gentlemen of fashion there.

Descending, Peregrine Melburry was admitted to the house with no surprise at all by the servant at the door. He recalled Lord Melburry from his previous visit.

"Is your mistress free?" Lord Melburry asked with some impatience.

"You wish to speak with her, my lord?" the man inquired with a proper air.

"Yes, I do. Ask her if she will see me," Peregrine said, handing the butler a crown with which to dismiss his carriage. With a slight bow, the man did as he was bid. He went first to inform his mistress of Lord Melburry's presence and then out to the hired coach.

"I'm not to wait then?" the driver asked with a leer. He knew what these places were.

The butler shook his head.

"Right then, I'll be off." With that, the driver whipped his horses and rattled off into the night.

Reentering the house, the butler was unfazed by Lord Melburry's arrival. He was quite inured to late night callers and ordered the cook to prepare a light meal for his mistress and her guest.

Late as it was, the evening was but beginning at another residence situated some distance away in the fashionable quarter of London.

The Honorable Percival Snogging lolled comfortably back in his chair, pushing himself a bit from the dining table and lighting up an aromatic cigar, one of his lesser vices. Looking across the still overladen table at his dinner guest who was engaged in a similar occupation, Mr. Snogging indicated the tray that was set before him, arrayed with many-colored liquors.

"Well, Giles, what will it be? Sherry or the port?" Mr. Snogging asked, every inch the solicitous host.

Eyeing the assortment, Lord Killingham allowed the blue-gray smoke from his cigar to curl carelessly from his lips, indicating wordlessly the port.

With a sigh, Mr. Snogging poured out a glass and brought it over to Lord Killingham, a sherry being his own choice which he quickly quaffed, immediately pouring another to replace it.

"Can't imagine why you prefer port, Giles," Mr.

Snogging said, a hint of disgust indicating his feelings. "Sherry is the only decent drink after a meal. Cleanses the palate, not to mention the soul."

Killingham grimaced as he quickly downed his drink. It seemed more of a punishment than a pleasure.

"That is the difference between the two of us, Percy, though there are others to be sure. Your youth and times assure you that sherry is the drink for the civilized man. In my age and times it was port. We must both be true to our upbringing." The smile on his lips was a trifle grim and not in keeping with what one would expect from a contented guest. "As for my soul, Percy, that is not going to come clean with a weak wash of sherry. It requires an ocean of port at the very least, though I must say that even that does not suffice on occasion."

Seating himself again, the Honorable Percival Snogging was quite convinced that he was nothing like Lord Killingham at all, contrary to what his guest might think. He enjoyed the man's company, his sneering and seemingly sophisticated view of the ton and of his own life; but no, he was nothing like Killingham, he decided. With that he settled down to finish his cigar and sherry.

An observer might have agreed with Mr. Snogging, for in appearance the two men were decidedly of different molds. Percival Snogging would have given a fortune to be able to top six feet. It was his unhappy situation to have been not above five and four inches, and barely that. With a tendency to underweightness and overpadding of his attire in the shoulders, he looked like nothing so much as an inverted triangle ambulating on toothpicks, his pleasant but vacuous face atop the whole.

Lord Killingham, on the other hand, was large in frame and had no doubt once been athletic in build. However, at fifty-one years of age he had developed a soft paunch encumbering his lordship when fitting his waistcoats where once muscles as strong as cords had been situated. The figure had run somewhat to seed due to advancing age. The face was so lined with dissipation and a gnawing, lurking hatred that if it had once been comely, it must have been in some age long ago.

Finishing his liquor and ridding himself of the stub of his cigar, Mr. Snogging rose, one elaborately embroidered waistcoat pocket disgorging a large, pretentious gold watch which he unfobbed with a great flourish.

"Are you trying to hurry me along?" Killingham demanded, starting on yet another glass.

"We have left Ann to sit alone for some time now, Giles. Women have little patience, as you well know, and Ann less than most," Percival remarked knowingly.

"In a moment, then. You can hardly blame me, such excellent port you have, Percy," Killingham complimented as he saluted Mr. Snogging with his half-full glass.

"And it cost enough at that," Mr. Snogging answered, his patience wearing thin.

"Had no notion you were concerned with the cost," Lord Killingham said with some note of surprise.

"What can you expect when Ann and I both play so badly at the tables?" his host asked irritably. Then, appearing to recall some matter, he continued, "And while we are on the matter of finances, let me say that you have cost me one hundred guineas which I could little afford, Giles."

This was said with such a petulant air that Lord Killingham eyed the small man dangerously.

"How have I cost you one hundred guineas then?" he asked quietly, his voice apparently reflecting calm.

"Why, you lost me the money when you lost the race to the Duke of Melburry. I bet his wretched imp of a brother that you would best the field and specifically that you would pound the Duke's bones into the turf. Since you did neither, so I lost abominably."

At the mention of the race, Lord Killingham had not moved a muscle, but once his host was done with his remark, he had risen from his seat to tower above Mr. Snogging, a deadly glint in his small eyes.

"Perhaps it would be best if you lead the way; we don't want to keep Ann waiting," Killingham said.

This was more a command than a suggestion and Mr. Snogging dared not refuse, noting the white face and set jaw of his friend.

118

Leading the way toward the antechamber, Mr. Snogging attempted to appease his guest. "If you ask me, it was luck that the Duke won," he said, glancing at Lord Killingham apprehensively. "The Melburrys are notoriously lucky in some matters."

Lord Killingham agreed, the very mention of the family name setting his blood up. "The Duke is himself lucky that authorities have not the power to accuse someone of his rank of any crime without excessive proof."

This snide remark went past Mr. Snogging who appeared to be more concerned with the younger Melburry.

"Peregrine would appear to be lucky in money, since as a second son he shouldn't have a groat to fly with, but some indulgent grandparents left the boy a fortune of his own," Mr. Snogging remarked, opening up the doors to the antechamber. Proceeding ahead, he went on, "Lord Melburry would also appear to be lucky with women. I have it from Francis Trent that Lady Aurora Trevelyn appeared much taken with him at the auction. I suppose you wouldn't know anything about that, would you Giles?" Mr. Snogging asked with mock innocence.

Before Killingham could answer, Mr. Snogging had passed through the chamber into the next. There, in the cozy light provided by several large candelabras, sat Ann Snogging, attired in salmon pink which she was sure showed her complexion to advantage, especially in the fire's glow.

Lord Killingham bowed before her and took the lady's hand, admiring as he did the compact and slim figure of his host's wife and the familiar lascivious glance which she bestowed upon him.

Theirs had been an interesting affair, starting before Ann had married Mr. Snogging, and there remained enough attraction throughout the years to warrant an occasional continuation of their interest in one another.

Bending over his wife and placing a chaste kiss on her forehead, Mr. Snogging did not see the speaking glance that Lord Killingham gave his wife. "Well, Ann, we are a pair of sinners, the two of us, leaving you

119

alone for so long. We were discussing mutual friends and lost track of time. I hope we are forgiven."

Percy excused himself politely, with what he supposed was adequate husbandly attention, then proceeded to ignore his wife for the most part, engaging Lord Killingham in talk until his manservant entered. Whispering discreetly in his master's ear, he conveyed his message and waited near the door to attend his employer.

Turning to his guest, Mr. Snogging apologized, "It seems that there are matters I must attend to for a few moments. Please, help yourself to more wine. I will return shortly." With that he left the room, the servant following behind him.

As soon as the steps were faint, Ann rose from her seat and came up behind Lord Killingham, placing small eager hands on his jacket as she caressed his shoulders.

"It has been some time since we were alone together, Giles. You have not come to see us in ages," Ann said, bending close enough for her lips to brush Killingham's ear.

When he did not respond to the gesture, she flounced away from him, miffed.

"I have had better things to do, Ann," Killingham replied tactlessly, his interest centered only on his newest *amore,* the intriguing Aurora Trevelyn. He might admire Ann, but he was quite used to her, and there was no novelty in used merchandise.

For his rudeness Ann gave him a scathing stare. "Well, you have been busy indeed, losing races and my husband's money for him, Giles."

The arch look she gave him was intolerable, but just as he would have made an ungentlemanly remark, an idea occurred to him for which he would need Ann's assistance.

"Forgive me, Ann," he said, rising and going to her, using his most persuasive tones. While her back was turned to him, he touched her bare neck with the familiarity of a lover and kissed the flesh at its base. "I am only irritable to a friend such as you because I have been preoccupied. Old enemies and new ones have appeared, and I am snappish."

The low growl in his voice chilled Ann a bit. Giles had always been prone to a strain of violence in his nature if her memory served her. Giles implanted another kiss on the flushed flesh of her neck and she dismissed the uneasy feelings she had.

She turned in the circle of his arms around her waist to face him. He was less handsome than before, but then Ann was not choosy this evening. Anything was better than the repellent fumbling and clumsy gropings of her husband.

"Who is crossing you, my lover?" she asked, curiously, "and why do you tell me of it? It is not like you unless you want my help."

"You have great understanding, Ann," Killingham replied, a tight smile gracing his lips as he drew her closer in his embrace. "You recall the Duke of Melburry?"

He saw that she did by the knowing look she gave him.

"He has returned, then?" she asked.

"He has. He was the man I lost to in the race, and his brother Peregrine can be credited with parting your husband from his blunt," Killingham answered, looking hard at Ann.

"I know, or rather I have met Lord Melburry. As for the Duke, I recall him only vaguely," Ann replied. "And you wish for me to do them a disservice for you, I gather."

Lord Killingham was surprised with her quickness. "You were always a fine girl, Ann," he said admiringly, his interest genuinely, if only temporarily rising. Her willingness to do as he wished pleased him greatly. "That is precisely what I desire."

"But how?" she inquired. "What is the key to it all?"

"That is simple," Killingham answered confidently, a wicked smile on his face as he spoke. "I cannot do anything yet with the Duke and his brother. Both are an irritant. However, you can do me a service indirectly. You are familiar with Lady Lettice and Lady Aurora Trevelyn?"

"I am, though I like them not," Ann responded, pressing her body passionately to Lord Killingham's

121

until she could feel the brass of his vest buttons painful against her breasts.

Mindful in case of detection, Killingham listened carefully for any signs of interruption. "Well, the Duke may have conceived a passion for the Lady Lettice and his brother definitely presumes a tendre for Lady Aurora. As you occasionally have the ear of both ladies, I am sure that you can think of something suitable to turn them from their suit. It is a small thing, but it will serve to unbalance my adversaries. Unrequited love has a way of accomplishing that."

Ann considered his words a moment. Then, with a wanton smile, she said, "And what will you give to me if I do this for you, Giles?"

The passionate kiss that was his reply and the whispered assignation were all that she required to consent to the deed. "I must leave now, but I will attend on you as promised later," Killingham assured her.

As he left, Ann stretched voluptuously on the lounge, fanning her heated brow and breast, smiling with anticipation. She had never liked any of the Trevelyn sisters. They were far too admired by far too many gentlemen when only she herself, she thought, was worthy of such devotion. What is more, the sisters would not put up with her tendency to insult and gossip about even those who were supposedly her friends, and they were increasingly turning a cold shoulder to her. Eventually they would stop seeing Ann altogether, so she lost nothing in doing what Giles wished. Besides, she had her eye on Lord Melburry as her next love, and it did not suit her that he should form a prior passion, especially for Aurora Trevelyn!

"Giles is not Peregrine, but at least for tonight he will do," she whispered to herself as she rose and quit the room to make her preparations.

CHAPTER 5

As MUCH AS Lettice detested the fashionable hour at Hyde Park, with all the simpering beaus and peacocks of the ton emerging into the light of day from their homes for the satisfaction of communing with their equals upon horseback, she found the fresh air and well-kept gardens a pleasure. Of course, her dislike was really an undue prejudice as some of her friends found the rounds a necessary part of every day, an opportunity to chat in semiprivacy among the trees or as carriages stopped on the pathways. Riding the horse with which the Duke of Melburry had gifted her, Lettice was secure in the knowledge that there would be no opportunity for anything more than a short run in the park. The Duke rode by her side on a stallion of superior carriage, never suspecting that her steed was anything less than he thought it to be. Glancing over to the left, Lettice observed Lord Melburry hardly urging his pair along, concentrating more intently on Aurora than on the curricle which moved at a snail's pace along the road. Noticing a small handkerchief fluttering from a passing carriage, Lettice waved her riding whip in response, the small wizened face of Lady Chompton peeping out of her dilapidated baroche as her gruff and partially deaf coachman continued along in the same manner he had for the past fifty or sixty years. For Lady Chompton, daily expeditions into Hyde Park were her whole life, now that her husband had passed away, and Lettice supposed here at least was a purpose for the park.

Correctly and, for her, somewhat primly attired in a habit of subdued green, Lettice was nonetheless striking with her statuesque figure and the style in which she rode, her horse easily keeping up the lazy pace that the Duke set. Acknowledging and occasionally halting to speak to acquaintances, Lettice was aware that the Duke had spoken very little that afternoon. He did, however, appear to be overly observant, watching her every move and listening attentively to every word which she spoke. Of course, there had been the usual flurry of chatter while leaving the house, the Duke and her papa having gotten along on quite an equal level when they conversed in the drawing room. Of course there had been Patrice's lackluster greeting, still moping over her damned lieutenant and not a civil word to utter to the guests.

Lettice blushed a bit at the remembrance, for she could not recall when she had ever been more mortified or more astonished at Patrice's behavior. A scant "hello" was the extent of her involvement. Perhaps even more irritating had been her own hesitancy on entering the room; the Duke's appreciative glance had been enough to set her afluster, a condition she was unaccustomed to, and somewhat shamefaced at.

Aurora had had no compunction about looking quite lovingly into Peregrine Melburry's eyes, an action which seemed to scandalize her father to some extent. Still, the fond look had been reciprocal, and the Earl was not blind. Such a passion might come to naught, but it was not harmful since the Earl considered the young to be fast healers in the area of amour.

Focusing her attention on her riding as her horse skittered a bit at a flapping duck crossing her path, Lettice observed the Duke's looking at her yet again. A small, nervous smile which disappeared quickly was all she could muster, and she was sure she was appearing a ninny. Quite suddenly, Richard leaned closer to Lettice and whispered.

"As I knew, the horse suits you far better than it could have ever done me."

The Duke smiled with satisfaction as he sat back again to view them both, the woman and the stallion so well matched that a porcelain reproduction would have been an appropriate manner in which to capture the graceful delicacy they presented. The thought pleased him and he smiled again.

He is being decidedly pleasant, Lettice thought as

124

she smiled in return. It was an easy gesture, and one which she was surprised that she enjoyed performing as it begot a grin from the Duke in response.

"Richard," a voice from the curricle called out loudly, the carriage slowing to a halt on the path. Peregrine Melburry's head popped absurdly round the corner of Aurora's small bonnet that she had worn to shield herself from the bright sunlight. Peregrine's action reminded Lettice of a child's playing hide and seek. "Richard," he repeated earnestly, his bright blue eyes pleading, "Lady Aurora wants to stop and look at the flowers. I am sure that you wish to continue the ride, so I suggested that perhaps you might like to go on and come back for us a little later."

"Circumnavigate the park perhaps?" the elder Melburry suggested. Lettice thought she could detect the laugh in his voice as he teased his brother. "Of course, what if we should not find you again? It begins to grow late and I wouldn't want Countess Trevelyn to be unduly worried."

This remark was said with such a straight expression that Lettice wanted to laugh herself as Lord Melburry's face fell.

"I am sure Lord Peregrine can be trusted to return Aurora safely to my mother, Your Grace," Lettice assured the Duke. "Shall we go round a bit and return in half an hour?" Lettice felt tolerably inclined toward the Duke today and knew that both Aurora and Peregrine would enjoy a tête-à-tête. This suggestion produced a nod of assent from Richard, and without another word the Duke and Lady Lettice turned their horses onto another path, Lettice observing the broad smile with which those words had been greeted by Lord Melburry.

Left to their own devices, Peregrine gave himself a well-deserved pleasure, staring with unabashed admiration at the young lady beside him.

"And will you sit and stare all afternoon, then?" Aurora asked playfully, looking shyly up into those enormously appealing eyes that Lord Melburry possessed.

"I could very well do so and not have a care for the time," Peregrine admitted frankly, grinning as Aurora was put to the blush very prettily.

"Well, I wish to see the flowers, Lord Melburry, and I shall not be denied because of your strange fancy," Aurora said, unyielding to the young man's appealing gaze.

With an exaggerated sigh, he assisted Aurora to descend from the curricle, careful of the height of the vehicle. They walked over to inspect the newly blooming flowers along with the other people who had also decided to view the beautiful plants. With another sigh, Lord Melburry resigned himself to being among the milling people as Aurora discussed the virtues of one variety of rose over the other with some young chit of a girl in a white *pelisse*. Wandering off a bit from the crowd to get a better view of the statues strewn about the area, he was astonished to feel a slight tugging at his sleeve. Turning abruptly he found himself looking into dark brown eyes fringed with thick long lashes. Stepping back a pace, he recognized the woman and looked about anxiously.

"There is no one to see us, Lord Melburry," the woman said with a whisper that belied her confidence. "I would not have approached you here, but when I saw you I had decided just an instant before that I am more interested in your offer than I had believed on the previous evening."

Looking at the diminutive figure beside him, Lord Melburry noted with a practiced eye that she was tastefully attired. Neither too loud nor too dowdy, she appeared to have more than a modicum of tastefulness in choosing her gown. Dark brown hair set high on her head with a cluster of pearls strung through here and there, the woman appeared younger than she was, an asset in her chosen profession.

"We cannot talk here. I am sure you realize that," Peregrine said at last, unaware of the light tread of slippers approaching from behind their turned backs.

"Where shall we meet?" the woman inquired anxiously.

"I shall come to you tonight. I am sure that things can be arranged to your satisfaction."

The woman had not appeared to have heard him as she pointed to one of the larger trees in the clearing. "I daresay that tree has been there some time, perhaps since the park was granted," she said in clear tones.

This unexpected comment and the warning look in her eyes took Lord Melburry aback for an instant, then he heard the slight cough behind him and he turned about with feigned delight to hide his unease.

"Lady Aurora, I was just wondering where you had gone off to," Peregrine said as he observed the speculative look in Aurora's eyes as she viewed the stranger beside him.

"I was looking at the flowers, as you know." Aurora's reply was a trifle cold, and her demeanor was decidedly so, as Peregrine took a stab at explaining his actions.

"Been talking about the trees," he offered lamely. "Interesting things, these trees. Some of them are as old as the park itself."

This bit of information did nothing to ease the situation at all, and Aurora was torn between suspicion and trusting in her own feelings of affection for Lord Melburry.

"If you will excuse me, I must be leaving. My escort is waiting for me by my carriage as you can see. I must not leave him waiting. Fiancés are such particular creatures, they will take a notion on occasion to become offended if a girl talks too long to anyone, you know." The woman indicated a rather handsome gentleman who indeed appeared to be waiting on her by her sedate landaulet. "Charles doesn't like the park, you see, and will not walk with me, only ride in the carriage."

This was added with a light laugh and she left without further words, a nod of Aurora's head and a mumbled farewell accompanying her away.

Lord Melburry looked apprehensively at his companion to see if there were to be any hard words to endure. However, the blue eyes that met his had been reassured by the presence of a fiancé, and Aurora gazed at Peregrine with affection. "You should not have gone so far away. I was a bit worried," Aurora said as the two walked back toward the curricle.

"Afraid that gypsies had made off with me?" Pere-

127

grine quipped, watching the landaulet leave out of the corner of one eye.

"Of course," Aurora replied impishly, "that would have been a pity, for then I would have had to return home alone. Mama would have been appalled by your lack of consideration, Lord Melbury. Allowing yourself to be abducted by a few paltry gypsies. It wouldn't do at all."

"As you can see," he grinned, "I am here to do my duty and thus avoid your mother's black books entirely."

Reaching the curricle, Peregrine assisted Aurora to ascend, and then took his place beside her. Aurora's good humor had returned in full where but a moment ago jealousy had reared its unseemly head.

"Have you had quite enough of the flowers for one afternoon?" Peregrine inquired, "or would you prefer to see more?" His voice was not at all encouraging.

"That is quite enough, I think," Aurora decided, mercifully. "We should be returning if you are indeed to succeed in keeping out of Mama's bad graces."

Lord Melbury sighed a sigh of relief too soon as he started his pair, for by his side Aurora soon perceived the Snogging carriage, Mrs. Snogging at the leads, high poke hat embellished with multicolored feathers nodding in the breeze like a proud woman to the multitudes. Aurora frowned. Ann must have come from the same part of the park where they had just been and Aurora would liefer have avoided the woman altogether. As it was, she had to acknowledge Mrs. Snogging as she quite passed them up, coming dangerously close to scraping Lord Melbury's wheels with her own. Aurora thought she could hear Ann shout with vulgar loudness that she would visit the family later in the week, and was not pleased at the prospect.

"Damnable skill if you ask me," Peregrine swore softly as he kept a firm hand on the pair before him. "Shouldn't be allowed to drive in the park."

Lord Melbury's irritation was great as he frowned at the disappearing carriage.

"Some gentlemen have admired her skill, actually. She can go between two phaetons with only an inch to spare between them and never nick either," Aurora commented, waiting with interest for her escort's reply.

He appeared to be something of a sportster considering that he had engaged in the daredevil race, and Aurora was not entirely sure that there wasn't something to be admired in Ann by some men. Fortunately, Lord Melburry's reply was as abrupt and to the point as she could desire.

"Some gentlemen," he concluded with disgust, "are total sapskulls, and I am not among their legion, or did you think I was?"

Taking Peregrine's arm Aurora shook her head, a pleased smile on her face as she leaned a little closer to him. Lord Melburry found this so enjoyable that he was inclined to hope that the Duke and Lady Lettice would not find them along the path at all.

As it was, Richard might have obliged his brother on this occasion. He was himself having an enjoyable time, far surpassing his expectations in fact. For the most part there was no real reason he could pinpoint for this feeling, he only knew that he was indeed enjoying himself. Though the Duke had been unable to give his mount full rein, Lettice had engaged the Duke in a short canter. For such a spirited girl she had seemed unusually reluctant to race her horse against his, but he put this down to some definite, if minute, maidenly propriety within her makeup. They had talked but little and then the conversation had been limited to upcoming events and parties, all of which Lettice intended to attend and at none of which the Duke planned to be present. Richard was acutely aware that Lettice found his reluctance to talk about himself limiting. Such confidences might later lead to more probing questions, and he was not terribly sure that he desired such an eventuality. He was sure she had not yet been apprised of his past and there was no use in starting an acquaintance if she would later be repulsed.

Though he had not said very much, Lettice did not appear to be nonplussed by his lack of conversation. She rambled on wittily as they met mutual acquaintances on the path, stroking her new stallion absent-mindedly with one kid-covered hand as she made an amusing remark to Lord Simmons or gave Percival Snogging a deliberate set-down.

129

As they moved their horses slowly away, leaving the gaping Mr. Snogging and a laughing Lord Simmons by the wayside, Richard observed the slightly amused look on the lady's visage.

"Such behavior will not win you many admirers, Lady Lettice," he admonished her, his smile pulling Lettice into the game.

"I know, but I can't seem to control my wretched tongue. You see, it will give vent when it knows that certain parties really deserve a debunking," she sighed, a gesture with her hands emphasizing the futility of it all. "Besides, I do not care if Mr. Snogging is numbered among my admirers."

"Because he is otherwise engaged?"

"Because he is a buffoon," Lettice responded with a gay toss of her head. Her hair glistened in the receding sunlight, hints of blue highlighting her curls as she threw back her head in laughter. The smooth white column of her neck was devastatingly inviting, and the Duke found that he was staring too pointedly yet again. Tearing his eyes away, he looked ahead at the path.

"A buffoon has his advantages, nonetheless," Richard pointed out. "At the very least he is amusing."

"He can also be an embarrassment to some. Of course, I am not such a one as to be embarrassed *by* an acquaintance, though I have on occasion been embarrassed *for* a few. No, I do not find buffoons entertaining in the least," she asserted.

Stopping, she looked about. They had circled the park and should soon be meeting her sister and Lord Melburry.

Reluctantly, but as if a man compelled, the Duke asked, "And what of me, Lady Lettice? Do you find me 'entertaining'?"

Though his inflection was flippant, the expression on his handsome face was serious enough.

"You are good company, Your Grace. I do not find you entertaining as I would a pet monkey or lap dog performing tricks," Lettice replied solemnly.

She did not know what prompted her to do so, but as she spoke she reached over across the space between them and touched his arm. While Lettice had hoped vaguely that this gesture would indicate to the Duke her friendly intentions, it seemed to have an adverse effect instead. Richard withdrew a bit into himself, apparently perturbed by her actions.

Lettice removed her hand quickly, looking away in embarrassment. They rode on in silence until Richard felt it necessary to say something, appalled by his own inexplicable conduct.

"It is kind of you to say that you enjoy my company," he began, finding his words awkwardly. "I am aware that I have not been terribly talkative." Lettice made a motion as if to object but the Duke continued: "You will appreciate that I have been away from home for a long time. I have found it difficult to readjust to London, to the people." Lettice did not speak. She listened intently to the Duke's words.

The hesitancy with which he spoke was utterly incongruous with his previous demeanor, and Lettice was amazed.

"I am taking a mull of this," Richard said at last. Then he seemed to collect himself. "What I wanted to say was that though I may not appear to appreciate your company, I do nonetheless. I am simply, how shall I put it, occasionally struck inarticulate."

This last was said with a familiar, self-depreciating manner, only half mocking.

"Your Grace, if you do indeed enjoy my company, will you grant me a small favor?" Lettice asked, her face grave as she spoke.

"If it is within my powers," he agreed instantly, the sparkle back in his disposition.

"Try to be a little kinder to yourself," she pleaded, the charitable look in her eyes forcing Richard to turn away.

"I am as kind as I can be under the circumstances," he responded. His voice was not harsh, but tired. "That is enough of me," he said, suddenly brisk. "There is Peregrine." He pointed to an approaching curricle.

They halted their mounts and waited for the vehicle to catch up with them. As they watched, the Duke glanced at Lettice by his side.

"When will I have the pleasure of seeing you

again?" he asked, the brightness in his attitude making Lettice wonder if the conversation just a few moments ago had been imagination.

"Are you sure you wish to see me again?" she countered. "I have a feeling that I make you uncomfortable on occasion, and I don't think I will be able to curb my inquisitiveness."

She said this by way of a warning, but Richard appeared to be unfazed.

"Perhaps, in my way, I welcome your questions."

Lettice found this maddening.

"You sidestep and haver and caver, Your Grace, if you don't mind my saying so," she said with exasperation. "But if you do wish to continue with the inquisition, you will no doubt be able to avail yourself of the opportunity at the garden tea which my sisters and I are attending three days hence. That is, if you decide to overturn your decision to stay away."

"I shall be delighted, I am sure," Richard replied, taking Lady Lettice's hand in his and kissing it briefly but meaningfully.

Lettice's expression was at once incredulous and skeptical, but over it all she was very pleased, and greeted Aurora and Peregrine with a brilliant if somewhat confused smile.

"Well, we have found you at last," Lord Melburry called out, drawing the carriage up close to the couple. "As you can see, we are none the worse for our separate excursions, and we have just enough time to spare before Countess Trevelyn calls out the watch in search of her two stray daughters."

Eyeing his brother curiously and noticing the odd look he received in return, Peregrine perceived that something was up, but he did not have time to investigate, if he was to return his valuable charge to her mama.

"Yes, by all means let us be off," Richard agreed heartily, though he did not in reality wish to leave Lettice's presence. Escorting the women home, the brothers left them at their doorstep, Lord Melburry and Aurora showing their reluctance to part more evidently than did the Duke and Lettice. The parting formalities took on meaning that the buzzards of propriety would have deemed scandalous. The simple kiss on the hand conveyed such a passionate longing on Lord Melbury's side and such a reciprocal feeling on Lady Aurora's that Lettice and the Duke were almost put to the blush by it, hardly knowing which way to look.

Entering the house, Lettice attempted to admonish her sister, but it was as if she spoke to a stone wall.

"That was hardly seemly, Aurora," she scolded. "I knew not where to look, and on the street in broad daylight."

"You needn't act so scandalized," Aurora retorted blithely. "It was nothing improper, just a kiss on the glove, you received one from the Duke as well."

"I don't need to have that pointed out to me," Lettice responded, a bit huffily. "It was nothing like the salute you received. You are lucky that Mama was not watching."

Looking about at the empty drawing room, Lettice's eyes widened. All about there were boxes and packages strewn, as if something were preparing for a departure. Aurora noted the disarray as well, moving slowly into the room and discarding her bonnet as she looked.

"What in heaven's name is happening?" Lettice whispered.

"I will go and find Mama. I am sure that she will have a rational explanation," Aurora assured.

"I would very much like to hear it," Lettice answered as Aurora went in search of the Countess. Walking amidst the disarray, Lettice recognized her mother's trunks. "Well, wherever she is going, it will be for some time," Lettice remarked to the empty room, counting up the large cases and musing to herself as to the nature of her mother's departure.

In a moment she had her answer as her mother entered the room, her face wreathed in a blissful smile.

"You have a question for me, my angel child?" she cooed, her demeanor distinctly unlike her usual self.

Glancing at her sister, Lettice saw by Aurora's expression that she too was as mystified by this change in temperament. Only the previous day the Countess had been all frowns and irritation over Patrice's sulking and Lettice's stubbornness, and now Lettice found herself endowed with the dubious title of "angel child". It was beyond conjecture, so Lettice came speedily to the point.

"Mama, what are all these boxes doing down here? Are we going away?"

"We are not going away, at least not all of us," Countess Trevelyn said airily, waving her silk scarf in the air with a dreamy expression on her face. "I am traveling to France with your father in a few days' time."

"France!" Aurora exclaimed. "I do not want to go to France," she protested vehemently.

"I always thought you enjoyed France," Lettice said, surprised.

"Yes, yes, I do enjoy it but there are reasons for staying in England just now," Aurora insisted frantically.

"But *you* are not going to France. I thought I made that perfectly clear," the Countess said, surprised at her daughter's silliness. "Your papa and I are sailing four days hence and you will all remain behind with your Aunt Amelia."

Though their mother's voice was one of finality, Lettice's curiosity was decidedly aroused by this hasty journey. "Mama, why are you leaving so abruptly? And what reason? Is it business for Papa?"

"No. It is not business, for once," the Countess replied, the loveliest of smiles still lighting her features. She looked to be a young girl again and Lettice could now guess the reason.

"Ah, I see. How gauche of me to forget. You and Father visited France when you were first married, did you not?"

The shining in her mother's eyes was sufficient reply for her daughter.

"A second honeymoon, then? How terribly romantic, and France is the best setting for such things," Lettice approved wholeheartedly of the idea as did Aurora who no doubt could understand the feelings with more personal experience.

"Yes, Mama, and you mustn't worry about us. We will do famously while you are away," Aurora commented enthusiastically. "Aunt Amelia is a wonderful choice for chaperone. She even looks the part of a guardian, all those benevolent but slightly admonishing

134

smiles she gives the gentlemen!" Aurora's ebullience over her mother's happiness and her own flowed over. To her the whole world was in love or ought to be by all rights.

"Yes, Amelia will quite do the trick," the Countess agreed, as her daughters giggled a bit at her slip into the vulgar slang. Recalling herself, she added seriously to Lettice, "I shall depend upon you, rather than Amelia, to watch over Patrice. I have said that she may not see Lieutenant Torquill and I do mean it, so you must keep your eye on your sister!"

This most unwelcomed admonition was irritating indeed, but though she might not like the duty, Lettice was aware that she was the only person who could be placed on watch. Though Patrice was ordinarily docile in nature, this passion of hers was such that only an equally stubborn and alert person could be placed on guard over her. Aurora was far too involved with Lord Melburry to be expected to be ever vigilant, though to be sure she would do her part to keep her sister from such a disastrous marriage. This left the bulk of the assignment to Lettice.

"And will you build me a watch-house as well, then?" Lettice jested bitterly. "Is not Amelia enough to curb Patrice?" She did not need the look her mother bestowed on her to tell her she could not shirk the responsibility. "Oh, very well. When will you return home?" Lettice asked glumly, "for I want to know how long my sentence is to be."

"We will be on the Continent for at least three or four months," her mother answered. "We will be visiting all of our old haunts, and there are quite a number of them."

Old memories seemed to hold the Countess's attention for a moment, and the expression of rapture she wore was so unusual that Aurora found it difficult to remember that the ecstatic woman before her was her own mother.

"Four months," Lettice spoke with the accents of one condemned. "I do not relish the idea of being Patrice's jailer, but then there is nothing for it, I suppose," she said fatalistically. "And just where *is* Patrice? I have not seen her for the entire day, and I know she would have come down to greet us, even as sullen as she has been for the past week."

"Well, it is surprising, my dearest, but Patrice was in a remarkably good humor this morning. I do believe she is beginning to see the wisdom of my decision," Countess Trevelyn commented, somewhat bemusedly. "She even consented to attend a small party with Lord Ringwood this evening. That is why she has not greeted your arrival."

"Well, Mama, if she is indeed becoming more complacent with your desires, then why must Lettice watch her every move while you are away?" Aurora asked not unreasonably.

"Simply because girls of Patrice's age are so susceptible to handsome military men. She could slip back into believing herself in love quite easily and I cannot say that I altogether believe this sudden acquiescence," the Countess replied, the doubtful look on her face increasing as she dwelled on the idea.

"There is no worry at least for tonight," Lettice commented, walking toward the hallway to prepare for supper. "I am sure that Stuart will keep Patrice occupied so that she will hardly think of the lieutenant. It will not be the first time that an infatuation perished for want of attention."

Lord Ringwood himself was thinking much the same thing as he noted with what revived energies Patrice defeated him in a harmless game of silverloo. She seemed in high croak and he was glad of it as she appeared to have gotten over her tendre. She had talked animatedly during the early supper. And now, standing by her side in the music room, turning pages for Patrice as she executed a charming piece on the pianoforte, Stuart began to wonder what could possibly have wrought such changes in so short a time. Only the day before she had been all frowns and heartbroken sighs. Try as he might, he had been unsuccessful in making her smile, and tonight she was her usual good-natured self. The other guests applauded enthusiastically as Patrice completed the little tune and Stuart guided her toward the small side table for refreshments, wondering how to phrase a few tactful questions that he knew he must ask.

Patrice looked expectantly at the crystal punch bowl. Lord Ringwood hurriedly filled a delicately cut glass with the aromatic, sparkling gold liquid, slopping a bit over his fingers in his haste to fulfill Patrice's smallest desire. Patrice did not titter or even appear amused by this. This was a characteristic which Stuart Ringwood appreciated more than he could say. With a small sigh, he mopped his fingers with a napkin and presented the glass to Patrice who accepted it with a pleasant smile.

"There you are, such as it is," he murmured, somewhat abashed, clasping his hands behind his back as she sipped the punch to refresh herself. Once more he was struck by her happy, contented face; and that unsettling feeling that something was afoot prodded him. "You seem in high croak tonight," he said at last.

"Do I?" she asked brightly, looking up into Lord Ringwood's face happily. "I feel quite fine as a matter of fact, Stuart. I know I haven't been much company this past week, but that is over now." At that, Patrice's smile sparkled so that Stuart was dazzled by her beauty. He found himself staring so pointedly that he had to turn away, and picked up a few candies from a bowl to occupy himself.

Looking down into his hand and rolling the confections about, he could not look at Patrice as he asked, "And what of Lieutenant Torquill?" Suddenly a horrible thought struck him. "Your parents, they haven't reconsidered the match?" he asked, appalled at the idea as he said the words.

"No, Mama has not reconsidered," Patrice replied, her eyes darkening a bit as she spoke. Then, straightening resolutely, she regained her composure. "But I will not think of it anymore. One cannot sulk forever, and there are parties to go to and people to meet," Patrice bubbled, her nonchalance somehow unconvincing. "Mama and Papa are going to France. Did I mention that to you?"

"Oh?" Stuart replied, his mind racing ahead as best it could to the dreadful possibilities this new development conjured. He knew something of the workings of the female mind, having lived with two older sisters for most of his boyhood. He was aware ladies tended to take advantage of any situation that was presented, and that Patrice, as sweet and innocent as she normally was, would still be capable of the average female logic.

"Patrice," he said, screwing up his courage and attempting not to melt utterly as she gazed attentively into his eyes as was her wont, "you and I are friends, ain't we?"

Patrice looked upon the young man with a sisterly affection that smote his heart. "But of course, Stuart," she answered, placing a friendly arm over his.

Lord Ringwood instantly lost his grip on the candies which scattered on the highly polished floor. There were a few good-natured jests as the other guests observed the two young people stooped over and retrieving the elusive comfits like little children, before a footman took the job in hand.

Stuart looked totally disheveled, his cravat more than a little askew and one of his shirtpoints sticking up into the air by his ear. Taking him by a sticky and sweaty hand, Patrice led him into another room to help him put himself to rights.

Deftly, she straightened the collar and adjusted Lord Ringwood's cravat until he looked as he had before. "There, all fine as a tulip," she said, patting a few loose strands of her own hair back into place, as she surveyed her handiwork.

"Now, you were saying in the other room that we were friends," Patrice began again, "and I was about to agree with you. I am extremely fond of you, Stuart. Haven't I always told you my troubles? You are my confidant for I know you never make fun of what I say. Is that what you wished to hear?" she asked, tilting her head as she looked at him again.

"Yes, I suppose it is," he admitted, hoping that Patrice would attribute his high color to his recent activity. "I wanted to hear those words before I asked you a question that has been rattling around in ma head."

"What is that, Stuart?" Patrice inquired. "It must be quite serious for I seldom see you so grave."

Lord Ringwood squirmed uncomfortably, unsure if he really had the right to question Patrice. Though he felt a responsiblity to Lettice as one of his dearest friends, he also had to ask this question for his own peace of mind and to assuage his own inner turmoil.

"Patrice, I am only concerned for you when I ask this, and I would never mean to offend you."

"Go on, Stuart, say what you must," Patrice encouraged gently, mystified.

"I know the Countess has forbidden you to see Lieutenant Torquill, but have you received some communication from him? I know it is possible, since ma sisters were ever receiving letters; the chambermaids would bring them."

As Stuart spoke, Patrice's eyes wavered, then lowered. He knew before she spoke that his suspicions were confirmed.

"We are friends, and you must promise not to tell anyone what I am going to disclose to you now. You have to promise, or I cannot speak of it. I want to. I am so excited and happy that I would like to tell you for you have always been my friend since I have known you," Patrice said, looking back up into Stuart's green eyes. "Promise me," she repeated.

Lord Ringwood nodded; he could not speak because his heart was in his throat for what he thought he would hear.

"You are right, Stuart," she began, "I have been receiving letters from Basil. Mama has been so busy preparing for her trip that it was not difficult to pull the wool over her eyes. Basil and I have pledged our love to one another." Reaching into the reticule she had carried with her all evening, Patrice withdrew a small sparkling ring of gold filigree. Lord Ringwood was shocked.

"He gave you that without asking permission from your parents?" he asked, his sensibilities outraged, "and you accepted such a gift?"

"Do not tell me that I should not accept it," Patrice warned proudly. "I am no toy that he is indulging with a trinket."

"I never said you were," Stuart said, his concern for Patrice overcoming his usual awkwardness with her. "But he must know that 't'ain't proper for him to present you with such a ring."

"I did not hear you lecture Lettice when she received a horse from the Duke," Patrice reminded him indignantly.

" 'T'ain't the same, as you well know," Lord Ring-wood pointed out primly, with severely pursed lips.

"No one knows of this engagement but Basil and I, save yourself, and you have promised not to speak of it to anyone," she said, growing more upset.

"But what is to come of it?" Stuart asked with despairing tones, unable to make heads or tails of such a situation. "There can be no wedding without your parents' consent. This engagement smacks of impropriety, and I am thinking only of you when I say that it is not right."

His vehemence would have surprised Patrice had she not already been so heated by their discussion. "Basil says someday we shall marry. He says that my parents cannot be a barrier to him. He says that they will grow used to the situation in time," she said with conviction.

"And what do *you* say to all of this?" Stuart asked abruptly. "Enough of what Basil wants or believes. What do you want and what do you believe?"

For a moment Patrice was stunned by the straight-forward question and was speechless. Then, anger flared in her eyes and the Trevelyn temper could be seen to emerge. It did so rarely in Patrice, that Stuart had ever seen, but when it did appear Patrice could be as implacable as either of her sisters. "I wish to be escorted home, Stuart. I see that you are not as much a friend as I had believed or you would want for me what *I* desire. That is what Basil wants and I do not wish to discuss this personal matter with you any longer. I only hope that I may trust you to keep my confidences as I asked."

Stuart could only give a curt nod of his head and followed as Patrice led the way from the room. He cursed himself as he drove Patrice home in silence. He should have known that anything he might say against Lieutenant Torquill would be futile at this time. Though Basil Torquill was known to be in need of an heiress and Patrice had her own fortune aside from her dowry, Stuart might have known from personal experience with his sisters that women were damned funny creatures about matters of the heart.

As he rode along, his temper cooled, and he was left with a longing to make amends. If he could not be

140

loved for himself by Patrice, he at least wished for that small morsel of friendship that he had let slip away in his incautious words. But he found himself mute. As so often occurred with Lord Ringwood, he could not compose a decent sentence in his head, and Patrice did not wait to hear his sputtering attempt at apology as she descended the carriage and entered her home.

He did not see the hot tears streaming down her face as she ran past the footmen once the doors closed, stumbling a bit as she blindly ascended the staircase to her room. Throwing herself onto her bed, she wept and could not think why. "He makes me all confused," she said aloud, resentment in her voice as she lay on her back and stared up at the patterned ceiling. "I thought he was my friend. How could he not understand?" she wondered despairingly. Taking a handkerchief and wiping her teary eyes, Patrice hurried to her vanity and reached around the back of the mirror against the wall, withdrawing a small packet of letters tied with a satin ribbon.

She felt a quick moment of guilt at her deception, the covert messages to Basil delivered by her chambermaid, an incurable romantic. However, all things were fair, she reflected, as she hurriedly selected the last note which the lieutenant had sent her. It was easily identified as it was well crumpled. She had read the letter at least a hundred times, poring over every line. Her gaze flew to the most important section of the note, where Basil had set up a plan to see Patrice at the garden party:

Meet me by the willows at the far end of the garden. We shall make the final arrangements for our elopement.

Patrice clutched the missive to her breast tightly. They had often talked of the day when they would be married, but this new resistance of her mama's had provoked Basil into the extreme decision to elope for Gretna Green. It was a daring idea, one which appealed to the romantic sensibilities within Patrice, but she could not help feeling somewhat frightened by the impetuosity of the plan and the improperness of such a

141

marriage. She had heard of other women speak of such unions with disdain, the heroines being converted to hoydens in gossip, and Patrice did not wish overmuch for this to happen to her.

These fears were uppermost in her mind, and if the very thought of marriage made her uneasy, the thought of marrying such a perfectionist as Basil was even more disturbing, though she would not permit herself to doubt that theirs would be a marriage made in heaven. After all, she reflected as she replaced the letter with its fellows behind the mirror, the marriage was what she really wanted, and Stuart was only being biased by Lettice's dislike for the lieutenant.

With a deep breath, Patrice attempted to calm her nerves. "Once we are wed, I am sure Stuart will become more used to Basil," Patrice said aloud to herself as she prepared to retire early, unaccountably weak and exhausted. That her sisters and her friends did not approve of Basil was quite clear, though she might try to convince herself otherwise. The knowledge that she was quite alone in her decision to elope with her lieutenant preyed on her mind.

She did not bother to ring for her maid to assist her and soon crawled between the cold covers of her bed. Try as she might not to worry, tranquility was definitely at a minimum for her. Deception was not her nature, and she felt that she had lost her only possible ally in Stuart Ringwood.

Well, there is no use in worrying, I must save my strength for the elopement, and I must be calm so that no one may suspect our plan, Patrice thought, pulling her covers up to her chin and attempting to sleep.

The next few days were hectic for all the family, preparations going full ahead for the Earl's and Countess's departure for France. The house was to be closed down for the few months they were to be away, and many of the servants were put to the task of covering the furniture and packing the necessary articles for the trip.

Lettice and her sisters found themselves busily transferring their clothes and other possessions of import to their aunt's home in advance of their arrival. This in itself was a major operation and everyone was feeling quite beside himself with exhaustion and frustration as the day of departure drew near. Nevertheless, other duties of a social nature could not be neglected during such a domestic upheaval.

The Countess and Patrice found themselves obligated to return a visit for breakfast though every attempt was made to cry off since the packing was but half done. There was no begging the issue and the two of them had gone. Likewise, Lettice was summoned by special courier to attend on the Duke's mother, much to her utter astonishment and forboding. It had been Lettice's understanding that the dowager had voluntarily taken up residence in the country, leaving the townhouse vacant for her two unattached sons. She preferred to mourn in privacy rather than in the glaring light of London.

For Lady Melburry to have returned to the city and requested Lettice's presence, a direct entreaty must have been made by Richard for her to play hostess, and Lettice could not be but flattered and somewhat bewildered by such pointed attention. That the Duke should single her out from among so many for such a distinction, knowing her as little as he did, was to Lettice no less than incredible, and she knew not what to expect by way of greeting from the dowager as she was ushered into the main salon for an early tea.

Apprehensive lest she be confronted by a dragon of a woman or perhaps a possessive mama resenting her intrusion into the family circle, Lettice entered the room with a hesitant step. Her fears were dispelled as soon as she beheld the smiling face of the former Duchess of Melburry. Lettice saw that she was a tiny, delicately fragile woman of perhaps fifty years dressed in pearl-gray mourning attire.

Lettice's eyes were instantly drawn to those of the dowager and she found herself looking into the originals from which the Duke's were drawn. Warm and clear like hot spiced punch, the woman's hazel eyes echoed the welcome that she now made with her lips.

"My child, welcome to our home. Richard has spoken of you so often since my arrival two days ago that

I feel I should know you among a crowd," she said, rising slowly from the couch she had been sitting on.

Lettice hurried to assist her as she saw the pain with which the lady rose.

"Please, do not get up on my account," Lettice insisted, helping her to sit again.

"Thank you, my dear," the dowager said as she settled back into place, a slight smile still on her lips despite the discomfort. She observed Lettice with an astute eye. "I see that Richard was quite correct," she murmured.

"About what, madam?" Lettice inquired. That the Duke should discuss her with his mother at all was of intense curiosity to her.

"My son has told me that you were different from the other young ladies of his acquaintance. Of course, for the most part they have been French girls, but besides that difference, you are certainly not in the common way, my dear. You are, how shall I say it?"

"Imposing in stature?" Lettice suggested ruefully.

"Let us say that you are singular in appearance," was the kindly answer.

This comment caused Lettice to blush deeply. She was a little unconventional in her dress, not altogether caring for the latest fashion but more concerned for what she preferred herself.

Richard's mother, however, observed that Lettice had the good sense to dress just a tad differently from the mode. Sitting before her, Lettice wore the current rage of a round dress cut very fully in the skirt and high at the waist, however, she had wisely shunned the frilly ruffle at the neck and hem which would have been more suited to a cherubic face and slighter form.

With a cryptic nod of her head which Lettice hoped was approval, the elderly woman served tea and the afternoon passed pleasantly. Lettice found that the dowager had many tales to tell about her two sons, and was not the least bit reticent in revealing these family reminiscences.

She learned that the Duke as a child was so much fond of animals that he would bring many of them home to live.

"He secreted them all about the house, even placing

one small fox kit in one of my hat boxes. Imagine my surprise at finding such a creature! I almost wore him to a rout!" she laughed, relishing the memory.

Lettice was certain that this recounting would have caused the Duke some discomfort, but she was glad to hear of it. Lettice especially wished to remember that Lord Melburry had kept rabbits for pets, certain that Aurora would find this interesting as well. The Duke's mother left no amusing aspect untold, right down to the years Richard spent at Cambridge.

"So the Duke misbehaved a great deal?" Lettice had inquired, and was not surprised to learn that such had been the case.

"Richard had been sent down to 'rusticate' any number of times. I recall one occasion in particular where he rearranged the Dean's garden one winter so that in the spring there was total chaos in the man's flower beds. He was not caught for that one, but he told me all the same for he knew that I enjoy such things," the lady confessed.

Things went smoothly, the only moment of unease occurring after Lettice had made a vague reference to the late Duke. She had thoughtlessly wondered aloud if he had approved of his eldest son's antics at school.

"My husband was not an angel, either, to be sure," she said, then went on to other subjects.

They had just finished their tea when a knock sounded on the door and a servant entered to announce the Duke.

"I asked Richard to come and show you about the house since he was unable to join us for tea," the dowager explained as Lettice appeared uncomfortable at the surprise. "Though the townhouse is not so fine as our country estate, there are yet quite a few things I feel would interest you."

The Duke stood before the two women, an encouraging smile on his lips as he bent to kiss first his mother's cheek and then Lettice's fingers. The appreciative gaze he bestowed on her caused Lettice to blush once again.

"Am I on time?" he inquired, assisting his mother to stand.

"Prompt as ever," she responded, looking at her son

with such fondness that Lettice wondered how she could have borne his absence. Turning to her guest, she motioned for Lettice to take her other arm and they walked from the room.

Moving through the house, Lettice wondered at all of the heavy, oppressive furniture. The house was rather darker than was her liking until they reached a small room near the back of the main hall. The dowager opened the door and the dim hallway was suddenly flooded with light pouring through the windows within. "This was my sewing room, but as you can see Richard has decided that he must redecorate. I am rather fond of it the way it is presently, still he is the one who must live here now as I rarely visit anymore."

Lettice looked with delight at the difference that the small room presented.

Gone were the heavy drapes, replaced with what appeared to be sheer white silk, embroidered lightly with gold and silver threads. The room had been redone in white and rose tints, and it seemed to Lettice that it must be some new French influence. However, when she inquired if it was so, the Duke hesitated, reminded of his long stay in France.

"No, this is original, I fear, so only I can be blamed for the effect."

"It is quite lovely," Lettice murmured as she saw that the dowager had not missed her son's hesitation.

"Well, let us go on shall we?" his mother encouraged, finishing the tour with the gardens. "That path," she said, pointing with one hand off toward what looked like a set of small shacks, "leads to the stables. We had them built for our carriage horses, though I am sure that Richard is housing a few of his racehorses there now. Perhaps you would like to see them? I would go with you but I fear that while I am in London I have acquired a most unforgivable but necessary habit, that of taking an afternoon rest."

"Of course, I would like to see them. I hope I haven't tired you out too much, madam," Lettice said, concerned as Lady Melburry did not appear to be tired.

"Not at all, it has just become a ritual with me."

The Duke motioned for one of the footmen who instantly appeared to escort the dowager upstairs to her rooms.

Before leaving, the woman turned to kiss Lettice lightly on either cheek in the French mode. Accepting the friendly gesture, Lettice was undeniably pleased with the lady's pleasant reception of her.

"I hope to see you again soon, Lady Lettice," the dowager said as she turned to go, "and," she added as she left, "I hope that Richard had the sense to fill in any of the missing pieces of his history that I have neglected to tell you."

With that she departed, and Lettice marveled at such a parent who could have reared such an unusual son.

The couple walked to the stables with only a few comments to spare between them. Lettice was acutely aware that the Duke looked her way from time to time, and that his glance was distinctly appreciative.

"It was good of your mother to have me to tea," Lettice said cheerily, hoping to stimulate some sort of conversation.

"I suppose it was good of her at that, though to be sure, I asked that she do so," Richard noted with a wicked smile.

"And I imagine I should ask to what purpose," Lettice responded with more bravado than she felt.

The Duke paused solemnly, then announced with a whisper, "Well, if you must know, she hopes that I have decided to pay you court."

Halting outside the stables, Lettice's eyes widened with surprise at his reply. "And are her hopes well founded?" she demanded, moved to laughter by the Duke's impudent grin.

"I sincerely hope so," he prayed fervently, making himself out the clown.

Lettice was aware that he would only be so amusing if he were masking his discomfort at making such a serious announcement of his intent, and after a moment, Lettice followed Richard into the stables, a serious expression replacing her mirth.

"If you are truly intent on what you say, then I must tell you something which has been preying on my con-

147

science for some time," Lettice commented as she surveyed the Duke's horseflesh. It was in fact this fine assortment of animals which had caused her to recall her deception of Richard at the auction.

"Then you had best speak for I truly am intent on paying you court, Lady Lettice," he maintained, totally serious as he spoke.

Taking hold of her courage, she admitted all of her crime to the Duke, and as he listened, his face unchanged, she wondered if perhaps she would have done better to let the matter rest. Still, she finished the confession, never once faltering as she gave her reasons for deceiving him.

"So you found me obnoxious," Richard said as she finished speaking.

"Intimidatingly so," Lettice admitted. "But then it was not just the things that you said, but the arrogant, flippant manner in which you implied that I should need all the assistance I could get to pick out a few horses. You must agree, Your Grace, that it was hardly fair of you to judge me by my outward appearance," Lettice insisted with spirit, not wishing to appear to grovel for forgiveness.

Richard thought for a few moments, then looked at her. "I had not meant to put you off, believe me," he said at last, looking perturbed, "and I admit that I may have been too hasty with my words, but that does not excuse your behavior in any case."

Lettice's chin went up a fraction as she awaited any scathing words the Duke might wish to throw at her. She was strong enough to take them, though she did not relish the prospect. Richard witnessed her defiance, daring him in a way to set her down.

"However," he continued, "as I have learned to admire your spirit, and because I have grown to like you, there is nothing for me to say. I am sure the horse will be an excellent brood mare, and I say it again, the beast suits you."

Lettice was stunned, then asked, "You forgive me, then?"

"I hadn't realized you asked for any forgiveness, but if such was the case, how could I possibly deny you?" the Duke replied. His voice was almost a caress and the helpless attitude in which he motioned with his hands shook Lettice to her very foundations. Such a declaration! And from the Duke of Melburry whom she had thought so proud. Lettice's head swam.

"That is a relief to me," Lettice said when she could speak, "for I felt I must clear my conscience to you." That matter settled, Richard and she finished looking at the animals housed in the stable, then returned to the house. As Lettice prepared to go, she suddenly recalled the dowager's parting words.

"Your Grace, it would seem that your past history remains a mystery to me still, even though your mama was so desirous of a disclosure," Lettice jested, yet the Duke caught the meaning behind her banter.

Taking her hand before she left, Richard smiled warmly. "Endure my company a little longer, and like Scheherazade, I will tell you it bit by bit."

Gazing up into his eyes, Lettice could not help asking, "And do you think I would forsake you if you simply told me all, as that poor unfortunate feared?"

The Duke could not respond, and she smiled a bit sadly and departed.

Richard stared after her a long while before entering the house. His mother awaited him in the sitting room. They did not speak for a time, Richard staring down at the carpet while she worked a little on some small embroidered adornment. Finally, he spoke.

"I did not tell her, Mama. I can almost hear the question in the room as you sit there stitching away. I did not have the heart," Richard said as he looked to her as if for guidance.

"Not the heart or not the courage?" she replied rather hardly. "You must be honest with the girl if you even contemplate offering for her. She is definitely not of a color to stand for anything secret."

Her son did not reply to this, and she knew that he would do what he felt best in his own time, as he had always done. She rose and extended her arm to him.

"Let us dine now. There is time yet."

There were not enough hours in the day, however, or so it seemed to Aurora who found the task of purchasing a departure present for her father most time-consuming.

Browsing on Bond Street in search of the perfect gift for her father, Aurora was attended by one of the footmen as she gazed into an interesting shop window. She did not frequent this area, but she was in desperate straits having found nothing which she could truly call appropriate as a gift.

Peering through one of the small panes of glass, Aurora did not note the approach of a gentleman on the street and was startled as well as repulsed as she found herself accosted by none other than Giles Killingham.

"Lady Aurora!" Lord Killingham exclaimed, coming forward to make his bow.

The footman was as startled as his mistress by the appearance of this gentleman in the middle of a public street. It was not a person whom he knew to frequent the Trevelyn townhouse and he waited to see if Lady Aurora would decide to acknowledge the man. He gave every appearance of being a Bond Street lounger, one of those obnoxious troublemakers who found it amusing to rouse the watch in the middle of the night.

It was something of a sight to see—the aging roué tightly braced in his waistcoat and the fresh and unsullied beauty that was Aurora Trevelyn in a walking dress of saffron edged with tan eyelet lace—and the footman watched the scene with interest.

Holding her parasol before her, Aurora did not present her hand for Killingham's salute, and she effectively used the delicate sunshade as a bar to his coming any closer to her physically.

Aurora decided that she could not ignore the man entirely, though her every instinct cried out for her to do so. She had, after all, exchanged an introduction, albeit unwanted, with the man.

"Lord Killingham, I see you are out and about this morning," she remarked in her most uninterested manner, hoping to put him off. "It must be quite an effort for you to be up at this hour, considering your age."

Her footman made a point of hiding his amusement, though it was difficult, to say the least.

This remark had a definite effect on Lord Killingham who was already aware of the discrepancy be-

150

tween their ages. Still, it did not deter his interest and
Aurora found herself trapped into a conversation that
lasted all of fifteen minutes. This was far too long for
Aurora's liking and she was relieved when she could at
last take her leave. Hurrying along, Aurora was becoming more and more irritable as she thought about
the manner in which Lord Killingham had forced his
company upon her. He appeared to enjoy her disdain,
almost relish it.

He is mad, Lady Aurora thought with a shudder, for
she was sure that no sane individual could enjoy another person's scorn, especially as ill-disguised as hers
had been.

And he was showing unnatural interest in the subject
of Lord Melburry, she recalled as she tried to concentrate on selecting a snuff box from among a multitude
presented to her in one small establishment. She was
distracted at the remembrance of Lord Killingham's inquiry. Aurora had mentioned that she would be seeing
Lord Melburry at the Cadbury home on the morrow.
She had hoped this would be sufficient to encourage
Lord Killingham to shift his attentions elsewhere,
seeing that she was occupied. However, Giles Killingham had not seemed overly concerned at the glowing manner in which she had referred to Lord
Melburry, praising his appearance and congenial and
engaging demeanor as much to irritate Lord Killingham as to state the truth as she saw it. His reaction
was quite the contrary to what she had anticipated. He
appeared almost satisfied with the fact that young Melburry would be in her company.

Her attention was recalled to the selection before
her, and Aurora chose a small oblong snuff box of silver as her gift to the Earl. With a heartfelt sigh of relief at having at last found something to her
satisfaction, Aurora stepped into her carriage and was
soon home with her prize.

She could not dismiss the meeting with Lord Killingham from her mind as she entered the library in
search of Lettice, hoping to discuss with her the
growing unease she felt on the matter. Though she
would have been loath to admit such a thing, Aurora's
disgust of the man was mixed with some fear. Possibly

this was a result of her ever-increasing conviction that Lord Killingham was not in his right mind, and though Aurora could face any normal gentleman without the slightest hesitation, she could not find it easy to deal with a madman.

"Lettice!" she called out, moving into the hallway. "Where is Lady Lettice?" she asked the butler who had hurried forward upon hearing Aurora's voice.

"Lady Lettice and Lord Ringwood are, I believe, with the Countess in the drawing room, Lady Aurora," the butler responded quickly. "Lord Ringwood was only just now inquiring after you, my lady."

"Thank you," Aurora responded, moving toward the drawing room, wondering what Stuart could have to say to her. She would have preferred to speak to Lettice alone and so Aurora decided to retell the tale of her encounter when a more private moment presented itself. Arriving at the chamber, Aurora entered upon the typical tableau that occurred whenever Lord Ringwood chanced upon the family at tea.

Sitting awkwardly on the small chair too tiny to accommodate his frame, which chair the Countess always insisted he take, Stuart balanced the absurdly tiny cup on his saucer while attempting to consume his jam tart. Upon noting Aurora's entrance, he rose somewhat clumsily to his feet, unsure of where to place his half-eaten tart. He ended by making his bow with one hand clutching the pastry, the other balancing the cup of tea.

Aurora knew not where to look, for she did not wish to offend Stuart with her amusement, but he was well aware of the figure he must be cutting and was resigned to looking absurd when most he desired not to.

Oddly enough the Countess was not as critical of the spectacle that Lord Ringwood presented this day. Probably so pleased with her journey that even Stuart cannot ruffle her calm, Lettice reflected as she poured her sister a cup of tea.

The conversation was filled mostly with talk of the trip, who the Countess and Earl intended to visit while on the Continent, and what sort of changes they might be expected to find since they had traveled last. Countess Trevelyn was particularly concerned that her wardrobe be on an equal level with that of the French women for she vividly recalled her first visit when she had found it necessary to purchase an entire new wardrobe after an embarrassing party which she had attended in what was considered the previous season's fashion.

"Lord Ringwood, I am depending upon you to ask your friend, the Duke of Melbury, to tell me about all the latest changes in the mode," she insisted. "He and I must talk about it all when he comes to call on us. Of course, he has not responded to the invitation I issued, but then I should imagine he has quite a lot of things to take care of and straighten up considering the late Duke's ill health has left the estates more or less unattended."

"Richard has not responded?" Lord Ringwood asked with surprise, his thick eyebrows rising and disappearing into his shaggy locks. "That is most unlike him, I can assure you," Stuart asserted, a worried look on his face. "Course, can't say as Richard would know that much about the toggery the ladies sport in France. I mean, not if he is like ma self. Never really know what's the crack from season to season."

"Well, I shall ask nonetheless," the Countess informed the young lord firmly, "and I daresay he must have seen something of it, having lived there for such a long time."

Lord Ringwood squirmed uncomfortably so that both Lettice and Aurora were aware of his discomfiture. One would have to be a fool not to smell out some sort of a mystery afoot, Aurora reflected, but there were other matters more pressing for her to consider than what could be going on with the Duke of Melbury. She would much rather concentrate on his brother when it came right down to it.

"Stuart, why don't you come upstairs and I shall show you the miniature Lettice finished of you. It will be your sole opportunity since Patrice will in all probability have it enshrined in her room for the masterpiece of art that it is," Aurora jested, leading her friend out of the Countess's way.

He went gratefully as Lettice made a face at her sister's remark.

Inside, however, Lettice was really glad that she now had an opportunity to speak in private with her mother about a matter on which she hoped the Countess could shed some light, the mysterious circumstances under which Richard Melburry had left England four years ago.

"Mama, about the Duke of Melburry," Lettice began, hoping that her tone showed none of the burning curiosity that she felt within. "You knew him before his move to France, did you not?"

The Countess glanced up from the French periodical she had been studying in her lap as she savored her tea. "But of course, my dear, we knew of him, although we were not acquainted with him personally. It is difficult not to know of an eligible young man who has the potential of receiving ten thousand a year on his majority, not to mention the Dukedom."

"Mama!" Lettice admonished disapprovingly, "I had no knowledge that you cared a jot for fortunes."

"I do not care an' you mention it, Lettice. One must consider practical matters when entering a marriage. I could not countenance one of my precious jewels living in abject poverty. Think of the disgrace! No, my dearest, much as I detest having to consider the monetary side of such things, it is necessary for someone to do so to insure the best possible matching of two people."

The Countess looked upon her statement as the most natural thing in the world, and Lettice did not care to continue in the same manner for she had pressing questions which required immediate answers.

"Mama, why did such an eligible young man, with so large a fortune and so much to enjoy in London, leave England for France? I know it would be natural to go for a short visit, but to live there for so long, I know there must have been extraordinary circumstances warranting such an occurrence," Lettice said with certainty. She waited patiently as her mother finished the last of her tea, seeming to search her memory for an incident long past.

"There was a scandal, I daresay Lord Ringwood has told you as much," the Countess began. Then, noting the crimson flush that rose to Lettice's face, she added knowingly, "You see I know you better than you would believe, you are not half so readable as Patrice, but there are a few things I have learned of your character."

"Well, Mama, you have found me out. I have my reasons for desiring to know of the Duke's past," Lettice admitted, aware that her mother must realize her interest in Richard Melburry.

"I approve," the Countess replied unsolicited, and continued before her daughter could do anything as inelegant as contradict her supposition. "You are aware that a scandal does not last long, another comes along to take its place. They happen even in the best of families, so I would not hold it against the Duke if I were you, my dear," she counseled sagely, aware that Lettice might not approve of such a history in a husband, even as she might not have a care should it pertain to an acquaintance.

"Depend upon it, that I should not mind what the gossips would say, but I care for myself what the Duke's character might be, and if you are able to elucidate on his past behavior I would find it most helpful," Lettice replied with a hint of the willfulness that had always plagued her mother.

With a sigh, the Countess resigned herself to her task. "If you will know, the scandal involved a married woman, someone who was known to be somewhat indelicate in her personal affairs. There was to have been a divorce, and the Duke would have no doubt been brought forward as a corespondent, but he left the country instead and nothing ever came of it."

Lettice considered these words, her face a study in thoughtfulness, then she looked into her mother's eyes. "Is there nothing more than that? Surely there must be something you have not told me."

The Countess hesitated and Lettice instantly saw that she was correct in her assumption. "Come now, you must tell me all you know," she insisted inexorably.

"Indeed, my dearest, you are mistaken," Countess Trevelyn faltered, then saw that she must blacken the Duke's character further. "Do not make yourself uneasy my love, but there was a death involved in the

155

entire matter. The woman in question, Lady Killingham, committed suicide on the night of the Duke's departure. It was the talk of the town for months after."

"I can imagine," Lettice commented, her face expressionless. "How did she do it?"

"How?" the Countess repeated, astonished at her daughter's morbid curiosity.

"Yes, what did she do precisely? Was it laudanum?"

The Countess shifted as uneasily in her chair as had Lord Ringwood in his before she was compelled by her daughter's baleful stare to speak. "I am afraid she chose to make use of one of her husband's dueling pistols."

Lettice's eyes widened at this information. "She discharged the gun upon herself?" she asked incredulously. "She must have reached the heights of despair indeed, poor woman."

"She but brought it on herself," the Countess offered. "She had quite a few 'diversions' before the Duke of Melburry." This explanation sounded lame to herself and she looked away from her daughter's unshifting eyes.

"Thank you, Mama," Lettice said, rising thoughtfully from her seat and brushing the crumbs from her gown with a perturbed air. "You have told me a great deal, and I suppose I shall now know better how to deal with the Duke's attentions." Observing her mother's concerned face, Lettice sighed impatiently. "You needn't look like that. I have decided nothing on the matter of the Duke. I cannot reconcile what you have told me with what I know of him so far, but never fear, I shall do so eventually."

"Many of the finest husbands are reformed rakes, Lettice," the Countess assured her daughter faintly and without much conviction.

"We do not know that he is a 'rake' as you put it," Lettice corrected her mama abruptly. "However, if he is, how can you utter such nonsense as you have just spoken? Would you have married Papa if he had been a rakehell?" Lettice asked, her chin rising as she looked down on the seated woman.

Her mother could not answer and Lettice continued,

"It doesn't matter in any case. Before I would condemn the Duke I would know the truth from him."

"And if he could not choose to speak of it?"

Lettice paused. "Then he doesn't regard me as he has led me to believe, and there will have been a dreadful mistake on my part." With that, Lettice quit the room.

"Daughters!" the Countess exclaimed to herself in despair, ringing for the servants to clear the tea things away. "If it is not Patrice and her overbearing, insulting lieutenant then it is Lettice who is bent on spinsterhood. Thank goodness Aurora seems content to form a tendre for an acceptable young man. She at least has sense enough to behave and allow me to plan my journey in peace."

The very thought of France caused the Countess to smile as she recalled distant memories. She hardly could credit that she had ever been quite so young, that every morning in those early months had been filled with such wonder, as she had awakened to look out on the city of Paris beside her new husband. There had only been the two of them in those days, Roland and herself, and then had come Lettice and the rest of the children, and it seemed to her that there had not been a moment's privacy since. She still felt a little guilt at leaving her children behind, but they would all soon wed, as they were of age, just as she herself had done. Besides, it was time that she and Roland become acquainted once again with the young couple so much in love that they had been so long ago. The Countess sighed loudly and turned her thoughts elsewhere. Enjoyable as she found it to reminisce, she had the present to deal with first, the most outstanding matter being the selection of a gown for the garden party on the morrow. This concern occupied the Countess for the remainder of the day, but her pains were not unappreciated the following day.

The Trevelyn family attended in its entirety, the Countess dominating conversation among the dowagers with talk of France, and as ravishing as she could desire in a gown of cream silk over a pink underdress, falling in waves to the grass at her feet. Lettice found herself

157

searching the grounds for a sign of the Duke of Melburry, Aurora by her side.

Her previous night's repose had been an uncomfortable and halting affair as she had weighed the pros and cons of what she had heard from her mother against what she had gleaned of the Duke's personality herself. She was prepared to meet Richard on this day, but she was not one such as would run and hide from a confrontation simply because she was unsure of what would occur.

Aurora, on the other hand, was quite sure that any meeting with Lord Melburry could not help but be delightful in every aspect as moments spent in his presence so far had been heaven for her. If she had felt a modicum of jealousy that day in the park, it had been duly quelled with remembrances of time spent with the young gentleman, of their similar humor and love of adventure.

Turning to her sister who had chosen to don an exquisite gown of French lace with a *pelisse* to match, Aurora remarked on the beauty of the flowers and the ingenuity with which the various fruit trees had been decorated with colorful ribbons round their trunks and in the lower branches.

"It is quite remarkable, really," Aurora exclaimed, wondering how long it had taken to achieve the festive air that was present. "I should imagine that Patrice will appreciate the novelty of it all, she is forever complaining of the lack of color at most parties."

"I have not seen Patrice in some time now, I wonder where she has gone off to?" Lettice remarked suspiciously, hoping that it was only lack of sleep which caused her neck to tighten with irritation. Not only had she to concern herself with the unmistakable feelings of growing affection she felt for the Duke, but she must also contend with Patrice and keeping her out of mischief. The entire tale that she had heard from her mother was so incredible that Lettice knew not what was truth and what was the gossips' fabrication. The only true historian must be the Duke himself, and she was not at all sure she wished to pry into his affairs. Of course, the fact that it had been Lady Killingham who was the supposed center of the scandal made Lord Killingham's behavior all the more understandable—the blatant hatred for Richard and all connected with him. Lettice felt herself shiver a bit at the remembrance of the hostility that Lord Killingham had exuded at the auction.

And now he will have another Melburry to deal with if his attentions to Aurora thus far are any indication of his interest, Lettice thought, sure that such a man would not stand for any rivals and ultimately must clash with Lord Melburry. It was as inevitable as the fact that the strange game that Lord Killingham was playing with the Duke would soon come to a head. The more that Lettice considered it, the surer she was that all was not forgiven by the Duke or his adversary, that it was not finished, and could not remain so indefinitely.

Who am I to involve myself? Lettice thought abruptly. I have other matters to consider, such as Patrice. "I shan't be a moment," she said aloud to Aurora who still strained her neck in search of Peregrine Melburry. "I must find out what Patrice is up to."

With that, Lettice moved off to find her wayward sister while Aurora continued her search, greeting friends as she went along, pausing only for a few seconds to talk.

Though she found the company pleasant, she longed to find that one face that would make her day completely enchanting. Of course, she had already noted certain faults that Lord Melburry had. She would not pretend that they were not present, however, there were many more things admirable about him, so Aurora was well pleased.

Walking toward a large group of people at the far end of the garden, Aurora found herself being hailed by the familiar and unwelcomed figure of Ann Snogging who hurried toward her, osprey feathers fluttering disparately in the breeze as she attempted to reach Aurora's side. Aurora debated whether or not to outmaneuver that annoying woman, but decided against it. Perhaps she had seen Lord Melburry. No avenue must go untrodden in her search to find him, so she waited patiently until Ann had succeeded in catching up to her.

159

"Aurora, how good to see you!" Ann exclaimed with her usual animation.

The smile she wore was surely affected and Aurora observed that Ann had chosen to apply her cosmetics with a free and heavy hand, the lacquer showing the areas which that lady considered flawed on her complexion.

Ann observed the wandering eyes which Aurora presented, still looking for Lord Melbury, with satisfaction. Giles was right, she shall be meeting him here. All the better, I have gotten to her before him, Ann thought, her purpose decidedly malevolent as she smiled with false friendship.

"Aurora, you are not attending to me," Ann remarked as Aurora found herself called to attention. "Who are you looking for with such determination? Some young beau I will warrant, though you have beaus enough. It never hurts to have a few more, eh?" Ann laughed, the sound was particularly vulgar as the woman threw back her head. "Who is this new gallant then? Surely someone I know," Ann inquired in a conspiratorial whisper which Aurora found somehow nauseating.

Straightening, Aurora made no attempt to lower her voice, and in this way denied any sharing of a secret with such an individual as Ann Snogging. "I have been looking for Lord Melbury, if you must know, and I would hardly refer to him as a 'gallant'; he is an acquaintance," Aurora answered, regretting that she had not at least made an attempt at eluding Mrs. Snogging's company. Vain was the hope that Ann might know of Peregrine's whereabouts, she decided, with vexation at her own foolishness.

"Lord Melbury!" Ann cried in tones of horror; then, as if to cover her reaction, she murmured, "Well, I suppose you know what you are doing, but I am surprised that you should desire such an acquaintance."

"What objection could you have to Peregrine Melburry?" Aurora inquired with apprehension, surprised by such a response.

"Nothing, nothing at all, my dear. Please do not even recall that I said anything. Only, well my dear, you do know of his reputation. He is, after all, a Melburry and there is a tendency among the Melburrys toward profligacy."

"I had not heard of it," Aurora replied with incredulity, knowing that Ann was hardly a reliable historian or judge of character. "And on what grounds do you base such a statement?"

"There is no need to become indignant," Ann said with a hint of amusement which irritated Aurora beyond all bounds. "After all, I should have thought it was common knowledge to one and all that Lord Melburry finds those of the demimonde most agreeable. Why, you yourself were witness to his familiarity with one such bit of muslin only a week ago in Hyde Park, that woman to whom he was speaking. I happened to be nearby in my carriage when I recognized you or I should not have noted it."

The pitying manner in which Ann looked on Aurora made her pale, then redden visibly with a mixture of rage and embarrassment.

"If you will excuse me," Aurora said coldly, turning to go.

"Of course, my dear. I can see this has been a shock to you," Ann said, the slight smile spreading on her face as Aurora quickened her step.

As incriminating as Ann's words had been, Aurora found herself seething more from the woman's impudence than from any belief that Peregrine could possibly be guilty of such an act as deception. Walking determinedly away from where Mrs. Snogging stood, Aurora could not believe that Peregrine was anything less than he appeared, however she could not deny that she felt some unease as she recalled the strange encounter in the park. She was loath to think that she had been so completely duped, and that Peregrine was possibly toying with her affections for his own cruel pleasure.

It was at this precise moment that Aurora heard her name called out. Turning, her face brightened as she saw the figure of Lord Melburry approaching her with quick strides. The sweet smile on his handsome face eased the suspicions within Aurora's breast, and then did quell them entirely as the young lord bent to kiss her hand with a passion and tenderness that would have been difficult to feign.

"Lady Aurora, I have found you at last after toiling through the greetings of at least twenty persons who were disappointingly not you," Peregrine said as he neglected to release Aurora's hand from his. Cradling it as if it were the most precious of jewels, Peregrine seemed almost unable to believe his own good fortune in being in her presence.

"Peregrine," she replied, using his Christian name as he had entreated her to during their last encounter, "I have been searching for you as well, but had the misfortune of finding that wretched woman, Ann Snogging, instead," Aurora told him, watching him carefully.

Aurora was unsure of what she thought she would see, but was unaccountably filled with relief when Peregrine replied, "Oh, Lord, you unfortunate child. To be cornered by the town wag! You are to be consoled by me for the remainder of the afternoon. It is the only cure for such an exposure."

"I suspect you are entirely correct," Aurora admitted with a smile to match his. "She had spoken some nonsense about that woman you met when we were in Hyde Park the other day. Something about your having known her before. I'm sure she was mistaken."

Aurora deliberately allowed a questioning tone to enter her voice as she spoke, and she did not miss the look in Lord Melburry's blue eyes as he heard her words. Was it guilt? Aurora felt suspicions rise within her.

Before she could inquire further, they were interrupted by the arrival of Lord Simmons, dressed to the nines in his quiet way: an elegant spencer coat of manila with dusky brown gloves to accent his strong but slender hands well suited him.

Making his greeting, Lord Simmons noted that he had apparently intruded on the couple amidst a disagreement or argument. This he assumed since Lord Melburry looked distinctly like some guilty party while Aurora had that speculative look she always wore when her suspicions were aroused. This state of affairs suited Lord Simmons down to the ground as he would by far prefer Aurora to discover Peregrine's infidelity on her own without intervention on his part.

"Well, it has been some time since I last saw you, Lord Melburry," Lord Simmons remarked as he watched the young man shift his weight a bit, obviously wishing that Simmons would absent himself. This Lord Simmons had no intention of doing, and he engaged Peregrine in a discussion of thoroughbreds which Lord Melburry little wished to participate in. They thoroughly spoke on the various young 'uns to be found at the races, who was to bet on which, and what the chances of a win were, until Peregrine was completely talked out.

Aurora did not speak much herself during this time, preferring to listen rather than comment. She watched as Peregrine stewed in his own juices for a bit. She had no doubt that he believed her to be displeased with him, but she was unsure whether he was distressed over the fact that he was indeed guilty of some misdemeanor, or simply appalled by her displeasure. She could not be sure, but as the conversation waned between the men, she resolved to give Peregrine the benefit of a doubt. After all, Ann was a dreadful gossip, and was more often than not incorrect in her tales, and Aurora would not take her word that Lord Melburry had wronged her.

"If you will excuse us, Lord Simmons, I would like to speak with Lord Melburry in private," Aurora said as she took Peregrine's arm and led him off a ways.

Peregrine appeared wary of this new development, but said nothing as Aurora faced him, her expression serious.

"Well, Lord Melburry." He noted that she chose to be formal at that moment. "You have not told me if you did indeed know that woman."

"Is it important if I did?" he asked apprehensively.

"Only an' you have done something which would be considered reprehensible," she replied without hesitation.

"I knew the woman vaguely, but I have done nothing to wrong you, nor would I willingly do so, for a single hard word or slighting glance from your eyes would surely preclude such a thing," Lord Melburry assured the young woman. "Your displeasure just now causes me incredible pain. You must know that it does."

Aurora looked into Lord Melburry's expressive eyes, so evocative of her reciprocal feelings, and was convinced enough to smile a bit ruefully and wag her finger at the repentant young man.

"You should have told me that you knew her," she said.

"You would not have liked it if I had," Peregrine replied, and Aurora knew that he was correct.

"We will speak of it no more, then," she said, discounting entirely the rest of Ann's story as she recalled the respectable air about the lady she and Peregrine had spoken to. That could be no courtesan surely.

Lord Melburry, at being forgiven, took up her hand gleefully, and a little ways off, Lord Simmons witnessed this with a frown. Biting his lip, he turned away abruptly lest he be tempted to say something unwise.

In another part of the garden, Lettice found herself in a situation of less bliss than her sister. Searching vainly for Patrice so that she might carry out her loathsome obligation as her dragon, Lettice was suddenly confronted by the familiar figure of the Duke of Melburry.

"Lady Lettice, we meet once more," Richard said as he greeted her with a smile which could only have been described as fond. Lettice recalled with what good fellowship they had parted on their previous encounter, recalling too the feeling of closeness that had resulted.

"Your Grace, it is extraordinary how we seem forever destined to meet with one another," Lettice replied with a faint smile of her own. "You will have to bear with me, I am looking for Patrice. You haven't seen her by any chance?"

The Duke shook his head. "I am afraid I have not, but you are welcome to enlist my aid in the task of finding her. I know how younger siblings are, and understand your plight entirely."

"She may be with a military man," Lettice told him as they searched about the garden for some trace of Patrice.

Looking about, the Duke thought he perceived a

patch of red and directed Lettice's eyes across the garden only to be told, "That is not him. My sister's lieutenant is far handsomer than that individual."

As they walked, Richard seemed as if he wished to speak, and Lettice had the distinct impression that it was something of import as the Duke cleared his throat intermittently. Halting, Lettice turned to him.

"You wish to speak?" she inquired, not sure if she was correct in her perception.

Richard stood before her and Lettice could see that he had resolved to speak to her, no matter that the setting of a garden party was hardly the most secluded of places for a disclosure, for such she felt it must be.

Lettice awaited his words anxiously for she herself had resolved to break with the Duke if she felt he were truly but dallying with her affections as he might have with Lord Killingham's wife. However, before he had an opportunity to speak, there was a commotion close by them. The sound of harsh words and weeping could be heard faintly among a cluster of small trees, and Lettice knew without a doubt that her worst fears were realized.

Hurrying forward, Lettice had to go round a large oak tree to discover the source of the din. As she had suspected, there stood the Countess admonishing a teary Patrice. The lieutenant was nowhere to be seen, no doubt making good his own escape, leaving Patrice to bear the brunt of the Countess's anger.

"That my own child should practice such a contemptible deception is beyond belief!" the Countess exclaimed, bosom heaving with agitation. Seeing Lettice's arrival, the Duke behind her, the Countess continued to give vent to her feelings, regardless of their presence. "I can see that you cannot be trusted to remain with your sisters while we are away in France," the Countess continued, her words causing Patrice to flinch as if struck. "You will have to travel straight away to the country to stay with the dowager until we return. You may attend the country parties for I will not have you shut away as some other mothers might. Your grandmama will have strict instructions not to allow you to see Lieutenant Torquill, or indeed any military man for that matter. There will be no secret messages sent by any such go-between as I suspect there has been already."

Taking Patrice and Lettice by the hand, Countess Trevelyn barely nodded to the Duke in farewell, and Lettice could but hurry silently behind her mother, not daring to glance back at Richard.

Lettice could tell that Patrice felt the humiliation of being caught in the midst of a clandestine tryst quite keenly as they waited for their carriage to be brought round. A footman was sent to summon Aurora who, upon arriving, was totally astounded to hear the details concerning their sudden departure.

Ascending into the carriage when it came at last, the Countess's expression was one of immense irritation, Patrice was red-faced and sniffing, while Lettice's and Aurora's appearance could best be described as dissatisfied. There was a distinct feeling of business unfinished as the carriage rattled away, and Lettice for one was sure that matters were still unresolved for all of them.

$\approx$ CHAPTER 6

PULLING the lace-edged curtains farther apart so that she might better observe Patrice and Stuart in the garden making their good-byes, Lettice could faintly hear the Countess out in the front of the house, marshaling the servants in loading the trunks onto the carriages.

"I still do not see why Mama insisted that Patrice leave on the same day that she and Papa are to depart for France," Aurora sighed as she hurried into the sitting room to join Lettice. Picking up several small knick-knacks as she scooped up the last stray bandboxes with one hand, Aurora sighed loudly to no one in particular. "The woman has no consideration, that is

166

what!" Turning to Lettice who had not responded to Aurora's comment, she added vehemently, "And Mama is not the only person without any consideration, either. You could at least say something to me instead of looking out the window as if I did not exist."

Turning from her observation, Lettice apologized, "I am sorry, I was lost in thought. My mind has not been one moment calm since Mama decided to send Patrice away."

"Nor mine," Aurora agreed, plopping down, packages and all, into a comfortable chair. "Between that worry and thinking of a certain gentleman who has not once contacted me in the last week, I feel I shall go mad indeed." This confession came as no surprise to her older sister who had daily seen Aurora waiting hopefully for some missive from Lord Melburry. This she had observed so frequently because she herself had hoped for a like message from the Duke.

"We each of us have our own problems and diversions," Lettice said with a sympathetic smile. She was privy, of course, to the details of Aurora's attachment to Peregrine Melburry and could feel a closeness in feelings with her.

Abandoning the packages altogether and ignoring the distant cries of the Countess for her to hurry along, Aurora looked out the window which Lettice had quit and could see that Lord Ringwood was finding it difficult to part company with Patrice. He was shuffling a foot as he stood beside a tree and gazed at Patrice who was dressed in a traveling cloak in preparation to leave.

"Poor Stuart!" Aurora exclaimed, hating to see her friend so appalled. "If only he could let Patrice know of his feelings."

"No doubt he has tried in his way, but you know Stuart. He would misstate his own name if required to announce himself," Lettice declared somewhat ruefully, a little embarrassed herself by Lord Ringwood's verbal ineptitude. As Aurora sighed yet again, she and Lettice picked up the remainder of the packages and hurried off to appease their mother whose voice had been raised to new heights in her attempts to coerce her daughters into making an appearance.

167

In the garden, Stuart doubted that he could continue to think of adequate small conversation much longer, though he very much wished that he could remain with Patrice. Once again, as if he would never tire of the occupation, Lord Ringwood gazed at the young girl seated on the stone bench beside him.

Dressed in a black traveling cloak, Patrice's blond hair shone brightly against the fabric as she sat and listened to Stuart's chatter with a small, pathetic smile. She knew that Stuart was attempting to keep her spirits up and she was grateful for his efforts if nothing else. She considered him to be a good friend and was even somewhat consoled by what he was saying.

"The country can be jolly good fun, you know," Stuart said as he gesticulated broadly with his knobby hands. He tried to inject some enthusiasm into his speech. "All that fresh air and the routs and hunts. And you will be with your grandmother whom I know you like."

"But she will be the only person with whom I will be familiar," Patrice interrupted, but Stuart went on gamely.

" 'T'won't matter a whit. You are sure to make an impression on the fellows there. I mean, stands to reason that a dozen or so are going to flock about you in no time at all," he assured Patrice more heartily than he felt. Though he had no doubts as to the veracity of this statement, he wished with all his heart that it would not be so.

"I do not care much for many beaus, and well you know it, Stuart," Patrice commented wistfully.

"Don't see why not. It always does a young lady well to have a lot of admirers. I have it on the highest authority that it is so, too. Ma sisters were forever saying so," Stuart countered vigorously. Then, hesitating only slightly, he joked nervously, "You have me in your group of admirers, for what it's worth. Can't say as it would be very prestigious, however."

If there were ever a more veiled and vague declaration of adoration, Lord Ringwood did not know it, and he wished he could slink away as Patrice seemed oblivious to his intent.

"But you shall not be there to impress anyone,

168

Stuart. I will be quite alone and miserable," Patrice responded not a little bitterly at her fate. To go from the expectation of becoming Basil's bride to that of communing with cows was lowering indeed. Then, to be utterly alone with only an aging grandmother, no matter how kind, for company! It was all too discouraging.

Stuart was beside himself in misery as he could tell that Patrice was more distressed now than when he had come out to try and console her. Sniffing unobtrusively into her kerchief, Patrice was near tears. Suddenly an idea occurred to him and with a deep breath he plunged into a convoluted explanation of how he happened to have a friend who lived near to Patrice's grandmother who had been requesting his presence for some time.

Utterly bewildered, Patrice halted his rambling explanation with one delicate hand raised. "Stuart, what are you trying to say?"

"Why, I have a fancy to rusticate. I suppose what I am saying is that you will have ma company at least while you are in 'exile'," Stuart said in his ungainly manner.

Patrice looked at him oddly, but did not speak for a time until Stuart began to feel quite out of place. Her gaze was so intense that he could not tell what she thought, nor look her directly in the eyes, so he stared at the ground.

After a moment, Patrice spoke. "You would do that for me?" she asked in amazement at such a show of affection on Lord Ringwood's part. Then, overwhelmed by his gesture, she rose and placed her arms about the astonished young lord, hugging him briefly.

"By Jove!" Lord Ringwood exclaimed involuntarily, his face starting to redden, much to his dismay. "It's time you were going in. No doubt the Countess will be mad as blazes that you haven't left yet," Stuart said quickly, nearly tripping over his own feet as he led the way back to the house.

Patrice followed behind, a thoughtful look on her countenance as she considered how odd it was she had never before noticed what a broad set of shoulders her dear friend had developed.

She was still contemplating this as she allowed

Stuart to assist her into her waiting carriage, loaded to the utmost with Patrice's wardrobe. As Stuart handed her up, she was surprised to feel as though there was really nothing so horrible about going to the country after all, and she actually smiled and waved as the coach left so that Lettice turned in puzzlement to Lord Ringwood who stood beside her, a strangely blissful appearance to him.

Suddenly there was a flurry of servants pouring out of the house to make their last farewells to the Earl and his wife, lining up in their starch whites and livery. The Earl came out, his wife on his arm, and made last-moment orders to the various servants. The Countess left the Earl's side a moment to talk privately to Lettice and Aurora while her husband, spying Lord Ringwood, motioned the young man to come forward.

"Your lordship," Stuart nodded.

"Lord Ringwood, I have a particular favor to ask of you, presuming on your friendship for my daughters," the Earl remarked, moving a little closer with an air of secrecy. Stuart was surprised and not a little nervous over such a request, but allowed the Earl of Trevelyn to continue.

"As you know, the Countess and I shall be away for some time, and our lovely daughters are, in a sense, our most valuable treasures. Lettice and Aurora I have little worry over, but Patrice. Things have gone badly between her mother and her. I would ask you to watch over Patrice while we are away, protect her from harm. I would not ask but for the fact that I feel you are to be trusted with her safety. Will you do this?" the Earl asked. The lines of worry he bore looked peculiar on him, and it was only then that Stuart realized how much he did love his daughter.

"As a matter of fact, I had a fancy to rusticate, and Patrice was already counting on me to bear her company," Lord Ringwood replied softly.

"Excellent, excellent," the Earl declared, turning to see if the Countess was ready to leave. "I am sure that you will be able to protect Patrice from any folly she might contemplate."

The Countess appeared to be finished with whatever motherly duties she had felt obligated to make, and returned to her husband's side, her daughters following to give their father a hug and a peck on the cheek. Arrangements, the Earl told them, had already been made for the two sisters to stay with their aunt, and as he kissed each one of his daughters, he advised, "Mind you stay out of mischief, the both of you. It is extremely bad to drive one's parents mad, doubly so if it should occur on foreign soil, and it shall be if we get word of any scrapes." With that, the Earl chucked them affectionately under the chin and slipped to each of his daughters a small satin bag, each filled with pin money, not knowing or caring that the Countess had done much the same, and departed with true regret.

Both Lettice and Aurora felt more than a twinge of sadness as they watched their parents leave, especially when there still existed such bad feelings between the Countess and Patrice. The Earl had made his peace with Patrice the evening before, and though he did not like what she had done, he had forgiven her completely. The Countess on the other hand had not yet given Patrice any sign that she had changed her attitude. Though both Aurora and Lettice knew in their hearts that their mother did not enjoy such a punitive role as she played, there seemed a need to discipline Patrice for her own good.

Suddenly, as if recalling his presence, Lettice turned to Stuart who was preparing to leave.

"Stuart, what did you do that put Patrice in such good humors?" she asked curiously.

"Do?" Stuart responded evasively, "Naught that I can think of." Hurrying over to his gig to make sure all was secure, he sprang lightly, almost jauntily, into the seat.

"And where are you off to in such a hurry?" Aurora added as she followed him. She was not one to be denied an explanation from one so easily persuaded as Lord Ringwood. Nevertheless, she went without a satisfactory answer on this occasion.

"Must be leaving. Visiting friends, you know," he offered over his shoulder as he departed, not even recalling to take leave properly.

"Will wonders never cease? Here I might have expected Stuart to be downtrodden at the thought of Patrice leaving and he goes off as easy as you please looking none the worse. I cannot comprehend it in the least," Aurora declared, throwing up her hands as if to abdicate further responsibility for his strange behavior.

Turning to go back into the house, Lettice sighed. "I don't feel in the mood to attempt to plumb the depths of Stuart's bizarre behavior. I have had quite enough problems for the time being without taking on that task. At least we have heard the last of that Torquill fellow. What an utter cad he was, to leave Patrice in the lurch," Lettice said scornfully. The expression of distaste on her face reminded Aurora of sucking on lemons.

"Patrice is better off in the country. She will more easily get over that man there and I am sure with reflection she will realize that it is all impossible," Aurora said, knowing all the while that she herself would never react in the manner she had just described, but believing with conviction that Patrice was cast in a different mold than her own unyielding disposition.

"Well, I daresay Stuart is relieved that the lieutenant is out of the way now, poor dear," Lettice continued, shrugging off the feeling that something was amiss.

"Yes, and I must say that so am I," Aurora added with unaffected pleasure at the thought that there would no longer be any intrusions from that most disagreeable individual.

With that, the sisters parted at their doors to finish packing, consciously absorbing themselves in the endeavor so as to forget that neither of them had heard from either the Duke or his brother Peregrine.

Some miles off, Patrice sat on the soft leather seat in her carriage and also attempted to cease thought, but try as she might, she continued to recall Basil Torquill's face when she had seen him last, vowing with an intense gleam in his eyes that they would be wed, that it was meant to be so and that his very nature demanded that it would happen.

She shuddered a bit as she thought of how she had received no message at all, not that she could have with Mama watching everyone like a hawk, but there had not been the slightest attempt. Pulling her heavy cloak more closely about her, Patrice was giving herself up to despair. Not even the comforting thought of Lord Ringwood's presence in the country could console her as she thought of an opportunity lost to her. She would not now have a runaway marriage with all the romantic trappings she had so often dreamt of and read in the novels she had secreted away from her disapproving family.

Shifting a bit in the seat, Patrice heard something fall softly to floor of the coach beside her warmly wrapped feet. Bending over, she was astonished to find a sealed letter.

Perhaps it is from Mama, she thought brightly, hoping that her mother had decided to forgive her after all. Tearing it open, she eagerly read the words and was struck still by what she saw.

My wife, for so I will always consider you. It takes only the act to complete what I know must be. I will come to you in three weeks' time, so long for they must not suspect, and then it's off to Gretna Green. You will meet me at the parish church on the third at sunset.

Basil

For a second, Patrice could not think, her senses refusing to respond, and then her first thought was, It is settled. He wants me to come to him on the third. The feeling of finality somehow sat uneasily with Patrice who knew by all rights that she should be totally elated.

"Well, we have beaten them all," she declared to herself in the empty carriage. Then with a hand that moved unnaturally to the act, she located, secreted in her traveling gown, the ring which Lieutenant Torquill had given to her, so austere even in its intricate design. The geometrical shapes which decorated it were hardly soft and rounded. "A token of our love, you said," Patrice murmured as she held it in her hands. Then, because she somehow felt she should, she kissed the ring and thrust it back into its hiding place, deep within the folds of her traveling gown. Settling back, she could not even begin to plan on what she would do to prepare for the flight. "But I have time yet," she told herself. The thought was comforting, for her mind was in a whirl, and she wished to be clear of head when she walked before the vicar as a bride.

"A bride," she murmured as she closed her suddenly weary eyes. "I shall be married." The smile was brief as Patrice attempted to rest.

In London, on Bond Street at one of the more fashionable jewelers, the smile on the face of the owner of the establishment lasted much longer than a few seconds. Some would find it appropriate, though no doubt Lettice would have described it as nauseatingly ingratiating. Mr. Clark, too, was thinking of marriages, and of how very profitable they were when prospective grooms were forever purchasing small tokens for their blushing brides. On this occasion, one indulgent fiancé had ordered quite an extravagant little pendant, expensive even by normal standards, for his beloved.

Standing before the purchaser, Mr. Clark watched as the gentleman inspected the heart-shaped bauble of blood-red rubies set in white gold.

"Is it to your specifications?" Mr. Clark asked nervously, as the gentleman had not spoken for some time.

"Yes, it is," the man replied at last. "Have you engraved the words I ordered?" he demanded.

Mr. Clark was taken aback by the sharpness of the gentleman's speech and hurriedly burbled, "Only look at the back and see," indicating that all had been done as the gentleman had asked.

Turning the pendant in his hands, Killingham read through narrowed eyes the inscription: "To my bride, Aurora. No one can ever part us. Giles."

"Excellent," Lord Killingham said with satisfaction, placing the necklace in his pocket as he informed the jeweler to put it on his bill.

Bowing quite low, Mr. Clark was all willingness to do as he was told. He reflected as Lord Killingham left that perhaps there would be more purchases once his lordship was wed, for wives were forever wanting this and that for a party. Rubbing his hands together, Mr. Clark continued with his business. He did not see Killingham as he paused outside the shop to look once again at the large jeweled heart, so vivid against his slightly yellowed skin. Reading the inscription, the lord suddenly clenched it in his fist as if he would crush it. "No one," he hissed, "especially not another Melburry." Thrusting his hand into his pocket, Killingham stalked away, face as grim as murder as he walked through the streets.

Lord Killingham was not the only individual to acquire a new bauble that day as Marquess Wainfleet soon discovered upon reaching for his snuff box. Finding it missing, Wainfleet swore mightily with near-apoplectic rage.

"That . . . that little ruffian has stolen my snuff box!" he bellowed furiously, disregarding entirely that he was within the hallowed confines of White's. "A bump into me and then gone, the rascal!" he continued to howl, recalling the small urchin who had so inconvenienced him in the street earlier.

Francis Trent ignored this gentleman's ravings as he daintily spooned himself up some lukewarm kidneys, left over from the morning's breakfast selections which the club so conveniently made available to its members.

"When I get my hands on that little dog, I shall wring his neck for him!" Wainfleet continued, making appropriate clenching motions with his hands as if to demonstrate more visually his intent, should the young reprobate ever come within his powers.

"I shouldn't think you would care," Sir Francis commented at last, popping a tender if greasy morsel into his mouth. "You don't use snuff, as I recall it. What you were doing with a snuff box I can't imagine, can you Simmons?" Sir Francis asked, turning toward his other companion.

Lord Simmons appeared to give the matter some thought and then with a laconic smile replied, "Perhaps you intended to store your bile pills in them for you seem to have a deal of it and logically must needs medicate your ills away, Marquess Wainfleet."

This remark caused Sir Francis to titter, holding an immaculate square of lawn to his lips, lest his sputterings soil his cravat with grease. Marquess Wainfleet was far from amused as might be expected, and appeared exasperated by all this ill-usage.

"That is quite uncalled for," Wainfleet said with stiff-lipped anger. "That snuff box, if you must know, was meant as a gift for a friend. As much as I abhor the practice, he is much addicted to it."

"You can always get another," was Sir Francis' flippant reply as he peered about the sideboard for something further to consume, rather like a bird of prey about to stoop.

"Francis is correct," Simmons agreed, and Sir Francis' eyes popped with surprise. It was not often that his arch rival in fashion agreed with him on any matter. "It is bad luck you were robbed," Simmons continued with a philosophical tone which he knew would irritate Wainfleet no end, "but there must be something else bothering you for you to carry on so. I wonder what it could be?"

If Wainfleet heard the speculative tone in Lord Simmons' voice, he did not wish to gratify his curiosity. Sir Francis, however, would not allow the subject to drop as he had gotten wind of Simmons' implication. It was not very remarkable a feat on his part as all of the town was agog with the gossip. Everyone knew that Wainfleet had been totally cut out by Lord Melbury for the attentions and no doubt for the affections of Lady Aurora Trevelyn. It was no secret either that Wainfleet was mad as blazes about it and a very bad loser as well.

"I will warrant that Marquess Wainfleet has had other losses of a more 'personal' nature than he cares to speak of. If Lady Aurora were less of a beauty or more susceptible to that pap you imagine to be witty conversation, I should think that then you would have stood a chance of besting Peregrine," Sir Francis said with a visible smirk of glee.

"There was not so long ago a time when you, too, vied for the lady's attentions," Wainfleet snapped waspishly, harried beyond endurance as he saw that Peregrine Melbury had just entered the club and had spotted his friends standing in the corner.

"Your information on the subject is a bit stale," Lord Simmons interjected, well aware of Peregrine's approach but continuing nothing loath. "Francis has been fascinated by the charms of the widow Carsden for some weeks now and is no longer a contender upon that fair field of Trevelyn."

At this, Sir Francis was at last able to tear his attention from his platter of kidneys to note Lord Melburry's arrival. "Peregrine! So you have returned to the fold at last."

"I hadn't been aware I had left it," Peregrine replied, smiling. Turning to Lord Simmons he smiled more broadly for he liked the gentleman. "And did you think I had made off and away from the city too, Simmons?"

"Hardly. I am not such a one to suppose that you would long be away from Lady Aurora's side," Lord Simmons answered, gesturing languidly to the bottles of wine which were laid out. Lord Melburry declined the offer of refreshments.

"I can only stay a moment. I have business elsewhere. I have been very busy with our lawyer this past week and that is why you haven't seen me about."

"But we will be seeing you, no doubt. There are a great many people waiting on your call," Simmons remarked, remembering that Aurora had made mention of not having heard from Peregrine in some time.

"Oh, you shall see him," Sir Francis interrupted, waving his napkin like a banner before him. "That is, if you are going to the Cyprian ball as you did last year. Peregrine and I are going together." Turning his eyes upon Wainfleet, Trent added with wicked intent, "Perhaps you would like to come too? You could use a diversion to take your mind off your losses."

Wainfleet did not reply to this volley and turned on his heel and left.

"Rude fellow," Sir Francis quipped, not really caring and glad to be able to consume his meal in peace at last.

Lord Simmons and Peregrine moved a little way off together as they had no desire to join Sir Francis in his gastronomic throes.

"Well, will you really be going, and with such poor company as Francis?" Simmons inquired, a little disbelieving. He himself had often been involved at the Cyprian balls, the event which had become something of an institution. He had attended many of these masquerades, enjoying in his turn the charms of the various courtesans, both famous and infamous, who attended them as well, but oddly enough, he could not stomach the thought of Aurora's loving Lord Melburry an' he not be as pure as she must picture him to be. The thought sat uneasily on his mind as Peregrine replied to his inquiry.

"Yes, I shall be going, and only with Francis because his gig has broken down quite inconveniently," Peregrine answered absently, his mind elsewhere. His preoccupation was obvious, and Lord Simmons guessed that Peregrine had come to the club for some peace and quiet, a commodity at a minimum at his home since his brother was known to be redecorating at a furious pace, carpenters and *drapiers* having come in and out in a constant stream for this past week.

"I must be leaving now," Simmons said after a few moments of silence, aware that Peregrine wished to be alone. Lord Melburry did not protest and Simmons took his leave quickly, leaving White's at a jaunty pace as he drove his tilbury along the street. If he hurried he would be on time for his appointment with Lady Aurora.

As he drove his pair, Lord Simmons was in something of a quandary. He was not a prude at heart and his was hardly a spotless record, yet he was aspiring in his own unobtrusive manner for the affections of Lady Trevelyn, just as Lord Melburry and Marquess Wainfleet were. But, he reflected, Aurora was well aware of his feelings. She had known of his past for he had been quite open about his vices under the auspices of their friendship. She was, he was sure, quite unaware of Peregrine's associations with the demimonde.

Now the difficulties and problems. Should he tell her? Well aware that such a revelation might ruin Lord Melburry's suit in her eyes, Lord Simmons had half an urge to tell her for that reason alone, but more importantly to him, he did not ever wish to see Aurora hurt. He would, in all probability, die a thousand times over if he were to see her day after day in an unhappy marriage. Though he did not make a spectacle of himself as Wainfleet did, wearing his heart on his sleeve, this did not mean he did not have a true and serious passion. Oh, he reflected, he would be urbane to the end. She would never know to what extent he cared for her, for he knew she did not love him in that manner. But should he approach her on the subject of Lord Melbury? Now would be the perfect opportunity, when she had reason to feel his neglect of her. Simmons just did not know, so he continued on his way, undecided.

Lettice and Aurora were by now firmly established in their Aunt Amelia's townhouse, having been welcomed with a warmth that was not surprising considering that good woman's unhappily childless state. Fortunately, at the ripe and glorious age of forty-three, Lady Amelia Braden had little else in her life to rue for hers had always been a love match and so it had remained. Her husband, Lord Alton Braden, was as attentive as he had been from the first moment he had become enthralled with the young beauty that had been Amelia during her first season.

Watching her aunt as she poured tea, Lettice could still see much of that incredible beauty that had won Lord Braden's heart. As she witnessed the tenderly familiar gestures and glances that this long-married couple bestowed on one another during tea, Lettice grew not a little envious.

Shall I ever be so loved? she wondered, and the recollection that the Duke had not called upon her since she had moved caused her to feel more melancholy than ever.

Turning to her favorite niece who sat so silent, Lady Amelia could not know that her obvious happiness was particularly painful for Lettice to witness. "We are quite happy that both you and Aurora have decided to stay with us while your parents are abroad," she said, white hands with tapering fingers gesturing so gracefully and grasping Lettice's with such warmth that one could hardly misbelieve her words. "We are only sorry that Patrice could not join us. Are we not, Alton?" she added as she reached across the small space separating her from her beloved, and took his hand.

Lord Braden agreed heartily with his wife for he was

particularly fond of both Patrice and Aurora. "I am selfish enough to wish that Patrice could be added to this happy party," he admitted with a charming smile. "But where is Aurora?" he asked with concern. "As I recall it, Aurora used to enjoy her tea quite a bit and here she is not present."

"She is still up in her room preparing to leave with Lord Simmons. They are to attend a dog exhibition this afternoon. It was Aurora's particular request as she is so fond of the tiny creatures and Lord Simmons could not, of course, disappoint her," Lettice explained with a slight smile.

Lady and Lord Braden smiled in return for they well recalled the irresistible charm which Aurora possessed when she chose to make use of it. "She is not a lady to be denied easily," Amelia observed, a twinkle in her eyes.

"And Lord Simmons is of a yielding disposition when it comes to the fairer sex," her husband added knowingly as he sat back comfortably with his saucer and cup in hand.

"You know Lord Simmons well?" Lettice inquired, unaware that any other member of the family was familiar with any of their male friends.

"We frequent the same club," her uncle replied with a shrug of his shoulders. "I suppose that means we are acquainted but not, how would you say it, 'bosom beaus'. I have seen him quite often in the company of Lord Ringwood whom I perceive as having a passion for our Patrice an' I not mistaken it. Lately he has also kept company with the newly returned Duke of Melburry and his brother, Peregrine."

Lord Braden was in the middle of sipping his tea, else he might have noted the new attentiveness with which Lettice now favored him. She scrutinized him intensely as she asked, "Do you know the Duke of Melburry very well, Uncle?"

"Not any more than Lord Simmons, I fear," Lord Braden replied, finishing the last enjoyable drops of his tea and rising as though thoroughly refreshed. "I fear I must go now, much as I wish to stay and chat with you. I have an appointment at the club."

Lady Braden also rose and extended her hand to her husband who looked, to Lettice, to be regretting his need to depart all the more. Taking his wife's hand, Lord Braden kissed it gently. "Never fear that I shall be late for dinner," his lordship said as he was walked to the door of the room by Amelia Braden. "I know how you detest tardiness, my love," he teased.

With that he was gone, and Lettice was left with the tangible impression that the little scene that she had witnessed was a far more restrained version of how Lord and Lady Braden usually parted company, even for the smallest fraction of time.

Returning to the couch, Amelia Braden patted the vacated seat beside her, inviting Lettice for a comfortable tête-à-tête, should she be desirous of one. Lady Braden was sure that her niece would wish to have one at that, for she had not missed Lettice's unusual interest in the subject of the Duke of Melburry. "Much as I shall miss Alton, this does give us a few moments alone with one another," Amelia said as Lettice took her place beside her aunt. "I have not been to see you in ages, I'm afraid. You have changed since last I saw you. You are quite the woman now."

"But you are still the same, still as lovely as ever and still so very attached to Uncle Alton. It is a pleasure to see you together," Lettice said, looking down into the fabric in her lap.

"Yes, some things do not change, fortunately. How is your Mama?"

"Mama is Mama. I do not know how else to explain it," Lettice answered. "She has gone off without us to France as is her wont. She and my father still dote on one another, but it is a little different than what you and Uncle have."

"It always was," Amelia replied matter-of-factly. "But tell me about you, now. I haven't seen you in so long I hardly knew you when you walked in the door with Aurora."

"It is difficult to tell what is different now," Lettice laughed. "I have gotten even taller, yes taller, and the mamas always take the opportunities to tell me of it as if I were not already aware of it."

"You are more imposing in height, that is true, but that can be an advantage," Amelia encouraged. "You are more readily noticeable and you are certainly not too tall."

"I sincerely hope not, for I do wish to be attractive enough to get by without being labeled a 'creature'," Lettice admitted lightly, and Amelia knew that there was more concern than was expressed in her niece's voice.

"There was a time you did not care," Amelia said. "Have there been new developments, then? Have you formed a tendre at last?" Lettice's reluctance caused Amelia to wheedle in her most persuasive manner, for she so enjoyed being privy to her niece's confidences. "Tell me, do, for you know how I long to hear these things. Is it perhaps the Duke of Melburry?" At the astonished look on Lettice's face, Amelia raised her hands to her lips as she burst out laughing. "Did you think I could not see it? I have known you a long time, all your life, in fact."

"Well, I had hoped I was not that obvious."

"And you are not. But I was paying close attention," Lady Braden pointed out. "If you have formed an attachment for the Duke of Melburry, then I see your taste has become quite outspoken as you have grown."

"Then you like him?" Lettice asked, her question more a plea.

"Do you need to hear that I do?" Amelia asked, puzzled. "I would have thought it would not matter a whit."

"Until recently, I would not have thought I should care for others' opinions, but there are special circumstances. I hardly know him, and find it difficult to decide what to do," Lettice replied. "I need your help, Aunt."

Lettice could see that her aunt was deeply touched. "You have asked your mother? No, don't tell me. It doesn't matter," Amelia said, glad that her niece had asked for her help, no matter if she was one of many. She paused to think, then nodding her head slowly she answered. "Yes, I do like the Duke. I have always thought of him as a good-natured if a bit rambunctious individual. He never slighted a plain girl presented to

182

him for a country dance, always brought out the best in everyone. At least that is what I recall of him before he left for France." Her aunt hesitated at that. "You know of the scandal, of course?"

Lettice nodded. "I know of it only a very little from Mama."

"It was a long time ago, and I am sure that no one but the Duke and perhaps his brother know the truth of the matter," Lady Braden sighed.

"Mama said that Lady Killingham killed herself because the Duke left the country. Is that true?" Lettice asked, half not wishing to hear.

"She killed herself, that is true, but I do not know if it was because the Duke left the country. You cannot know what is in another person's mind all of the time. Do you love him, Lettice?" Amelia watched her niece closely, seeing the struggle on her face.

"I believe that I might," Lettice said, anguished. She looked away from Amelia. "But would he be suitable for me? Would he be faithful? Constancy means a great deal to me. How could I love a man who would be so craven as to run from the country at the threat of further scandal?"

"Is that why you think he left?"

"I can think of no other reason."

"But you don't wish to think it."

"I do not."

"And what has the Duke said of the matter?"

"That is just it, he has said nothing, though I know that he grows more involved with my life as each day passes. I have not heard from him in a week and I do not know why," Lettice said, the sadness in her voice only a small indication of the depth of her feelings.

"Was it perhaps a flirtation, then?" Amelia asked. She did not wish to hurt her niece's feelings, but neither did she wish to ignore all the possibilities.

"It did not seem like one. And if he comes back to me, and his intentions are honorable, what shall I say?" Lettice asked, unable to decide the thing herself. This was quite a novelty in itself, for one who had always had the most definite opinions on every matter.

"I ask you again, do you love the Duke?"

Lettice was silent as she weighed and judged her

feelings, her love fighting with suspicion. "I fear that I do love him, God help me," she said at last, looking desperately into her aunt's eyes for guidance. "Is it wrong?"

"To love him?" Amelia asked, astonished. "How could that be wrong?"

"Mama would not say he was not the thing, but I feel she thinks of his title and money."

"It is not that important that the gentleman be 'suitable' in my opinion. It is my opinion you ask?" Amelia queried. Lettice nodded and she continued, "You must have love; it is the most important thing. Only think of life without it. It would not do for one so passionate as I know you to be, Lettice."

"Love, Mama has said, is not everything."

"Yet your Mama loves her husband," Amelia pointed out. "Many things can be endured if there is love."

Lettice could not look at her aunt at these words for she was certain that she referred to her childless state which would have been difficult indeed had hers been a marriage of convenience only.

"Then it is still up to me. This is what you are saying of course." Lettice was sure that her aunt would be honest with her.

"It always was up to you. But should the Duke return, he must be the one to tell you everything that has happened. Only then can you make a decision. My only advice is to hear what he has to say first before deciding."

Lady Braden took Lettice's hand in hers, comforting the young lady. "And don't look so glum. I am sure there is a good explanation for why he has not seen you this past week. Perhaps he, too, needs time to reflect."

Lettice found some sense in what her aunt said, but it did little to ease the ache in her heart.

It might have consoled Lettice somewhat, had she been aware that Richard was also suffering, even if he did not admit this fact to himself. Standing in the hallway of his London townhouse—a steady stream of workmen weaving in and out of the rooms like worker

184

ants—Richard had immersed himself in the redecoration of his home in an effort to ease his longing to see Lettice—without success. Try as he might to block the persistent pressure he felt about his heart, he could not. His misery was increased as he was besieged with the various workmen all wishing for specific instructions at the same moment. Of course, this was at his own request as he wished for the metamorphosis to be all a new bride could possibly desire, but it was draining nonetheless.

"Your Grace, the furniture for the dining room has arrived. Shall we unload the things? Where shall we put them while the room is being cleaned?" one man asked as he shuffled his feet before the Duke of Melburry, hat in hand. Another wished to inquire as to the colors to be used for the master bedroom, another asking about the library shelves.

Just as it seemed that he was to have no peace, Richard observed his brother descending the stairs.

"Peregrine," he called out, motioning for his sibling to come to him. "I need you to direct these two gentlemen to where we will store the furniture until we are ready for it," Richard said, indicating the men before him. Peregrine, obliging though he generally was, seemed reluctant, but gave way, leading the men off as the Duke dealt with the remainder in turn. Peregrine returned to Richard's side as the last of the men were dismissed to attend to their work, and he turned to his brother a little reproachfully.

"It is about time you lent a hand, you know, Peregrine. There has been little enough evidence of your presence in the last few days. I perceive you are about to leave even now," the Duke commented, eyeing his brother's apparel with an experienced eye.

Peregrine was aware that his rather flash outfit of canary and white did not meet with his sibling's approval, but grinned in any case.

"I realize this ensemble is not to your tastes, Richard, but I assure you, it is the latest thing."

"I daresay," the Duke replied doubtfully, "but where are you off to in it?"

The question was not unexpected and Peregrine studiously avoided answering as he excused himself.

"Can't stay to chat now, Richard, must be off," he re-marked as he headed toward the open door.

"To see Lady Aurora Trevelyn, perhaps?" Richard inquired. His guess, though incorrect, effectively halted Peregrine in his paces.

"I have not had that pleasure in some days now. I can tell you that the lack of her company has been a sore loss to me." Peregrine's face as he spoke was indeed a picture of longing, but also of determination which Richard could not fathom.

"Well, I am off," Peregrine said briskly. "Off to the lawyers if you must know. Personal matter." With that, he was gone.

Richard paused at the threshold, watching his brother drive off. Of course, Peregrine knew he was preparing the house for Lettice, even though nothing was certain about even an engagement. In fact, Richard had several times thought of going back to France to live, and leaving all his entanglements behind, but he had not even required any comment from Peregrine to realize that it was not what he truly wanted. With a sigh, the Duke turned back into the house. There was still a great deal to do and Richard hoped that it was not all in vain.

Peregrine, hurrying along now as he was late due to the delay, was more certain of the outcome of his own endeavors than the Duke, at least he prided himself that he was. The delays were particularly annoying now that Richard was beginning to despair. He had met so frequently with the family lawyer that he could have aroused suspicion in Richard, had he not been so preoccupied with the house; but now it was almost over and soon Peregrine would be able to turn his mind to other matters.

His only regret in truth was that he had not been able to do as his heart demanded in seeing Lady Aurora. It had been a fight from the start to keep from going to her, being with her. Peregrine knew himself better than anyone else could, and he was well aware that once his passionate nature overcame his sense of duty, there would be no concentrating on what had to be done to guarantee Richard's exoneration. He could not success-fully do both at once, of that he was sure, so it had been necessary to deny himself. At times he had felt he was refusing himself his life's blood in such a banishment, but he had known enough to do it regardless.

And there was no denying that things were getting out of hand for Richard. The time for action was near. Only yesterday a close associate of Peregrine's had heard Killingham refer to Richard as a blot on the family name. If things continued in that fashion, there would in all likelihood be a duel. If it was not initiated by the Duke, then by the increasingly irrational Killingham. Peregrine had even heard from Francis Trent that Lord Killingham had taken to whispering to himself when believing himself alone in a room. Sir Francis had been astonished as he had heard the one-sided conversation just before entering the empty billiards room at White's. "Empty, that is, save for Lord Killingham and his phantom friend."

Peregrine felt foreboding as he drove on. "Well," he murmured, "soon we shall take care of you, sir, an' I have my way."

Urging his horses on, Peregrine continued to concentrate on his problem with Killingham, unaware that he might have more to do with Giles Killingham than Richard's entanglement with that gentleman. So busy was Peregrine that he could not suspect that Lord Killingham was ardently pursuing the same lady, even after her rejection of him at the auction; or that Killingham, so much enamored, had decided that his marriage to Aurora was a certainty, deluding himself into believing there was a reciprocal feeling on Aurora's part.

Lord Killingham had no doubt that Lady Aurora was playing a coy game with him as he ascended the steps to the Braden home. He had discovered where Aurora was staying from one of the servants who had remained at the Trevelyn home to close it. It was with narrowed eyes that he observed Lord Simmons' vehicle at the front of the house and his irritation rose as the doors to the house opened. He was halfway up the stairs as Aurora descended on the arm of Lord Simmons. He halted, barring their way momentarily.

"Lord Killingham," Simmons nodded his head in a faint acknowledgment of the man's presence. Before

Killingham could speak, Lord Simmons continued, aware of Aurora's tense body beside him and her almost visible revulsion for the man before her. "You have come, no doubt, to visit. Pity that we will not be able to stay and chat with you, but do go on in. Both Lady Lettice and Lady Braden are at home and would like nothing better than your company, I am sure." A swift touch to the brim of his top hat and Lord Simmons made his way down the steps just ahead of Aurora, clearing an unresistible path for her to pass Killingham and shielding her bodily on one side. Aurora did not even attempt to acknowledge the man, and it was her right not to, as she chose. She did not look back at him, but Lord Simmons did, gratified to see Giles Killingham was speechless as well as motionless before the threshold of the manor.

He did not go in, abandoning his plans and leaving quickly. There would be other opportunities, he thought. Eventually he would break through her little game. And he would deal with Simmons another day.

Taking his place beside Aurora in his curricle, Lord Simmons was aware of the animosity he had aroused. He was not one to put Lord Killingham's hatred off lightly, but as Aurora placed a grateful hand upon his, Lord Simmons felt not the slightest regret.

Aurora felt that it was unnecessary to say anything to Lord Simmons. He was very knowing, and she was sure he knew of her dislike for Lord Killingham enough that she need not express her thanks in words. Leaning back in her seat, Aurora attempted to put her mind in a more favorable attitude. She had not begun the day well, thinking of Peregrine Melburry all morning. She had alternated loathing him altogether for his dreadful treatment of her, and finding herself totally in love with him. This did nothing to insure her good nature for the afternoon's entertainment which she had been looking forward to for some time. It was just another little thing to heap blame upon Lord Melburry for: If not for him, she would be quite ecstatic riding to the exhibit.

Lord Simmons knew of her mood, and of how it could change if given the uninterrupted chance to do so, and was quiet as he drove. His silence was well rewarded as Aurora began to chat about the exhibit, and did he think there would be a good representation of canines?

They chatted amiably, and frivolously, the time soon passing. When they arrived at the exhibition, they found themselves immersed in the innumerable barkings and yowlings of what seemed to be countless dogs, penned up in groupings of breeds all about them. Lord Simmons could see instantly that Aurora was enchanted as they walked about the large area where the creatures were being shown. Many of the owners did not wish strangers to handle their animals, warning of the possibility of bites. However, Aurora worked her usual magic, and even the largest dog there, a bull mastiff of incredible dimensions, came gently under her hands. This caused no little admiration for the young lady among the canine fanciers and she seemed to cause as much of a stir as the most exotic animals there, much to Lord Simmons' pleasure and amusement.

There was almost a carnival air about the place, children darting in and out of the pens, patting a small terrier here, a large wolfhound there, a docile bulldog too old to care. After a few short hours, Lord Simmons thought to stop, and produced a small ice in a paper cone for Aurora to refresh herself. With her wide-eyed enjoyment he felt as though he were entertaining a precocious but delightful child rather than a young lady who was very downy indeed. Looking at her as she continued to observe the dogs, Simmons was once more struck with that uncontrollable despair to which he was prone whenever he reminded himself that Aurora, however pleasant and sweet she was to him, saved her affections for an undeserving wretch such as Peregrine Melburry. As he stared, unheeding of the impropriety of his gaze, Lord Simmons felt the urge to speak grow within him. She must know of Peregrine's infidelity; he would tell her. If she chose to have him all the same then she would at least have chosen with the full knowledge of what Peregrine was.

The last of Simmons' reservations were dispelled as Aurora turned to look up into his eyes. She had, with her uncanny sense, felt Lord Simmons' eyes upon her, and as she looked at him now, she was for the first time fully aware of the affection which he bore her. It was all in his eyes, so much so that Aurora could not doubt what she saw, though his sudden glance away and the mask which dropped over his face tried to belie the fact.

"Enjoying yourself?" Lord Simmons asked, leading Aurora to a more secluded spot behind some of the vacated pens where a few wooden benches provided a place to rest.

"Very much, thank you. It was good of you to bring me here today. I am thoroughly grateful to you," Aurora answered.

Her hesitancy and reserved air made Lord Simmons even more determined to speak. "You were not so happy when I first saw you this afternoon," he said, trying to find the words he needed. "I had the distinct feeling that you still were upset with Lord Melburry. Is he in your black books?"

"Where else could I place him after such neglect?" Aurora inquired. She was not sure how to reply.

"I feared you may have locked his image away in your heart. It is not unheard of with a person as faithful as yourself. Forgive me if I am intruding, but we are friends, are we not?"

"I believe we are," Aurora replied, looking at her dainty hands as she could not look into that familiar face with her newly acquired knowledge. "And perhaps you are not far wrong. Perhaps I do retain some feelings for him."

Lord Simmons sustained this blow without any sign of upset, and managed even to smile a bit. "Is that wise?" he asked in a kindly manner. "My dear, there are a few things that you do not know about Lord Melburry, even if you think you are up to every rig and row."

"And of what am I so ignorant?" Aurora countered cautiously, aware that Lord Simmons had a purpose to this little talk. "Has Peregrine done something illegal perhaps?" she laughed nervously.

"I do not want to vex you, but it is possibly far worse than a little simple smuggling or some such thing," Lord Simmons answered, the serious expression on his face quenching any light laughter to which Aurora might have resorted.

"Then let us have it in the open, Lord Simmons. I do dislike secrets when they are kept from me," Aurora said with a steady voice. She was braced for his words, but the explanation he gave for Peregrine's unsuitability caused her to blanch all the same. It was one thing to hear Lord Melburry accused by one such as Ann Snogging, a common gossip and known liar, but to hear from a trusted and honest friend that it was so was devastating.

"I cannot believe it of him. I cannot!" Aurora exclaimed, her eyes watering momentarily before she could get a hold on her emotions.

"Why can you not? Because he looks the innocent?" Simmons asked bitterly. "Dear child, his is just the sort most able to conceal such behavior. They look the veriest angels, it is true. It is also true that Peregrine attends the Cyprian ball this week. I have been there. You attend not to watch but to participate. I do not try to absolve my own past behavior, but I find it appalling that he should conceal his true nature from you." The agonies of jealousy and hurt could not be concealed, and Aurora felt torn.

"Take me home," she said tearfully. Her appearance was so distraught that Lord Simmons immediately complied with her wishes. They were silent on the ride back; a few watery sniffs were the only sounds to be heard.

Aurora would have entered the house without a word, but Lord Simmons could not let her leave without some sign that she did not hate him for the news he had given her.

"Do you forgive me?" he asked, and she looked at him with reddened eyes.

"There is naught to forgive. You have been a good friend in telling me what you believe is true. All that is left is to see if what you have said is in fact the truth."

With that, Aurora entered the house, leaving Lord Simmons to ponder these ominous words. He could not decide what she meant, and left wondering if perhaps he would have done better not to speak.

Within the house, Aurora paced her room where she had again taken refuge. It seemed to her that she was forever seeking a quiet place to face herself with facts. She was pacing the length of the small chamber like a caged animal, Aurora thought. Then, hurrying over to her clothespress, she rummaged about in wrapped parcels until she discovered the one she was searching for. Untying it quickly, she gazed at the costume which she had worn in a play she and her sisters had produced for their parents' pleasure some years ago. Lifting the soft white material that had been fashioned into a Greek toga, Aurora held it before herself, and looking into her reflection she whispered fiercely, "I will know the truth!"

CHAPTER 7

"DON'T PULL on the reins as if you were struggling to hold on," Stuart admonished gently as he attempted to loosen Patrice's death-grip on the leather lengths in her hands. At these words and the calmness with which they were said, Patrice did as she was instructed.

Taking a deep breath and allowing the air to escape slowly, Patrice found that Stuart had been correct all along, as the horses gradually fell into a steady, easy pace of their own accord. At first she was inclined to think it a fluke, that although for once she was indeed controlling a carriage and pair, the horses before her would rebel against her in her inexperience. However, as they continued for a mile, Patrice discovered that she was actually beginning to enjoy the occupation.

"Why, this is fun!" she exclaimed, turning to the young gentleman beside her with amazement. "And I never thought that I should ever be able to do it! Only think what Lettice would say an' she could see me!"

"Eyes forward," Stuart reminded her. Patrice turned back toward the road. "I hope you won't tell her that I taught you for if you should have an accident she would no doubt tear me with her teeth," Lord Ringwood chuckled. "You have only to be a bit more observant and you should do quite as well as Lettice, with practice," he continued confidently, his own surprise at Patrice's accomplishment well hidden.

The past three days had been nothing short of bliss for Stuart Ringwood as he had had Patrice's company primarily to himself. He did not, of course, allow himself to think of Patrice's lieutenant. Even if she no longer had anything to do with that gentleman, Stuart could not forget with what loving eyes she had always viewed Basil. He was also aware that she had never looked upon him so adoringly, and believed she never would. Still, he could not live without her friendship, and continued in her company. He congratulated himself that on occasion he was even able to think of her merely as a friend when not in her actual presence. Of course, he could not achieve this when he was in her company, but he sincerely believed that in time it would come as well. Patrice would not wish to make him suffer if she knew of his feelings, of that Lord Ringwood was sure, for she was a tender soul. For his own good, or for what she would undoubtedly feel was for his own good, she would banish him from her company. This thought was unendurable, so Stuart had resolved to aspire to nothing more than Patrice's friendship.

Looking at Patrice with unwavering eyes, for her own concentration on the road ahead afforded him that opportunity, Stuart found that at least for the time being, his heart, hungry though it might be, could be contented with crumbs. And as he observed Patrice's driving ability, he was struck with a thought.

"Why have you never tried to drive a pair before?" he asked curiously, glancing from the road to the driver frequently. "After all, I know both Lettice and Aurora were taught. I imagine you could have been as well, so why have you hesitated so long?"

"Lettice and Aurora were asked if they wished to

193

learn, I was not," Patrice replied quietly, her face contemplative. "Of course, I did not wish to learn," she added quickly. "Made quite a point of letting Father know that I expressly did not wish it, but they did not encourage or attempt to persuade me. Perhaps if they had, I might have reconsidered."

"Why in the world did you say you didn't wish to learn how?" Stuart exclaimed. "You can't beg non-interest, for you wished to do it when I mentioned it to you."

"Yes, but you see, I did not think it would look right," Patrice explained. "You understand, do you not, that both Lettice and Aurora have always been expected to be a bit more, shall we say, intrepid. Papa was forever taking them with him fishing and hunting."

"But he asked you, of course, he is a fair man," Stuart interrupted speedily. Patrice raised one hand to silence her companion, and Lord Ringwood, in order to avoid another such dangerous maneuver, was quiet.

"Certainly he did, but he did not really wish it. He rather liked the manner in which I was delicate. He always said I was his pretty little china doll. You see, china dolls do not learn to drive a pair."

"So you did what you thought he wanted?" Stuart asked, more than a little puzzled by such behavior. "You should have done what you wanted instead, then you should have been an experienced horsewoman rather than an amateur. But," he added tactfully, "you are a very good beginner."

"Thank you, Stuart, for the compliment," Patrice replied, her green eyes giving Lord Ringwood a fond look which caused him to look away at the quickly passing trees.

Patrice kept her eyes and attention on the road ahead after that, though her thoughts, had she given voice to them, would have been quite a revelation to that gentleman. For the past three days Patrice had experienced something quite amazing; she could remember feeling something similar to it when she was a child playing on the ground about her estate, but that was only an imperfect replica of what she felt now. She had racked her brains to describe the feeling which had

194

grown steadily within her breast as she spent more and more time with Lord Ringwood. She had first believed that it was contentment, for she had always enjoyed the quiet country. But as the days had passed, she realized that contentment would not have occurred, had Stuart not been present. She had always enjoyed his company, of course. Even in London he had been her particular favorite, though he could not perform the figures of a quadrille with any adequacy. But in the country she had begun to notice many of Stuart's qualities that she had not been aware of before.

An excellent example was the patience which he was presently exercising in teaching her to drive his gig. He never raised his voice, did not grow impatient, or attempt to make her perfect on the first trial. There was something different in the manner in which Stuart treated Patrice, which was only becoming apparent now that she paid him more attention. Patrice could not quite think what, but there was definitely a difference between the way Stuart spoke to her and treated her and the way her family or even Basil did.

Finding that she was growing a bit weary of holding the reins, Patrice wordlessly handed control of the horses over to Lord Ringwood, who had sat silently beside her for some time now. Stuart turned the horses about and Patrice soon found that they were very close to her grandmother's home.

Nearing the front of the house, Stuart could see that there were several other carriages there. "Guests again!" he observed. "I must say your grandmother is keeping you well entertained," he said, halting the gig among the rest of the vehicles and removing his driving gloves.

Looking at the other carriages, Patrice identified them. "I see Mr. Danby is here. Only look, Stuart. I do believe he has attempted to imitate you. He has painted his wheels yellow," Patrice noted with some amusement. "It doesn't look near as well, I must say."

"I should hope not," Lord Ringwood commented roundly, his senses somewhat offended by this attempt better to please Patrice. He was sure that the renovation of Mr. Danby's chariot was due to the fact that Patrice had viewed his gig with great admiration.

195

Though the young man was thoroughly likable otherwise, Lord Ringwood found that Danby had not as yet made the slightest inroads in his jealousy over Patrice.

That Patrice had never before paid such complimentary attention to his carriages did not occur to Lord Ringwood. Nor did he note the fact that she had been more attentive to him than usual, and that her glances had become a little different toward him. Such was the studiousness with which he had guarded his own secret that he did not even imagine that Patrice's feelings might have changed toward him.

This did appear to be the case, however, and Patrice was only just now beginning to realize the fact herself. Sitting before her guests, Mr. Courtfeld, Mr. Danby and his gracious mother, Patrice was startled to find herself comparing Stuart with the two young men. She was even more surprised when she discovered that he showed favorably against the gentlemen, though many would have preferred their more regular features and gregarious natures. Patrice's grandmother, who was the dowager Granvill, was occupied with Mrs. Danby sorting embroidery threads in one corner of the room.

Mrs. Danby, though full of smiles and knowing looks whenever the elderly lady should look up from her labors, was nonetheless quite put out. She had expected a woman of magnificence, considering her title, but this drab little old squab of a woman who sat relentlessly bent over her work was not at all as she had imagined a dowager to appear. As a member of that solitary group known as young widows, Mrs. Danby could have been described as quite conscious of her appearance. At an age where gravity waged constant war on her full features, the widow Danby was fighting back the tide with unabated vigor. The lacquer and rouge applied artfully, if a bit liberally, confounded the eye as best they might, and her figure was still quite impressive if a trifle full blown. She showed to advantage in a brown puffed muslin robe, gathered into compartments, over a simple dress of white china silk. The effect was quite as striking as Mrs. Danby could have hoped, but it was still a pity that she was so stylish and had no one of consequence to admire it.

Of course, Mrs. Danby would never have consented

to come except for the persistent requests made by her dear boy. Head over heels for Patrice, the young gentleman was aware that the dowager's sense of propriety demanded the presence of his mother.

That Mr. Danby had to contend with Mr. Courtfeld's persistent rivalry as well as his mother's objections to having to spend an afternoon with the dowager was unfortunate, but unavoidable. He did not resent the problems as much as he might have, however, for he felt the price well paid if he could have but a few moments in the Lady Patrice's company.

There was a long silence now as none of Patrice's guests spoke. Lord Ringwood seemed wholly absorbed in looking at a book of pictures and Mr. Courtfeld felt the lack of conversation acutely.

"And where have you been to?" Mr. Courtfeld asked Patrice. "I had thought to come a bit early so that you might consent to come riding, only to find you gone, to my infinite distress."

Mr. Courtfeld's facial contortions which no doubt were meant to convey his feelings were nothing short of ludicrous, but Patrice's composure did not give way. Instead she replied not without some hint of pride that she had been out driving "Stuart's" rig.

It would have been too much to say that Mr. Courtfeld's eyes bulged in surprise, but Patrice reflected that they did at least start momentarily. "Pardon my amazement, but I hardly pictured you behind the reins of two such bruising young 'uns as are harnessed to Lord Ringwood's gig!" Mr. Courtfeld remarked with no little admiration.

"Nor I," echoed Mr. Danby. "I had better imagined you dancing the waltz, or perhaps tending your roses in some garden. Certainly not coursing about in such a high-spring vehicle. Trifle dangerous for one so delicate as yourself, an' I may be so bold, madam."

Lord Ringwood, having been silent all this time but attentive to what was being said, could be silent no longer. Looking up from the picture book, he cleared his throat. "She did tolerably well for a green hand at it," he commented with a clear and precise voice. "I can't see why you can't imagine Lady Patrice behind the reins, for I can, and," he added, turning in Patrice's direction, "besides which, the Trevelyn women have always been exceptional horsewomen."

Lord Ringwood was basking too much in both men's cowed silence, or he would have seen the warm glow in Patrice's eyes as she looked at him.

Why, she wondered, had she never noticed before the consideration with which Stuart consistently treated her? Patrice could not have been more touched by any other person's praise, of that she was sure. Her father had always compared Patrice to her sisters, but found her lacking, or so she believed. In any event, it was wondrous to her ears to hear Stuart praise her driving abilities, to acknowledge that she was indeed a Trevelyn as much as her sisters.

Mrs. Danby, noting her son's unusual silence, turned from her tedious task. "Thomas, do show Lady Trevelyn what you have done with your curricle. I am sure she will be favorably impressed." Turning to Patrice even as her son reddened at his mother's gauche reference to the deliberate change in his vehicle, Mrs. Danby added with a sly look, "Tell me if you don't think it is better than any other you might have seen. Thomas has labored so long on it, I am sure that it must be superior."

"We saw it as we came in," Lord Ringwood remarked with uninterestedness. Patrice was certain that he did not miss the meaning of Mrs. Danby's words—that she felt that her son's carriage decidedly outstripped his own.

"And do you not think it just the thing, Lord Ringwood?" Mrs. Danby pressed, unable to allow the point to rest. This question was unwise, as Patrice could see Stuart's irritation rise. This occurred very seldom and the thought that his anger might be somehow connected to some affection he might still hold for her caused Patrice to catch her breath. She knew not why, but she hoped there was a little jealousy for her within Lord Ringwood's breast. Why she would desire such a thing at this time when she would soon be off with the man to whom she had already bestowed her heart, she could not explain even to herself. But she waited anxiously to see what Stuart would say next.

In response to Mrs. Danby's smug inquiry, Lord

Ringwood did not forget he was speaking to a woman, a very vexing woman, but nonetheless entitled to some courtesy, a point his own mother had made certain he learned. "Mrs. Danby, if you feel that your son's carriage is all the rage, then it must be, to you at least, for a mother is never wrong about her children."

"Only I have asked your opinion since, as a member of the Four in Hand Club, you would know," Mrs. Danby responded, a trifle annoyed that Lord Ringwood should try to put her off.

Stuart scratched his nose, a contemplative look on his face that signaled Patrice of his intent at last to put the woman in her place. "Ma opinion, Mrs. Danby, since you seem to wish it so much, is that your son's carriage, while a good imitation, lacks a certain thing which members of the Four in Hand Club value: uniqueness. I ma self value it, and must now needs change ma own carriage, I am sorry to say, especially when I got it the way I like it."

Lord Ringwood seemed not the least concerned that Mrs. Danby was livid at his words, possibly because Patrice's grandmama, the dowager Granvill, was amused by his comments. She was hiding a smile behind a piece of embroidery. It was an amazing fact, but the aged woman seemed most impressed with Stuart. She had said it was his straightforward manner, also his refusal to allow most strangers to put his nose out of joint. It wasn't cruelty at all, it was simply a refusal to be pushed or knocked about like a doll.

"Perhaps," the dowager said hurriedly, interceding before any more mischief could be done, "you and your son would like to go out in the garden with my granddaughter? The flowers are in bloom and I know, Mrs. Danby, that you are possessed of a green thumb."

Mrs. Danby opened her mouth in a most threatening way, but was cut off by her already mortified offspring. "Yes, Mama, I believe we have had quite enough of Lord Ringwood's company."

"Your servant," Stuart said, bowing slightly as he had been raised to do. Mrs. Danby glared, her son grew rigid, the dowager herself could be seen to smirk, and Mr. Courtfeld knew not what to do at all. Sweeping her robes regally about her in a huff, Mrs. Danby held on possessively to her son's serge-covered arm and followed Patrice into the garden with Mr. Courtfeld trailing the entourage. Lord Ringwood, deciding that the best course for himself was to remain behind, glanced a bit apprehensively at Patrice's grandmother, severely clad in the colors of mourning. He had heard that she had adopted that mode of dress so as to be in perpetual mourning for her deceased mate, though what bearing her clothing could have on the matter Lord Ringwood's limited facilities could only speculate upon.

"Lord Ringwood," she called out, observing the young gentleman's eyes upon her, "you must come and sit beside me for you have been a ray of sunshine in my life."

Coming forward to do his duty, Stuart's puzzlement was obvious. "I am glad I brighten your day, madam, but I hardly know how for I have no wit. Have been told so to ma own face on several occasions by persons in the know."

"You are nonetheless amusing, Lord Ringwood, and I have been interested in what sorts of gentlemen Patrice had finally decided to keep company with. I must say that it is a relief to me that she does not seem partial to those of a disagreeable nature," the dowager replied, an aged but still-sharp eye kept trained on Stuart. "Tell me, what do you know of Patrice's reasons for 'visiting' me down here at this time?"

"I know all about the affair. At least I believe I do," Lord Ringwood replied cautiously, unsure of just how much had been told to her.

"And what did you think of the lieutenant? Your own personal opinion is what I require, sir." As Stuart hesitated to speak unkindly, the dowager wagged one withered finger at him. "And I will have the truth, please. I do not have the time any longer to waste on poppycock!" she warned.

"I did not like the man ma self, truth be told," Stuart replied with his straightforward manner.

"He was not up to snuff?"

"He was not fit altogether. Not good enough for Patrice," Stuart said emphatically, his jaw raising a fraction and the dislike he felt in his heart appearing with vivid clarity in his eyes.

The dowager looked Lord Ringwood up and down carefully, as if assessing a prize bull she would purchase, then nodded, satisfied. "You have told me what I wished to know."

"About Lieutenant Torquill? I could say more."

"No, you have told me all I wish to know about you, sir. That is what I required and I thank you for your assistance. I suggest that you now join the others in the garden for I am sure you do not wish to be long from Patrice's side."

Stuart felt uncomfortably as if he had been found out, and the stubborn streak that lay deep within him made him openly defy the dowager's dismissal. "You had a purpose to your questions, madam, and I don't like being the hare in a chase. What do you think you have discovered?"

"Only that you love my granddaughter. Do not mistake me, Lord Ringwood. I am happy that you do, and you have my blessings. I shall dance at your wedding."

"Only you are the one who mistakes, at least a little, madam," Stuart said with alarm at his having been found out. "Patrice don't favor me in the least, so there will be no banns for us."

"Nonsense, she likes you very well," the woman contradicted with that confidence which is bestowed with age.

"As well as she likes anyone else, perhaps," Lord Ringwood insisted stubbornly, his cheek twitching with his agitation. At this time his main concern was to extract a promise from the dowager to keep his secret, for he feared exposure of his more tender feelings above all else after Patrice's seeming uninterestedness. "You must give me your word that you will say nothing of this sort to Patrice, madam. I entreat you to consider ma feelings an' she should begin to pity me. I could not countenance it. I am sure you can understand that."

"I feel you are wrong, Lord Ringwood," the dowager began, and then seeing the agony on his face, she considered again. "Very well, I will not expose your secret, but you shall see for yourself that Patrice shares your feelings," she forecasted.

At this, further discussion was curtailed as Patrice and the guests reentered the house. From what Stuart could hear, there appeared to be an outing in the planning as Mr. Courtfeld and Mr. Danby tried their utmost to persuade Patrice to attend either a hunt on the morrow or participate in a fishing expedition on the lake.

"You must come fishing, you would enjoy it I am positive," Mr. Danby insisted to the right of Patrice with something of a nasal whine which grated on the dowager Granville's nerves.

"But you would really rather be hunting. I am sure you would prefer it over the fishing," Mr. Courtfeld pressed.

"The merits of fishing overcome those of hunting twofold," Mr. Danby maintained with dogged determination.

"And the hunting is not to be compared with such a paltry form of entertainment as that," Mr. Courtfeld repeated firmly.

The dowager watched and listened to this continue, Patrice's lovely head swiveling first to one gentleman and then to the other. Mrs. Danby was of no assistance whatsoever as she staunchly agreed with her son, pressing Patrice for an answer in favor of the fishing. "It is quite genteel, I assure you. My son would not urge you to anything that would not assuredly delight you."

Finally, an imploring look was cast toward Stuart by a totally confused Patrice. "What do you think I should do, Stuart?" she said, the familiarity with which she spoke his name causing Mrs. Danby to frown deeply.

Lord Ringwood pondered this question as if it were the most important one he had ever heard. He answered decisively, "You must do what you wish to do, Patrice. That's the thing. Can't always be doing what someone else thinks is right for you. I mean 't'ain't right."

Patrice's eyes widened with surprise. "You mean you won't give me your opinion?"

"Oh, well! Ma opinion is that the fishing is something you might enjoy only if you like being wet and cold," Stuart replied swiftly and with a matter-of-factness which quite put out Mrs. Danby. "But if you're asking me to decide what you should do, I can't do it, Patrice, or rather, Lady Patrice," he stuttered at the last, aware of his familiarity in using her Christian name before the dowager.

All eyes turned to Patrice for her decision. Patrice, nothing loath, made one of the few decisions that had ever been requested of her. "I shall go hunting, then," she announced, a small flush of pleasure coloring her cheeks as she savored her own decision. "And I am sure I shall enjoy it greatly," she added, allowing Mr. Courtfeld to bow over her hand before taking his leave of her and her grandmother.

"Well, child, I hope you do not have cause to regret your decision," Mrs. Danby said as she also took her departure, a dejected and thoroughly discouraged Mr. Danby accompanying her to the carriage that awaited them in front of the house.

Lord Ringwood made his exit as well, though as usual with a reluctance that reflected his deep attachment to Patrice. Patrice for once also felt reluctance and would have asked him to stay but for the fast approach of dusk.

"Will I see you then, tomorrow?" she asked as he took the reins of his gig in his hands. Gazing down into that familiar face which he carried in his mind and heart at all times, Stuart replied cheerfully as he knew he was expected to.

"Of course. Can't disappoint a friend, can I? Besides, what sort of a person would I be to leave you in Mr. Courtfeld's company for an entire day? He would have you jaunting after some mighty strange game, I'll be bound." With those playful words, he deliberately tilted his hat so that it sat jauntily on his head. Patrice had to laugh at the sight although there was some inner disquiet which would have quelled it; and Lord Ringwood left satisfied that he had at least retained the capacity to amuse his dearest friend.

So intent was Patrice on watching his carriage that

she was startled as her grandmother spoke from behind her.

"That is an unusual young man," she remarked as if to herself.

"I am aware," Patrice responded as she continued to watch the carriage.

"I do not think you are," the dowager replied with a severity which surprised Patrice. "I do not think you are aware of a lot of things, but perhaps you will come to understand in time." The woman motioned for Patrice to hurry into the house. "The damp is not good for a child of your constitution," she said as she clucked over the slippers that Patrice had muddied in the garden.

As they entered the house, the dowager paused for a moment and then remarked, "Oh, Patrice. Your friend, Lord Ringwood. He is unmarried?" Patrice nodded to this, her face turned from her grandmother as she was removing her soiled slippers. "That is splendid. I would like to introduce him to a few young ladies in my acquaintance. I am sure they would appreciate such an introduction, for Lord Ringwood is quite personable in his way. Don't you agree?" Her eye was quick, but Patrice had no response to this ploy, and her grandmother was answered with an unsatisfying "yes" from Patrice as she rose to change her things.

"You have no objections to my doing that?" the dowager called out, vainly hoping for some dissent to confirm her own growing feelings that Patrice was indeed deeply in love with Lord Ringwood as he was with her.

"I have none."

Patrice's mild reply started the dowager to doubting her own perspicacity.

"Possibly there is some deserving young girl among your friends' children," said Patrice. "Choose them with care, for I would want Stuart treated with kindness, as I am fond of him. Perhaps they will even treat him with more kindness than I myself have shown to him, for he deserves more."

As Patrice left, the Duchess gave vent to her exasperation. "You foolish children!" she exclaimed, not

believing that two people so much in love with one another could deny themselves the wonder of that feeling.
"Well, I shall not interfere, at least not at this time. It
wouldn't be appreciated, I warrant." Sitting down to
her embroidery once more, the dowager's irascible temper would not settle down. "I should hope that your
sisters are not grown into such unreasonable creatures," she muttered to herself as she attempted to finish the piece which she had set out for herself.

Unfortunately for Amelia Braden, at least one other
Trevelyn sister was being most unreasonable. Seated
before the pianoforte, listlessly executing an exercise
scale, Lettice was concentrating all of her energies on
being as stubborn as was humanly possible, and Lady
Braden for one was finding it most difficult to tolerate.
This incredible display of contrariness was due to
the fact that for the past two days Lettice had received
both letters and appeals by messengers sent to the
Braden home on the behalf of the Duke of Melburry
and had refused them in turn. This behavior confounded Amelia who had even asked Lettice personally
at least to read the Duke's letters for an explanation.
Lettice, however, appeared bent on a course of ignorant revenge, and would not yield to this request.
"Let him wait as long as I have and then we shall
see if he still sends me messages and expects a reply of
a decent sort!" Lettice had cried out in exasperation at
the pesterings of her aunt only the day before. She had,
of course, instantly apologized for such rudeness, but
that did not change her attitude toward Richard Melburry.
Lord Braden had not had any suggestions to make
for he found it difficult enough to fathom the mind of
his own wife of many years, much less the workings of
a young relative. "You had best let Lettice handle the
matter in her own way, my dearest," he had advised
the evening before at dinner. Lettice had decided to
dine in her room, finding her aunt's insistent eyes a de-
terrent to her company. "She is of a different suit than
yourself and I do not think any amount of persuasion
will sway her while she is so resolved."
"But this is ludicrous!" Lady Braden had insisted,

the crease in her brow threatening to leave a wrinkle due to the diligence with which she frowned. "Lettice is a proud girl, I understand that, but it is about time that she allowed the Duke an audience. It doesn't make it right for her to put him off simply because he has neglected her. Especially when she does not know the why and wherefore."

"She will never send for him in her present mood, so why not leave her be?" Alton Braden had pleaded, a bit weary of the entire matter. Unknowingly, he had hit on an idea which his wife was quick to realize.

"There is no necessity of Lettice sending for the Duke," Lady Braden had said in the sweetest of voices. "After all, he has not yet called upon me, and I do wish to meet him. You will ask him to come, will you not, Alton?"

Lord Braden was not easily persuaded to perform acts which might endanger the peace and harmony of his home, but he was also not one to deny his better half any boon which was within his grasp to grant.

So it was, with great trepidation, that Lord Braden now sat beside his persuasive spouse listening to Lettice's rendition of an old Scottish lullaby, aware that at any moment he would hear of the Duke's arrival. He waited anxiously for the knock at the study door.

It was not long in coming, a servant entering and announcing the Duke of Melburry, requesting the privilege of being allowed to intrude his person on their quiet group.

"Pray, let him enter by all means," Lady Braden said quite gaily, ignoring the first startled then outraged look on her niece's face as she rose to greet her visitor.

Lettice would have asked to be excused, even contemplated an escape into the garden. But it was far too late for that as she espied the Duke through the half-open doors, and he entered the room before she could act on any of her thoughts.

"Your Grace!" Amelia Braden exclaimed with utter delight, watching her niece's reaction from out of the corner of her eye. "How good of you to come! We were just wanting for some lively company."

"Then you may be sorely disappointed for I am hardly lively, but I will do my best," Richard remarked in an attempt at humor which he could observe had no effect on Lettice's calm and cold face. Turning uneasily to Lord Braden, he extended his hand, meeting a firm grip in return. "It was good of you to ask me to come."

Lettice threw her uncle something of a disdainful look for his part in her present predicament but said nothing, motioning for the Duke to be seated.

"Yes, do sit down, Your Grace," Lady Braden said with a smile, steering him into the seat beside Lettice on the low couch. "I am sure that the two of you must have a great deal to discuss for Lettice had told me that you knew one another, and you have not been about lately. Lord Braden and I shall be in the library for there are a few things we must look after that cannot wait. I am sure you will forgive us if we leave you alone a bit."

All this was said with an unhurried but insistent manner. The chance for a refusal was missed as Lady Braden scurried quickly from the room with Lord Braden following behind without question.

Amelia Braden would have liked to listen outside the doors as she left, but her husband, feeling that he had quite enough to do with going against his niece's will, unrelentingly dragged his wife off to the library.

Richard and Lettice watched as the doors closed softly behind their hosts, leaving them in a silence so heavy as to liken the room to a mausoleum.

Lettice would not look up from the contemplation of her skirt for a few moments, though she knew the Duke's eyes to be upon her. Richard was thus allowed to look his fill, but as he gazed at her he knew that he would never be able to satisfy his eyes in looking, no matter how long he should do so. It had been a very little time, really, but Richard's longing to see Lettice again, to be near her, had grown into an irresistible impulse that had forced him to seek her out once more, breaking all the resolves he had made to forget her and go to live in France. It was as if he had been denied her company for a much longer amount of time, and Richard did not know how to begin.

Her silence drew out, the minutes passed, until Lettice finally looked up into his eyes. "Well, sir," she said, her voice shaking just a little with the anger she felt at this deception, "are you not ashamed to come here in such a manner?"

"I deserve your anger, but only for my past behavior," Richard answered, never taking eyes that were hopelessly loving from Lettice's face. "What I have done to see you again could not be helped any more than I could help being in love with you."

Richard watched as the anger slowly seeped away from Lettice, and she stared with eyes wide and half disbelieving.

"Surely, you have known that I love you," Richard continued, daring to take Lettice's hand in his as he spoke. He had to be sure that she returned his feelings if he was to say what he had been considering almost constantly all of the time he had been absent. "God knows, I have dared to love you though I have tried to stop during these past weeks. It only made it worse, to know you were here and yet not see you."

Though Lettice turned her head away, her heart pounding at the suddenness of his declaration, she listened still to his words, and they were as a balm to her wounded heart. She had been too proud even to admit to herself that there was a wound, that any man had been skillful enough or devastating enough to inflict such a blow. Now Lettice could feel her excitement grow as she became certain that she too had made her mark upon the Duke's heart.

"I had thought you loved me. I was not certain, and then not a word from you for so long," Lettice said, turning to look once more into Richard's eyes, at the warmly insistent pressure he exerted on her shoulders. He wished to see the truth in her face. "Oh, why did you not write?" she asked suddenly, the anguish of so many days returning for a moment to haunt her. "A letter would have been so little to you and so much to me if you care as much as you say."

"And do you think my pain was any less than yours?" Richard spoke as if the words were pulled from the depths of his soul, and his grip on Lettice's shoulders tightened as if he would never release her. His face was so close to hers that Lettice was dizzy with his nearness. "If you were hurt because you did not receive a letter, only think what it cost me to deny myself even that contact. You say it would have meant so little to me, but for days now it has been my entire existence, and I had denied it to myself until I couldn't bear it any longer."

"And now? What do you have to say to me now?" Lettice asked, her breath uneven as Richard slowly released his hold on her and stood back from her a pace. Lettice could still feel where his hands had lain and she crossed her arms across her breast, hugging her shoulders.

"Now, I have to tell you a tale about a young boy. Young, not only in years, mind you, but in his attitudes and his experiences with life. He had not lived long enough to be able to know what to do when he was required to play the man." Richard turned his back to Lettice, walking over to the pianoforte and looking down into his reflection in the polished wood as if at a stranger. "This young man enjoyed light flirtations. They were harmless and enjoyable, especially with the more knowing among the married ladies. And it was exciting, I admit that it was exciting, to have the touted beauties of the ton paying heed to one so ready to be recognized." Richard turned abruptly back to Lettice, his face grim. "Then one day one of the young man's flirtations grew serious, desperate in fact, for his company. She wished to leave her husband, to flee to Europe with her young admirer who had not bargained for such an eventuality. Still, the young man might have done as she wished if other persons had not intervened, for could it not be possible that he was really responsible for leading the lady astray to her destruction? No matter, in any case the husband discovered the 'affair'. Husbands usually do where there is nothing in reality to be found out. He threatened the young man's family with a court hearing, a scandal. He was a cuckold, you see, and he would extract his pound of flesh publicly if needed be."

"And so the young man fled," Lettice interrupted, unable to be silent any longer.

The Duke started. "You know. How long?" he asked, coming back to her side and searching her eyes.

"I have known since before that day at the garden party," she replied, reaching out and touching Richard gently on the shoulder. "And so the man fled. You must continue with the story."

"The young man did not flee, at least not then," Richard corrected her, continuing to look at Lettice intensely. "He did not leave until his father, a man of ill health at that time, insisted that he go to France for the good of the family."

"And being young . . ."

"And quite foolish, I see that now," Richard continued, placing his arms tenderly about Lettice, shyly as if he feared that she would escape from him like some wraith, "the young man left the country as he was told, only to return some years later when his father died. He returned to put the estates in order and ended up falling quite hopelessly in love with a proper young lady of his class."

Lettice would have objected to the description of herself, but the Duke shushed her with a finger upon her mouth. Tracing the curve of her lip and caressing a smooth cheek briefly, Richard tilted Lettice's head up until he could look into her soft brown eyes.

"He fell in love, as I said, but then began his dilemma. You see, the husband was still living. He yet accused the man, now no longer so young, in every place he dared, of the death of his wife, for she had committed suicide when the young man left."

"It was not the young man's fault," Lettice reasoned, attempting to make sense of this muddle. "He could not have known that the woman would do such a thing."

"Perhaps not, but he wonders sometimes, even as he is whispered about, if perhaps he is not rightfully accused. He wonders if she might not have lived, if he had stayed to bear the scandal with her. And he wonders too how he can possibly ask that young woman he loves so dearly to share such an existence, where her husband is open to every foul accusation made by a man, no matter how mad, who might have just cause."

Looking up into Richard's eyes, Lettice answered, for she was sure now of her feelings for him. "He has just asked, and the lady can do naught but accept. She is as madly in love as he is, and there can be no choice for her, really."

Gazing down at the shining brown eyes, bright with love, Richard drew Lettice tight against his breast, bending his head to her lips in a long and passionate kiss. Feeling his lips so demanding and insistent upon her own, Lettice returned Richard's embrace measure for measure, never wishing it to end. Finally, their lips parted, and Lettice laid her head against the smooth fabric of the Duke's coat, cradled in the hollow of his broad shoulder.

"Killingham will never stop until he has what he truly wishes," Richard murmured, looking down at those lips he had so recently kissed.

"You must not duel with him," Lettice replied. "Of that I am certain. It would be as if you were admitting that what he says is true."

"Isn't it?" Richard asked, the agony in his voice, the doubt, causing Lettice to hold him tightly to her, as if to give him her strength.

"It is not. You must believe it because I believe it," she responded with conviction. "We will face it together."

"Well, then," Richard said, the tenderness in his voice and the love with which he looked upon her spurring Lettice's joy to new heights, "if you believe it, then it will be so for me. The world is a paltry thing against your love."

Lettice, still held close in his embrace, did not speak further. They would decide how they would continue later, but for now it was enough that she held him close, and she allowed tears of joy to trickle unheeded down her face. She had found her true love at last, and no power could take him from her, of that she was sure.

Patrice could truly say to herself that she was exhausted, not merely tired but totally and thoroughly "burnt to the socket", as Stuart would have said. She had risen at the break of day to ride to the hounds and had grown weary steadily as the day had progressed. However, tired as she was, her sense of accomplish-

211

ment burned bright inside her. She had never before hunted after the elusive fox, and did not truly care if the clever creature were ever captured, for that was not the point for her at all. At first she had thought to herself, I will go on. I would not want Stuart to think me such a milksop as to stop so early. But then, near the end, Patrice realized that she was continuing as much for herself as for Stuart's benefit. She found that her stamina, though not as strong as that of her sisters, was still sustained by her sense of will, a sense she had not until now had avenue to cultivate.

Stopping finally before the manor, the sun's red glow in the distance, Patrice heaved a triumphant if weary sigh. Lord Ringwood halted his horse alongside, and dismounted in an easy motion that Patrice envied at that moment. He had to assist her in dismounting, for her joints were stiffened and cold from all the riding.

"You did very well," Stuart said as Patrice brushed the nettles from her skirt folds. She had ridden through some interesting terrain and had done nothing to improve the appearance of her riding dress of French merino.

"And were you proud of me, then?" she asked seriously. "I was not an embarrassment?"

"Definitely not!" he protested, aghast at such an idea. "You rode well to the hounds, much better than anyone expected I'll warrant. You surprised the lot of them." Stuart's voice rang with such pride at her accomplishment that Patrice's heart leapt.

"I am glad. I did not want to disgrace you in front of all those people, especially since Mr. Courtfeld and Mr. Danby were expecting a spectacle," Patrice said, knowing all too well how close she had come to fulfilling their expectations not less than three times, nearly falling from her horse in the beginning as she was becoming accustomed to her steed.

"Courtfeld and Danby don't know you like I do," Stuart replied. Then thinking such a statement a bit familiar, he added, "After all, both your sisters can stay astride a horse, it is only common sense that you can as well."

Patrice suspected that she understood Lord Ringwood's meaning, and her hopes, vague in her mind but still there, were raised. "Stuart, come into the house and stay a bit," she suggested. Her melodic voice had an almost hypnotic effect on Lord Ringwood's senses, and he might have gone but for a prior commitment.

"I would like to, but I must be getting back. I have to leave for a few days, and I have to prepare," he said, drawing back a few steps from her side. Even in the gathering darkness she was lovely, and Stuart could not help feeling rooted to the spot, for all his protests.

"But you said you would bear me company here!" Patrice exclaimed, a sudden panic rising inside of her. "Why must you leave?"

"Ma sister, you know, the one married to that Baron or some such," Stuart began, unaware that Patrice's reaction might be anything more than a desire to have familiar faces about her in a strange place. "Well," he continued, "she wants me to help her in London. Hosting a rout, and I have to come since her husband is away."

"It is a family obligation, then," Patrice said, unaccountably relieved.

"Yes, in a way," Stuart answered. "She must have someone else from the family there and I am the one chosen this time. Besides," he added, "you are doing quite as fine as can be. It is exactly as I said it would be. An' do not contradict, for it is true. All the town and countryside ring with the compliments of every young gentleman in the area. You don't need ma help anymore, and ma sister does right now, so I will be off."

Patrice could not but hear the bitterness in Lord Ringwood's voice. She was unable to know what to say.

"But I do like to have you near me, Stuart," she protested feebly, her past behavior toward Lord Ringwood returning to her shame. "And what do I care for all the countryside?" she added desperately.

"No. I suppose you save your cares for another," Stuart replied quietly, then as if freed from his invisible bonds, Lord Ringwood quickly mounted his horse. "Anyway, I cannot deny ma sister her request and she has invited several young ladies for me to meet, as is her usual manner. She has been severely tried by ma lack of interest, feels I should marry soon, I suppose." He paused, looking down into Patrice's pale face.

"I will be back, never doubt it," he said, and then was gone. Part of his brain told him to stay, even as he had spoken the words. But, because what he had said was true, Stuart did not feel that Patrice would be long alone. There were too many admirers. What was the use if Lieutenant Torquill was gone when there were all these minions to continue his torture?

Patrice stood motionless and speechless. He did not love her, she thought. She had destroyed any love that there might have been through neglect, as a rose dies without careful and loving attention. Patrice suspected that she would not be able to win it back if she were so inclined.

By all rights I should be thinking only of Basil, she thought, but as Stuart rode off, Patrice was aware of a feeling of acute loneliness.

It was as if a weight were burdening her shoulders as Patrice entered the house and made her way to her room. Finding the door ajar and the warm glow of firelight streaming through the crack, Patrice entered slowly to find a large package on her bed, unopened.

"My lady, you startled me!" a chambermaid exclaimed as she looked up from the linen drawer, her arms filled with fresh sheets.

"It is a bit late for you to be doing that, isn't it?" Patrice inquired.

"It was only ironed today, and I thought that as you were away. I will only be a moment and then off."

Patrice's interests were not on linen at this time. Walking to her bed, she looked at the package, and inquired, "What is this doing here? Who has sent it?"

"A messenger brought it down from your sisters in London, I believe. They said you left one of your gowns and they posted it to you," the young girl said as she completed her task with haste. "Will that be all, miss?" she asked as she closed the drawer gently.

"Yes," Patrice murmured, her expression strange.

"You feeling all right, miss?" the chambermaid

214

asked curiously, observing that Patrice was quite drawn-looking.

"Fine. I am fine. I would prefer to be alone right at this moment, please," Patrice said. With a bob of her head, the girl was gone and Patrice opened the strange package. On top of the tissues covering her gown was a note, a single sheet of paper with familiar writing upon it.

"At midnight tonight, my future wife." It was signed Basil. Patrice sat carefully on her bed. Basil had no doubt bribed the messenger to slip the note in with the parcel.

"I had forgotten, it is tonight," she said to herself in a low voice. I have promised to marry him, she thought dully, hardly caring, now that she felt she had lost Stuart's love entirely.

Then, desperately, Patrice clutched the note to her. "I loved you once, Basil, and you love me still. If I marry you, perhaps I shall begin to love you again. It is better than this solitude I face. You do love me, I know that you do," she whispered, her words half choked by her sobs. Thrusting the note into her cape pocket, Patrice began to select things randomly from her wardrobe, flinging articles onto the bed and occasionally wiping a tear from her cheek. She would need a few things at least if she were to leave tonight with Basil, she thought. Looking into the mirror and attempting to repair her ravaged face, Patrice stopped, and speaking to her reflection said with a tinge of irony, "Smile now. After all, this is the happiest day of your life. You are to be married." The face in the mirror crumpled and Patrice flung herself down on the bed, giving way to tears once more.

~~~~ CHAPTER 8

AURORA HAD chosen the most secluded part of the garden to sit in the sun, an occupation which had never failed before to calm her nerves whenever she was agitated. Today, however, it seemed to be ineffective. Sitting under the shade of a tree, skirts spread about her in expansive folds which gave her a feeling of territory and privacy from intrusion, Aurora nervously created a daisy chain, winding it with several others that her busy fingers had automatically produced as she had sat. Holding up a thick garland of the sweet-smelling flowers, she let it drop with a sigh of impatience.

"I must get hold of myself," she said to herself, trying to soothe her nerves. "I have done bolder things in my day, and this is no different."

That on this particular occasion she was contemplating actions of a possibly scandalous nature did not do anything to help abate her agitation. Her decision to attend the Cyprian ball and discover for herself the truth of Lord Simmons' words was one she knew she could not overturn, though the consequences, should she be found out, were devastating. For a woman of her rank to be found at a common trollop's yearly gathering was social suicide. Of course, she was not even supposed to be aware of this annual event where the butterflies and most exquisite flowers of the demi-monde came out to dance upon the floors of the Argyle Rooms. She was not supposed to know, but did know of it, as did many other young ladies. They simply did not ever acknowledge that they were aware of the ball to anyone for it would not be good form to recognize such women, or to have any knowledge of their goings on.

She had heard that the event was a veritable orgy.

These women would affect the behaviors of the ton in caricature. Aurora did not know what was truth and what a lie, but in her disguise, she was determined to seek Peregrine Melburry out and observe him.

Aurora had gone over her plan in her mind so many times that she felt as if her head would burst. Knowing, however, that a level head was essential to her scheme, she had come out to the garden to try to relax. Closing her eyes, Aurora chose not to think, but to empty all her thoughts from her brain awhile. She had thought of nothing else for days, and realized with a start that she had not even given any consideration to her sisters. She had not heard from Patrice as yet, and wondered now if she were suffering the pangs of loss over Basil Torquill. Aurora could have a little sympathy for Patrice if such was the case, but her own feelings tended to overshadow all else. Of course, she hoped for the best for Lettice. She had seen the Duke's carriage arrive and this appearance had also encouraged her to take herself off and leave her sister some privacy.

Aurora's absorption in her thoughts had been such that she had not detected the footsteps which had brought a figure close behind her, hidden from view by tall hedges along the walls of the garden.

Aurora opened her eyes with a start. She had heard a sound behind her, and turned quickly, rising to a kneeling position on the grass, her blue eyes wide and questioning.

"Lady Aurora." A voice she recognized as that of Lord Killingham met her ear. She saw him then, half hidden among the hedges where he had been for some time.

"Lord Killingham!" she exclaimed with surprise, rising to her feet as quickly as she might in the soft grass, a hand going involuntarily to her breast as she felt the uncomfortably intense stare Lord Killingham favored her with. "You have startled me, sir!" she continued, gathering her wits as she stepped back against the tree. Lord Killingham was advancing toward her slowly, so tall that she felt her head tilting up uncomfortably as she watched him warily.

"I beg your pardon, then," Killingham said, coming close to her side. "I had not meant to startle one so

217

lovely as yourself." Taking Aurora's hand, he kissed her on the wrist, a gesture which caused her to shudder slightly and draw her hand quickly away.

"You are most improper to come to me here in the garden, Lord Killingham. Where is my aunt? Why is she not with you?" she demanded, suddenly outraged that she should have to cringe within the confines of her own aunt's home. "Well, sir?" she demanded when he did not answer. "Can it be that she is not aware of your presence?"

"She is not. I admit that. But you cannot blame an ardent admirer for coming to you. You encourage such boldness by your very beauty," Lord Killingham remarked, attempting to charm her.

Aurora's mind could not comprehend such incredible rashness, such utter disregard for her privacy. "How long have you been here?" she asked suspiciously. "Have you . . . have you been watching me?" she asked suddenly. The very idea of being observed in secret made her almost physically sick. She did not wait for an answer. "How did you gain admittance? I am sure that no servant of my aunt's would be so persuaded. How dare you?" she demanded, her rage overcoming her fear.

"I do not beg your indulgence. I am sure you know why I am here. Let us not play games when we are so close to being betrothed." Killingham attempted to come even closer, ignoring her anger.

Aurora evaded him, moving away from the tree to open ground. He was not inebriated on this occasion, Aurora could see this, and she was suddenly more afraid than she had been on their first encounter, for he was a large man, and his sheer size was intimidating.

"Betrothed!" she exclaimed incredulously. "There has never been the least possibility of such a thing." Stepping back, all of her revulsion on her face, Aurora looked Lord Killingham up and down, her disgust at him causing her to shiver.

Killingham, however, did not seem to see the loathing with which Aurora viewed him, or did not wish to. Walking slowly toward her, he reached into his pocket, drawing forth an object which glittered in the sunlight.

"You jest," he said, his tone more a command than anything else. The glint in his eyes was like the shining in the eyes of demons. It was then that Aurora realized the enormity of the truth. Lord Killingham was in fact mad. He had been perhaps close to it for some time, and now was he totally apart from normal reasoning.

"We are to be betrothed. This is a gift from your most loving husband," Killingham continued, holding out the fabulously fashioned locket to Aurora. "See here, on the back," he insisted. "To you, for we are to be wed." It was as if the words inscribed on the polished surface were all the proof that he needed to make his fantasy a reality. "Take it!" he commanded, as Aurora made no move to accept this token.

She did not move. Her hesitation seemed almost to drive him farther into his insanity. He moved forward. Aurora was positive he intended to force the locket upon her. For a fleeting second she observed the man, as if suspended like a picture on canvas. This huge, hulking man, whose labored breathing and agitated features forced home the demented glimmer in his eyes. His face was sweating and shining red as if he were about to have a fit or go into a frenzy. The locket held in a clenched fist.

"Take it," he hissed, coming closer, reaching out as if to grab Aurora by her arm.

"Never!" her voice rang in her ears. She flinched away violently from his hand, as if his touch would burn her. Then, turning before he could move quickly enough to detain her, Aurora ran wildly back toward the house, never looking behind her for fear that she would see his form bearing down upon her.

Lord Killingham did not attempt to follow. He was too enraged to move from the spot where he stood. Staring down at the locket, a spark of certainty ignited in his brain. "Melburry," he said slowly, his voice a hoarse whisper. "We will see if she continues to prefer you, once she is with me. It will not be difficult. I have watched her until now. I will find the right moment."

Looking up and realizing that servants might be sent out in search of him if he remained, Killingham stealthily made his way out of the garden.

Halting just outside of the house, Aurora at last

looked behind her. Dragging gasping breaths into her lungs, she waited until her breathing was more even before entering. It would not do for her to appear so agitated before her aunt and uncle. It would only cause concern and possibly disrupt her plans for that evening. She was determined that nothing would prevent her from attending the Cyprian ball. Glancing at her hands as she reached out to open the door, Aurora noticed that the trembling that had possessed her in the garden as she had fled from Lord Killingham had ceased. Swinging the double doors open, Aurora walked quickly into the study only to find that she had interrupted Lettice and the Duke in a passionate embrace. She would have turned and left at that point, but the couple had parted, embarrassed a bit but still looking at one another with unabated ardor.

"I am sorry, I did not realize that you were 'occupied' still," she apologized, a trifle flustered herself.

"That is quite all right, Aurora," Lettice replied, smoothing her rather crumpled skirts and turning her flushed face away from her sister's scrutiny. "The Duke will be staying to dine with us," she added, looking up at Richard as she spoke.

From the way in which the Duke accepted this informal invitation, Aurora was sure that things had finally worked out for her dear sister, at least. Forgetting for the time being the evening facing her, Aurora smiled broadly at the couple, pleased that they had at last decided to make a match of it.

"Well, I am sure that I will want to know much more about you now, Your Grace, than ever before. Now, that is, since I have the definite feeling that you shall be among us for some time to come," Aurora remarked saucily. Richard and Lettice smiled at this, and Aurora led the way to the parlor to await the serving of dinner.

While Aurora was guaranteed a more pleasant dinner than she had first anticipated, the company of the Duke helping to distract her thoughts until the time came for action, Patrice had no such aid to settling her agitation.

Seated beside her grandmother, picking periodically

at the food before her, Patrice listened with half an ear to the dowager as she droned on about the oppressive weather that had suddenly appeared, and about how the joints and bones in her legs always reacted poorly to such atmospheric changes.

"I will have to have Beford heat a brick for my feet later," the elderly woman moaned as a particularly violent twinge was felt by her somewhere in the region of her large toe.

"That is a good idea," Patrice remarked automatically, failing to look up from her fast-cooling dish of veal.

The dowager raised one thin eyebrow, observing the lack of attention her granddaughter was exerting on their conversation. "Of course it shall probably scorch the bottoms of my feet."

"Naturally, just so, Grandmama," Patrice replied without hearing.

"And then the sawbones will be summoned to remove what is left of my poor feet," her grandmother added outrageously, in tones as conversational as she had used previously. "Wake up, child!" she snapped as Patrice appeared to be ready to make another ridiculous reply.

"I am sorry, Grandmama. I do not know what is wrong with me tonight," Patrice apologized nervously. "Do go on with what you were saying. I shall try to listen better."

"It is of no concern, child," she reassured Patrice, the bizarre behavior still unexplained. A thought then occurred to her. "It is a shame, is it not, that Lord Ringwood could not remain for dinner," she remarked nonchalantly, sure that Patrice must be missing his company already. She seemed melancholy, which was always a sign that a young man was involved in some way, and the dowager firmly believed that Patrice must have formed a tendre for Lord Ringwood.

"It is too bad, that is true," Patrice noted, picking up one of the ripe peaches from the garden and skinning it with the small pearl-handled pocket knife that she wore on her belt at her waist.

"But he will be back in a few days. He can come to dinner then," the dowager remarked, observing that

Patrice's features continued to droop rather unbecomingly. "Perhaps it is a good thing," the good lady continued as Patrice remained silent, all her attention on the fruit before her. "It will give your other swains a chance to see you without his being present."

"Grandmama!" Patrice exclaimed, shocked, "Stuart is not a 'swain' and I do not think of the gentlemen who visit me as such."

"Then what are they called, now?" she asked with asperity. "Gentleman callers, beaus, admirers, it's all the same. Don't tell me that they are not more than a little attentive, for they are, as is Lord Ringwood if you had eyes in your head to see."

This outburst was greeted with silence, Patrice sectioning her slippery peach with difficulty for her fingers seemed to have gone numb and lacked sensation. Indeed, her whole body lacked sensation, as if she were not really present in fact.

Her grandmother was put out for a moment, not sure of what avenue to try next. Obviously it was futile for her to expect Patrice to admit her affection for Lord Ringwood. The dowager felt that perhaps a little jealousy would do the trick.

"It is time that the boy went back to London though I still feel he likes you above half," she said. "Naturally, I can't blame his sister for throwing lovely ladies in his way. Time he was married and all of that. Marvelous state, marriage. I recommend it highly. I would imagine that his sister would be able to put quite a few eligible beauties before your friend, and they would all be lucky to have him come up to scratch too. Of course, they would probably be silly chits as well. He could be fooled into an unwise marriage."

Patrice pursed her lips around a comment she would have liked to make. The dowager waited anxiously for the result of her ploy.

"Stuart would no doubt pick the correct girl, Grandmama," Patrice said slowly, choosing her words carefully.

"And how would you feel about that?"

"I would wish them well, of course," Patrice replied quietly, her face never changing as she stared at the sliced peach before her.

"Harrumph!" The dowager's inarticulate noise, indicative of her great displeasure and skepticism, did not daunt Patrice who proceeded to eat the fruit without any apparent distress.

Lady Granville was in ill humor, and rang the silver bell by her right hand for the table to be cleared. Her mood did not lighten as the evening wore on, even though Patrice was required to read to her grandmother from a book of stories for some time, and then pressed into service winding yarn for a sweater the dowager intended to make for one of the needy tenants' children. Only once more did her grandmother attempt to elicit a response from Patrice as to her feelings for Stuart and it was a poor one at that. As Patrice rose to make her way to bed rather early, begging the excuse of a mild headache, the woman inquired solicitously, "Has Lord Ringwood's departure quite distressed you that much, poor child?"

The hopeful note in her voice was dashed as Patrice replied, "No, Grandmama, I have other things to think of tonight." With that, Patrice left after kissing her lightly on the cheek.

Setting her work down in her lap a moment, the dowager could not but feel discouraged and a little disappointed. She liked Lord Ringwood, and she liked Patrice quite well too, enough to wish them both as much happiness as could be had in a world she had always found to be wanting. There was no doubt that the two young people were meant for one another, they fit together quite well in personality, though there was a definite discrepancy in appearances, she had to admit. If Lord Ringwood's features were not perhaps as even as might be desired, he was still quite the most amiable, sensible young man she had observed for some time, rather like her late husband in many respects. And of course, she had to admit to herself that she had been looking forward to a wedding, almost any wedding would do. She felt in need of a little excitement, and had definitely been hoping to be knee-deep in wedding arrangements. Well, there was little likelihood of that, at least for the time being, with Lord Ringwood going off to London on the morrow.

Picking up the sweater in her hands again, she stored the half-finished garment with the balls of yarn Patrice had helped her to wind, shoving the whole unceremoniously under the divan. The dowager rose carefully to her feet but was penalized nonetheless as the joints in her legs complained of such treatment. "I see there will be little sleep for me tonight. Patrice is not the only one who is ailing," she said as she made her way slowly up to her bed.

Patrice's headache was growing steadily worse, but she could not put off what she had to do tonight in any case. She had sat tensely in her room until she heard the manor grow quiet after her grandmama retired, the muscles in her neck throbbing painfully as she strained to hear every sound. Dragging herself wearily to her feet, clothed in a dark travel cloak and carrying only a small satchel of necessities that she had finally put together out of the chaos of things she had thrown onto her bed, Patrice padded lightly along the dark hallway and down the grand staircase. In a moment, she was out of the door, hurrying along in the shadows as the hour drew near when she was scheduled to meet Basil. That she had continued to think only of her last conversation with Stuart and could not separate the image of his face from her thoughts Patrice found distressing in the extreme. Why she should feel something akin to desperation when she thought of what she was about to do, she did not know. After all, she could not be so fickle as to fall out of love with Basil in a few short days. Certainly, Stuart was someone she had known all of her life, but he had no similar feelings toward her.

When I see Basil again, I will feel differently, Patrice thought as she hurried her pace even more, wanting her thoughts to be true and rushing to make them so.

Arriving at the rendezvous point, Patrice found no sign of life. Not a sound but the night noises she had always found so pleasant, the crickets, the sound of leaves rustling. Then, everything was silent, unusually so, and Patrice felt a presence.

"I knew you would not fail me," a firm voice from the shadows spoke out. In the gloom, Patrice's lieutenant made himself visible, dressed in his ever-impressive uniform, just as she remembered him, yet not just so. Even as she rushed to embrace him and he returned it in his usual brusque manner, Patrice was aware that a certain excitement was missing, a thrill, a vitality that had been present before. It was so strange and confusing that she thought she must be mistaken.

"I have come, as we agreed, Basil," Patrice whispered, though there was no longer a necessity for secrecy.

The lieutenant looked at Patrice for a moment, as if sensing some difference himself.

"You do not seem overly pleased to see me," he remarked, perturbed at Patrice's lack of enthusiasm. "One would almost say by the look on your face that you find no pleasure in my presence at all."

"It has been some time since we have seen one another," Patrice said lamely, attempting to explain and cringing at the displeasure in Basil's eyes. It seemed to her that she was forever cowering at one thing or another that she had done to displease him.

"I know what it is. You are feeling strangely because we are to be wed. Let me assure you that it is a most natural state. All women are destined for it, so you will soon feel comfortable in the role." Basil seemed to satisfy his own mind for the time being without inquiring with Patrice as to the validity of his assumption. It was unnecessary for, within his knowledge, he had never been wrong about any issue at any time, and could not be wrong now. Taking hold of her limp hand, he added, "Soon, you shall have taken a new name and be part of my family. You have reservations, but you will be the perfect wife for me as long as you do exactly what I tell you. Naturally, there can be no question that your behavior will be exceptional."

Basil did not wait for a reply; he seldom ever did, and did not bother to observe that Patrice's hands were cold as ice as he guided her briskly over to the carriage which he had hidden up the bank by the side of the road. "You can be quicker than that!" he admonished as Patrice hurried to keep pace with him, her slippers becoming liberally soaked as she passed over the damp grass. "At last," he said, a hint of impatience in his voice as he almost pushed Patrice up into the small hired carriage.

Patrice observed the shabby vehicle. Military men did not have the means to purchase better transportation, and she imagined that she should be grateful that they did not have to go by mail coach.

Looking up into Basil's face as he took up the reins in his gloved hands, Patrice saw that he was as handsome as he had ever been. Nothing had changed, no new line or scar had marred his near perfect appearance. Suddenly, she was moved to ask, holding tightly onto one red-clad arm, "Basil, you do love me, don't you? Tell me that you do before we go."

The lieutenant, impatient to be off, patted Patrice's hand lightly. "Of course, of course. Would I be here if I did not? Be sensible now and sit back. We will be making a few stops tonight until we reach the border."

This undemonstrative manner did not sound very loverlike, but Patrice had to be satisfied with Basil's answer. Burying her face in his side, she felt the carriage begin to move.

Basil Torquill allowed her to remain in that manner, glad at least that Patrice had chosen to be silent, and Patrice was careful that no sound escaped her, even as she wept quietly into the rough material of his coat.

Leaning forward on the brocaded seat-covering, careful not to crumple the delicate wings attached precariously to the back of his costume, Francis Trent selected another small candied violet from among the comfits in a silver candy dish. Popping the liberally sugared sweet past red-colored lips, painted in an exaggerated bow for effect, Sir Francis gave a smack of satisfaction. "Lovely!" he exclaimed, reaching for yet another, ignoring the Jordan almonds and bonbons. "Peregrine, where did you get these? I vow that I have never had the like," he declared enthusiastically, proceeding to pick all the tiny hard candies from the shining dish.

Lord Melburry, arranging the last touches to his own costume, looked up at Sir Francis with a quizzical eye. "Don't know where they are from, really," he answered, attempting to tie the high lace Roman sandals he had chosen to wear. "Mother brought them when she was visiting. Don't see how you can stand to eat them, either. They taste dreadfully if you ask me, and have little to recommend them other than they make one's breath reek of violets," Peregrine concluded, successfully affixing a neat knot to the top of his muscular calf.

Sir Francis was hardly listening as he began to deposit the sweets in the only pocket present on his ludicrous costume. "I find them refreshing," Francis asserted, his conscience quite clear as he took the last of the violets. If Peregrine did not even like them, then it was clear that he must save them for his own appreciative consumption. "They go with my image tonight," he added, rising from his chair and fluffing out the swan feather wings he had so ingeniously designed. His quiver of gilt arrows complemented the small bow he carried, the natural trademarks of Cupid.

"You mean your breath is as sweet as a zephyr?" Peregrine asked, tying a light cape about his shoulders to complete his costume.

"Precisely!" Sir Francis answered. He enjoyed feeling the part as well as dressing it, and would also enjoy the stares of admiration he fully expected his masterpiece to elicit from the crowds at the Argyle Rooms. He was sure that his concept was the most original, and looked at Lord Melburry's rather common costume with a little pity. Peregrine was dressed as a Roman athlete, a short white tunic of cotton falling in folds about him. His hair was adorned with the classic laurel leaves and he carried a large, wicked-looking javelin. Lord Melburry's muscular build possibly gave more credence to the likelihood of his chosen identity than would Sir Francis' puny figure had he decided to dress in a like manner.

"Well, that's everything, I think," Peregrine declared, checking to see that all was in order before ringing for his valet to clear the debris he had created in his haste to make himself ready.

Lord Melburry had been late to home, having spent the bulk of the afternoon on Bow Street, arranging for some very special services from those stalwart individuals who constituted the "runners".

If everything worked out tonight as he planned, Lord Melburry's efforts of the past few weeks would all come to fruition. Tonight was very important to his plans, for the last essential piece of difficult puzzle would fall into place.

Making his way to the Argyle Rooms, Trent rambling on at his side as the cold night air whipped those feathered wings about in wild disarray, Lord Melburry again found his thoughts straying as they had frequently throughout the past week. Then three other gentlemen appeared wearing near facsimiles of Sir Francis's own costume, complete down to the last arrow.

"And my tailor told me that there were no others like this!" the unfortunate gentleman fumed, turning to demand of Peregrine whether or not the law could prosecute him as a person of the nobility, should he take it upon himself to eradicate his costumer for such flagrant lying. However, Lord Melburry had disappeared from his side without a word, having important business of his own to attend to.

Peregrine made his way toward the back of the hall where the private boxes were situated on the balcony level overlooking the noise and bustle below. A dour-faced servant stood sentinel over the staircase as the boxes had been rented for exclusive use. Presenting a small card to the man and adding an inducement of several gold crowns, Lord Melburry was allowed to ascend the stairs.

Though Sir Francis might have lost sight of Peregrine, there were another pair of eyes watching his every movement from a small alcove. Hidden by heavy drapes, Aurora watched as he disappeared from view, the musky smell of tobacco smoke filling her senses as she began to move slowly through the crowd.

Aurora had been at the ball for the last half hour at least, having skipped past the watchful eyes of the man at the entrance with a group of loud and boisterous young women of questionable character. The women had been too foxed to realize that a stranger was in their midst, and the footman had not found Aurora's more conservative garb too unusual. Many of the most famous courtesans chose to underplay their treasures, both material and natural, and the thin veil of material that Aurora wore gave her an air of mystery which the servant was sure would appeal to quite a few of the gentry.

In the short time that Aurora had been there she had been accosted by no less than three gentlemen, all rather "up" in the world, the drink heavy on their breath as they had attempted to persuade her in turn to either dance, dine, or accept their protection, all of which she was to be "reimbursed" for richly. Aurora had declined all offers as best she could, stunned that such things should occur in reality. Of course she had always known that gentlemen often took mistresses. It was a fact which disgusted her no end, but to see with what unabashed openness these overtures were made, and with such a casual air! It made her senses whirl.

It was an education, to say the least, but Aurora was not so missish that she would faint at such attentions. Though she felt scorn for the women who were there, she had other things to attend to than to stare at and censure them. Her eyes were ever attentive for the presence of Peregrine, though in her heart she still prayed that Lord Simmons had, by some incredible chance, been wrong about him. When she had seen Lord Melburry enter, her spirits had dropped to their lowest possible ebb. Her fears were being confirmed. But after the initial shock of seeing Peregrine's handsome face among the crowd, Aurora felt her resolve harden. She might have left then, but for her determination to see the thing through. She would confront him before his mistress, and moved with deliberation toward the private boxes to do so. Aurora could feel the dampness of her eyes and refused to cry yet, blinking back the unruly tears. As she drew near the footman at the stairs, she wondered at her own boldness. Why, she thought, should she wish to torture herself? To see Lord Melburry in the arms of another woman could do nothing but deepen the wound he had already inflicted by the sheer fact that she loved him. It was then she realized that actually seeing him with another woman, with her own eyes, was the only way in which she could ever hope to go on. She wished to destroy her love for him entirely, if this could be done at all. She had to witness his deception.

"I am sorry, Madame, but you are not allowed to go

229

up," a voice spoke to Aurora and she realized that she had stopped before the footman guarding the steps.

"It is all right, I am expected," she replied, her voice low as to disguise it, holding out a coin to the man. He accepted it cautiously, but did not allow her to pass yet.

"I have been counting. Every couple is already upstairs. All the boxes are filled," he said, a suspicious look entering his eyes as he watched her carefully. It would not do for anyone to disrupt the persons above, many of whom were more powerful than he dared to cross for so little as a crown, but Aurora's quick mind came up with an answer.

"You have never heard of a *ménage à trois?* Do not be so naive," she laughed, moving the man aside gently with one delicate hand and proceeding up the steps. He did not see the reddening cheeks as she left.

Entering the dimly lit hall to which the boxes were connected, Aurora was faced with the dilemma of finding the one which contained Lord Melburry and his lady love. As she passed each one, she could hear a variety of sounds behind the closed doors. The two on the far right were not to be considered for the occupants had not yet drawn the drapes overlooking the ballroom and Aurora knew that they did not contain the one for whom she searched. Finally, she heard a voice that was familiar, a woman's voice, the woman she had met in the park.

Halting before the door, Aurora could hear the woman speaking in a low voice.

"Well, Lord Melburry, you have come as we agreed, and I place myself completely under your protection. You have been persistent, perhaps the most persistent gentleman I have ever encountered, but you have already gained what you want."

Aurora felt her throat tighten, her heart pounding as if it would burst. The realization that she had been thoroughly betrayed hit her with a violence that she had not herself expected. With tears of rage streaming down her face, she wrenched open the door, allowing it to swing free with a bang on the opposite wall as she rushed through to confront Peregrine Melburry.

What she saw startled her into a frozen attitude, for

230

the room did not hold Lord Melburry and the woman from the park alone. No scene of languorous longing or passionate embraces met her eyes. Rather, the lady was dressed for travel, and two gentlemen dressed in plain, unobtrusive blue stood at either side as if to escort her. She turned her head a bit to see Peregrine, who stood as if turned to stone with utter amazement.

"Aurora!" he exclaimed, astonished and not a little horrified at seeing her in such a setting. "Take her off now," he said, turning to the two gentlemen in blue, hoping somehow to put things in order, but Aurora blocked the door, a determined expression in her lovely eyes.

"Lord Melburry. There is no denying that I am confused as to what is going on, but I feel that I am entitled to an explanation," Aurora insisted, not caring if he agreed or not.

Peregrine was torn between the joy of seeing Aurora again and a fervent wish that she not have chosen to appear at such an inopportune moment. "Please, Aurora. I shall explain in good time, but it is essential that this lady be allowed to leave in the protection of these gentlemen for the time being," he pleaded, the appeal of his eyes so strong that Aurora almost felt herself persuaded. However, the lady in question was of another mind herself.

"I think that it would be better if we told Lady Trevelyn all, Lord Melburry," the dark-eyed beauty said, her voice as refined as Aurora remembered it. Turning from Lord Melburry before he could protest, the lady motioned for Aurora to be seated, she herself sitting most wearily.

"I do not know if you have been aware, but Lord Melburry's brother, the Duke of Melburry, has been persecuted by a gentleman out of his past, one Giles Killingham."

"I am aware of that entire story," Aurora interrupted, and she noted the start Peregrine made.

"Is Lady Lettice aware, then, as well?" Peregrine asked with surprise.

"It is from Lettice that I have heard all," Aurora replied. Turning back toward the strange woman, she waited for her to continue.

"Then you know of the scandal, of Lady Killingham's 'suicide'," the woman went on. The manner in which she spoke the word made Aurora wonder.

"You speak as if you do not believe it was," Aurora said, looking first from the lady to Peregrine.

"I have always believed it was not," Peregrine burst out passionately. "For a woman of such vanity to shoot herself in the head is not sensible or likely."

"So he came to me for the answer," the woman interrupted.

"To you?" Aurora asked. "But why to you? What can you know of the affair?"

"Let us say that I knew Lord Killingham well, at that time. I was privy to his innermost secrets, and on one occasion, soon after his wife's demise, he admitted to me that he had shot her himself out of jealousy."

"Can it be?" Aurora asked, too astonished for words.

"Yes, it can, but there was no proof of his crime at the time," Peregrine said. Coming to Aurora's side, he knelt by her chair, taking her hand in his. "Richard had gone, and there was no one left to ask any questions of. I was in school then and Richard stayed away, believing that he had caused the woman to kill herself."

"All these years. But why do you come forward now?" Aurora asked, puzzled by this change of heart.

"Let us say that I am tired," the lady responded. It was then that Aurora could see the weariness was deep in her eyes as she spoke. "I have quite a lot of money now. I have earned every penny. But I cannot rest easy. You see, I have known Giles Killingham better than almost any other woman, and I know to what lengths he would go if he thought I was going to betray him. Naturally, there had been no reason to fear him when the Duke was living in France, but now that he has returned . . . I have received letters, threats upon my life if I should speak."

"Then why risk it when you have so much to lose and are in such dreadful danger?"

"My dear," the lady answered, as if trying desperately to make her understand, "he is quite mad. He may kill me even if I do *not* speak. Lord Melburry has offered me protection as you see," she said, motioning to the large men who were instantly at her side.

"So you will testify against him in court?" Aurora asked, the truth dawning on her. "Will your testimony be enough?"

"It will," Peregrine assured her, looking into Aurora's eyes with a confidence she had never seen before. "That and the other proof I have accumulated. Killingham did not cover his tracks well enough, you see. I have the man who sold the weapon to him. Killingham had testified at the inquiry that his wife had been possessed of the weapon prior to her demise for some year and a half, keeping it for protection against intruders. I have proof that Killingham purchased it only a few days before for the express purpose of murdering her. You see, there is nowhere he can run to now."

"Your lordship, we must be leaving, it is getting late and they are expecting us at the inn," one of the blue-clad gentlemen spoke, his eyes concerned as he glanced at a small pocket watch.

Peregrine looked at Aurora for her answer. Rising from her chair, she took the strange woman's hands in hers, helping her to leave her seat and staring into her eyes for a long moment before allowing her to pass into the protective guard of her two companions.

The woman left without further word, closing the door behind her as she was led away by her escorts. Aurora felt Lord Melburry come close behind her, placing his hands lightly on her shoulders.

"Are you satisfied?" he whispered gently into her ear, his warm breath brushing her bare neck as he spoke. Aurora turned her face to his, her lips invitingly close to his as she gazed into his eyes.

"If you are asking if I believe you, I do," Aurora replied softly. "Is that what kept you away for so very long?"

"I could not think with you near," Peregrine admitted frankly, his loving eyes erasing any doubts that Aurora might have felt at any time.

"I was a fool ever to think that I could stop loving you," Aurora said, coming closer to him, the languid look in her blue eyes issuing an irresistible invitation.

Peregrine longed to caress her, more than he had ever wanted anything, but he was suddenly aware of the crowd below. The din had increased as the ball was becoming a bacchanal, the sounds of raucous laughter tainting the very air. He looked down at Aurora's delicately pale face. This place was not fit for her, and Peregrine was more disturbed than he would ever have guessed.

Aurora observed Peregrine's visage as he flinched a bit at a particularly bawdy song that had begun below, and realized the problem, those expressive eyes revealing all to her.

"Let us leave," she suggested, pretending to be ignorant of what was occurring below, for his sake.

"Through that crowd?" Peregrine spoke doubtfully, imagining what they would see if they had to make their way past all of the couples. "There is a back exit we could use. My curricle is out there," he said eagerly, recalling the door connecting to the rear of the building that the runners had evidently used.

"I would love another ride in your curricle," Aurora said, a mischievous smile appearing on her face as she took Lord Melburry's arm lovingly.

Returning her smile with one twice as broad, Peregrine led the way and they were soon out in the crisp night air. It was not very late yet. The ball would continue until the small hours of the morning, so there were few people to see the young couple hurrying between the carriages, searching for Lord Melburry's curricle so that they might depart.

Aurora could not help giggling a bit as she helped Peregrine search in the darkness, the joy at having dispelled all of her suspicions making her giddy. She was pleased to see Peregrine was not above laughing as well, and Aurora found that Lord Melburry had a very silly giggle indeed as he stumbled over a small stone in his laughter.

"We'll never find it in the darkness," Aurora whispered, though why she did so she could not imagine for there was no one to hear but the horses who stood together.

"Yes, we shall. We cannot be left stranded here," Peregrine contradicted as he searched. "There, I think

I see it!" he said, pointing ahead in the darkness and moving forward. Aurora, having moved away for a moment as she had been searching all around, turned back in time to see two shadowy figures leap out from behind a carriage and set upon him. One of the men struck Peregrine with a bludgeon. Aurora screamed, but a hand reached around from behind her to muffle her cry.

"What shall we do with him now?" one of the footpads asked the man who held Aurora captive.

She heard the low reply as she stared helplessly at the unconscious form of Peregrine. "I have a score to settle with Lord Melburry. Thrash him well. Perhaps then he will learn his place." She could hear one sickening thud, then another, as the two ruffians began carrying out their orders. She struggled wildly to help him as she felt herself being dragged toward a waiting carriage. Turning, she managed for an instant to get a glimpse of her captor. What she saw struck terror deeper within her heart for she found herself staring into the hard cruel eyes of Lord Killingham, and they were quite crazed.

꧁ CHAPTER 9

LORD RINGWOOD WAS finding it difficult to relax though he had performed every remedy he knew of to evoke the feeling of slumber he so desired. Warmed milk had failed to do the trick. The half-empty cup sat on the small table beside his elbow giving evidence that he had at least tried. Sitting in the plush chair directly opposite the cozy fire, boots removed and allowed to pile upon one another in disarray by the footstool where Lord Ringwood had propped his lower limbs, Stuart continued to read the book before him. It was a sensational little novel which he had paid only a penny for on the street, received from an enterprising little urchin with grubby hands and a quick smile.

Sighing, Stuart allowed the book to fall to his lap as he rubbed his weary eyes. He had not expected to be easy of mind, but he had hoped that he could stop thinking of Patrice for at least a fraction of an hour. It was not to be, and he finally gave in, allowing himself to dwell on the memory of her countenance. As usual this occupation caused him exquisite pain, an agony he had almost become accustomed to but which now held a new poignancy since it was even more clear to him than before that Patrice would never dream of considering him a suitable mate.

He had thought to say something to her about his feelings a dozen times, but had not found the opportunity or the words to do so. He was not a charmer, unable to be articulate or to flatter, but that did not mean he held no feelings, that he could not appreciate beauty with as keen an eye as the most verbose of suitors.

"I've made a mull of it now," he groaned, recalling his parting words to Patrice that afternoon. He had a right to be bitter, he thought, but no right to allow his frustrations to make him abusive to Patrice, and he regretted what he had said. Patrice had always been kind to him, though he was a clumsy sort of a fellow, and Stuart knew that other women would not have been so indulgent of his lack of finesse. She had even admonished some of her friends not to poke fun at his nose, a sore point with Lord Ringwood as it was so prominent.

No, it was hardly Patrice's fault gentlemen found her so attractive, and Stuart continued to chastise himself, savaging his cravat as he pulled it roughly from his throat and loosened the collar of his shirt.

At that moment, Stuart became aware of a commotion in the outer room. The strident tones of the innkeeper's wife's voice arguing with someone, apparently insistent upon an audience with him. Straining his ears, Lord Ringwood's eyebrows rose, startled.

"The dowager?" he asked himself disbelieving but his doubts were dispelled as the lady swept through the door, the innkeeper's wife still protesting and looking with worried eyes toward Lord Ringwood.

"She wouldn't listen to me, sir. Came in as bold as can be," the woman apologized, wringing her hands.

"This woman obviously doesn't know your nature, Lord Ringwood," the dowager said with her crispest manner. She had a determined expression and it was aimed directly at an astonished Lord Ringwood. "Reassure her that my intrusion is all right," she commanded, indicating the concerned woman.

"It is fine. Leave us, will you?" Stuart asked. The woman, still unsure as to what was about, hesitated a moment. The dowager would have none of it.

"Get along, woman! I do not intend to do anything but talk to the young man. That cannot possibly necessitate your presence!" The good woman hurried from the room and Patrice's grandmother did not wait for the door to close fully before speaking.

"Lord Ringwood, I do not have a lot of time to spare, so bear with me. If I have my way, you shall have even less time than I do now." The dowager ignored Stuart's motion for her to be seated, and she went on, looking at him as though she would see his deepest thought. "It is Patrice," she continued. Stuart gave a small start, then continued to look at the dowager, silent. "She has run off. I went to check on her. She was acting so oddly this evening that, well, I was worried that something might be wrong. Perhaps you had argued or some such tosh. It sometimes helps to talk about such things, even with an aging grandmother such as I am. She was not there. Some of her things were gone, and her travel cloak was missing."

"But where can she have gone off to?" Stuart interrupted, unable to be quiet any longer. "She would not run away just because I said a few unkind things to her this afternoon . . . would she?"

The horrified note in the young man's voice caused the aged woman to reply hurriedly. "No, no! I found some letters, from that lieutenant. What was his name?"

"Torquill?" Stuart asked, astounded.

"Yes, that was it. The last one spoke of an elopement, tonight. From what I gather she has been gone a good two hours or more," she said, holding out a folded parchment to Stuart's hand.

Taking the note, Lord Ringwood read it, then slowly handed it back. "I imagine they have gone to Gretna Green, then—a runaway marriage," he said dully.

"Well?" the dowager demanded suddenly. "Aren't you going to *do* something about it?"

"I?" Stuart asked. "What can I do? She has decided to marry the man."

"I had thought because you loved Patrice you would wish to stop her from doing something which could ruin her entire life, not to mention so paltry a thing as her reputation!" Lady Granville said with a difficulty of control. "Are you forgetting that there must be no involvement with the local people? If there is to be an avoidance of scandal, who else can I turn to to bring her back? Be reasonable. I know that you love Patrice. You cannot wish to see her tied to an impoverished officer for the rest of her days. I daresay he is naught but a gazetted fortune hunter."

The dowager was silent a moment as Stuart considered his choices. It was true that he was the only person likely to keep such an event a secret, truer still that he did love Patrice and did not wish to see her married to Lieutenant Torquill, but if it was what she truly wished, he was not such a one to deny her true happiness. He was torn until he recalled his promise to Patrice's father, that he would watch over Patrice and keep her from harm. If he could not make up his own mind what to do at this time, he would at least keep his pledge. "Very well, then, I shall go after them, but I cannot guarantee that I will be able to overtake them. They have two hours head start and may have taken any route. I will have to assume they would take the direct route as it is the quickest, giving up secrecy for speed," Stuart said, pulling on his boots hurriedly and calling out for the innkeeper to harness his gig.

"At last, some action," the dowager said with satisfaction, allowing herself to sit only after Stuart had bolted out of the door, pulling on his greatcoat awkwardly as he leapt into the seat of his carriage and sped away. Rubbing her arms, Lady Granville found that this was ineffectual, that she was still freezing cold from the exposure she had sustained in the night air. She moved with stiffened gait to the fire, easing herself down into the chair Lord Ringwood had so recently vacated. Holding her cold hands toward the fire, the dowager could not help worrying.

"Patrice's travel cloak was made for more temperate weather. I hope that lieutenant of hers at least had the intelligence to hire a closed carriage so that she will be warm enough." The woman shuddered a trifle as she heard the wind whistling outside, and leaned a little more into the fire, glad of its warmth.

The light travel cloak was, as the dowager had feared, less than adequate to shield Patrice from the cold. However, her grandmother's concerns over whether or not Lieutenant Torquill had hired a closed carriage were now academic, as that unworthy vehicle had expired on the roadway not far out of Granthem, a victim of the deep ruts in the ground caused by the passing of so many wagons.

The horses had broken loose from their rigging before the lieutenant could extricate himself from the carriage, bolting away into the darkness and leaving the couple stranded on foot. Basil's raging and cursing at this ill fortune did nothing to alter the fact that the curricle was immobile, tilted drunkenly to one side as one of the wheels had cracked and splintered, leaving it useless. It only served to horrify Patrice who had not before heard such profanity from Basil. With a futile kick to the carriage, he had taken a lantern and lit the way for them. They had walked the last four miles to a posting house in silence, Patrice clutching her satchel as the night air cut into the bare skin on her hands, her cloak flapping wildly about as she attempted to keep up the military pace. Though she did not speak, Patrice's mind was more than amply occupied with her thoughts. They were difficult ones to deal with, but there was no time left to dawdle, to put off decisions which would affect the rest of her life.

Tramping a few paces ahead, face grim, Lieutenant Torquill at last broke the silence. "There. I see the posting house," he said, turning about to see if Patrice was still keeping up with him.

She came abreast with him, the lantern's light causing her to squint slightly as she looked up at her

239

companion. "Will we be able to rest here for a while?" she asked, feeling sorely the need for some time to think and rest.

"A while, I suppose," Lieutenant Torquill responded curtly. "But I hope to hire another carriage here, and this time I will be sure that it can stand the strain," he added irately. It was clear that he still fumed over the inconvenience that had occurred, and Patrice suddenly thought of how she would feel if she had to look upon his face, as it was now, for the rest of her life. Pale jaw grinding with irritation, tight-lipped and angry, it was clear that he would be making things difficult for someone.

Why, she thought, Basil does not even appear attractive in the least at this moment. She allowed her jaw to drop as she stared, and Lieutenant Torquill gave her a look which spoke of a little distaste.

"You could have made yourself a bit more presentable, you know," he reprimanded her coldly. "I wouldn't be surprised if the proprietor of the establishment wondered at us coming in so late, and you looking so untidy. Straighten your hair or something."

Patrice's free hand instantly went to her hair, pushing back the few stray strands under the hood hurriedly. "Of course, Basil, but that is the style, a few tendrils or *guiches* at the side. I thought you liked my hair the way it was," she said, a pathetic note in her voice.

"Yes, yes. But that was when you were in London," he remarked as he made his way toward the doorway to the house. "The country people out here will only think it untidy. Besides, you are about to become a married woman, and you will have to begin to dress appropriately, more maturely. Soon enough you will be the mother of my children, and they cannot have a child for a mother. Recall that to mind and conduct yourself with propriety." This last was said as he knocked vigorously on the door. He did not look to Patrice to see her reaction or he would have seen the outraged expression she bore at being told how to conduct herself.

Patrice held her tongue as the portal opened, an elderly gentleman dressed in a nightshirt and woolen

240

vest looking at them with candleholder outstretched for light. "It is quite late," he wheezed. "We were expecting no one until the morning."

Pushing his way inside with authority, Basil reassured the old man. "Our carriage broke down a few miles from here and we need a place to rest as well as a place to hire another carriage."

He can be so charming when he desires, Patrice thought, and realized that she felt nothing at all as she watched her "intended" convince the old man to allow them to warm themselves by the fire. The innkeeper looked at Patrice, but said nothing as she stared circumspectly at the floor.

Leading Patrice over to the fire, rubbing his own hands vigorously as well, Basil Torquill asked conversationally if there was any chance of a carriage's being available.

The proprietor scratched his head. "I believe there is one in the stables," he replied slowly. "Are you sure that your missus will want to ride on tonight? Seems mighty weary to me." This acknowledgement of Patrice's existence caused Lieutenant Torquill to look at her. She did indeed appear drawn, but Basil did not consider it a bar to further travel.

"It is just the walk here that has exhausted her," he answered for Patrice. "She will be fine after a rest. When can the carriage be made available to us?" he asked. He was ready to leave at an instant, that much was obvious.

"It will be an hour, sir, at least," the old man replied. "I have put the horses out in the shelter on the far pasture and must fetch them myself as my wife and children visit relatives tonight. This is not a much-used posting house, and we run the place ourselves."

"Well, then, you had best be off to get the beasts, I suppose," Basil said, then turned away to inspect the contents of a small pot on the side of the hearth. "Stew," he remarked, then sighed. "I suppose it will do." He turned to look at the proprietor. "Well, off you go. We must leave as soon as can be arranged," he said, placing the pot on the fire's embers.

"Basil!" Patrice exclaimed. "You could at least help the poor man." She watched as the proprietor shuffled

241

off toward the door, candle still in hand. "He is so old! I am sure the cold weather is not healthy for him at all."

"It is his living, Patrice," Basil replied sharply, casting a piercing, critical eye upon her, then turning back to the fire, the matter settled as far as he was concerned.

This was apparently the last straw for Patrice who had been holding much back within her breast since they had begun their flight. "Basil," she began, clutching her hands together as if to calm herself, "we must talk."

"You have my attention," Lieutenant Torquill murmured as he squatted down by the hearth to pick up the hot container of stew.

His inattention bothered Patrice, but she had to continue. "You said just now that I should act with more propriety. I had not known that I had not. You used to say that you liked the way I was, only tonight you seem displeased with me altogether, even with my appearance. Say that it is not true. Say that I imagine it, only please do look at me!" Patrice pleaded, her voice shaking and uncertain.

Basil glanced up from his position at Patrice's agitation. Then he rose and came to her, that familiar charming smile appearing on his handsome face. Sitting down next to her he took her hands in his. Patrice leaned anxiously forward to look into his eyes, hoping desperately to see there what she most desired.

"My poor Patrice. You are distraught by the excitement of all this," he said softly, all concern for her feelings of a sudden. "Else why would you doubt that I love you? Of course I do, but it is a husband's duty to help his wife to do *her* duty to *him*. Perhaps I started too soon, but it is only looking to our future happiness," he assured her with a small kiss on her cheek.

Patrice had longed for a passionate embrace, some proof of his love, and she searched his eyes for a sign and saw none. She stared into his deeply blue eyes and there was nothing there. They were as ice.

She could think of nothing to say, and sat back and stared. The golden curls on his head were still as

242

golden as before. He looked as handsome and masculine as ever. His voice was as persuasive as ever it was with its deep baritone richness, but Patrice could not see any love in his nature. It was as if God had stayed his hand when it came to endowing Basil with that quality.

"You do not really love me," she whispered, shrinking back from his nearness. "I have made a dreadful, dreadful mistake."

Lieutenant Torquill's eyes narrowed at these words. "You are hysterical!" he said flatly, and Patrice shrank back even more. She was familiar now with the initial signs of Basil's going into a rage, and this quiet, commanding voice was first. "We will be leaving soon, and in a few hours we will reach the Scottish borders and Gretna Green where we will be married." The manner in which he spoke was meant, no doubt, to convey a feeling of inevitability. Patrice was not being left with a choice, but her instincts demanded that she react, even if futilely. She did not want to think that.

"I wish to go home. Take me home," she said in a low voice, staring steadily at the man before her.

It was as if he had not heard her as he continued in a businesslike manner. "You must have some of this stew first, you will feel better then," he said, rising quickly and fetching the pot.

"I wish to be taken back," Patrice said again, her voice slowly rising in volume, her eyes beginning to become wild as she realized the full consequences of what was now occurring.

Lieutenant Torquill stopped, placed the pot on a table, and came back to Patrice's side, grabbing her wrist with a deliberately harsh grip, forcing her to look up. "You and I shall be off, and married, and then we shall set up a house, perhaps in London. I will resign my commission, of course. It would not befit my station at that time. We will have to see your lawyers about a 'fitting' allotment, and you will naturally need to have me take over all responsibilities for your welfare and that of my children."

Patrice wrenched her hand away. She was sure that it was bruised. She could say nothing. It was all clear to her now. If she fought him, he would most assuredly think nothing of striking her, and there was no help for her here. Her mother's and father's words returned to her; even Stuart had warned her that Basil might not be all he appeared, and she had not listened. It pained her most of all that she had accused Stuart of all people of being against her.

Lieutenant Torquill left her there a moment, searching for a dish and setting. Patrice thought furiously, her wrist throbbing as she cradled it with her unharmed hand.

"My family, they will never accept you, she stated irrevocably, her voice daring to be proud.

"It doesn't matter. You are independent of them. We will not socialize with them at all," Basil replied, rummaging in a cupboard unruffled. He now felt that things were under control.

"And if I will not say that I will marry you when we reach Gretna Green?" she threatened, the pain in her wrist goading a flash of defiance from her.

"You would change your mind soon enough," Basil Torquill replied ominously. Patrice did not need to have him describe what he would do in detail. She knew. He would force himself on her, and she would submit and marry him on threat of such a violence.

She was trapped, but could not give herself up to tears yet, though she was weary and frightened. All she could think of at that moment, as incongruous as it might have struck her at one time, was Stuart, and how gentle he had always been with her. Even when he had been incensed, even when he had said angry things to her, he had always been tender, and she knew at that instant that she loved him more than she had ever believed she had loved Basil. Now it was all too late. She longed to see him, to tell him everything that was in her heart, even if he did not want her. Given the chance, she would willingly spend her whole life trying to make him love her and proving how much she truly adored him.

A clatter of a bowl set before her roused her to stare up at her captor, for that was now what Basil had become. She did not wait for his order, and picked up her spoon with a trembling hand. Basil turned away to attend to his own needs, and Patrice now attempted to choke down a bit of stew, her throat constricted with despair. She felt like a prisoner, and her jailer was one from whom she had no hope of escaping.

Aurora was in similar straits as she found herself sitting across from Lord Killingham in the swiftly moving coach she had been thrust into only a few short hours before. At first, she had attempted to struggle from Killingham's grasp so that she might see what had happened to Peregrine, so frantic was she with worry, but this endeavor only served to give Lord Killingham a feeling of pleasure. He increased the pressure of his grip over her until she ceased, whereupon he released her, a triumphant expression on his face that gave Aurora a subtle hint on how best to manage herself. She recalled the mad glint in his eyes as he had stared at her from across the carriage, the excitement he had felt as she had struggled, making his breath come heavily until Aurora thought she must shudder in disgust and fear. However, she knew instinctively that to keep Lord Killingham from overstepping the last few shreds of humanity he pretended to hold true to, she must behave as though there was no doubt in her mind as to the correct course for him to take. She had forced herself to sit erect in the fast-moving carriage and look directly at Killingham, willing herself not to shrink from his presence. This behavior had intrigued him.

"Do not attempt to look out of the window or call out for help," he had warned, his voice as sinister as his intent. "If you do, I will have no alternative but to bind and gag you, and I would not wish to do that to my future bride."

Aurora had not shown the least little fear, rather, she managed a scornful expression, as if such behavior was beneath her. "I am not so silly as to do such a thing," she had replied proudly. "I do not waste my energies on futile gestures. You have obviously planned this entire thing to perfection."

Killingham had been somewhat suspicious of the calmness with which Aurora had appeared to accept, even if grudgingly, her fate.

"Yes, I have," he had said slowly, and Aurora realized that she had almost given herself away when he had continued, with a sadistic gleam. "I have killed two birds so to speak. I have 'persuaded' you to come with me, and I have arranged for a suitable revenge against Lord Melbury for daring to presume to keep you company. Never fear that he will be killed, my dear," he commented, reading the concern in Aurora's face. "He will receive the thrashing he deserves, but I fully intend for Lord Melburry to be present to witness our marital bliss. No doubt he will be tortured by it," Killingham added hopefully. "Yes, I believe I have been altogether successful this evening. Hardly the workings of a madman, wouldn't you say, my dear?"

She had been silent at that, refusing to discuss further the matter, but never altering her expression or her attitude which seemed so successful in keeping Lord Killingham at bay.

He had talked idly for the next few hours, and Aurora had only found it necessary to either nod or be silent. He rambled on incessantly about what their life would be like in the future, until Aurora could have screamed, but she had resisted this urge—to buy time. She was certain that someone would soon discover her absence, and there was a chance, however slim, that someone had witnessed her abduction. If there was a chance for rescue, she would do everything in her power to delay her fate at Killingham's hands.

So she continued to sit quietly, feeling nauseated as she inhaled the sickly sweet fragrance of the gardenias which were hung in bouquets about the carriage interior. No doubt it was to make the carriage more festive in anticipation of their "marriage". Aurora became aware suddenly of the carriage's slowing, and a rough voice from the driver's seat called out to Lord Killingham at their approach to an inn where they had arranged for a short rest and a change of horses.

"Recall, your behavior must be most circumspect when we arrive, as befits a bride. Recall also that a struggle would be futile. I have told the people at the inn that you are a crazed relative I am conveying to a confinement house outside of London."

"Would they believe it once they have seen me?" Aurora inquired, a feeling of hopelessness engulfing her once again as she realized that she would no longer have the darkness of the coach to hide her from Lord Killingham's ravenous eyes.

"But of course," he laughed. It was a hideous laugh, somehow obscene. "I have applied my blunt liberally. They will believe anything I say. Besides, I have purchased a private sitting room so you will not have the opportunity to appeal to anyone." Aurora could feel Lord Killingham's eyes upon her even in the darkness, and she felt her color rise. The vehicle came to a halt, and Aurora was handed a long cloak to cover her costume. She wrapped herself in it to the neck. "I have forgotten nothing," Killingham whispered close to Aurora's ear as he handed her down from the carriage. She squirmed from his grasp, an action which caused him to laugh. Her face was still burning as she walked with an even stride to the door of the inn, lights still lit, as they apparently did expect Lord Killingham's arrival.

The door was opened by an unctuous-looking innkeeper who stared fearfully at her, as if expecting some sort of frightful fit. Yes, Killingham had thought of everything. As Aurora passed through the door into the hall, she could hear the innkeeper's rough-looking wife as she wondered aloud at how normal she appeared. Aurora lifted her head proudly as she passed into the private room which had been set aside for her.

There was a fire in the room, and as Aurora entered she looked to see if there were any tongs or a poker, but they had been removed purposely, or so she deduced as she sank wearily into a chair by the hearth. Killingham had seen her eyes wander toward the fireplace and smiled as he took a chair and placed it beside hers.

"Warm yourself well," he advised solicitously, the flames illuminating his unhandsome face as he spoke. Aurora had now the opportunity to peer more closely at Lord Killingham as he continued. "We will make another stop outside Granthem for late supper and then not another until we reach Gretna Green."

"I suppose you have told them the same wild story!" Aurora demanded bitterly. She could not help herself, such was her feeling of helplessness.

247

"Of course," Killingham replied, smiling. He was enjoying all of this immensely, and it showed.

Aurora could feel his eyes on hers as she watched the fire, holding her cloak close about herself as if it were a shield against his gaze.

"You will be more comfortable if you remove your cloak," he suggested. Aurora did not move. "I can assist you with it if necessary." It was a subtle threat, and Aurora removed the cloak casually, as if she did not care.

She heard him chuckle a little, and it made her shiver as she rubbed her hands on her bare arms. She was aware that her simple costume, that of a wood nymph, was more revealing than she would have liked, considering her circumstances, and she was ever aware of Killingham's eyes upon her.

"That is what I enjoy about you," he said suddenly, leaning closer to Aurora who did not flinch away due only to her steely self-control. "You are so proud. My first wife, she was proud. Some would have said vain. I like that in a woman. It makes you fit to be my bride."

Aurora did not respond to his remarks, nor did she look at him, but she could see him in her mind's eye clearly, the aging face with its lines of dissipation. There were still the remains of alcohol on his breath as he hovered close to her, not yet daring to presume upon her, only because her demeanor commanded it, and it was her proper behavior which he prized so, or so she had deduced.

"You are as beautiful as she was," Killingham continued, seemingly thinking of times past as he stared at her with unseeing eyes.

"What was she like, your wife?" Aurora asked in a low voice, as much as to lengthen their stay and increase delay as to learn something of the woman who had taken Lord Killingham willingly.

"She was beautiful. As I said, a trifle vain, but then she was my wife and of course surpassed other beauties of that time," he commented, lost in thought. "She was regal, proud like yourself, but not so calm. She was always highly strung, nervous, prone to fits," he continued without prompting, "and she knew of her charms all too well."

248

Aurora was tired of playing this quiet game, and Lord Killingham appeared to be becoming more amorous as he came ever nearer to her. She decided to try another tack. "Other men were aware of those charms, or so I hear," she commented dryly.

"Eh? Where did you hear that?" he asked sharply, sitting up in his seat and thus putting more space between himself and Aurora.

"From several people," Aurora continued vaguely. "She had lovers, they say."

"She was a slut!" Killingham roared suddenly, his expression changing in an instant to one of rage. Aurora was left speechless at the change. She realized that this radical switch was due to his madness, and she remained stiff in her seat as Lord Killingham stalked about the room like a driven creature. If he had been distant before, he was no longer aware of her presence, of where he was as he now spoke.

"She had lovers, oh yes she did. She would deny it one moment and then flaunt them in my face the next. And yet she had everything she could want, carriages, jewels, clothing, everything, every little whim was granted. If we had . . . problems, well, so does every married couple." He paused at that, as if remembering insults hurled in anger. "She lied to me, even to the last. She told me that the Duke of Melburry was not yet her lover, but that she would run away with him. They had been together all along, and she was going away to France with him."

"But you changed their plan, didn't you?" Aurora asked, the irresistible desire to know from Killingham what had occurred causing her to ask.

Lord Killingham hesitated. "No one leaves me unless I wish it, and I will have my way in all things," he said slowly.

"You killed her, didn't you?" Aurora whispered, the horror of it all causing her to shrink back in her seat as she gazed into the vacant face of Lady Killingham's murderer. Though she had known, to hear it confessed made it all the more real to her.

He murmured a few words that Aurora could not make out. It was as if he was commiserating only with himself. Then she could hear what he was saying. "She was sleeping between sheets of white satin, in all her nakedness, waiting for her lover, I have no doubt. She ordered me from the room. She had such red hair, and then there was the red of the blood when I shot her, all over the covers."

There was silence, Aurora barely moving as she took shallow breaths of air, then Lord Killingham looked at her once again and seemed to recall where he was. He reached out a hand toward the lovely girl before him, desiring to touch the throat that glowed white against the fire. Aurora could feel her heart pounding as if to burst as she pressed hard against the back of her chair in a futile attempt to escape his touch, loathing and dread in her eyes. She was paralyzed and unable to flee, but a knock on the door stayed Lord Killingham's hand at the crucial instant. "Come in," he bellowed with irritation, letting his hand fall reluctantly. The innkeeper entered hesitantly, staring blatantly at Aurora's strange costume and at the flushed and still-wild face of Lord Killingham. This unreal tableau caused the proprietor to wonder which of the two was truly insane.

"Your carriage is ready, your lordship," he said, wringing a cloth for cleaning between anxious hands. He had left the door open when he had entered, and Aurora could see his curious wife standing not far off.

"We will be only a moment," Lord Killingham assured the man.

The innkeeper wavered a moment at the door, then backed out. The door remained open, but the proprietor hurried his wife out of the hallway to wait.

The intrusion seemed to have been enough to cause Killingham to think better of his plans, whatever they might have been. Instead, he reached into the pocket of his coat and extracted a familiar object that glittered like fire, suspended from its golden chain.

"The locket you once refused. Put it on," he commanded, holding it out to Aurora. She could not make herself take it, for she would never willingly accept this symbol of their impending marriage. Killingham waited a moment, then rose, unclasping the chain and approaching Aurora. She did not move as he placed the locket about her neck, his hand caressing her bare shoulders briefly. He stepped back, eyeing his handi-work with approval. "It suits you, as I knew it would," he said. There was a small noise out in the hallway. "Make yourself ready to travel," he said abruptly to Aurora as he left the room to settle his account with the innkeeper.

The moment he left, Aurora's hands went to her throat, tearing at the thin chain about her neck as if it burned her. The soft metal snapped instantly at her at-tack and she hurled the locket onto the braided rug on the floor, raising both hands to her throat and shoul-ders as if to erase the memory of Killingham's touch. Hurriedly, Aurora draped herself with her cloak again, making sure that her neck and breast were totally cov-ered so Lord Killingham might not discover what she had done. Pulling the hood up over her head partially to conceal her face and her agitation, she quitted the room.

Killingham was waiting for her in the hall, and they were soon off again. The clatter of the horses as they started, pounding with Aurora's heartbeat, was like a clock that marked off how much time she had left, be-fore she would no longer have any choices. Aurora prayed fervently for a miracle as she sat once again across from her captor.

Sir Francis was not entirely foxed but quite near being foxed, as he took another sip from the glass of sherry held by a creature who had proclaimed herself Mab, queen of the fairies, or some such. In any case, the ravishingly lovely young creature seemed willing enough, and Sir Francis wondered why he had ever hesitated to come to the Cyprian ball to begin with. Leaning back on the lounge, heedless of the conse-quences to his winged costume in his semi-inebriated state, he allowed the fairy queen to pour the sherry in a thin stream into his mouth. She did so with a laugh that reminded him of a fountain's splashing, then sud-denly she seemed to take it into her head to play hide and seek, and left his side, darting out of a side door into the back of the building where the carriages were kept.

Well, strenuous activity whets the carnal appetite, or

so I have been told, Sir Francis thought doubtfully as he roused himself from his reclining position to give chase. Once in the darkness, he could see little. There was a moon, but it was obscured by clouds, peeking out only on occasion to light up the carriages which had been placed in little rows as with a militia of men. Suddenly, he heard a giggle of laughter, and turned to see a glimpse of the lady's green costume darting between carriages as she hurried along on tiny feet. A ballet dancer perhaps? he wondered, then left that academic question for later as he hastened off after his quarry, as quiet as he might be, considering that his wings scraped the sides of the coaches as he passed through particularly tight spaces. He was losing feathers here and there, but could not stop to retrieve them as that tinkling laughter was still ahead of him. He passed a familiar crest and recognized it as Lord Melburry's curricle. He had not seen Peregrine of late, but then the evening was yet early. Perhaps there were pressing considerations that he had to attend to, but for Sir Francis, his concentration and energies all were focused on his elusive fairy queen.

The unfortunate Lord Melburry was at that moment being held up by the arms, barely conscious, by two ruffians of unknown parentage. He could faintly hear their voices as they discussed what next to do to his restrained form. It had been some minutes since he had heard the last rumblings of the carriage which had whisked his beloved away, and he had been subject to an inept thrashing of sorts by these two hooligans. He had been a handful at first, struggling to reach Aurora's side as he had become aware that she was being dragged toward a vehicle, but he had been pulled back and thrust to the ground, remaining there to be kicked repeatedly.

"What'll we do wit' 'im now?" asked the smaller of the two, turning with a slightly swollen fist to his partner. Bound by the wrists behind his back and gagged with a filthy rag, Peregrine had a moment's satisfaction that the man had hurt himself worse than he had Lord Melburry in his endeavors.

Looking down at Peregrine's still-open eyes, the light of defiance and revenge shining in those blue orbs, the other man rubbed his chin a moment. He liked to see a man break before him; it was what he enjoyed most about his work. "High and mighty, ain't he?" the rogue snickered. "An' oi' suppose that clock oi' 'is makes 'im a one for th' ladies, I'll be bound." There was a movement by the larger man, and suddenly Peregrine was aware of a flash, the glint of steel. The man fingered the blade of his knife gingerly. "Th' gentleman said not to kill ye, but oi' believes we can yet make ye a little less proud," he said grimly, placing the razor-sharp edge of his hunting knife against Peregrine's right cheek.

Suddenly, his partner released his grip on Lord Melbury, raising his hands to his face, as if to shield himself from some horrific vision, letting loose with a terrible shriek. His larger partner watched amazed as his friend fell to his knees in an attitude of prayer, then turned to look behind him at what had caused such an incredible transformation. What he saw coming toward him in the darkness caused him to allow his knife to clatter to the ground from numbed hands. Floating toward him, wings outspread in the attitude of an attacking falcon, was a ghostly specter, a creature or monster, and as it wove an unsteady path toward him, feathers fluttering in wild disarray about it, the ruffian took to his feet, leaving his immobile cohort to his fate, never looking back lest his soul be spirited away.

Francis Trent watched after the fleeing man with a slightly besotted expression, then looked down at the kneeling, frantically praying figure before him for some moments before looking to the bound figure that he recognized as Peregrine Melbury. Bending down to release his friend, wings awry and moulting, Sir Francis cried out in surprise.

"Peregrine! Good God, what in the world has happened here?" Sir Francis, in his hurry to release Peregrine, and in his less than sober state, failed to secure the second assailant who, realizing that this was no avenging angel but a costumed cove, made good his escape.

"Damn you, Francis!" Peregrine gasped brokenly, the pain in his ribs where he had been kicked beginning to intrude as the muscles got over being numb.

253

"You have let him escape," Peregrine complained as Francis struggled to loosen the cords which bound Lord Melburry's hands.

"You could at least thank me," Trent replied, kicking the sodden gag aside fastidiously with his foot as he knelt to see better the ropes. Finally Peregrine was free, but he was unsteady, and a sudden wave of weakness overcame him as he leaned heavily against the already unsteady Sir Francis.

"They have taken her off!" Peregrine murmured vaguely, the very trees about him beginning to swim as another sharp pain in his ribs made itself known.

"Yes, yes," Sir Francis burbled helplessly as he began to feel the heavier weight of Peregrine begin to slide down toward the earth against his feeble struggles. "Who has been taken off?" he asked as he finally gave way and Peregrine slid down, lying on the cold ground, barely conscious.

"Aurora, she has been abducted. Must go after her," Peregrine managed to gasp before he was lost in darkness.

"Aurora?" Sir Francis repeated blankly, his fogged brain taking an inordinately long time to digest this information. "By Jove! I believe he means Lady Trevelyn!" he exclaimed, then, as if galvanized to action, hurried back toward the Argyle Rooms. Bolting through the darkness, unable to see clearly, he barreled straight into the burly form of one of the footmen.

"Ah, just the man I want," he exclaimed as he was propped back up on his feet. He had fallen, sprawled to the ground on impact, the servant unmoved by so little a projectile. "You must go to Lady Braden's house and fetch back the Duke of Melburry. It is most important that it be done with all speed. His brother, Lord Melburry, is hurt and the Lady Aurora Trevelyn has been abducted by persons unknown." He thrust a five-pound note into the man's hand and promptly allowed himself to collapse on the cold stones of the terrace in exhaustion, the effects of the drink coming on him of a sudden.

The servant hurried off, pausing only to inform his superior of what had occurred. Sir Francis could hear someone shouting for a physician, and then a number

254

of footsteps, but he was now leaving the rest of the details up to everyone else for he was quite exhausted, falling off to sleep, leaning up against a granite carving of Pan.

As it was, Sir Francis' presence was not required, Lord Melburry reviving in a short while to the sight of both his elder brother and the eldest Lady Trevelyn who looked down at his prostrate form as a physician finished binding Peregrine's chest.

"Aurora!" he exclaimed, barely aware that the word had been no more than a croak.

"Give him some water!" Lettice said, anxious concern in her voice as she waited for Peregrine to speak.

"What is this I have heard!" Richard asked tensely as Peregrine pushed the glass away from his lips after scarcely a sip.

"Aurora, she has been abducted. It was Killingham, I heard his voice as he was taking her away," Peregrine replied quickly. The doctor admonished him to lie still, but Lord Melburry was having none of it. Sitting up tentatively, he winced a bit at the pain, but found it bearable enough. "I must go after her," he said in deadly earnest.

The Duke would have pushed his brother back to the ground, but for the look he saw in his eyes. "I will go with you," Richard said at last, assisting Peregrine to rise.

"But where to?" Lettice asked with dismay, horrified at the thought of her sister's being in Lord Killingham's power. She was aware of what sort of a demented man he was, and was as determined as they were that she would not be left behind.

"He can have taken her to only one place," Peregrine said, his breathing shallow, as it pained him.

"Gretna Green?" Richard asked, helping his brother on with the heavy coat he had brought with him.

"It was a traveling coach he dragged her into," Peregrine said grimly, his face murderous as he recalled the scene to mind. "I heard him instruct his coachman to that effect."

Richard instructed an eager footman to bring the

carriages around to the front, post haste, and as they waited, turned back to Peregrine, his face serious.

"And now if you can manage to tell me what Lady Aurora was doing here, I would appreciate it," Richard said with gravity.

Peregrine saw no reason to hide his activities further. His suspicions had all been confirmed about Killingham, so there was no remaining hint of doubt as Peregrine explained.

"Aurora suspected that I was having a liaison with a courtesan and she had followed me here tonight to discover if it was true."

"And was it?" the Duke asked bluntly, not wishing to mince words.

"Of course not," Peregrine replied instantly. "I was placing Killingham's former mistress under the protection of the runners. She had promised to testify against him in a court of law."

"Testify to what?" Lettice asked, totally mystified by all of this.

"That Lord Killingham murdered his wife out of jealousy. He confessed it to her, and I have other proof that is enough, along with her testimony, to hang him," Peregrine responded, and from the look on his face Lettice was convinced that he would have relished witnessing Killingham's demise at that very moment.

This incredible news stunned Richard so much that he could barely find his voice, and there was an uneasy silence, broken only by the arrival of the carriages as they halted before the waiting figures.

Peregrine refused his brother's shoulder to prove to himself that he could walk alone, wincing only slightly as he went.

"I want you to travel with me in the carriage," Richard said as their vehicles were brought forth. Lord Melburry's racing curricle was there as well.

"No, I will be faster if I go alone in my rig," Peregrine replied stubbornly, his face grim.

"But the pain," Lettice protested.

"The pain will keep me awake and alert," Peregrine interrupted brusquely. "Do not argue, every moment we stand here talking puts them farther away." So saying, Lord Melburry mounted his carriage with only an

256

instant's stiffening of his body to show what it had cost him.

"I will follow behind, then, after I have taken Lettice home. And Peregrine," the Duke hesitated, "thank you, bantling."

Peregrine looked into his brother's eyes a moment, nodded once, then whipped his horses into furious action, the clatter of hooves loud against the cobblestones as his curricle careened out of sight toward the city's limits.

Peregrine, his chest throbbing at first, was glad of the cold air which hit him; as the chill set in, it numbed the pain somewhat. His teeth were clenched until his jaw ached with the rage he was saving. That he would find Lord Killingham he was sure; wherever he might try to hide and no matter how swift his horses were, Peregrine intended to dog his tracks. And once he did catch up with him, it would no longer be his brother's score he wished to settle, but his alone. His only fear was for Aurora, and he fought that, as well as time. He was certain she would try to delay Killingham, but the fact that she would also use every ounce of her strength to resist him, mad as he was, caused Peregrine to fear for her safety. "If he harms her, I will kill him," Peregrine swore softly in the voice of a man to be taken seriously at his word. It was well that Richard could not look on his brother's face, for if he had ever doubted that Peregrine had the ability to take a life, his mind would have been changed forever. Killingham had taken the one thing which mattered more to Peregrine than life or honor, and he would have her back or see Killingham die in agony.

Richard watched his brother leave, but his mind was still on the truth that Peregrine had told him, trying after all those years to believe that it was true. The Duke felt a hand slip into his.

"Now you know the truth," Lettice said, glad in her heart for Richard, but unable to control her worry over Aurora. "Richard, you must take me with you," she pleaded.

"I cannot. It is a long journey and I will go faster

without you," he said, trying to ignore the appeal of Lettice's apprehensive face.

"Then I will follow you in another carriage," she insisted, almost frantic. "Recall, you knew from the beginning that I was headstrong, and I cannot sit quietly at home when my sister is in so much danger."

"I had known you were stubborn," Richard admitted grudgingly. The minutes ticked by as he hurried to make a decision.

"My aunt will say nothing. I daresay she knows me well enough to know that I would insist upon going," Lettice said hurriedly, her words persuading the Duke.

"One scandal at a time, I suppose," he said abruptly, and Lettice hurried to seat herself next to him in the carriage. "I only hope that a scandal is all that we have to deal with when we at last catch up with Killingham." With those words the Duke started up his horses and followed after Peregrine, determined to be there at the kill.

CHAPTER 10

STUART HAD been driving for some time now and felt distinctly like a man whose goal was forever retreating from him. He had reached the posting house outside of Granthem in short order but there had been no sign at all of the runaways, and the proprietor of the house had only stared with some amusement and surprise at this young gentleman flying madly about the countryside in the dead of night with high Hessian boots more fitting for the hunt than for driving.

Stuart had hurried away from there in embarrassment, feeling the staring eyes upon his bare neck where his cravat should have been. As he had continued along the same road, he began to have doubts that the couple had not chosen a more devious route, or that the lieutenant had decided to sport the blunt to hire horses to be changed at some prearranged spot along their route so there would be no need at all to stop. This idea had gnawed away at his mind as he had continued with no sign of anyone. After all, if he himself had been considering such an expedition, he would have planned it well, arranging for the fastest horses and the quickest route befitting the precious cargo he would have been absconding with. In any case, even if he did find them, he was not at all sure what he was going to do once he had. He had tried to imagine himself taking Patrice back to her grandmama against her will, and it had caused him more than one shudder, this not even considering the lieutenant's natural objection to his plans.

Lord Ringwood was deep in his thoughts as he continued, so much so that he suddenly had to swerve his carriage to avoid crashing directly into an object blocking the road ahead which he had failed to see until the last instant. His gig's springs shrieked at the strain as he pulled back onto the road, small stones slipping about the wheels.

Sitting a moment to settle his nerves, Stuart had visions of the Four in Hand Club's expelling him from their ranks for his lack of skill, then dismissed the fantasy and breathed a sigh of thanks as he walked over to see what had occurred on the roadway. He discovered a hired chaise whose wheel and axis had apparently given way. Tilted at an extreme angle to the side, the riggings torn away by the no doubt terrified horses, it looked quite badly off, and in an instant Stuart guessed that this had been the vehicle used for the elopement. Just as suddenly the idea intruded itself that perhaps someone had been hurt in the process. He looked frantically about for some sign of such an occurrence, but found none. He calmed a bit when he found no evidence to support his fears, and even chided himself a bit as he went back to his gig.

"Never do to go off in a tizzy," he said to himself as he again started on his way. "Shoddy carriage to plan an elopement in. Could have broken their necks." The lieutenant must be quite run off at the legs if he could afford no better than that, and Stuart liked the idea of seeing Patrice married to such a man less than he ever had. The thought of Patrice's being taken advantage of for her dead relatives' rolls of soft caused Stuart to clench his teeth, and he wondered if the officer would pay his bride much mind once he himself was plump in the pockets from her inheritance.

Stuart reckoned that they could not have gone far on foot, and on such a night as this. The nearest inn or posting house was a scant four miles away, and they must hire a new rig and pair if they wished to go on.

He hastened the pace as he began to feel that perhaps he might now have a chance to catch up to the couple, allowing himself to nurture an anger within himself as he went, dwelling on how Torquill might have killed Patrice with his bird-witted scheme and his damned hired carriage. He himself might be something of a clodpole about certain things, but Stuart knew that he would never be so bacon-brained as to hire a vehicle that was about to fall to pieces for a journey to the border.

Lord Ringwood was not alone in these feelings as Patrice was also harboring something of the same resentment toward her lieutenant. Poking at the cold stew before her, she reflected that the entire affair was in no manner exciting or the least romantic. She was enraged at Basil, and at herself for having been such a fool as to think she loved him. She had done with trying to make herself believe that things would be all right once they were together again. Patrice did not love him in the least, as handsome as he was. At first numb with the realization that she would not be allowed to return to her grandmother, Patrice had tried not to think, but thoughts had continued to come as she had sat waiting for the new carriage to be prepared, and she had found to her complete surprise that she had become increasingly rebellious. Though she knew a struggle would be useless, she had the desire to resist in any case, however futile the effort.

The lieutenant was watching out of the window the old man's progress in hitching the horses up. He was impatient to be off for he wanted the entire deed done as quickly as possible. Lifting his watch out, he unfobbed it and gazed at the time. The hour was late, and the possibility of someone's coming in search of them was great. Patrice heard the sharp snap as Basil closed his watch and rose from his seat to come to her. The time had come for her to make a stand and she fully intended to do so, as she had made up her mind. It was a frightening idea, more frightening than when she had defied her mother, but a great many things had happened since that small step. Patrice could no more help her decision to resist Basil than she could help being hopelessly in love with Stuart, for she had come to the realization that she was in love, and had known it for some time now deep in her heart.

She did not turn but could feel Basil come up behind her as she remained seated. Suddenly, he kneeled beside her chair, his face close to hers as she continued to stare down into her bowl.

"You must forgive what I said before, Patrice," Basil said, his voice as persuasive as she knew it could be. "But you were acting in a manner most contrary to what is your normal mode. You and I are both a little tired out, but it will be all over in a little while and things will be back to normal." The lieutenant looked at Patrice expectantly, fully believing that she would fall headlong into his embrace as she had on other occasions, but was surprised to find himself looking into defiant green eyes.

"You and I need no longer tread about softly," Patrice replied sharply, rising to her feet, eyes flashing. "I know why you wish to marry me now. You made it plain enough, I vow. But if you think I will go along tamely, you are mistaken!"

Basil rose to his feet slowly, unused to having his proposals scorned. "And do you really think that you will receive any help from that tottering relic outside?" he asked tauntingly, angry himself and tired of trying to persuade Patrice to come along willingly. He grabbed her roughly by the hand and she began to struggle frantically to free herself.

"Let me go!" she demanded, her pulling ineffectual against his greater strength. A sharp pain went from her already bruised wrist up her arm as Basil began to pull her toward the doorway.

"Stop struggling, you are acting like a hoyden," Lieutenant Torquill commanded, exasperated at such contrary behavior. He was totally confounded as Patrice had never before been so defiant. Where now was the complacent young girl he had decided would be his bride? He wondered momentarily how he could have misjudged her so. He had not thought to have any problems at all bending her already pliant personality to the desired shape, but this screeching, struggling, wild creature before him was much more than he had bargained for. He hesitated by the door, not knowing what to do, and Patrice, noting that he had halted, looked up from her struggling to see doubt in Basil's face.

"Why, you are afraid to allow that old gentleman to see you dragging me off to the carriage, aren't you?" she exclaimed, the truth revealing itself in the officer's red and now blustering face.

"That is ridiculous," he barked, but made no effort to open the door nonetheless.

"You are nothing but a coward!" Patrice exclaimed, glad of it but surprised that he was, nonetheless. She had not considered him capable of being so afraid of what the world should think.

Before he could answer, the door to the posting house was suddenly thrust open and a disheveled Lord Ringwood entered the room, a look on his face that did not bode well for Lieutenant Torquill's safety.

"Stuart!" Patrice cried with joy, her face lighting up at seeing his dear sweet face, no matter that he looked a veritable sight dressed so oddly, and with his hair blown about.

Lord Ringwood, who had been expecting some resistance on the part of Patrice, was taken aback as she threw herself into his arms, Basil having let her hand fall as he saw that the game was up.

"Oh, Stuart, I am so glad to see you. You cannot know what I have gone through these past few hours!" Patrice said, holding him closer to her, heedless of how it might seem to him.

Lord Ringwood did not dislike the experience at all, in point of fact he was beginning to enjoy it immensely, though he did not know what could have caused such a change of heart. This entire turn of events made it difficult for Stuart, who had rehearsed what he would say all the way there, and now was at a loss. Placing his arms protectively around Patrice, he glared at Lieutenant Torquill afresh.

"I had come prepared to give Patrice the free choice of coming back to the safety and calm of her grandmother's side or continuing on with you, sir," he said with a barely restrained hostility toward the man. "I can see now that it will be unnecessary," he added as Patrice looked up trustingly at him. "I think you had best leave, unless you question ma authority to tell you to do so."

Lieutenant Torquill glared at this unwanted intruder with overt hostility. "I most certainly do question your authority," he asserted heatedly. "I also question your ability to interfere with my plans."

Basil reached out as if to pull Patrice away from Stuart's side and she cringed from the lieutenant's grasp. There was no need for her to have done so for Stuart took that opportunity to land a quick, neat blow to the lieutenant's jaw. He was in no mood to debate and was afforded great satisfaction as Basil was knocked over by the punch.

Stuart was prepared to continue, both hands clenched in efficient-looking fists, but the lieutenant seemed to have had the fight knocked from him as he rose to his feet, rubbing his chin gingerly.

"I give you one last chance to leave with me, Patrice," Basil said as he brushed his clothing off. "Lord Ringwood would bring you back to your grandmother, to be ruled by your mother again. Come with me." Basil extended his hand to her in a most compelling fashion, but she would not take it.

"And be ruled by you instead?" she asked doubtfully. "No, I will return with Stuart."

There did not seem anything more to say. Gathering up what little remained of his dignity, the lieutenant quit the room.

"Are you all right?" Stuart asked concernedly. "Has he harmed you in any way?"

"No, no. I am quite all right now that you are here, but I do not know what would have become of me if you had not come," she said, shuddering a bit in his arms. "Oh, Stuart, you and Lettice were right about Basil, even Mama was right. He only wanted my inheritance. He didn't care for me at all."

"But I thought you loved him," Stuart said, puzzled but hopeful as he looked down into her pale face.

"I only thought that I did. Tonight he showed his true colors. I realized I did not love him at all," she answered, enjoying the feeling of being protected by Stuart.

"Well, I am sure that Mr. Danby will be most glad to hear that you are free," he said hesitantly, unsure of what all of this meant, but suddenly filled with joy at the possibility of what Patrice's words implied.

"Stuart, you know I don't care at all for Mr. Danby—or any other gentleman. It has been you all along, only I never knew it until a few days ago, and then you were so cold," Patrice replied petulantly, but not releasing her hold on his lapels as she looked up into his face.

"I!" he exclaimed, "Cold?" Stuart's head was in a whirl.

"I will forgive you if you will only tell me that you feel the same way that I do," Patrice promised, looking anxiously up at him.

Stuart was almost struck speechless with joy, but managed to sputter, "Of course I love you, it seems I've loved you all ma life."

"Then we ought to do well, you and I, don't you think? Both loving one another as we do."

Patrice smiled at Stuart who could not quite believe his great good fortune, astonishment and happiness so apparent on his face that she had to laugh a little. It was exhilarating for her, and suddenly very much more romantic as Lord Ringwood bent to kiss her tentatively on the lips, still curved in a smile. His kiss was fully returned as he felt Patrice's arms wrapped round his neck. When they parted he felt as if his heart would burst with the rapture he felt.

He continued to hold her for a few moments, oblivious to their surroundings, until they heard the door to the house open and the proprietor totter in, frozen almost to the bone in his nightshirt and counting a few crowns in his hand.

"Has the lieutenant gone?" Patrice asked him as he seemed about to pass them on his way back to the warmth of his feather bed. The old gentleman looked up in surprise.

"Why, I thought you had left with him!" he said as he stared with a confused and somewhat disapproving eye at the young couple who remained locked in one another's arms.

"This lady is ma fiancée, if she will have me," Lord Ringwood told the man, to allay any concerns he might have.

"Yes, well," the man coughed mildly, "the other gentleman has gone off in the hired carriage, and I am off to sleep myself. Tomorrow is almost upon us and I have to be up and about."

The couple took the hint and thanked the man for his hospitality, Lord Ringwood slipping an extra crown in his hand as he departed. Assisting Patrice up into the gig, Stuart saw the bruise marks about her wrist.

"Did he do that to you?" he exclaimed, his temper rising as Patrice put her arm through his, leaning comfortably up against him.

"Let's not think of him any longer, Stuart," she begged, "I only want to go home, and in answer to your question, yes."

"Yes?" Stuart asked in confusion, his mind still on what he would do to Lieutenant Torquill if ever he should encounter him again.

"Yes, I will most certainly have you. And, your sister will have to cease all of her activities to find you a more suitable bride, for I am sure that I shall be most incensed if she does not," Patrice said mischievously.

"Well, by Jove!" Stuart shouted. "You're sure now?" he said, hardly believing what he was hearing.

"Quite sure. This time I will not be changing my mind," Patrice assured him, shyly giving him a kiss to help convince him. Lord Ringwood was thoroughly overjoyed at this, and as he started up his gig, directing the horses back toward Granthem, he made a mental note to write his sister at once to stop all matchmaking plans, for he had found someone suitable on his own, at last.

Lord Melburry's chest was beginning to pain him again, and as time continued he was finding it more and more difficult to ignore it. It seemed to Peregrine that every jolt in the road and every move he made corresponded with an ache somewhere in his body, but he had gone on, nevertheless, stopping at several posting houses and inns to inquire after Aurora. There had been no one to tell him what he wished fervently to hear, and he had to settle only for a change of horses at one place so that he might make better time.

He was nearing Lincolnshire, and making good speed considering the darkness, but it was not good enough to catch up with Killingham's coach. That he would eventually catch up with him, Peregrine was certain, Killingham's coach being heavier and more cumbersome. But as time passed, Lord Melburry's vision began to blur more frequently.

He hit a particularly nasty bump in the roadway that tossed him about in his seat, an occurrence that would never have happened ordinarily but for his exhausted state. Peregrine gritted his teeth against the pain which threatened to overcome him, and was glad of a sudden that he was nearing another posting house. It was one of the larger ones that operated throughout most of the evening to catch the mail coaches which sometimes ran at night, and Peregrine drew into it at such a fast clip that he was almost unsuccessful in halting his course, the horses pulling the curricle faster as they recognized a place where they too might rest.

The proprietor came running out at the din in time to see Lord Melburry nearly fall out of his curricle in his attempt to descend.

"Here now. Don't you know better than to come in like that?" the man demanded, rushing to the young man's side to assist him all the same.

"Unforgivably bad driving, I know," Peregrine said as he straightened himself and declined the man's arm. "I have traveled from London this same night and have had little rest."

"Well, you had best come in and warm yourself,
266

then," the owner of the establishment said gruffly. He could see that Peregrine must be exhausted, and though he was dressed so incredibly, the greatcoat over his costume for the ball, the curricle he was driving indicated someone of the gentry. He led the way inside, and shushed his wife before she could even open her mouth. There were a few travelers present warming themselves by the fireplace, and the proprietor led Peregrine into a separate room with a private fire. Throwing a new log on the dying embers after assisting a hesitant Lord Melburry to sit, the man left to see to Peregrine's horses. Half lying on the low couch, Peregrine closed his lids momentarily, allowing his weariness to flood over him. Though he was as determined as ever to go on—there could be no question of stopping—Peregrine was now beginning to wonder if his body would continue to obey him, if he had the physical stamina. At that moment, Peregrine wished he were stronger, that he would at least last long enough to rescue Aurora or stay their progress until Richard should arrive. He continued to think along those lines until he heard the door to the room open and someone enter.

"I brought you some food, your lordship." The proprietor's wife set a plate of cold meat and a tankard of cider on the table. Peregrine was loath to move from where he was.

"Are my horses being attended to? I must leave soon," he mumbled. The effort of talking was even too much energy to expend at that moment, and he did not open his eyes to look at the woman as she answered.

"Oh, yes, my husband is doing it himself. We have had a lot of traffic this evening."

Peregrine opened his eyes slowly to ask if she had seen a young girl with an older man pass through, when something glittering caught his eyes on the braided rug before him. He leaned forward and reached for the sparkling object and found it was a locket constructed of rubies.

"What have we here?" he said, turning it over in his hand to read the inscription. The proprietress craned her neck to see, her eyes widening.

Lord Melburry suddenly sat bolt upright, his greatcoat opening. It was then that the woman saw he was dressed almost as strangely as the young woman who had been there earlier that evening, the boots and coat being the only thing usual about him.

"Were a young woman and an older man here previously?" Peregrine demanded, but he knew the answer even before the woman could speak. "A young girl dressed as I am, in costume?"

"Why, why yes, but the gentleman said she was mad, taking her to an asylum or some such," the woman replied with some confusion.

Peregrine was instantly on his feet as if galvanized to action. He took hold of the startled woman's shoulders and looked at her intensely. The wild look in his eyes frightened her dreadfully, but the hypnotic brightness of their color only made her speechless.

"How long ago did they leave?" he demanded, the agony of having yet missed them causing him almost to shake the woman for a reply.

"Not but two hours ago at most," the woman responded nervously, wondering if all of the inmates of Bedlam had suddenly broken free and agreed to meet at her home.

"Go and tell your husband to hurry with my horses," Peregrine commanded. She was astonished to see him so revitalized where only a moment before he had been about to fall off. With a bob of her head she was gone, glad to be dismissed. Peregrine began to pace the room, his blood rushing in his veins as he felt himself nearing his goal. All fears that he would fail in his task to Aurora were dismissed as he allowed anger to supply him with the will to go on.

A few miles away, the Duke and Lettice continued to follow in Peregrine's wake, stopping only briefly at each inn and posting house to see if Peregrine had already passed on and how long ago. At the last, they appeared to be only a scant hour behind the young man.

For the most part, Lettice had kept her thoughts to herself, preferring to allow Richard to concentrate his full attention on the road ahead. However, she was aware that he was also concerned about her worry over her sister, as he would periodically draw her closer to him as if to comfort her.

Stopping yet again, Richard motioned for Lettice to remain seated in the carriage while he went to inquire within. The proprietor came out to speak to Richard who remained lighted in the doorway for some minutes as the two men spoke, and when Richard returned to the carriage Lettice could tell by his face that something had occurred.

"What is it, Richard?" she asked as he started up the horses again at an even quicker pace than before. "They have passed through here, haven't they?"

"Yes, they have, and Killingham is telling everyone that your sister is insane so no one will heed her if she tries to escape him," he replied slowly, glancing at Lettice with concern. He had not wished to tell her that, but knew she would not wish to be kept in the dark about it.

She was silent a moment, her anger mixed with fear for her sister as she tried to imagine what Aurora was doing at that very moment, with no one to help her and everyone believing that she was legally in the care of Killingham. They would question nothing that he told them.

"How—how horrible," Lettice said at last, feeling her words with every fiber of her being. "Even if she should cry out for help, no one would come to her aid. Who would care about the ravings of a madwoman?" Lettice asked bitterly, appalled that Killingham should be taken at his word. "I am sure he paid them liberally." The impotent rage in her voice was hard for Richard to bear. It echoed his own feelings, but he could think of nothing to console Lettice.

"I will do everything in my power to save Aurora, as will Peregrine," the Duke said quietly so that Lettice barely heard him above the pounding of the horses' hooves. Lettice looked up at Richard, and saw that he was as determined as his brother had been.

"Believe me, I have confidence in your abilities, Richard," Lettice said, willing him to believe it, for it was true. "It is just that I recoil whenever I think of Aurora with that man, so much that I believe I will lose my mind if we cannot find them soon."

"It will be soon," the Duke assured her with a firm voice. It must be soon, he thought to himself, for time would be running out for Aurora the longer she remained in Killingham's power. He knew the man, and the more time passed the more likely it was that he would fly into an uncontrollable rage or force himself upon her. Lettice was aware of all this herself, and to talk about it further would only serve to agitate her more than she might be able to contain, as she was now doing, by sheer strength of character. That she had not flown into hysterics and had been able to calm the entire household of her aunt before leaving with him was to her credit. He knew of no other woman who was as level-headed or who could be of so much use in a crisis. The knowledge that here was a person who could be depended upon as well as allow herself to depend on others made Richard love her all the more. It also made it imperative to the Duke that he deal with Killingham as quickly as possible. Killingham had become not only Richard's personal concern, but their mutual enemy. If he had dealt with Killingham years ago, rather than flee to France as he had been ordered, perhaps none of this would have ever come to pass, and it was this that the Duke kept in his mind as he hurried toward Granthem.

Lord Killingham was less than pleased by the delay which had occurred on the road. Due to the dense darkness of the evening, the coachman had moved with more caution than he had previously, the roadway being in a state of disrepair and more likely to cause accidents. So it was that the coach at last pulled into the inn outside of Granthem a little behind schedule, the innkeeper hurrying outside to take the horses in hand.

Killingham assisted Aurora to descend, though she was loath to allow him to do so. The hours alone with him in the coach were beginning to take their toll on her nerves, and she felt them drawn as taut as strings as she shuddered against the feeling of Lord Killingham's hand against hers. He had not spoken much, but he had never taken his eyes from her all the same.

"Your lordship and the lady must be cold and I daresay you would no doubt look forward to a little supper. My wife has prepared a few things and they are waiting within," the innkeeper said, allowing a stable boy to lead the coach to the back of the inn and show the coachman to the kitchens where his vituals also were waiting.

Aurora watched the proprietor's face as he spoke, glancing nervously from Lord Killingham to herself, and knew that Killingham had spoken truthfully about the story he had spread about her. This man too thought her mad, and she was half tempted to give the man something to worry about and throw a fit. The rebellious thought was quelled in an instant as Aurora knew that such an outburst might cause Killingham to continue on his way more quickly than he intended, and Aurora would lose valuable time. As she followed Killingham into the inn, Aurora's faith that somehow she would be saved was beginning to waver.

Ushered into yet another empty room provided with a fire, Aurora gathered her cloak tightly about her. Killingham moved to take it from her, but she turned abruptly. "I am still very chilled and would have it on awhile," she said, her face not defiant but straining to look as complacent as possible.

Lord Killingham paused a moment. "Very well, but I shall move the table closer by the fire and you shall soon be warm enough," he said with a faint smile. He wished to look upon her person once again but decided that he could wait until after he had supped.

The table was already laden with small dishes of succulents that the proprietor's wife had prepared, but Aurora barely nibbled at any of them. Lord Killingham ate heartily and with speed, then sat back to watch Aurora, wine glass in hand as he took an occasional sip of sherry.

Aurora did not glance up from her repast, but knew Killingham was staring at her anyway. In her mind she found herself praying fervently that someone would come, but particularly a conviction lay deep in her breast that somehow Peregrine would arrive to help her in her hour of distress.

Killingham finished the last of his drink, setting the glass carefully on the table and focusing his entire attention on Aurora. He had wondered if perhaps he would grow tired of her after a time, but now, regarding her in the fire's glow, he could not wish for a more desirable woman. Her skin was pale and smooth-looking, and he recalled a rounded shoulder and white arms.

"That damned cloak," he said softly. Aurora looked up from her food at his words. "Surely you are warm enough now. Take it off. I find it obscures my delight in you. As a bridegroom it is my right to look upon you as I please," he commanded, still in that soft, dangerously tense voice, as if here were a panther, waiting to pounce. Aurora made no move to do as she was bid, and the silence in the room grew tense with only the crackle of the fire to be heard.

In the room directly next door to that containing Aurora and Lord Killingham a young woman was humming quietly to herself. She did so because she was quite fabulously happy and could not contain her joy and had to release it in a little tune. Patrice sat warming herself by the fire as if nothing in the world would have pleased her more greatly. Stuart had insisted upon stopping at this inn as he had sworn that her wrist was more swollen than before. His concern for her well-being and comfort was like heaven to Patrice, and he had been adamant upon stopping so that he might fetch a doctor to attend to her. Though Patrice was certain that it was nothing more than a sprain, she had agreed, not wishing to be home and alone so soon. Adoring Stuart and having adoration returned, Patrice found that she hardly ever wished to be out of his presence, but Stuart had gone off half an hour ago to fetch the surgeon while she had contented herself with nibbling on the little selections of dainties that the innkeeper's wife had presented to her. Picking up a jelly tart from the tray before her, Patrice was suddenly startled by what sounded like a roar from the next room and the sound of a chair falling over. Her hand went immediately to her breast as she felt her heart pounding.

Aurora had done much the same, so startling had Lord Killingham's reaction been when she had finally answered him with a low-voiced "no".

Towering above the still-seated woman, eyes flashing with barely controlled wrath, Killingham seemed about to strike her. "Since you do not seem to understand the request I have made," he said with a voice shaking with fury, "I shall assist you." So saying, Lord Killingham walked swiftly round the table and reached for the tie at Aurora's throat that secured her cloak. Aurora had attempted to elude his grasp, rising herself and overturning her chair in the process, but she was not quick enough and Killingham seized her by the arm through the thin material of her covering.

"You resist too much," Killingham remarked suspiciously. "Before, you removed the garment willingly enough. Let us see what you have to hide, my Lady Trevelyn." With that he pulled the cloak roughly from her and found her neck bare of any adornment.

"The locket, it is gone!"

Aurora broke away from his grasp, using every last ounce of her strength. Her own fury and disgust had risen to the point where she could no longer restrain herself from saying what she felt. She looked on Lord Killingham with revulsion as she backed away from him as she would from a rabid animal.

Patrice, hearing the commotion in the next room and uncertain as to what could be going on, had risen from her comfortable seat by the fire. She could not make out the words that were being said, but it sounded as if someone were very angry. Walking over to the door, Patrice opened it a crack, then walked into the hallway, determined to fetch the innkeeper to find out what was amiss. Once in the hall, she could hear quite clearly what was being said, for the door to the adjoining room was quite thin.

Within, Aurora had moved as far away from Killingham as she could, and she felt herself run up against the small table in the corner of the room. Wine decanters set in a row rattled together as her back moved against it. Killingham began to move forward, as if stalking her.

"Where is the locket?" he snarled, his anger showing in the scowl he wore on his face.

"I do not know nor do I care," she suddenly shrieked, the room reverberating with her scorn. "I hate and despise the very sight of you. Do you really think that I would accept, let alone wear, any token of yours? I find you odious, monstrous! No wonder your

273

wife turned to other men. She could not but have found you as repulsive as I do!"

Killingham came forward and was almost upon her. Aurora reached quickly behind her without turning, her slim fingers tightening around the neck of one of the heavy crystal bottles.

Suddenly there was a frantic pounding upon the doors. "Aurora! Aurora!" Patrice shouted through the door which Killingham had locked. Patrice had heard her sister's voice while out in the hall, and at first had not believed it was she, thinking that her own senses must be faulty. But at hearing the loud rantings, she had become convinced that it was indeed Aurora and that she was in some sort of danger.

"Aurora, are you all right?" Patrice fairly screamed as she pounded even with her injured hand. Killingham hesitated a moment when he would have grabbed Aurora, and she saw an opportunity to strike.

Quickly she lifted the full bottle and swung it in an arc at Lord Killingham's head. The crystal weapon flashed in the air, but just as quickly, Killingham's hand stretched out and grasped Aurora's hand, there was a brief struggle and the bottle came crashing to the floor.

"Patrice, run, get help!" Aurora cried out in despair. She knew not how Patrice came to be there, but had recognized that familiar voice herself. It was her only hope of salvation now, as Killingham dragged her to the door, his greater size all too large an advantage for her to resist.

In the hallway, Patrice hesitated with indecision. She had no idea of what was occurring within the closed room, but she did not wish to leave Aurora alone even for a moment. Then the door flew open and Patrice stepped back a pace. She was faced with the raving visage of Lord Killingham and could see Aurora behind him, caught in his hold.

"Get out of my way, woman," Killingham roared, thrusting Patrice aside like a doll so that she struck her head against the opposite wall and was stunned.

"Patrice!" Aurora cried with horror as she watched her sister lying dazed on the floor of the hallway. Killingham pulled relentlessly at her arm, and Aurora began to lash out viciously with her free hand and with her foot, trying in vain to loosen herself. It was as though the man felt no pain in his crazed state as he dragged her out of the house into the rear yard and toward the coach he had brought her in.

Inside, Patrice was coming round to the sounds of the innkeeper's wife squawking and squealing for her husband to come to her, rushing back and forth as if she were uncertain what to do. Her husband, hearing his wife's cries as she stood on the front porch, came running from the stables to see what the matter was, his face anxious. He had been helping Lord Killingham's coachman to select some fresh horses if any were fit.

As he neared his hysterical wife, his ears were assailed by the sound of a carriage approaching. The noise of wheels and hooves clattering was almost deafening and the man soon found why. Not only was there a curricle and pair, but the young gentleman who had gone for the doctor had returned as well.

Stuart had to move his horse quickly to one side as the racing curricle thundered past him at a mad pace, and he was startled for a moment and unbelieving as he thought he identified the driver as Peregrine. The doctor's house had been dashed difficult to find in the blackness, but he had found him at last and the doctor had promised to come in his wagon. Not wishing to wait, and wanting to be with Patrice as soon as possible, Stuart had gone on ahead only to find the inn where he had left her in total chaos and to meet Peregrine in this of all places.

The innkeeper's wife was still shrieking incoherently when her husband reached her side, Stuart clattering to a halt beside the curricle in time to call out as Peregrine leapt from his seat, every muscle in his body ready to spring into action despite the dull aching he felt. "Peregrine, what are you doing here?"

Lord Melburry stopped in his tracks and spun round. "Stuart," he said in astonishment. "I have never been so glad to see anyone as I have you," Peregrine said, grabbing his hand in a firm handshake, then turning back to the clamor that was being raised. "I have no time to talk now. Lord Killingham has abducted

275

Aurora and I am giving chase. Richard and Lettice are following not far behind me, I suspect, but I must discover if Aurora and Killingham have been here."

With that, Peregrine broke into a run to reach the door to the inn, Stuart hot on his heels. As they reached the frantic woman, Stuart heard her babbling something about Patrice.

"She was struck on the head, I think," the woman said, fluttering her hands nervously in the air as she responded to her husband's inquiry. "That man with the crazy niece, he is the one who did it. He must be as mad as she is. They have gone off in their coach, along the back road."

Peregrine did not hesitate any longer upon hearing those words. Sprinting quickly back to his curricle, the animals having hardly caught their wind, he whipped them up and guided his carriage around the back in time to see the faint outlines of Lord Killingham's coach disappearing through the darkness. Snapping the reins almost wildly, Peregrine gave chase, determined to end the drama once and for all.

At the inn, Stuart had rushed to Patrice who appeared to be groggy but otherwise unharmed. The small bump on her temple attested to the violence that Killingham had perpetrated upon her person, and Stuart hoped that when Peregrine caught Killingham he would leave enough for him to settle accounts.

"Stuart, we must go after Aurora," Patrice said with dismay as soon as she had been able to stand.

"Peregrine is already after them," he replied reasonably, though he himself would have liked nothing better. It was not feasible with Patrice so injured, however, or so he thought, but she was not to be put off.

"Please, tell them to bring your carriage around to the back," she pleaded. "We must help Peregrine. He may not be able to best Lord Killingham alone."

"Then I will go ma self," Stuart said as he hurried to the front yard to bring his curricle about. However, Patrice followed doggedly in his tracks.

"Stuart, it is my decision to go with you," she said adamantly, holding fast to the horses' harness.

Lord Ringwood looked her straight in the eye.

"Very well, then, if you must. Allow me at least to drive the damned thing," Stuart declared as he helped Patrice to mount.

At that moment, another carriage rattled into the courtyard, and Stuart realized that it must be Richard. It had barely come to a standstill when Lettice looked across and saw her sister.

"What!" Lettice could not say a word further as Stuart broke in on her.

"No time for the what and wherefores. Killingham's off in his coach with Aurora, and Peregrine is hot on their trail. Follow me," he shouted, and Richard automatically pulled up behind Stuart as they thundered off in pursuit.

It was only a few minutes later that Stuart could see the two vehicles up ahead. The clouds had cleared, and the moon was shining dimly in the sky. It was getting nearer to dawn, and the night was more deep gray than black, giving the entire panorama a ghostly quality.

"There," Stuart called out, pointing up ahead. "Do you see them?"

Patrice looked around to see Richard nod. "He sees them, too," she confirmed. "But how will Peregrine stop him? There is no room to pass on this tiny dirt road," she observed, not a little panic-stricken.

"I don't know," Stuart replied, mystified himself. "He would have to be a magician to manage it from what I can see."

Peregrine was thinking much the same but could not give in to despair. He had finally managed to catch up with Killingham, driving directly behind the coach so that he could even see Aurora seated beside him.

Killingham had not been aware of anyone's giving pursuit until Aurora had caught the sounds of the other carriage, turning in her seat to see the face of her beloved a scant distance away.

"Peregrine!" she cried, reaching out with her arms to him.

Killingham turned briefly to glance behind and, upon seeing his adversary not only apparently unharmed but close behind him, lashed viciously at the team of horses. They plunged wildly forward under the stinging pain of the whip, the coach lurching about unsteadily.

277

Lettice caught her breath as she watched Killingham's coach make a turn around a bend, sliding precariously on the uneven ground. Richard had felt her tense beside him, and heard the slowly released breath as the coach did not crash but continued on its rapid course.

"He will kill her, the fool," he muttered, and Lettice clutched his arm as if her will alone could prevent it.

The path ahead was lined with clumps of trees, and Peregrine was determined to pass Killingham's coach for that was the only way he could see of stopping him. Up ahead, he could detect a short stretch of the roadway where there were only a few short bushes. It was there that he must make his move.

Aurora, seated beside Killingham, had deduced Peregrine's intent, for she herself was aware that the only possibility of halting Killingham's progress was to bar his way. At the rate at which the coach was moving, it would be dangerous for Peregrine, and Aurora was suddenly sure of what she must do to assist him.

As they neared the vacant stretch of land, the wind stinging her eyes, Aurora reached out and began to struggle with Lord Killingham for control of the reins, clinging tenaciously to his hands as he attempted to maintain possession.

"Let go!" Killingham shouted viciously, striking Aurora with the handle of the whip. The coach weaved unsteadily and slowed as he took his eyes from the road, Aurora sustaining the blow and holding fast.

Peregrine saw the opening he had been waiting for, and thundered past Killingham's coach, the brush and rocks nearly jolting him from his seat. Peregrine began deliberately to slow his curricle, but Killingham struck his horses heedless. There was nowhere for the beasts to go, and the coach swerved off the road, crashing through the trees and coming to a halt as it slammed heavily against a fallen log. The horses plunged desperately against their harnesses, throwing Killingham to the ground as he tried to rein in.

Aurora looked down at the bulky form on the ground as she remained on top of the coach, too afraid to move from where she sat in the still-lurching vehicle. He did not move, his leg sprawled at an odd angle.

278

Then suddenly she was aware of footsteps running toward her over the bare ground and she could see Peregrine hurrying to her. As if freed from a spell, Aurora dismounted the coach, and raced into his arms, holding him tightly.

"Oh, Peregrine, you came. I knew somehow you would," Aurora sobbed in relief.

"I had to! You are my life," Peregrine said, looking into Aurora's eyes swimming with tears. The kiss which ensued was such that the young couple was barely aware of the arrival of Lord Ringwood and Patrice and the subsequent addition of the Duke and Lettice to their ranks.

With more of a head for details, Stuart walked over to Killingham to see what condition he was in.

"Out for the count, he is, and I think one of his pins is broken. Pity that I have too many scruples to kick an unconscious man or I should do it, for what he has done to Patrice," Stuart remarked seriously, the angry look which lingered on his face causing Patrice to lead her intended away from "that dreadful man".

Richard waited apart from them all as Lettice flew to her sister's side to embrace her as well as Patrice, and then walked over to Peregrine.

"Well, this is a pretty night's work," the Duke remarked, looking at the still-unconscious form of Lord Killingham. "It seems that it took an impudent young 'un to settle all the old scores," he added, not a bit ruefully.

"Let's just be glad that it is done," Lettice said thankfully, taking Richard's arm in hers.

"Or soon will be, once Killingham is handed over to the authorities," Stuart added matter-of-factly. "But then I will still have to answer to your father, I am afraid, Patrice," Stuart said glumly. "I have not done a very good job of keeping you out of trouble nor from harm as he requested. This is going to be a scandal that will beat the deuce out of anything you might have been threatened with, Richard."

"An' it comes to that, we are all of us going to be the talk of the town," Lettice remarked, not seeming to care in the least.

"And that doesn't bother you?" Richard inquired with astonishment.

"I would hardly think it would," Aurora answered for her sister. "I am sure you shall take her nonetheless, scandal and all. After all, it runs in the family."

"You hear that, gentlemen?" Lettice announced. "You are forewarned. Now is your one and only chance to flee the fate of mixing your blood forevermore with that of the tainted Trevelyns."

"Those scandalously willful women," Aurora added gleefully.

"Who run about the countryside with heaven only knows whom," Patrice added, not wishing to be left out when at last she had found she had a voice.

The gentlemen looked at one another, and then proceeded to eliminate any further ridiculous statements by silencing those fair Trevelyn lips with their own, to which there were no objections whatever.

ABOUT THE AUTHOR

ADORA SHERIDAN is a native of San Francisco and shares her home with her two dogs, a miniature dachshund named Elva and a Pomeranian, Leslie. Among her interests are horseback riding, embroidery, calligraphy and collecting stained glass.

Ms. Sheridan began writing romantic novels at the age of twenty to entertain friends. Recently, her first book, *The Signet Ring,* was published. *The Season* is her second work and a third will be published shortly.